# PRAISE FOR AND THE TRAIN KEPT MOVING

"Michael Kiggins' impressive first novel, *And the Train Kept Moving*, begins like a modern noir. Something bad has happened in the webby darkness of Memphis and the first person narration opens the story: hot, immediate, intimate and spiky. The book then shifts gears, moves into the past, and what follows is a dodgy but passionate love story, which is both moving and unsettling. Kiggins' Memphis is beautifully drawn and his supple prose up to all the emotions he puts his full-blooded characters through. The book is a realistic paean to the city in all its funky beauty, and all its raw danger and poverty. All in all, it's a great read, tough-minded and heartfelt and brave. Kiggins stands at the threshold of a bigtime literary career."

— COREY MESLER, AUTHOR OF
*MEMPHIS MOVIE, AND THE WORLD IS
NEITHER STACKED FOR NOR AGAINST
YOU: SELECTED SHORT STORIES.*

"From the first page, Kiggins establishes a kinetic tension between doubt and truth, danger and arousal, what's seen and hidden, that provokes us to turn another page with an irresistible impulse, like the myriad irresistible impulses Kiggins brings to light in the careful, detailed language and observations of his troubled, obsessive-compulsive narrator. And what a compelling, refreshing narrator Bryan is —with his fixation on a singular thought, his forgivable fears and weaknesses, his seductive vulnerability—wrought from the mind of a brave, exacting debut novelist."

— PATRICK EARL RYAN, AUTHOR OF THE FLANNERY O'CONNOR AWARD-WINNING COLLECTION *IF WE WERE ELECTRIC*

"A dark and seedy book that left me feeling the need for a shower and an AA meeting. *And the Train Kept Moving* is a meandering revenge tale mixed with a heart wrenching family drama with surprising insight on the HIV/AIDS epidemic that preceded events in the book. An intriguing read."

— JORDAN KING, AUTHOR OF *WHITE OAKS*

"A slow-burn study in compulsion and obsession whose climax will unsettle you for days."

— ANTHONY OLIVEIRA, AUTHOR OF THE FORTHCOMING NOVEL *DAYSPRING*.

# AND THE TRAIN KEPT MOVING

## MOVING

### A NOVEL

## MICHAEL KIGGINS

*For Randall*

# CONTENTS

# OPEN-ENDED

When I pulled into The Lookout Inn's parking lot, it was well past last call on the final night I'd ever spend in Memphis, and Adam's body had certainly been discovered by then. How many cops were swarming Club Fugue and how pissed were the employees after getting detained and questioned? Somehow, I had escaped without getting any blood on my hands, but on the drive home the reflections of taillights and fluorescent signs compelled me to double-check my chapped fingers whenever I could take my eyes off the road.

The Lookout Inn was a two-story motel that sat on the bluff's southern stretch and would have overlooked the Mississippi River if not for the towering trees surrounding it on three sides. My actual destination was the Old Bridge, which lay beyond the thicket on the far right.

Most of the lights in the motel's parking lot and along its breezeways were burned out or flickering. The gray brick had once been painted white. Few cars were parked out front, but the rear lot was crowded.

I parked my roommate's hatchback near a dumpster and

got out, my breath fogging. This early in the morning, the chilly air sharpened my mind, which definitely needed it. Most car and pickup windows were frosted over, and as warmly as I had dressed, each burning breath felt like the hour was simultaneously much too early and way too late. Or that could have been the dumpster, which reeked of beer and rum and sour milk, smelling too much like rotten eggnog. The song was titled "The Most Wonderful Time of the Year," and that ever-present sentiment ignored everyone who didn't celebrate Christmas and how many people white-knuckled it through the holiday's expectations only to kill themselves early in the New Year, their final resolution permanent once they pulled the trigger, cut deep enough, found the right pharmaceutical cocktail, or leaped from a towering height.

It was two days after Christmas and 2004 couldn't get here soon enough. I had no idea where I'd be when the ball dropped in Times Square, but it couldn't be as bad as everything I was leaving behind.

Chris's used car gleamed showroom-shiny next to a jalopy with side-panels Swiss-cheesed by rust. I hoped it would be all right. Then I shook my head. I'd effectively stolen his car after committing several felonies, and now I was worried it might get vandalized or stolen again.

Though I laughed at myself, my heart kept racing because I worried somebody would notice me. I didn't see anyone else in the parking lot or anybody peering at me from behind thread-bare curtains, but if I were caught before I got beneath the bridge and dropped a few pieces of evidence into the river, I'd be fucked in more ways than I already was.

A slow 360°-turn confirmed no one had followed me, but I needed to keep moving. I dragged my backpack off the passenger seat, slung it on, and nearly lost my balance. After I tightened the straps, I crouched on my toes until I quit wobbling.

Someone in a second-story room was blaring a Blues song. I stood and glanced back. Half the lights on that walkway were out, and shadows glided past curtained windows. So many people were having a grand old time, and all I could think about was how many rooms were infested with bedbugs and how much DNA could be swabbed from every surface. Before I knew it, I was rubbing my forearms through my coat. No matter how freezing it was, my mind could generate a burning itch.

Standing still only intensified the feeling, so I got a move-on. Past a small gravel lot that didn't allow overnight parking and a lightly sloping field, traffic thrummed across the Old Bridge. There was much more headroom and much less rust down on the midway stanchion than you'd expect. It was windy and noisy as all get out, but peaceful at the same time if you climbed down in the right frame of mind. It was also the best place in Memphis to let go of the past, hurtling it to the Mississippi a hundred feet below.

During my first trip to the catwalks, I was hanging out with some friends from college whose indie band was breaking up. The rhythm guitarist and drummer were graduating and we were all drunk and high as fuck. One of them kept saying, "We should have shot a music video here." Another sat on the railing, hooked his ankles on a lower rung, and leaned all the way back, staring at the world upside-down and repeating, "Gorgeous," until we pulled him back up.

The next visit was when Curt and I had started dating. He'd asked me to show him some unexpected or ignored beauty. When we climbed down to the stanchion, with the heavy traffic rumbling across the bridge above and the river racing below, he said, "This place reminds me of you, Bry—a little obscure, a little unstable." Then he kissed me, and said, "Well done." After Curt had dumped me, I returned often to stare at the river and imagine what those churning currents could do to a body. Not long ago, my last visit here was during an afternoon trip with Stefano when I realized we couldn't have been more incompatible if we tried.

All of those trips had shared a common purpose, even if I couldn't see it at the time: I was always leaving something behind, be it friendships or secrets or my dignity. Still, I'd never carried as much with me down there as I was doing tonight, and I didn't know if I'd be able to abandon everything I needed to.

When Adam attacked me, I hadn't thought—I'd reacted. Part of me wanted to truly steal Chris's car and get the hell out of town, but between leaving Adam's body and arriving here, I made myself slow down. At that hour, barreling down the interstate was a surefire way to draw attention to myself. So I ignored my instinct, knowing I needed to come up with a plan before dawn.

Once I reached the bridge, I hurried along the eastbound walkway. The bridge's diagonal girders reminded me of longer pieces from an Erector Set, pill-shaped holes stippled along their length. The headlights of passing cars cast shadows, so I walked slowly with my head down, ignoring the view, like I did this regularly.

Before leaving my apartment, I'd dressed in a pair of dark jeans, a long-sleeved thermal shirt, another shirt on top of that, followed by a hoodie and a navy-blue pea coat. A pair of black leather gloves and a black sock cap were the finishing touches. Hopefully, besides the iridescent piping on my running shoes, I'd look as unremarkable as a shadow to any drivers speeding past like the year's final days. I would have worn my Docs, but I tossed them and the clothes I'd worn out to the club into a dumpster by the midtown Piggly Wiggly. As for the proof of the crime I'd committed, I would let it plummet into the river. Maybe those fragments of Adam Whittemore would find their way to the Gulf.

At the halfway point of the Old Bridge, I tried opening the access hatch, but it wouldn't budge. I remembered the westbound hatch was usually unlocked and started to make my way across. I misjudged the flow of traffic, barely dodging a dualie as I sprinted across the eastbound lanes and scrambled atop the five-foot tall concrete divider. My first thought was: *That fucker sped up.* My second: *Why in the hell are so many people coming to Memphis?*

"Focus, for fuck's sake," I said, steadying my perch. Real-life Frogger was not as fun as my ten-year-old self had imagined it, not when the "log" that kept me from getting T-boned was a few inches from the steady traffic hurtling past. I needed to time my next dash carefully. Otherwise, I'd get smeared along the divider or run over.

It was much windier here than in the motel's parking lot, but those gusts didn't lessen the exhaust fumes, burned oil, and the reek of the river itself. The roaring of super-powered transmissions and the sputtering of dying ones dopplered in both directions. Redshift and blueshift require a committed position to determine what's moving away from you and what's getting closer. I knew exactly where I was, yet I had no clue where I was going.

While waiting for a big enough gap in the traffic, I remembered a story of this guy who decided to kill himself during rush hour—except he stepped off the subway platform a second too late. The train corkscrewed him from the waist down. This both killed him and kept him alive until his wife had been summoned. She'd knelt, cupping his face in her hands, and they cried, prayed their last prayers, said their last goodbyes, and kissed their last kisses. Before the train was pushed away from the platform, they squeezed each other's hands tighter than they ever had, as if that pressure could possibly tourniquet his soul. But his final words were lost to an exhalation as a piñata's worth of gore spilled onto the tracks.

*Bry, Bry, Bry.* I took a deep breath. *Getting rundown by an eighteen-wheeler would be a mercy. How often does roadkill feel regret?*

When the last thrombus of traffic cleared, I leaped from the divider and raced to the safety of the walkway. Once there, I got my inhaler from my right coat pocket and took a hit.

The Frisco and Harahan Bridges were a few hundred feet north and many decades older than the so-called "Old Bridge." One freight train chugged eastward, another westward, both pulled cargo cars sporting graffiti, the overlapping tags beautiful but meaningless to all but a select audience.

A little beyond the state line, I pulled up the dark skid-plated hatch, the bottom of which was another palimpsest of graffiti. The metal screeched in protest as it opened to the right, and I was glad I was wearing thick gloves because I couldn't remember how long ago my last tetanus shot was. The ladder was on the right side, and the stanchion's red lights were almost bright enough to see by. I began climbing down, squeezing close to the ladder so my backpack wouldn't get snagged, and then I locked the hatch after me.

Once I reached the oblong top of the stanchion, I grabbed a flashlight out of my backpack and switched it on. There was graffiti here too, and a few empty beer bottles. I walked along the stanchion, my gloved hand on the waist-high railing that circled it, kicking the bottles into the river. I sat down with my legs hanging over the edge and opened my backpack.

First, I pulled out the latest letter I'd received from the Shelby County Health Department, which was unopened and red-stamped Urgent. Following that were a fifth of bourbon I'd stolen from Club Fugue, my journal, this week's *Midtown* alt-zine dog-eared at an article titled "Bluff City Plagues: Then & Now," and a grocery bag containing the neck-and-shoulders of a broken beer bottle and several shards of Adam's teeth. Stuffed beneath all of those were an older pair of running shoes, each wrapped in its own plastic grocery bag, several outfits in addition to all of my underwear and socks, and a toiletries kit.

Adam was dead, but he deserved it. I hadn't set out to kill him, not that that matters. I supposed few would miss him. Based on how many people had ignored me when I tried telling them certain truths, even fewer would miss me. Soon, I would leave Memphis forever, but I had to tell this story before my departure, if only for my benefit.

A train screeched across one of the neighboring bridges and a gust of wind knocked back my hood. Thankfully, nobody was expecting me anywhere for a while and only a few, if they had even been in town, would have ever thought to look for me here. In other words, I had all the time I needed.

I pulled my hood back over my head and tightened the drawstrings. Then I rested my elbows on the middle metal railing, feeling the cold through all my layers, as the train whistles faded, the traffic above me thinned, and the wind died. I opened the bourbon and took a few swigs. It wasn't top shelf, but never had any bourbon ever tasted that good, like the peaceful warmth of a hearth in an otherwise empty home, one never sullied by the presence of people you detested.

I screwed the cap back onto the bottle, knowing that if I ever hoped to piece these fragments together, I had to begin when I met Adam.

# PART I

*Mysophobia*: irrationally fearing contamination while simultaneously feeling ridiculous. It's watching logic drown beneath
waves of worry. How much had been tainted and how far had
that blight been smeared in spit and semen?

See also: ritualized distraction,
and situational promiscuity with varying levels of risk.

*One day, I'll be forced to reconcile my drunken choices
with all of my fears. Which is to say, why can't I give up
all the things that put me at risk in favor of those that
don't make me cringe whenever I see my reflection? If
regret is all I'm clinging to, fine, why not admit it? That
may not be the healthiest approach, but couldn't I be
happier if I were honest with myself?*

— 2 APRIL 2003

# CHAPTER ONE

When I raised the dishwasher's doors and rolled out the clean rack, steam condensed into a cold sheen on my face and arms. I rolled in a rack of rinsed but dirty plates and bowls, set the machine on a three-minute cycle, and popped my neck.

"Freud!" the newest sous chef yelled at me. I couldn't remember her name, so while I didn't mind her not knowing mine, I did mind her unearned shorthand.

I shut off the pre-rinse hose and held a dripping plate crusted with marinara.

"*Sigmund!*" she barked.

"What, *Jung?*" I yelled back.

"Your couch's getting crowded."

I hoped she meant the trash and not the shrimp bucket. I'd rather scrape clean the present backlog of plates and forks with my teeth than be drafted into peeling, de-veining, and butterflying another five pounds of shrimp. That reek took its sweet ass time fading.

"*Throat cancer, empty the trash!*"

"On it," I called back. Three brimful bags awaited me.

Since I gave up using my Bachelor's, I'd been working in restaurants. Apart from a suspiciously evanescent stint waiting tables, I'd been washing dishes at Café d'Esyal. Whenever I had to take out the trash, "BS" never felt anything other than perfect.

The sous chef said, "Sorry to drag you away from your favorite little ritual."

I thought, *Great, her first OCD joke*, but replied, "It wasn't throat cancer."

"Whaddya say?"

"Freud died of—"

"Terminal misogyny," she laughed, flambéing an order.

By then, I'd been living in Memphis for eight years. I'd majored in psychology from the start, not realizing how bad any prospects beside going straight to grad school were.

It was early April and already hitting the eighties, but when I opened the back door, it felt cool against my damp T-shirt. As I carried two bags to the dumpster, a shirtless guy on a mountain bike zipped into the neighboring Indian restaurant's Poplar Avenue parking lot.

He coasted down the shared driveway between the restaurants, staring at me while heading toward North Evergreen. Another nameless and gorgeous man on the periphery of my life. Flashes more intimated than seen, more gesture than substance, around for a night if that. I hauled over the third bag. Whenever I thought a guy might be relationship-material, he'd either disappear or realize we'd make better friends than lovers. I threw the dumpster lid open and heaved in the first two bags.

Soon, the guy pedaled back up the driveway, smirking. He hopped off his ride and leaned it against the wall, his drawl a dredging of the Mississippi: "I bet you'd know."

"What's that?" I tossed in the last bag. He wouldn't break eye-contact, not even when l let the lid slam shut. *Maybe it's my lucky day*, I thought. *Straight guys don't look at you that directly.* His eyes were as green as mine, but his hair was corn tassel blond while mine was bright red. Before I knew it, my lips mirrored his smirk.

"I'm a little lost," he glanced over his shoulder, tracing a route on a non-existent map with his left hand.

I scanned him from neck to calves. Several inches taller than me, at least six-foot-three, his chest and legs were covered in blond hair, darkened by sweat. He had a deep tan, and where his underwear had slunk the skin was bright white. *I'm a fuckin' cliche*, I thought. Of course, as soon as a guy who looked like him showed up, I was suddenly one more horny faggot. It'd be funny if it weren't so damn pathetic how eager I was to find some exception to all of my OCD rituals so I could feel this gorgeous man's hands on my body. In therapy-speak, now was the time I should HALT.

Was I *hungry*? Famished.

Was I *angry*? By default.

How *lonely* was I? Well, that was complicated.

And, last, was I *tired*? No, I just wanted a couple years of unconsciousness, and even then I'd probably still wake up wishing my slumber could have gone a decade longer.

Everybody was a cliche at some point, and there was nothing wrong with that. To hookup anytime, every time, I got the urge—I didn't think I could live in that headspace, but vacationing there wouldn't be all that bad.

"That's Poplar, right?" He quit drawing his map, pulled up the waistband of his cargo shorts. "Where's Cooper-Young?"

That neighborhood was a few miles away. I gave him directions, telling him, "You can't miss it."

Before I could stop him, he was shaking my hand. "My name's Adam." His smile was brighter than that sliver of hip.

If given the chance, I wouldn't mind wrestling that cliche into the ground for a couple hours. "Bryan," I said.

"Hold on." Adam rummaged through his pockets. A few seconds later, he uncapped a Sharpie with his teeth, grabbed my right wrist, and wrote his telephone number on my forearm. "Call me, if you want," he said, peddling away.

I wondered how much soap it was going to take to wash it off. But two days later his number was ghostly, so I called him before I lost both it and my nerve.

While getting ready for our dinner date, I had a couple beers and straightened up the apartment. My roommate, Chris, was visiting family in Atlanta for a few more days. He always kept the place tidy, because he never knew when he might bring a trick home. I carried a few empty beer bottles and a couple of fast-food bags to the kitchen trashcan, and then I washed the three plates I'd let pile up.

We lived in the second apartment building east of the Cooper-Poplar T-bone, on the front left corner of a third-floor walk-up. The building was shaped like a squared-off "C" and its dark red brick was accentuated by gray brick overhangs above the sunroom's windows and diamond designs on the street-facing stairwells. The "C's" arms stretched toward Poplar Avenue, and between them was a huge courtyard filled with big-leaved plants, wisteria shrubs, vines, and old trees casting plentiful shade. There were two stone benches placed in pleasant spots overlooking the busy street and the park beyond it, not that I'd ever seen anybody lounging out there with a book.

I'd met Chris over a year ago when we both worked at the Midtown TGI Fridays. He was biracial and a junior at the U of M, majoring in drama. On one of my last closing shifts, a mugger caught me off-guard. Before I knew it, Chris had swung his backpack into the fucker's head, knocking him to the ground. As he drove me to my shitty apartment, he said, "My roommate skipped town a few days ago. Only left me half of his next month's rent, but he did write a nice little note about how he was going to Taos to find himself." Before I got out, he added, "If you're looking for better digs, I'm looking for a new roomy."

Less than a month later, Curt had dumped me. "Thanks for making it so easy," he said while moving out. He made sure to let our septuagenarian landlady know I couldn't afford the rent by myself. The next time I saw her, she shook her head: "Curt warned me I shouldn't trust what you say." I wouldn't have been surprised if he'd told her I'd cheated on him. She lived on the other side of the duplex, and from the blaring TV I knew she loved her soaps. In other words, I was sure she'd scarf down any real-life drama.

When I toured this place, Chris met me in the parking lot, and we walked around to the front stairwell. "These apartments were built shortly after the Second World War. Back then, apparently, people were really tall and had tiny feet. You can tell that from the narrow steps and the twelve-foot ceilings." Less than a thousand square feet total, the unit was all hardwood floors and crown molding. "I know the kitchen's cramped, but its sink and sidebars are porcelain. I love it. None of the metal cupboards and drawers opens quietly, but you'll get used to those." Aside from the microwave, coffee maker, and toaster, it was archetypal, like an image on a stamp issued near the holidays. "Perfect, right?" Chris said.

Past the kitchen was a hallway that dead-ended in a nook on the left and the bathroom on the right. Chris's bedroom shared one wall with the kitchen and a short stretch with mine on the opposite side. The largest space was the living room, which lay to the right of my bedroom and was filled with Chris's huge TV, entertainment center, and game consoles. The living room flowed into a tiny sunroom. Through the bay windows, we had a nice view of Overton Park.

The old growth forest looked especially thick this spring. Ten minutes before Adam was supposed to pick me up, I exited through the kitchen door, locking the deadbolt and checking the knob three times. The porch was about eight feet by four feet. Chris had had a plant on the porch for a while, but the pot was now home to whatever weeds had found their way up here. The iron stairwell zigzagged between three floors, down to an alley that opened onto a narrow driveway which connected with Poplar Avenue. The driveway could accommodate a single car, but you never knew if anyone would be driving out as you were pulling in, so most people entered the parking lot from Cooper, braving the paving as cratered as the moon instead of having to back out onto Poplar.

Unlike the building's curb appeal, behind it the parking lot was crowded and sad-looking. The building's two dumpsters were constantly full of, or surrounded by, discarded furniture and mattresses. It looked like tenants were being evicted every week and abandoning all their worldly possessions. Not that I ever saw this happening. No sheriff's deputies, no loud knocking on neighbors' doors, no walks of shame. But some mornings I'd find another stripped mattress, a futon, a dresser with its drawers open, or a sofa stood on its end and leaning against the dumpster.

I paced the parking lot and before long a red Chevy Blazer pulled in. Adam rolled down the window, "You cruising?" He was smiling, but it didn't quite reach his eyes. "Think I found a cool place. Ever had tapas?"

"Are you talking about the restaurant right by the Cooper-Young gazebo?"

"Yep," he thumbed at the passenger seat. "I think it's called Ménage."

*They might have better luck if they'd named it that.* I buckled up. "It's Mélange, for now anyway." Adam made a face, so I explained, "That spot is cursed. I'm surprised that restaurant has lasted this long."

"So, what you're saying is, we should hurry?" He drove toward Cooper, not worrying about the potholes.

*Better order as many small plates as you can.* Dusk sharpened my reflection in the window. *Feast now because the famine could resume tomorrow.*

Soon, we were seated at a two-top in a back corner, his left hand near the wall, mine by the service aisle, and we talked and drank. Adam had one dimple on his right cheek. His forearms and the backs of his hands were outlined in blond hair.

Adam asked, "You in school?"

"I graduated in ninety-nine. What about you?"

"I have one semester left. What was your major?" After I told him, he asked, "So you wanted to help people?"

I laughed.

"Did I say something funny?" he asked.

"No, you just made me remember something that professors in the experimental and cognitive tracks used to say."

"Go on."

"If you're majoring in psychology because you want to help people, get your ass to therapy. Stat."

"Nothing worse than being idealistic, right? So you're a chef now?"

"I'm a dishwasher and occasionally I get to play line-cook," which was true in the loosest sense. "Honestly, it's not as bad as you think. The clientele is on the generous side, and thanks to the owner I get tipped-out on top of a decent hourly. But," I began lying outright, "I'm prepping for the GRE and thinking about applying to different grad schools. What about you?"

"I'm majoring in biology. I'd love to get into med school. Hell, who wouldn't—" His cell phone rang. He flipped it open and frowned. "Shit. It's Gillian. She's in the hospital right now. I got to take this."

"Of course," I said, not that he was waiting for my permission. I took a drink of wine and went to the restroom. After pissing, I turned the faucet to scalding and washed my hands. Each time I tabbed the soap dispenser, it snapped loudly.

Good as new. Lather, lather, lather, rinse. *Remember the cliche.* Snap, snap. Good as new. Lather, lather, lather, rinse. If I hooked up with Adam, would all this hand-washing even matter? I bit my lip. *Do you really want to do this?* My reflection was fogged up by the time the toilet in the last stall flushed. The man who walked out adjusted his tie. Times like that convinced me I had synesthesia, because I could almost see the stench of his nascent colon cancer outlining him. A real-life Pig-Pen in an off-the-rack suit from Dillard's, complete with matching tie and pocket square.

In the second sink, he squeezed a tab of soap and washed his hands for all of ten seconds. With his wet right hand, he shut off the faucet, grabbed some paper towels. "Son," he chuckled, "if you're not prepping for surgery, I'd wager you're done." He lobbed the paper towels at the trashcan, his shot going wide. After he was gone, I got three paper towels and dried my hands. Then I bunched those up and used them to shut off the faucet and open the door.

Adam was drumming his right fingers on the tabletop, but he stopped and smiled when he saw me. "Thought you'd high-tailed it. Don't worry, I turned my phone off, like I should've done in the first place."

"Is Gillian"—I sat, raised my wine glass, noticed fresh legs sliding down, took a drink—"all right?"

Our server returned with a new glass for him. Once she was out of earshot, he motioned at my wine, "My bad. After that phone call, I needed a sip to tide me over till the waitress swung back around. Where were we?"

"How's Gillian?"

"God love her," he rolled his eyes, "she's a hypochondriac. You'd think being in a hospital would be her idea of heaven."

"Who is she?"

"My mom, and before you ask, I've always called her by her first name. She's a hippy and didn't want an authoritarian relationship."

"The hypochondriac hippy?"

"Listen at me. How bad am I sucking at this?" he laughed. "My first date with a guy and I'm talking about my mother. Bet you and your psych degree could have a field day with that. Where were we?" He pushed the menu away.

"Your first *what*?"

"Yeah, I came out like two weeks ago." He sipped his wine.

"You're a quick study."

"C'mon, Bryan, you're not the first guy I've flirted with, only the first I don't have to lie to myself about why I'm doing it." This time, Adam's smile reached his eyes. "Know what I'm thinking?"

"Bound to be one of a few things. I could guess, but I can tell you like getting straight to the point."

"Seems like we have that in common. So how's about we finish our wine and go, get to know each other better somewhere a little more private? What do you think, and be honest?"

"I will, because there's nothing I hate more than a liar."

"Who doesn't?" he laughed, wiping his lips with a napkin,

his lone dimple reappearing. Then he reached his left hand across the table. I instinctively pulled mine back. He frowned and motioned around. "Nobody cares, man." I took a few breaths and flipped my hand palm up. His hand was warm, his grip firm, and I matched it until he asked me what was wrong.

"Nothing," I pulled my hand free and took a drink.

"Remember what you said about liars? And you never answered my question."

He had me there. After taking another drink of wine, I asked, "I'm fine with that plan, but where are we going?"

"Do you have a roommate?" I nodded, and he said, "Yeah, I've got two of 'em." He resumed drumming his right fingers on the tabletop, from pinky to thumb and back again.

I was about to make a suggestion, when our server reappeared. "What will you be having tonight?"

"One more round and the check," I said. As she slapped shut her waiter wallet and visited another table, Adam was smirking. "I have a roommate, but he's down in Georgia right now, and I have tomorrow off work."

"Ain't that convenient?" He arched an eyebrow.

"Coincidences do happen."

"I'll toast to that," he said, and as we did, I couldn't stop smiling.

# CHAPTER TWO

When it comes to bloody sheets, it doesn't matter how much red you see, it's always too much and it always hurts more than you expect. Whatever this hangover was, it wasn't from the wine. I knew that with as much certainty as I couldn't remember getting home. I was lying on my stomach, and the light coming through the blinds meant it was either dawn or dusk. The back and left side of my skull were sore, and when I rubbed my face, dried blood flaked off.

Worried but hesitant, I elbowed up and rolled my hips, which made every hair below my waist feel like it had been snagged in a zipper that never stopped. Even worse, the sheets were stuck to my ass and thighs with blood like a Band-Aid made from duct tape.

After I peeled those away, I swung my legs over my bed and stood. The hardwood floors tilted up to my elbow, shoulder, and face. From this angle, I noticed the lamp and a glass of water had been knocked off my nightstand. Books lay scattered across the floor and a chair was overturned.

The room listed left and right and trimmed forward and

back as I got to my feet again. I shut my eyes until the seas calmed a little, then I took two pumps from my inhaler. I shuffled to the bathroom as slowly as I could, keeping a hand on the wall. Before I saw my reflection, I knew I needed to be careful, to be ready for the gasp and clench and pause. My right eye was black. My right lower lip was swollen. While my face wasn't as disfigured as the first time I'd caught poison ivy, it was worthy of a "very special episode," one which my roommate would have gladly narrated if he were home.

I should have called someone, but that late morning or early afternoon, whenever, all I focused on was cleaning up. While I sat on my knees in the shower, the water ran red at first. I stayed in there for as long as I could stand it, but the water's temperature felt wrong whichever direction I dialed it. Because water races to the lowest point, there was no way to slow the rivulets that sought out the spans of skin that both needed and hated it the most.

Later that day, as I balled up the sheets and stuffed them into a garbage bag (I didn't want anyone in the building's laundry room seeing what I was washing), I searched for the used condom. Nothing, not even an open wrapper. I'd had plenty of hangovers, but none ever lasted two days. And none ever haunted me beyond that.

Over the next couple of weeks, I tried tracking Adam down —to demand answers about the missing hours and make him admit what he'd done. Every call went straight to voice mail. Could I have avoided all the pain and mess by simply letting go, letting it happen? Maybe I had tried to and failed. It didn't seem to matter either way. Two decades before Adam, after so much had been stolen from me, I'd tried acting like everything was normal. Once, a therapist had told me that letting go was a choice I could make if only I wanted it badly enough. When I couldn't forgive my abuser, it felt like I'd failed all over again.

Eventually, that therapist dumped me as a client. "This will sound blunt," he had told me at the end of our final session, "but I am not convinced you actually want to heal your traumas." Years later, I still worried his assessment had been spot-on.

Every time I flipped my cell phone shut, after yet another call to Adam went unanswered, I couldn't slow my pulse or keep the walls and ceiling from closing in on me. Once I'd healed, I would lace up my shoes and go running. My pace had never been better, but it didn't help because no matter how far or fast I ran, I returned to this same apartment, the bathroom mirror never letting me forget who I was and what had been done to me. *Again.*

Chris knew something was up when he got back to town, but he didn't press the issue, letting me hibernate in my bedroom. Every hibernation has to end at some point, though, so as the end of the spring semester neared, Chris said, "Let's do lunch. There's someone you should meet. He'll help you forget whoever you're moping over. Trust me, he's great, so it'll be great."

I should have told him about Adam then, but I didn't. At best, I could get laid by this supposedly great fellow, not that I had any interest in that. At worst, I'd meet somebody who seemed promising only for him to later disappear. All I said was, "I hate tautologies."

"And I hate all that astrological bullshit."

"Chris, they're not—"

"Duh, brainiac. And, please, you thrive on them."

"Fine," I gave up. "Tell me when and where to be."

At the university's older cafeteria the next day, I avoided the fast-food offerings and got a bowl of broccoli fettuccini Alfredo and a fountain Coke. While the cashier was counting out my change, I remembered my first-grade teacher, who was a great-grandmother but went by "Miss." After one vocabulary quiz, she'd chastised another student: "You are *not* kids. *Kids* are *goats*. You are *children*." She had also told my class, "Never put coins in your mouth. You have no idea where they've been."

For whatever reason, cash didn't bother me as much as coins or this particular cashier's fingers when he'd scraped those against my palm. When would the treasury stop minting coins? Think about all the people who'd handled them before you did. Think about how many times the coins had been dropped on the floor and stepped on.

After wadding the bills around the coins, I stuffed them in my back pocket. The thin paper cup of my soda was sweating. I grabbed the cup and lowered my hand, wetting my fingers and palm, which was the least I could do until I found a seat and was able to use my small bottle of hand sanitizer.

Crowds always made me uneasy, and the cafeteria was packed. Each student's blinks, the careful stroke of fine bristles removing the camouflage of history's detritus, grain by grain— as if the fossil could feel its piecemeal exposure.

Rationally, I knew strangers would notice little besides my right eye (but not my left) somehow missing out on a few nights' sleep. When I'd checked in the mirror, I could still trace the outlines of a bruise. Walking felt normal, unless I let my mind wander. Then I could feel sharp edges where none should be, a field of crystals folded in half and grinding against itself.

Across the room, there was an open four-top. It was between two tall windows and beneath an enlarged black-and-white photograph of Miss America '41, an alumna, who wore a crown and short cape. I walked toward Miss America until I noticed Adam sitting at a neighboring table. He was finishing off a submarine sandwich as a redheaded woman talked to him. He must have found whatever she said amusing, because he grinned and pecked her on the cheek. When he saw me, he took a sip from his soda.

I froze. My hands shook. Drink, bowl, and silverware slid to the edge. My jaws clenched. My lunch crashed to the tiled floor and my stomach turned itself inside out, a used sock, but I couldn't break away from Adam's stare.

He smirked but kept talking to the woman. His dimple, another smirk.

Funny, how much worse the inside of a worn sock feels than the outside.

While the woman rummaged through her backpack, he stared right at me. Winked. Took a longer drink from his fountain soda.

My hands dropped the tray, my legs bolted me out of the cafeteria, and my mind thought: *You're pathetic. And stupid. And pathetic. And stupid.*

Once I got outside Jones Hall, I gulped for air. I hit my inhaler as I rounded the Admin building and found an empty bench. For several minutes, I took slow, deep breaths. Clouds frayed across the sky, and the breeze was steady. The shock faded, replaced by anger. Part of me wanted to obliterate Adam's smirk with a determined patience, to shred it layer by layer.

I stood and started walking back to the cafeteria, deciding I was going to introduce myself to the woman I assumed was Gillian. Would she be more upset about Adam being bisexual or about him telling me she was his mother?

But as I raced across the lawn under a tree's shade, I tripped on an exposed root, and that resolve vanished. When I got back up, I promised myself, *The next time,* and began the trek to the corner of Poplar and Highland. While I waited for the bus to Midtown, I couldn't decide if him admitting what he'd done would be enough, but I'd start with that.

\* \* \*

A couple hours after getting home, I logged onto AOL. The Memphis M4M chat room wasn't that busy and nobody's screen name seemed like it could be Adam. I switched to Gay.com and then Manhunt and searched for his profiles, but every one of them was a bust. When I gave that up, I laughed at myself: *What? You really expected to find him advertising his cock on the web?*

Before I disconnected the modem, I logged into my email and found a spam asking me to verify my checking account at a bank I'd never used. At the bottom of the email was this string of nonsense:

*the Crown uses departmental murder as a principal, the national bodies party, so much cake... a crypt, the filth of finish is fitting for the empress of Disneyland regiment... not even Boltzmann could wrap his mind around this...*

You and me both, Boltzmann. This passage meant nothing except what I projected onto it, but that wasn't the point. I highlighted those sentences and dragged a text clipping onto my desktop. There were over twenty such snippets randomly juxtaposed from the spam I'd been receiving the past six months. I liked the symmetry found in the shared nonsense and *the filth of finish is fitting* had a nice ring to it.

I wrote down that line in my journal and continued: *So much filth is invisible—if not microscopic, then ignored because it's so commonplace. But what happens when the "finish" of a person or a thing is not only accepted but expected, a condition without which that person or thing is regarded as being somehow incomplete, and if not that, then disappointing? Without a doubt, that was how Curt saw me, and no matter how I phrased an apology, nothing would ever change. If I told him, "I'm sorry for being the sperm that fertilized the egg," he'd shake his head, and say, "That's a good start, but what else do you got?"*

Chris got home late that night, carrying a couple Seessel's grocery bags and our mail. When he saw me on the couch, he said, "Hey, dick. A heads-up would've been nice."

"I ran into someone and had to get out of there."

Chris set the bags on the coffee table. "Who pray tell?"

"Someone I went on a date with while you were visiting your folks."

"Go on."

"We came back here."

"The first guy you ever hosted and I missed it?"

"*Chris.*"

"Fine. I assume you were fucked up, but how fucked up are we talking?"

"Wish I knew the answer."

"After rooming with you, I wouldn't be worried."

"It's not that simple, Chris."

"Why not?" I didn't have an answer, or at least one I was willing to tell him yet. He continued. "It's been several weeks, right?"

"Yeah."

"Have any freeloaders hatched?"

"What?"

"Is gravy seeping from your dick or ass? Are there any blisters?"

I stared at the far wall, fingernails digging into my palms and feeling more pathetic after every question. While I didn't want to be interrogated, I wouldn't have turned down a hug. Hell, a hand on my shoulder would have been nice. But there was one thing I knew for certain: Chris would be more comfortable giving me a urethral swab than any kind of physical reassurance.

"What I'm getting at," he said, "and I say this with love in my admittedly atrophied heart, is knowing you, you're overre-acting. Sure, you have shit taste in men, but you're one of *the* most cautious people I've ever known. Wait a couple months and if nothing happens in the meantime, go get tested. Till then, you've got two options: worry yourself into a twenty-four-seven panic attack or try and live as regular a life as you can."

Like most people do when it comes to their own advice, he believed what he was selling. "It's probably nothing," I played along, "other than me overreacting," while thinking, *The next time I run into Adam, we'll see who overreacts.*

"What's the schmuck's name, by the way?"

After I told Chris, he picked up the grocery bags and headed to the kitchen, saying, "Ain't ringing a bell."

# CHAPTER THREE

I wouldn't meet my roommate's "Trust me, he's great" until the end of May when Chris dragged me to Club Fugue on a Tuesday night. The University of Memphis's theatre department had rented out the city's largest gay club for a cast party. Chris and Mr.-he's-great had had *small* roles in *Lysistrata Erotica*.

A couple hours earlier, Chris had poked his head in my bedroom door and said, "You can read Stephen Hawking any old time." I told him that was cute. "Which is exactly how you should dress," he said. "And believe me, whatever outfit you pick will be nowhere near as cute as the friend I want you to meet." He walked down the hall, saying, "Giddy-up or we'll be fashionably later than I was already planning on."

It was only when Chris walked into the living room holding up two shirts that I realized how quickly I'd showered, shaved, and gotten dressed. My haste, an unconscious enthusiasm. "Which shirt goes best with my jeans?" he held up two hangers. I told him the one on the left. He tossed that onto the sofa beside me and put on the other shirt. As he buttoned up and walked back to his room, I checked my pulse on my neck and steadied my breathing.

Before leaving the apartment, I dug out an old paperback copy of *Naked Lunch* that I kept buried under T-shirts in my dresser. I flipped through the pages until I found a tab of acid. I hadn't dropped any for over a year, but it might still be good. While I could handle hanging out with Chris, I knew I would need a buffer for the shit-ton of theatre-nerds and the gay bar itself.

Club Fugue was several thousand square feet of OCD triggers and bad associations. As we entered, Chris and I handed over our IDs. The front desk attendant took his time finding Chris's name on the guest list. The guy was average height and looked like a scarecrow who had been on too strict of a diet for too long. His dark brown hair was parted to the right and his bangs hung to his nose. "Found you," he said finally, stamping the backs of our hands.

"God," Chris whispered as we walked down the main hallway, "I hate that door-whore. Girl thinks she's a fuckin' manager and not a glorified coat-checker."

At the far end of the hallway, two glass doors opened onto a ramp, which led down to the club's cavernous dance floor. To the left of the ramp was a circular bar and to its right were waist-to-ceiling-high windows, beyond which were a wading pool and patio.

Halfway down the hallway and to the left was the video bar. The wall of TVs behind the bar played music videos and comedy clips and was manned by Puck, a fixture of Memphis's bartending and restaurant scenes.

Across the hall was the lounge, where generic jazz was played and the furniture was upholstered. Every time I'd been in there, I'd seen people lying across this couch or splayed on that love seat in ripped jeans, wondering how much a black light would reveal.

I hung around Chris for a while, but there were too many inside jokes for me to keep track of, so I talked to Puck, who was working the private party. It was odd seeing him serve drinks from behind any bar other than the video bar. I had met him when I worked at the TGI Friday's in Overton Square.

At that fine eating establishment, Puck's ever-present top hat was another piece of flair, the rest of which was frequently risqué. He'd taken me under his brim for the two months I needed to accept I'd never make it as a server. Half the time, I didn't realize what expression my face was making. That had made for awkward interactions with clients before I quit working in the mental health field, but it was a fatal shortcoming for a server.

What I liked most about Puck was that, while he might make fun of you for a tragic hook up, he never thought less of you. Sex was sex, and even if you didn't accept your consensual kinks come dawn, he did.

Instead of "Hello," Puck said, "Something's a bit off with you, Bry."

"What kind of *off*?"

"You have more than one kind?"

I hesitated, *Fuck it*, then asked, "Ever heard of an Adam Whittemore?"

Puck's eyes narrowed. "Taller than you?"

"Yes."

"Hitler's swampiest wet dream?"

I sighed.

Puck said, "Tell me you didn't."

I laid my forehead on the bar.

"This one's on me," he slammed a bottle next to my face.

When I sat up, he continued, "And keep your skull off my station. Where do you think you are, J-Wags?"

"Thanks." I grabbed the Heineken.

"Little use fretting now."

"Why's that?"

"I haven't verified this scuttlebutt from the queens around here, but I've heard tell he's an occasional rent-boy these days. Goes by 'Dex,' if I recall. I love seeing you, Bry." Puck walked toward a new pair of customers. "You always brighten up my day by contrast."

I took another drink.

"You're Chris's roommate, right?" asked a guy behind me.

When I turned around, I answered, "Guilty as charged."

He was taller than me and stacked, like a brown-haired Adam, sounding So-Cal-surf instead of dead-zone-Delta: "Chris told me your name a while ago, but I'm totally spacing. I'm Ian."

"Fitting," I smiled. If this was Chris's "Trust me," he had good taste and definitely knew some of mine.

"What?" he shook his head.

"Nothing. My mind wanders." As hot as he was, Ian reminded me too much of Adam, and I wasn't ready to trust anyone in that category.

"Chris did say you're a special case."

If Chris had told him that, Ian was apparently tactless enough to repeat it. I smiled and asked, "I'm a *what* now?"

"That sounded bad, didn't it?"

"You're quick."

"Dude, I'm sure he meant it as a compliment."

"Sure, that's right up there with, 'Bless his heart.'"

"What's the expression around here: 'I don't know you from Adam.'"

"I'm not a local."

For a moment, his face resembled a dog confused by a magic trick. "Alright. Do-over: I'm Ian, and I need people to feed me lines to keep my feet out of my mouth."

"That was a good one, actually."

"If only I'd come up with it."

I couldn't tell if he was flirting. "I'm Bryan and I suppose I'm a 'special case' because this place skeeves me the hell out. Present company excluded, of course."

"Cool. What did you think of the play?"

Was he the worst kind of actor, the narcissist waiting on stage for his next line instead of engaging? I asked, "How extensive were the fittings for those strap-ons?"

"If you ask my girlfriend," Ian chuckled, waving her over, "I don't need any more encouragement on that front."

A woman sidled up and said, "Are you talking about your dick?"

"Stop, Viv," he mock-whined. "*I* didn't bring it up."

"And you're never one to turn down a fluffer."

"I'm not—" I tried to interject.

"Sometimes, I swear," she said, "you're the gayest straight guy I've ever fucked."

Ian grabbed her by the waist. "Honey, I'll never need any fluffer but you."

"If you guys haven't already auditioned for a Tennessee Williams play," I said, excusing myself, "you should." They continued bantering without me, as I realized I *had* been a fluffer for what would have been some hot sex to watch. A shame I'd never be the right kind of invisible.

At this point, I intersected Chris's orbit. He pulled me into a small circle of guys, his familiar presence enough to hold me there. "Bry, let me introduce you to some folks," he said before explaining I didn't shake hands and rattling off names. "And last is Jason. He's a psych major, just like you were. Figured you'd have some gory work stories to share."

"Gory?" Jason asked, smiling. He was a bit shorter than me and dressed preppy cute, if you ignored his sandy ponytail and sparse attempt at a beard.

"Yes, Bry," Chris tilted his head, a serious expression on his face. "Tell him what he can expect."

"Chris," I frowned—thinking first, *If he's your trust me, we really need to talk,* and then, *I bet the poor fuck wants to help people*—but I said, "There are four things you don't talk about at parties: religion, politics, salaries, and the residential treatment of adolescent sex offenders."

That got Jason's attention. "You worked at Fresh Springs? I was thinking of trying to get a position there, work my way up. Would you recommend I—"

"Ever work at Fresh Springs Adolescent Residential Behavioral Treatment Center, Inc.? Nope. Nada. Never. Nein." I decided not to mention my tenure at the Memphis Forward Living Advocacy Group. If Jason was geeking out this much over a glorified juvenile detention facility where "therapy" was complete when the insurance ran out, I dreaded the black hole of pointless questions that would open up once he knew I'd worked at an HIV/AIDS agency. That had been my favorite job despite the deaths of too many clients for whom HAART's "Lazarus Effect" hadn't arrived in time.

"That's weird." Jason stood with the posture of someone who'd already submitted a job application. "I've heard nothing but good things about them. Maybe you weren't cut out for that line of work."

"No maybes. That's a fact. About four months in, I got transferred from the cottage full of teenage sex offenders to the sexually reactive boys' cottage. My first shift there, I had to break up a seven-year-old boy's number three. Nobody's cut out to see that."

"Number three?" everyone in the group besides Chris and Jason asked.

"'Sexually reactive' means they'd been molested and were either beginning to show signs of becoming a sex offender or they'd already offended before hitting puberty. Because of those factors, they could ask to take a number three, which is a jerk-off break."

"What," Jason asked, "you had to knock on the bathroom door and get the little guy to finish?"

"No, he was spread-eagle on the shower floor, using soap for lube as he flogged away. Apparently, he didn't do this unless he thought no male staff was working. A second grader. Hadn't learned cursive yet."

Jason was breathing through his mouth. Better shut it down now. "If you want to hear about the really awful days, I have a question: how squeamish do you get imagining a game of dodge ball in which you're always the target of bodily fluids and semi-solids?"

While the group was silent, a few acted like they knew where this was headed. Chris's eyes, meanwhile, were as wide as those of any final girl on a horror movie poster from the '80s, his lips sealed around the speared olives from his martini.

"And some of those wards slinging piss, cum, and shit at you," I pressed on, "have infections like hep B or worse, but your bosses won't tell you which ones have what since that would violate their privacy."

"You're kidding, right?" Jason wore the expression of someone who'd suddenly realized "this exclusive, amazing opportunity" following graduation was the worst kind of pyramid scheme, the mortar of which now made him shudder.

"The only upshot?" I said. "Free vaccinations against hep

A and B." Jason stared at me with his mouth open. Chris looked impressed as he sipped his cocktail. I had no idea what my face looked like. "And *he*," I thumbed back at my roommate, "bet me I wasn't as good of an actor as any of you. When's the next audition?"

Chris choked on his martini and slapped my back hard enough without making it obvious.

"Lord," a guy in the group laughed. "Where the fuck do you work now?"

"I wash dishes."

Everyone else started laughing. Someone patted my shoulder, saying, "Good one." And then all of the clique except Jason wandered off.

"Do you..." His forehead had condensed into a realization I wished my advisor had backhanded me with. "Do you think I should apply there?"

I finished my beer and then, in complete honesty, told him, "It will change your life." If he heard what he wanted to hear instead of what should have been obvious, then that was on him. If he was as much of a sap as I had been, he'd go through with it, but this conversation might help him realize there was nothing pure about Fresh Springs much sooner than I had.

"Topher!" shouted a younger guy who was entering the lounge from the patio with a middle-aged man.

Chris said, "About damn time," grabbed my arm, and towed me clear.

The younger guy shook the older man's hand and then strolled over to us. "I knew I shouldn't have gotten here on time."

"We've been waiting on *you*," Chris replied, then he whispered to me: "He's the one."

"Waiting on me?" he replied. He was five-foot-six, and he had ink-black hair and olive skin. He reminded me a lot of my ex. "Right, 'cause you're the most punctual person. I'd apologize for my tardiness, but I think I rocked an impromptu job interview."

"Bry, this is Stefano Malatesta, but he prefers to be called 'Stephen' because of the daytime-programming connotations, or some such shit." Chris continued, "Soap-Opera, this is my roommate, Bryan Meigs. At some point, you should ask about his gunshot wound. Either of y'all parched?"

In the same breath, we replied, "Please" and "Yeah."

Stefano's twice-broken nose made me smile. It suited his hair and small but muscular frame better than a never-broken nose ever could. *Scrappy* came to mind. He'd come out earlier that semester and was five years younger than me.

"I like the contrast," Stefano said.

"Sorry, what?"

"Your eyes and hair."

"You're the first person not to find this fire engine mop cringe-worthy."

With a blank expression, he replied: "I didn't say I don't find it 'cringe-worthy' by itself." When I frowned, he flicked at the few curls of copper that crept above my collar. "Contrasts are nice."

Chris returned, holding two beers in one hand and a new martini in the other. "Here you are, sirs. And now, I think I shall find some who are worthy of my intercourse."

"Like you ever have any problem finding a big enough foot for your slipper," I said.

"Ain't that an interesting metaphor? And careful now: I know where you sleep," Chris said over his shoulder. "Most nights anyway."

Stefano motioned toward the lounge's back door, saying, "C'mon." We stepped onto a covered porch. The patio, from this vantage point, resembled a backward "P." Down the seven steps from the porch, on the left, was a sidewalk between the small wading pool and the dance floor windows. Along the back edge was a serving island, now empty, where the weekend pool bar would be set up.

Heading back toward the lounge on the other side, the space broadened, with a sand volleyball court, two picnic tables, and a fenced-in and landscaped alley that extended along the back of the lounge.

Stefano walked around the empty patio bar twice, a calculating frown. When he turned his back to me, his traps and shoulders were clearly outlined in his shirt. After he caught up with me, we sat atop a picnic table, nursing our beers.

"I've never been here," he said, "or any gay bar, actually."

"Is it everything you ever dreamed it would be?"

"You'd think all of us drama fags could have filled it up with more people. Wouldn't mind seeing the club when it's open to the public. That dance floor looks fun."

"I don't come here often."

"Yeah... Topher told me about your hang-ups."

"*Topher?*" I said. "More like 'top her.'" Stefano snorted. I took that as a good sign and asked, "Speaking of my hang-ups, did Chris call me a 'special case'?"

"Not that I remember, and I don't think I'd forget that. Anyways, we've all got our own bullshit. I could judge you for yours, but then you'd judge me for mine. Besides, you're handsome."

I felt like I was the protagonist of a certain Carole King song.

"What're you smiling at?" he asked.

"Nothing," I chuckled. "Tell me about this job interview you aced."

"Pool bartender," he said, thumbing to our right. "Think I'm gonna do it."

Then, being hospitable, I asked, "You smoke?"

"Only pot."

I lit us up. He took a long hit, holding it down until he started coughing.

"You could have declined."

"When in Rome or on the patio of a gay bar," he said. "Anyways, Chris swears your scar is beautiful. But I have me some doubts."

I pulled my right arm out of its sleeve and lifted my shirt.

Stefano placed his palm on my chest, his fingers colder than I'd expected, and traced them across the hairless whorls of scar tissue inward toward my sternum then up and outward to my shoulder.

"How about we finish these," he raised his beer, "then split before Chris calls in his debts? I wouldn't mind seeing y'all's place, as much as he brags about it."

# CHAPTER FOUR

"**D**id you rob the whole fuckin' library?" Stefano laughed, meaning the uneven columns of books stacked a couple feet high against the far wall of my bedroom.

"Nothing's cheaper than reading except writing."

"Are these, like, your version of garlic and crosses? A way to ward off illiterates?" Then Stefano patted the top of my ten-inch black-and-white, rabbit-eared TV, saying, "Nice set."

"I bought that on lay-a-way, saving up my allowance," I explained. "I was nine and liked deciding what I watched, not caring if I had to watch it alone in my bedroom on a grainy screen. The reception sucks, so now it's more for meditation."

Stefano ran his fingers across book spines. "Your room's a metaphor made literal. Walls of words. Would I have to get a library card to check out anything from your collection?" Before I could reply to his joke, he pointed toward my door. "What's in the boxes?"

He meant the three long white boxes. "Comics," I answered, but he was on to something. Walls of words. Defenses composed of poetry, histories, biographies, memoirs, and outright fictions—lives mediated through the finality of a narrative, alive and dynamic, yet static all the same.

Stefano snapped his fingers in front of my face. "Still with us, Bry?"

Everything was kicking in. "Sorry." I plopped on my bed. My mind was a Newton's Cradle, except those steel balls were ricocheting off one another in every direction instead of shuffling in a single, clean line.

Stefano knelt between my legs, kissed me, and rubbed my thighs. "You know what I've never done?" His voice, a hand momentarily stilling that kinetic desk toy.

"That's a loaded question," I laughed, lying back. The acid, beer, and pot transformed my bed into a spaceship—hovering, revolving, and glorious. The ceiling fled from the floor like we were jumping to hyperspace. My bedroom's walls fell away, and gravity concentrated in my crotch.

Stefano unzipped my jeans and yanked them and my boxers down. My cock flopped out, and after a few seconds, I began doubting his inexperience, telling him as much between the pinprick shivers of ice and heat.

Mid-bob he joked, "Actors gotta commit."

I was lost in the contrast of his soft lips and callused palms, the quick upstroke, warm spit, and velvet. When I came, my mind was lost to a swirling exit from hyperspace.

Wiping his lips, Stefano asked, "Does that get me a library card?"

"Hold on," I laughed, pulling him onto the bed and kneeling in front of him.

A head rush walloped me, my mind wandering to the breathless moment the Eucharist was placed upon my tongue, where the wafer would remain dry for a split-second before it began absorbing my saliva from the center outward, an explosion, a blossoming. Mass after Mass, the priest stalled the blessing slightly, his gaze lingering on my open mouth. But then I'd paid attention: the priest did this with everyone regardless of age or gender. What private and inviolate transubstantiation was he witnessing?

After I blinked several times, Stefano asked, "You okay?"

I told him, "Never better." My mouth was open and waiting, eyes raised and unblinking. Stefano combed the fingers of his left hand through my hair and cupped my skull. I barely breathed as I sucked his girthy cock. My silence, a prayer.

After we'd moved onto the bed, my skull got knocked around while Stefano fucked my mouth. A part of me took leave during this, watching the scene from above. The part that stayed didn't think in words.

Stefano raised my chin and lightly smacked my face with his left hand. When his eyes narrowed, I smiled. He grabbed his cock in his right hand, a make-shift mouth-guard, which slammed into my nose and mouth harder and faster.

Though I'd already come, I matched his rhythm with my own hand, muttering gutturals. I shut my eyes, concentrating on the slapping thud of flesh, the wetness of spit and pre-cum. This lasted until one of Stefano's thrusts knocked my face to the bed. I laughed until I felt the familiar trickling warmth of brine.

"Shit! You okay? God, I didn't mean to—"

"I'm fine," I sighed, disgusted with myself. "It'll stop in a minute or two. Did I get any on you?"

For whatever reason, Stefano scanned his chest and shoulders for signs of red, "Nah, don't think so." Then he saw the stain on the bed where my face had landed. "The sheets weren't as—" Finally, he noticed his crotch. "Jesus, fuck!"

Naked, he raced down the short hallway to the bathroom —"Fuck!"—I was grateful Chris wouldn't make it home for several hours—"Fuck! Fuck! Fuck!"—and switched on the faucet.

I followed and tried to keep my nose from dripping. I slouched against the doorjamb, pinching my nostrils tight, and watched.

Stefano was tiptoeing—his forehead pressed flat against the mirror, his breath fogging the glass—while he soaped up his softening cock and washed off a few drops of blood.

Rationally, I knew how little risk he was in, but I couldn't blame him. At the same time, I wanted to tell him he'd be fine and that he was being ridiculous, then I caught sight of my face in the mirror. Before that moment, I would have said I looked calm, but my expression was as angry as I felt whenever I was in the middle of one of my rituals.

Stefano let out an embarrassed chuckle. "Sorry, man." His shoulders were held high and his calves were tensed. "Better safe than sorry." God, his ass was gorgeous.

I shut my eyes as he lathered up for a second time and pinched my nose harder. The blood was slick in my throat. I swallowed it and started to stiffen. "There are clean towels in the cabinet behind you." I walked to the kitchen. "I'm going to give you some space so I can take care of my nose. I'll have a beer waiting for you."

When I heard him say—"I'll be there in a minute"—I grinned, glad the night hadn't been completely ruined. If I had been in Stefano's place, I would have been out the door as soon as I had finished washing up.

# CHAPTER FIVE

The following weekend, eager for another chance to hook up with Stefano, I forced myself to go clubbing with him and Chris. We hit Fugue first, then a bar called Ntropé. The latter was nestled in a gully behind the Forest Hill Dairy plant on Madison and didn't close till a quarter-to-five with a wink to the MPD that they stopped serving at a quarter-to-three. At both clubs, I kept an eye out for Adam, trying not to make it too obvious because I didn't want Stefano to think I wasn't interested in him.

Throughout Ntropé's final drag show, Stefano and I sat next to each other at a four-top, our knees touching, while Chris talked to people at the next table. One performer couldn't lip-sync in time with the lyrics and her dance moves were several time zones behind her lips. At one point, the queen who was emceeing the show told a heckler, "You are *ka-rashing* my T-cells! You want me to die so I can't *kill?* Get the fuck outta here. No, *guurrl*, really. The door's right there."

Stefano clapped and laughed throughout the show. The next performer was a pageant queen, so I told him, "Watch where she points." When she pointed left and then walked that way, Stefano patted my knee and left it there, squeezing lightly. As entertaining as Ntropé's drag revue was, for most people the bar's real draw was how, whether on the dance floor, the patio, or in the dimly lit side hallway, you could find whichever party favors you desired.

After the show ended, Stefano and I made our way to the dance floor. Until the harsh fluorescent lights were flipped on and the desperate hit up the sidewalk sale, we danced, drinking from red Solo cups, illegally filled and refilled with cheap draft beer. Tonight's vintage was Icehouse. It could have been worse. At least they weren't serving Milwaukee's Best.

Stefano put an arm around my waist, pulled me close, and kissed me. After that, he stepped back and thumped my crotch. When Chris caught up with us, he and Stefano huddled close, conversing for a minute, before they left to get a beer. It was after three and the dance floor made me feel claustrophobic and filthy, but I was counting this drunken systematic desensitization as a step forward.

*　*　*

When it came to my OCD, ironically, a lot of it was about distrusting soap. Did it truly disinfect, or was that merely marketing? I understood how it was supposed to work, and even I couldn't deny its smell, its odor so crisp and so closely paired with the very idea of cleanliness. Still, I had to wash my hands with scalding water *at least* seven times after shaking someone's hand or rising from the toilet. As it did with the venal and mortal, my mind leveled all distinctions: if a sin was a sin, then a contaminant was a contaminant.

OCD was accepting that my hands have aged much more than my twenty-six years of life. It was hearing from strangers,

45

"Man, seeing your hands makes mine hurt," not that I could blame them. Most days, the skin between my fingers readily flaked away, and my knuckles were crisscrossed by fault lines that resembled sunbaked mud and stung when I was forced to resort to hand sanitizer.

It was reassuring those who asked: no, no, no—it's *not* a value judgment. How could I politely explain that it *was* a condemnation? Sometimes subtle, sometimes not, and pretty much never based in reality. Regardless, the whole process seemed much too simple: wet, lather, and repeat for the time it took to sing "Twinkle, Twinkle Little Star." Clean? Hardly.

\* \* \*

Across the dance floor, near the restrooms, there was somebody who could have been Adam. He was the right height and build, but I could only see him from the waist up and he wasn't looking in my direction. If that were him, I thought about tapping his shoulder and punching him as he turned around. Even if he didn't say, "I'm sorry," seeing him sprawled on the dance floor might be enough. I needed some sort of satisfaction, and I'd rip that from him however I could.

It took longer than I thought it would to make my way over to this possible Adam because I was doing my best to avoid touching people, which was difficult enough without the group of handsy twinks who were apparently rolling for the first time.

Finally, I was several feet away from the guy, and maybe the crowd had made me angry, but I wished I had a beer bottle to smash against his skull. When he turned around, I was glad my hands were empty, because whoever this was, his chin was too long and his hairline was receding. He grinned at me. I kept on walking.

The men's restroom was disgusting. There was only one

sink for two stalls and three urinals, the latter of which were crowded with guys pissing at a leisurely pace while they trawled for a trick. The stalls weren't much better. Yes, both had doors, but they got monopolized by faggles of two or three who needed privacy to snort a line. Luckily this time, the stalls were empty.

I walked into the first one, using a sandwich bag to close and lock the door and the bottom edge of my right shoe's tread to lift the seat. The music's bass bumped, whistles shrilled, and people clapped as I unzipped and waited for my pee shyness to subside.

\* \* \*

OCD was about anticipating triggers, in whatever form those presented themselves. Regardless, upon each, the periphery dissolved so I could focus on the minutia of a gesture or an action, or the potential of either. Sometimes at the urinal, no matter how careful I was, my piss ricocheted back, drops surely contaminated by the piss of every guy who'd stepped up, zipped down, yanked out, and sighed into his stream. Contaminated somehow even though the urinal had surely been flushed at least once before I started pissing.

It was about mapping where each pin-drop splashed—a finger, a forearm, sometimes my face—so like a leper who believed soap was the answer, I could monopolize the sink. And how many times had I seen a man exit a stall after hearing him unroll a tree's-worth of toilet paper, his stench a contrail, as he checked himself in the mirror, fingered through his hair, and left the restroom without wetting his hands under the faucet?

It was about opening doors with make-shift gloves (a sandwich bag, a folded paper towel, or a shirttail, in order of desperation) to prevent skin contact. Doorknobs and handles were outdated, dangerous. (Those always made me think about salad bars. Which cult was it, I couldn't remember, that sprayed *E. coli* on a restaurant's doorknobs and salad bar tongs as a test run for a biological doomsday-offensive? How people could trust salad bars was beyond me.)

It was about distrusting the flush handle of my toilet, no matter how many times I'd cleaned the bathroom with bleach and disinfecting foam that I sprayed from an aerosol can featuring anthropomorphic bubbles. On the bottle, they were pictured racing forward at an angle, their eyebrows raised over wide-open eyes. (When I was younger, I'd wanted to program a video game wherein I would *be* the bubble. I remember wishing that the scrub brush bristles were an all-around mustache, but back then I never stopped to consider how this mustache would be, once dry, clumped together by filth. Was that why I distrusted guys who only sported a 'stache?)

* * *

After I shook off and zipped up, I used the sandwich bag to unlock the door and my shoe to flush the commode. Yes, I was sullying the flusher with everything the sole of my shoe had walked on. Do you know how many men begin pissing into a urinal and flush it mid-stream using the same hand they'd been aiming with, which goes right back for the shake off? You'd never guess how many zipped up and left without washing their hands.

Thankfully, nobody was waiting for me to be done using the sink. With my trusty glove around the hand that I hadn't used to piss, I turned on the faucet and got a few pumps of soap. I pulled the bag inside out using just my left hand, pocketed it, and washed up. Once I was done, I wiped my hands on my jeans because there were no paper towels, and then used the glove to turn off the faucet. Yes, I got a few stares, but I came here so rarely I didn't care.

I made my way back to where we'd been dancing. Stefano waved me over, and I motioned I was getting a drink. While waiting for my turn at the bar, a shirtless guy several customers down was crying into his beer. Five feet tall and skinny, he was the kind of guy about whom Chris would say, "Girl, those aren't abs, they're ribs. Biscuits are your friends," which I thought about when my roommate walked past us toward the dance floor, shaking his head.

After the crying man was handed a red cup, he turned to his left and saw me. I stared in the opposite direction, but in the bar's mirror, the flash of strobe lights stuttered down his cheeks.

Once I got my drink, I chugged the poor excuse for beer, then found Chris and Stefano near the dance floor's back right corner. Chris wasted no time, getting right next to me and shouting, "Did Dire Duke try to tell you about his latest tragic happenstance?"

"Who?"

"That half-naked mess sobbing at the bar."

"Never gave him a chance," I yelled.

"Smart move," Chris laughed. "If you let him start moaning about his sorry-ass life, he'll never stop. He's a fuckin' siren."

I could be accused of doing the same, but I ignored that, concentrating instead on the scattershot beat and affected vocals. Huddling close to Stefano and Chris, I danced as unselfconsciously as I could, my fists clenched.

* * *

OCD meant being patient after I was unable to avoid shaking a jerk's hand. Strangers and acquaintances were so easily slighted and so terribly sensitive to rejection, less often real than imagined, that it simply saved time, breath, and their disdain to bow to convention. Post-firm-greeting, I'd hang my hand at my side, a slight inward curve to the fingers, and as soon as I could, I'd quietly excuse myself. My few friends knew I thought being forced to shake hands was a sign of disrespect, so while they gave me shit occasionally, they never expected a handshake or high-five.

It meant getting drunk or high enough to keep from worrying myself limp. But even then, while lying on my back as some guy wolfed down my cock, I *was* aware of which hand he was using on himself, making sure he didn't jerk me off with that one while I searched his body for any suspicious blemish, mole, or wart that would become proof the guy must be infected.

It meant doing almost everything left-handed: getting keys out of my right pocket (a habit I couldn't break), rubbing eyes, combing fingers through hair, buttoning shirts, zipping up pants, and fastening belts. Pretty much everything except writing.

* * *

Around me, people were shirtless and sweaty and in love with themselves. I'd love to be that carefree, but as much fun as they were all having, how many in the crowd were already dying? My would-be Adam was grinding his ass against another guy's crotch. The real Adam wasn't standing by the bar and he wasn't on the dance floor. Maybe he didn't come here. Maybe he'd been here earlier and I'd missed him because I was so focused on Stefano. It probably wasn't any of those.

The music was obnoxiously loud, or maybe that was because I didn't like it and didn't recognize anything the DJ was playing. I couldn't believe glow sticks, pacifiers, and facemasks were still dance floor necessities. When the fog machine went off, I heard the sloppiest chorus of whistles. The fog smelled sweet but wrong. I closed my eyes and let my head hang freely. I kept thinking about Stefano's naked body, him smirking as he looked up at me. My eyes were closed, but my mind translated the noise all around me into bursts of red and blue checkerboard and Technicolored Pollack splatters.

Someone ran into me hard and I stumbled into a couple, ruining their romantic moment. Strobe lights flashed, the mirror ball's reflections spun around the dance floor, resembling overlapping baby doll faces frozen in mid-tantrum, eye sockets and downturned mouths rendered in raccoon mask, forehead and cheeks and chin in white.

The couple I'd been knocked into was glaring at me with the same expression. The bigger guy shoved my shoulder. "Watch it, asshole." The more I tried to figure out who had knocked me into them, the thicker the crowd got. "What a fuckin' mess," the shorter one said.

I turned my back on them and kept trying to find the true asshole, but he was lost.

"Hey!" Stefano wrapped an arm around my shoulders. "We're starving."

# CHAPTER SIX

Fifteen minutes later, we were sitting in a window booth at the Midtown CK's, hoping a couple mugs of their horrible coffee would wake us up before Saturday dawned. The diner's restroom usually had soap, so as we left Ntropé I began cataloging itches and adjustments I'd make after I had washed my hands.

Chris had stretched his legs across his half of the booth, forcing Stefano and me to share the other side while we waited for the server to take our orders. Across Poplar Avenue, Sputnik revolved. It had been erected in 1962 and advertised with much fanfare, but over three decades darkness replaced its radiance, rust its alacrity.

Several years ago, the liquor store's proprietors restored the shiny red orb and pyramidal thorns illuminated by neon strips of blue, green, purple, red, white, and yellow. On an atypically cold but typically drizzly May afternoon, a sizable crowd had gathered, waiting for Sputnik to be set in motion.

There are sixteen thorns total, eight per hemisphere, arrayed in a starburst pattern: half near each pole and half near the equator. Both hemispheres revolve in a counterclockwise fashion, while the whole globe, if viewed from above, spins clockwise. Bright, giving swift chase, the thorns appeared like they were about to collide, but they didn't. Given how drunk I was, it was disorienting.

"Besides coffee, what can I get y'all?" the server asked, snapping me out of my reverie. After she'd scribbled down our orders, I shut my eyes and zoned out to the bacon and eggs sizzling on the range, other customers murmuring, and silverware clinking on plates. That peace lasted until an SUV with its brights on rumbled to a halt in the parking space nearest our window booth.

Its engine revved in crotch-grabbing pointlessness and a guy stumbled out of the rear passenger-side door, his feet and palms hitting the asphalt simultaneously. He stood too quickly for his mind, then brushed his hands off and staggered to the corner by the window on Chris's side.

"Nice," Chris exhaled, craning his neck. "The cap-and-khakis creep sure *is*."

While Creep shook off and zipped up, his three friends exited the SUV. All four wore nearly identical outfits, and they were drunker (or at least much louder) than us. Creep was the sloppiest of his group, his plaid button-down half-undone and untucked on the left side. His ball cap's fraying bill was a sloppy triangle, he'd shaped it that much. The hair curling from beneath the sides and back of Creep's cap was as bright orange as mine, and our faces were equally scattershot with freckles.

*Me-Creep*, I grinned at the thought of this doppelgänger who was maybe six-one, so an inch taller than me.

Two of their group sat a few booths behind Stefano and me. One went to the jukebox, feeding it quarters between leers. Creedence Clearwater Revival's cover of "I Heard It Through the Grapevine" started playing on the jukebox. The fourth,

Me-Creep, elbowed up to the counter and distracted the server while she was handing orders to the cook: "So, darlin', how long you been slinging them grits? You wouldn't tell me to kiss them, would you?"

*God help* me, *what are grits a euphemism for?* Returning my attention to our table, I observed, "You know you should really find a sponsor when..."

"—*ever* you wake up," Chris yawned, stretching his arms above his head. "Was that out loud? Sorry. Back on task: she's less a Monet and more a Francis Bacon."

A woman on the far side of the booth behind me was scarfing down a hamburger and pontificating about the size of a man's belt buckle: "If he's wearing one of those," she swallowed and licked her lips audibly, "and he ain't a professional bull rider, that'll be the least satisfying eight seconds of your life."

Her friend laughed, "That's why they call 'em tombstones for dead dicks."

Chris exhaled toward the window. "Don't you hate it when you've been cruising the wrong rodeos?"

Thinking I was being funny, I turned around and asked her, "What about guys who don't wear belts or those who opt for suspenders?"

She tilted her head and burped with her mouth mostly closed. "Next thing," she said, "you'll be asking me about real ties and bow ties." She took another chomp out of her burger.

"As if you," Chris mumbled, "are so upwardly mobile."

Her voice rose, "Why do *you* care?" Then she, her friend, and Me-Creep and his pals chuckled. Tina Turner's "What's Love Got to Do with It?" started blaring. When the song reached its chorus, the caps-and-khakis karaoked the lyrics, bourbon-fueled drawls flailing for a harmony. Everybody in the diner laughed.

Soon, I'd learn my laugh was too loud or too suspect. "I need to piss," I said, sliding out.

"And, Bry," Chris tapped his cigarette against the ashtray, "we'd thank you not to pressure wash the masonry."

The CK's restroom had a doorknob instead of a handle, so I was glad I had the sandwich bag. This restroom housed a urinal and a toilet, no partition between them, and a single sink. The walls were slick, the toilet was running, and its bowl was streaked. I finished my business in record time and got out without any cross-contamination.

While walking back to the booth, I heard, "Hey buddy," in a clipped tone reminiscent of every schoolyard melee.

*If I go sit down, whichever cap-and-khakis had said that will walk over.* I thought, *Better to meet him on my feet.*

As I approached their booth, Me-Creep stood, his fists clenched and chest puffed out. He was skinny-ripped, and if he wasn't being a homophobic fuck, he'd be handsome, which made me feel like a piece of shit. He kept glancing between me and his frat brothers. *Great: a tall schmuck with a Napoleon complex. They're so much worse than guys who aren't tall enough to ride the ride.* I figured the two of us would have been a fair fight, but I knew it wouldn't stay fair for long.

"Hey, buddy," Me-Creep said. "Giving you a heads-up, but after you're done eating, I'm gonna kick your ass."

"What?"

Me-Creep repeated himself.

"Alright," I asked, "why?"

"Don't worry about it."

"Kinda difficult not to."

"After you eat," Me-Creep smirked at his friends again.

One of those guys chuckled, "Dude, go sit down." I started to walk away, but he winked. I stopped in my tracks until Me-Creep piped up, "Ain't your food waiting?"

When I slumped in the booth, Chris said, "Let me guess, the john had a pube-festooned bar of soap and a hand dryer?"

Stefano glanced over his shoulder. "What's up with the aggro?"

"The public pisser," I rubbed my eyes, "has scheduled my beat down." My scrambled eggs and hash browns had arrived during my absence. I pushed the plate away. "At least I get a last meal." I felt idiotic. Most likely, nothing would happen, so why couldn't I stop my thighs from shaking?

"Why'd you go over there?" Chris rolled his eyes as he stubbed out his cigarette.

"Eat up," Stefano laughed. "We got your back."

"Mm-hmm," Chris lit a new cigarette. "More like you already had it."

"I meant like a straight guy would," Stefano said.

"Yeah, even better. They always got something to prove."

Not long after that, Me-Creep and pals left. He stared me down as he staggered past the window, his arms held out to the side, his mouth hanging open. When the Winker jerked Me-Creep by the collar, he fell hard on his right hip.

That made me smile, but my thighs were shaking and my jaws were clenched, and I still felt ridiculous.

I was ready to go as soon as Chris and Stefano had finished their respective coffee and waffles. When Stefano dropped us off at our walk-up, Chris hugged him goodnight and went in ahead of me. Once we were alone, I said, "Thanks."

"For what?" Stefano laughed.

I stared at the floorboard. "For making sure I had a good time, despite how gross the clubs are."

"I'm glad you came out with us," Stefano said, moving closer. "And if you didn't beat that frat boy's ass, I would've. Bet he's the kind of asshole who's never shaved his balls but expects his girlfriend to weed whack every last hair."

I smiled. "He probably wears the same underwear for several days in a row. But seriously, thanks. Most guys don't give me half the chance you have."

Stefano placed a hand on my shoulder. "Bry, I haven't been out that long, but most guys are fuckin' idiots." Then he kissed me. It was brief and sweet. After it, he bit his lower lip, checked his watch, and gently squeezed my shoulder. "I had a great time, but I've got to get some sleep. I'll call you soon."

After he drove away, I floated up the flights of stairs to my apartment. When I walked in, Chris said, "Look at you," but I didn't smile until I was in my bedroom.

* * *

Around one p.m. on the same day, which was nowhere near long enough after I'd fallen asleep, Stefano made true on his promise, calling me up and asking if I'd like to catch a movie.

"A friend gave me a couple of free tickets to the Highland Quartet."

My eyes were so scratchy I knew how bloodshot they looked. "What time are you picking me up?"

"There's a showing at two-thirty, so I'll swing by a little before two. That cool?"

"Yeah, but now I'm going to mainline some coffee."

After the movie, he drove up Highland and took a right onto Southern Avenue, heading toward Midtown. Behind the Circle K at the corner, there was a car wash.

He was talking about the movie—"Seriously, how long does it take for a cracked dam to burst?"—but his voice faded as the sight of people cleaning their cars made me anxious. The same had been done to every car in which I'd ridden shotgun, including this one. Family and friends had used the same vacuum hoses on floor-mats as they did seats, never washing their hands after picking up the mats, oblivious to the filth they'd tracked in from public restrooms and spreading that grime onto every surface they touched. And I'd opened passenger-side doors, rolled down windows, fastened seat belts, changed radio stations then touched my face without suffering any prominent infections or sores that wept for days. More precisely, none of either that I could clearly trace back.

All I'd ever caught from riding in other people's cars was a free lift here or there. A rational person would assume that would be enough to make me stop obsessing about microscopic threats, to free me from those compulsive loops, but it wasn't. Instead, the inconsistency between any perceived dangers and actual consequences made me feel justified, in both good luck and bad.

Stefano took a right onto East Parkway, and asked, "Feel like hitting 'Broso?" Cocina Sabroso served bland, overpriced Tex-Mex and was both an unearned mainstay at Cooper-Young and catty-corner to Mélange.

Like the matinee, it was an opportunity to spend a little more time with him. "It's late for lunch," I said, drumming my thighs, "but I'm sure I could eat a little to balance out a margarita."

The restaurant was busy, so the only open table was a two-top in the enclosed alley-patio between Cocina Sabroso and Young Avenue Deli. "Is that okay with y'all?" the hostess asked.

Stefano said, "No problem."

The table was wobbly, and despite the trees and the triangular cloth shades strung above us, the sun was too bright. Sparrows dive-bombed for every wayward crumb. Once we were seated, I looked around the patio twice. There was nobody who even resembled Adam.

"See anyone you like?" Stefano said.

"Just people-watching," I lied.

Our server, Drew, arrived with menus and waters. A little sloshed from the top of Stefano's glass. Drew's smile was forced and his eyes were wide. "Can I get your drink orders?"

Stefano and I ordered margaritas, and Drew started to walk away before he remembered to check our IDs. After he did that, he said, "I'll be right back with those."

"He's cute," Stefano said.

"You think so?"

Stefano shrugged.

"He's too nervous for my tastes," I said, "like this is his first day serving tables. Now him," I motioned across the patio, "he's handsome." The other male server was built, his skin was a warm brown, and his hair had an orangish tint, with the top grown out a little and the sides faded. The square jaw, the shirt hugging his torso, and the thick forearms didn't hurt, either. Sipping my water, I watched him maneuver between tables, checking on his guests.

Drew returned with our drinks and took our food orders, diligently writing our every word. I smiled thinking about the line cooks reacting to the novels he was sending back.

After he left, I said, "I hate that."

"Be more specific," Stefano chuckled before sipping his margarita.

"When I think about it," I began, pausing to sample my drink, "regardless of tense, people whose names are verbs annoy me. For example, I knew a guy in middle school named Drew, which wasn't short for anything. And as much as he liked comics, he couldn't draw, which was somehow disappointing."

"That reminds me of this kid at school whose first and middle names were Ricky Jack, not Richard John." Stefano laughed. "Think he's serving five-to-seven now."

"Sounds like that curse," I mirrored him, "christen your kid 'Blank Wayne Blank,' and he'll grow up to be a serial killer."

"I'm sure I would too, if my first and last names were 'Blank.'" Stefano's cell phone rang. "Hey, Topher," he said. "We're at 'Broso... Yeah, Bry's crushing on a waiter." He winked at me. "Nope, I suppose he's attractive." Stefano described him, then there was a pause before he laughed, "Hold on." He held the phone toward me, and said, "Say that again."

"I *said*, Bryan thinks he's hot," Chris deadpanned, "because of those forearms. He loves fellas who can really shovel through his Cracker Jack looking for the prize."

"If I hadn't felt the need to wash my hands before that joke," I pushed my chair back from the table, "I would have now. I'll be right back." When I walked inside, I didn't take my sunglasses off. My hands felt filthy and the restaurant itself wasn't too dark, until I walked into the restroom and everything went pitch black.

"Goddamn it!" I fumbled for the light switch.

In the darkness, a deep voice shushed, a belt buckle clinked, and fabric rustled.

I fumbled for the switch, which was placed lower and farther from the door than light switches usually are. When I flipped the lights on, a middle-aged man and a chubby boy of twelve or thirteen were huddled before the same urinal. The man zipped up his fly, shouldering me into the door as I asked, "What's going on?"

"Somebody," the boy blurted, "turned out the lights."

I echoed the kid but thought—*Why not turn them back on?* and *Why are you both using the same urinal?*—as he wet his hands under the faucet and fled the restroom.

I washed my hands until I broke the dispenser's tab squeezing out the dregs. Then I held my hands under the faucet until I couldn't stand the hot water any longer, shutting off the tap with my left elbow. I wished I hadn't forgotten my inhaler. Back at the table, I lay my hands palms-up on the placemat.

"What happened to you?" Stefano shut his phone and shook his head. When I didn't reply, he leaned across the table. "Were they out of paper towels? The unmitigated horror." He stopped laughing when he saw the steam rising from my bright red hands. "What the fuck, Bry?" After I told him, Stefano said, "I'll be right back," and stormed inside the restaurant.

I dropped my arms to my lap. Chitchat and laughter from other tables surrounded me, a large cloud floated past, a pleasant bit of shade, followed by a breeze and a sparrow landing on the table, cocking its head at me before taking flight.

Five minutes later, Stefano returned with two to-go boxes. "Let's get out of here."

In the main dining room, the man and the boy were sitting at a long table. The boy was leaning into the man's arm, as they and the rest of their family ate chips and salsa. My legs started to shake and my stomach folded itself inside out, but I said nothing because what exactly had I seen and who would I tell and why would anyone ever believe me?

Stefano shook my shoulder. "Bry, c'mon."

Or was my inaction—like the questions that flashed through my mind after I had flipped on the restroom's lights—an attempt to assign complicity to the boy so I'd feel less culpable?

No. As Stefano dragged me outside by an arm, I felt something I will never not regret: I could have helped that boy by doing something, *anything*, instead of a gawk-jawed, thigh-shaking nothing.

* * *

The following morning, I woke up with enough time for a leisurely walk down to d'Esyal for the brunch shift. I barely paid attention to the traffic during my commute, wondering if I'd have a message from Stefano waiting for me after my shift.

Before I'd gotten out of his car yesterday, he'd placed his right hand on my thigh and leaned in close, "There was nothing you could do." It didn't seem like he was pitying me. "Next time," he said, "I'll pick a better restaurant." I must have smiled, because he did too, telling me, "I'll call you soon." That made my hangover feel not as bad, even if I was about to be slammed at work.

Despite my OCD, being a dishwasher didn't bother me. Sure, my friends saw this as a contradiction in terms, and, yes, I'd have to agree with them, but handling dirty plates didn't spring the usual mousetraps.

The job was nothing if not mandatory, regulated rituals. I never could tell how busy any given shift was going to be, but slammed or not, eventually I'd catch up and the towers of dirty dishes would shrink with each batch I ran through the dishwasher. For everyone else, those rituals were obligations. For me, they were virtues. I wasn't altogether worried about the commonplace microbe. If any pathogen could survive the pre-rinse and machine wash with its virulence undiminished, clean hands or not, we'd all be fucked.

Near the end of Sunday's brunch, my cell phone rang during a smoke break. "How's your day going?" Stefano asked.

"A lot better now," I said. Outside, the sun blazed in a naked sky, Memphis's typical pit-drenching mug.

He chuckled. "So guess what?"

"You're not about to come out as straight, are you?"

"No chance of that," he said.

"Thank God. I hate it when that happens. So what's up?"

"I got the bartending gig! As soon as I pass the TIPS class, I'll be this summer's pool boy."

"How glamorous."

"I know it's only a start. Maybe one day I'll be scrubbing dishes."

"Touché," I laughed.

"I've got to run, but I just wanted to say hi. Let me know when you want to hang out later this week."

"Will do."

After hanging up, my shoulders loosened until I heard the manager yell my name. I walked back inside and immediately started emptying the trashcans. Better to dirty my hands than let others do it only for them to get distracted and answer the phone, roll up silverware, plate dinners, or serve a drink with a lemon-slice, all of which I was sure happened when I wasn't there.

As I slung the heavy bags into the dumpster, Adam zipped past on his mountain bike. I'd swear he smirked as he rounded the corner of North Evergreen. I sprinted after him, but there was nobody on the street in either direction. Beneath d'Esyal's awning, I stood for another minute or two, my fists clenched.

If I'd been able to catch up to him, I would have yanked his shirttail hard to the right. Maybe he'd break his forearm during the wreck. Maybe he'd get a concussion or chip some of those sparkling teeth. At the least, he'd scrape his leg. That wouldn't cost him as much blood as he had cost me, but it would sting. And while I stood over him, I'd make him admit the truth.

The restaurant's front door swung open. The head server, Pamela, asked, "You having yourself a moment?" She was a career-server in her early-forties whose love of wigs (this week's hue was burgundy) was surpassed only by her penchant for pot. We always had our own joints, so she was good company.

"I am. If you need a smoke break, give me a minute to wash my hands."

"A minute? Girl, I'll see you out there in ten."

When the door clicked shut, I walked around to the back and hid behind the dumpster. I steadied my breath, raised my gaze, and stared shut-eyed at the glare for a few minutes. Overwhelmed by so much stimulation, my retinas flashed outlines of spray-painted sketches and strobing colors. It'd be nice to think these outlines possessed more meaning than my eyes simply being overwhelmed. When a jet roared too low for comfort, I blinked away the glare, returned inside, and washed my hands.

With each lathering, I realized how every day I worked, every unnecessary trip I took to the sink, and every squirt of hand sanitizer I used erased years from my future, if my chapped hands and faded lifelines were any indication. Instead of worrying about that or the water's heat, I tried concentrating on the cool glob of relief that followed each tab of soap. But I couldn't keep my focus, because no matter how long ago I had scrubbed off Adam's number, I could see that dark ink resurfacing on my wrist and coiling around my forearm up to my elbow. How long would it be until I saw his script written across every inch of my skin?

"Pamela," I said as I shut the faucet off with an elbow, "I'm ready whenever you are."

# PART II

*Intermittent Reinforcement*: inconsistent rewards fuel the most resilient expectations. If pressing a lever always earned the rat a food pellet, it would lose interest as soon as its belly was full. The unpredictability is what keeps the rat coming back, compelled by whatever sliver of hope its minuscule brain can imagine.

See also: one-night stands, ex-boyfriends, and the "slot machine" effect.

*My least met expectation is being loved for who I am and not who others think I should be. Consider my relationship with Curt. Often, he had me wondering if I were some new breed of masochist. Sure, I could have been a sub searching for a dom, but I was probably just a glutton for punishment. Do I want trust and safety invoked with a word or degradation without a purpose?*

*Why can't I answer these questions, and why do I still miss him?*

— 20 JUNE 2003

# CHAPTER SEVEN

F riday night was busy. I had long ago sweated through my T-shirt, and my pants were plastered to my thighs and shins. The sink was full of dishes, with more stacked on the side, and while I was steadily washing them, that wasn't fast enough for the manager.

"Bryan, did you come here to actually work today, or what?" He was a thin middle-aged man who, when he wasn't dealing with the public, possessed all the charm of a feral cat. His voice was shrill, but his body reminded me of wilted celery, sallow and rubbery. He didn't laugh often, but when he did, it never sounded anything but angry. "Get a move on," he said. I ignored him.

The brand-new server entered with a full plate and sat it on the counter. The manager conferred with her, cutting off a piece of steak. "Who cooked table twelve?" he yelled. The chefs and line cooks kept working.

"Is this a rare steak?"

The sous chef said, "We're swamped right now, so—"

"Do you know what a rare steak looks like?"

She double-checked new plates which were about to be sent out. "Indeed I do."

He held the piece of steak in her face. "*This* is not *that*. Re-fire table twelve's steak au poivre now." He sat the plate on the line and walked off.

As I pushed a new rack into the dishwasher, a couple of plates shattered on the floor. When I turned around, that new server was kneeling, scooping up shards of ceramic and ruined food with her bare hands. I didn't wait for the manager to start screaming. I told her to stop and grabbed two smaller pieces of cardboard to scoop up the mess and dump it into the trash. While I was mopping, she ran out the back door, slamming it behind her. I placed the wet floor sign, then swept up the smaller shards from under a nearby table. The manager raced after her, slipping on the tile. He would have busted his ass if I hadn't been there to catch him, his body much smaller and lighter than I'd have guessed, too many bones for that blousy shirt. Back on his feet, he whispered, "Thanks."

It was half-past nine, which meant I had a good hour, hour-twenty left. I got back to work and was making headway when the manager returned.

"Pamela," he said, "take over for table twelve. Their server has quit in record time." He paused by the sinks and sighed loudly enough that I knew he expected me to ask him what was wrong, but I stayed silent, wondering how much weight I had sweated away that shift.

"Any plans tonight, Bryan?"

I rolled out a fresh batch of dishes. "A friend of mine is bartending by the pool at Fugue. My roommate and I are going to pay him a visit."

"Think I saw him last week. All he's serving out there is beer, by the way, but he's a cute little thing."

"He is," I said. "What about you?"

"Guess I'll curl up with a bottle of wine and read through the applications we have on file. Got to find somebody to replace whatever her name was." He walked off. "Wish I had it as easy as you."

\* \* \*

When I was done, Chris picked me up and drove us home. In quick order, I showered and changed into a T-shirt, jeans, and my Docs. We made it to Fugue shortly after eleven and headed straight to the pool bar.

I couldn't believe there were people actually swimming. Chris laughed at my expression. "For once," he said, "we're on the same page."

"Hey, y'all." Stefano waved when he saw us. "Do you want the beer bust or bottles?"

"What's in the keg?" I asked.

"Bud Light."

"I'll take that," I said.

Chris asked, "What are the other options?"

While Stefano refilled someone's cup, he said, "Coor's Light, Michelob Light, Rolling Rock, Heineken, Smirnoff Ice, and Zima."

"Give me a Zima," Chris said.

"Really?" I laughed.

"What? I like it."

We paid for our drinks and stood off to the side so we could talk to Stefano without hogging the limited seating.

"How's it going?" I asked.

Stefano filled two cups. "It's picking up, but I'm tired of people getting pissy because I only serve beer."

"And a tasty cooler," Chris said.

A shorter man wearing a polo shirt tucked into jean shorts walked up, yelling, "Stephen!" before taking a Polaroid of him.

After he'd walked away, Chris said, "Girl."

Stefano threw an ice cube at him. "Quit calling me that."

"You telling me you already got paparazzi, or is he a stalker?"

"Oh, I have a stalker, but it's not him. That's the manager." Stefano then served a couple new customers. A few minutes later, he said, "I'm sure he takes as many photos of all the new employees."

"Nothing creepy about that creeper creeping along," Chris said as Stefano got a surge of customers. "We're going to take a loop. See you in a bit. Make that bank, girl."

He pulled me through the door onto the dance floor. Directly ahead was the huge circular bar. To my far left was the ramp leading to the lobby. I followed Chris as he circled the bar and navigated through the crowd, past a cramped stage, and up a short staircase leading to the side hallway. It ended with a door marked "EMPLOYEES ONLY." To my immediate right were the men's and women's restrooms and a locked walk-in cooler. On the left were the windowed walls of Puck's bar, and in a corner near the stairs there was a cigarette machine.

Chris sat his Zima atop the vending machine and bought a pack of gold Marlboros. After he ripped off the plastic and tapped out a cigarette, he took a long drag. "That's better." He headed for Puck's.

"You forgot your 'tasty cooler,'" I said.

"No, I didn't." He opened the door to the video bar for me, and when we sat, Chris laid down a ten-dollar bill and ordered a Cosmo. Then he explained, "It was the most expensive drink Stefano's selling."

When Puck poured Chris's cocktail, he asked, "Working tomorrow?"

Chris nodded as he took a sip. Licking his lips, he said, "I'll be there bright-eyed and covered in flair for the easily impressed lunch crowd."

"And Bry," Puck placed his left fingers on his collarbone. "Can't believe I'm seeing you twice in so short a time. How *are* you?" Then he was off to another corner, taking three orders. As he completed those, he yelled over his shoulder, "So, Bry?"

The TVs were blaring clips from one of *In Living Color*'s "Men on Film" skits.

"I'm fine, Puck."

During a lull, he came back, put his elbows on the bar, and cradled his chin in his hands. "What about that whole Adam thing?"

Chris stopped sipping his cocktail. "Is that the guy you were moping over when I got back to town?"

"Don't think he was moping, Chrissy," Puck said before more customers demanded his attention. "More like mopping up."

Chris turned to me, "What was all that about?"

I chugged my beer and turned away.

"Nope," he grabbed my shoulder. "What's going on?"

I shrugged his hand off. "I already told you."

"You told me something, that's for sure."

"Puck," I yelled. "Beer me."

He returned with a frosty bottle and took my cash. Meanwhile, Chris was glaring at me. "So," Puck said, "not great?"

I stood up, telling Chris, "Let's get some air."

Once we'd sat at a picnic table between the pool and the sand volleyball court, he said, "Get on with it." So I told him everything. How the date went. What I saw and how I felt when I woke up the next morning. I took a gulp of beer. Told him why I'd ditched meeting him and Stefano at the cafeteria that day. Told him what Puck had said about Adam's part-time

71

job as a hustler. Another gulp. How I was seeing him every-where but finding him nowhere.

"Slow down, Bry. Have you gotten tested yet?"

"It hasn't been long enough," I said. "Could be a false negative."

"I've never woken up like that, but I've played the waiting game." Chris looked at the sky as if he could see any stars, then he stared at the dance floor windows. "Keep on living 'til it's been long enough. Then get tested. After that, go in whatever direction makes the most sense."

"Sounds easy enough," I shook my head, "when it's anything but."

"Bry, nothing's set in stone yet, and it may never be. This one time I hope you listen to me: please, tell your OCD to fuck all the way off."

I said, "Alright," but if I hadn't figured out how to do that before Adam, there was no chance of it happening now. Stefano had two customers sitting at his bar.

"Our boy could use some business," I stood. Chris frowned but followed me. "Don't worry," I told him. "I'm going to nurse the rest of this beer."

# CHAPTER EIGHT

A couple Mondays later, I was getting dressed when someone knocked on the front door. Chris paused whatever shoot-'em-up video game he was playing. I heard him unlock the door, and say, "Soap-Opera! What're you doing here?"

I finished buttoning my shirt and rolling up the sleeves, but as I was walking to the living room, I dropped my keys, and muttered, "Goddamn it."

"Everything okay?" Chris asked.

I waved hello to Stefano as I raced to the bathroom. "Be right back." With the faucet running, I couldn't hear anything else, so I only made myself wash my keys three times. After I dried them and my hands off on a fresh towel, I took a last look in the mirror, thinking I didn't look too anxious.

When I returned to the living room, Chris was leaning close to Stefano, and I thought I heard him ask, "And you're still going on a date?"

"Yes," Stefano said as he saw me. "Why?"

"Hey," I said. He smiled.

"Alrighty." Chris returned to the couch and grabbed his game controller, resuming mayhem on the TV. "Where are y'all going?"

"Molly's," I said.

"On a Margarita Monday? Good luck."

I slipped on my Docs and opened the door.

"Later, y'all," Chris said, jamming buttons on the controller.

After locking the deadbolt, I crouched and tied my bootlaces.

Stefano was smiling, his head tilted to the side. "It's amazing how your laces never touch the ground," he said. "It's almost as cute as you are."

I was wearing a dark blue button-down which I'd left untucked and jeans. Nothing special. When I stood, I told him he looked amazing in a gray baseball T-shirt with maroon sleeves and a pair of olive-green shorts that stopped above the teardrops of his knees. Amazing except for the Teva sandals.

"This ol' thing?" he said.

While we walked down the stairs, I asked, "So what was that about? You and Chris?"

"Nothing," Stefano said, "I hadn't told him we were getting dinner."

"Why would you need to?"

He got his keys out of his pocket, spun them on his index finger. "I don't, which is why I didn't." He squeezed my shoulder. "Sometimes Chris confuses looking out for folks with sticking his nose where it doesn't belong. Either that or he mistakes being out of the closet since he learned his ABC's with knowing everything about being gay, especially when it comes to other people."

"Damn, Soap-Opera," I laughed. "That's harsh."

He started down the stairs. "Oh, I've said it to his face. And what, you think he's never read me for filth?"

"So just now, was he trashing me?"

"No, Bry," Stefano smiled. "He's only looking out for both of us in his own special way."

*  *  *

"It's going to be fifteen to twenty minutes," the hostess told us, so we sat on a long wooden bench in the hallway behind her stand.

"You run all the time, right?" Stefano asked.

"Five days a week usually."

"I can't run that often, but I could use somebody who can push me."

A group of six guys sat on the next bench. A couple of them leered at Stefano.

"There are plenty of good routes in Midtown," I told him. "There's the park, of course, but the running path is less than a mile-and-a-half. I don't like running the same route out and back, so I usually hit the neighborhoods leading up to the park."

"Are those hilly?"

"Not too bad and there's some good shade. Let me know when you want to go for a run."

A commotion got our attention and quieted the other group's chatter. We all craned our necks back toward the hostess stand. A burly, sweaty guy wearing an apron walked out a lanky guy by his collar and belt. The erstwhile bouncer was easily six-six with a beard that reached his collarbone. I hoped he wore a hair net on it when he wasn't running security.

"I'm *going*," the lanky guy shouted. He was wearing a pale orange polo and khaki shorts. Behind them, a short twink in an identical outfit pleaded, "Stop! He said he's sorry."

A couple minutes after they were out the door, the hostess walked up with two menus. "It's y'all's lucky night. Follow me." She led us to a four-top in the smaller dining room. The table was still damp from being wiped down.

"What was all that about?" Stefano asked.

"The taller one kept grabbing the waiter's ass," she sighed. "He was warned but didn't listen."

"We'll behave," I said, "and we tip well."

Our table was the last one on the left, perched next to the corner doorway leading down three steps to the bar. Across from us was another arched doorway leading to the hallway we'd been sitting in. Directly ahead of us was the main dining room. The conversations from there were as loud and bright as the lighting you could read by, with so many jokes and comebacks fueled by half-priced margaritas.

I sat against the wall, next to the doorway to the bar. Stefano sat beside me so neither of us would have our backs to the steady foot-traffic. He inclined his head and narrowed his eyes. Behind me, there was a large framed photo of Chickie, the painting orangutan from the Memphis Zoo. Below her portrait was a typed biography that was flanked by two of her paintings. One was a reddish-orange with streaks of yellow, like a lion or tiger leaping toward an unseen prey. The other was mostly green with a few hints of yellow, resembling either a curving two or a "Z."

Our server took our drink and food orders, and soon Stefano was sipping on a margarita. I stuck with water. He sampled the chips and salsa, and before he was finished chewing, said, "This almost feels like I'm at the club."

He wasn't wrong. I'd say over half the diners were gay. And loud. I was sure most would be going around the corner to Ntropé for karaoke. "See any regulars?"

"Nobody I recognize, thank god." He took a drink.

"Do tell."

"The money's alright, but being completely sober and surrounded by obnoxious drunks and tweakers is annoying as hell."

I didn't see Adam or anybody who resembled him.

"Who are you looking for?"

"Nobody," I lied, "just people-watching."

He sipped his margarita then said, "You sure like doing that."

Our server returned a few minutes later with a new margarita. Stefano wasn't done with his first one yet. The server dropped it off with a note, saying, "You have a secret admirer."

Stefano opened the note and read it, shaking his head. He folded it back up and set it aside. He pushed the new drink toward me. "Do you want this?"

"Sure," I took it. "What does the note say?"

He slid me a ripped piece of paper that had been folded in half twice. The block script read: "Enjoy the drink, handsome. Didn't want you getting parched. No need to slum it with that guy. How's about I show you a good time?"

I tried keeping my face calm as I sipped the cocktail, but the room felt like a straitjacket. "Tasty, but awkward," I said. Stefano frowned and nodded slowly. I had meant the margarita and the situation, but maybe he thought I was talking about us. When he looked away, I assumed it was the latter, and said, "Stop it."

After he replied, "I will do that as soon as your face isn't stuck in mad," I realized I was actually talking about myself.

I relaxed my forehead, but my cheeks and neck were burning. While wondering how splotchy they were, I stared at the floor and took several deep breaths. The larger tiles were squares or diamonds, depending on your perspective, surrounded by flattened hexagons that abutted each other.

Our server walked up with two sizzling skillets. Stefano said, "Fajitas: the dish that screams, 'I'm a second child, pay attention to me!'"

He had a point. No matter how many times I'd eaten in a Mexican restaurant, I'd always stare at servers delivering them to other tables.

"Careful," the server sat the skillets down, "these are hot." A second server sat down the plates of ingredients and tortillas.

"Are you contractually obligated to say that?" Stefano asked.

"You'd be surprised how many people will hear the sizzling and see the steam and still touch 'em."

"I wouldn't," I said before taking another sip from my margarita. "On the bright side," I told Stefano, "a free drink's a free drink." I was glad the food had arrived because that kept us occupied and the conversation to a minimum.

As Stefano was finishing up, he wiped his lips with a paper napkin and forked around the leftover toppings. "They never give you enough tortillas."

I washed down a mouthful with some water and gave him my last one. He wasted no time making another fajita and didn't see the taller chubby guy who skulked past glaring at me. I let Stefano enjoy the last bites of his dinner and didn't point out his secret admirer.

When we left Molly's, the sky was overcast and a cool wind whipped the trees. Small groups of gays who were leaving at the same time were headed to Ntropé.

"What do you think?" Stefano asked. "Wanna sing karaoke?"

"Hell no," I said. "I'm less a singer than a vocal stylist."

"Whatever," he scoffed. "It's supposed to be bad."

"Says the theatre major who can probably belt out show tunes like the rest of us burp."

"I was kidding," he said as he spun his key ring, "but you're not wrong. What would you like to do now?"

"Molly's was my idea," I checked my watch. It was a little after nine. "What are you thinking?"

Of all the things I thought Stefano might suggest—"Wanna hit up 'historic crime-free Beale Street,' and make fun of tourists?" Or: "There are some decent bars on the Highland Strip, if you ignore all the frat boys"—I never expected him to ask, "What do you think about zombies?"

"Are we talking about the philosophical or cinematic variety?" He frowned. "Okay," I said, "the cinematic."

"I've had some tequila, so thanks."

"Those movies can be fun. But when they have zombies moaning 'Brains' and an undead Michael Jackson getting electrocuted, not so much."

He unlocked his car and we got in. "You didn't like *Thriller?*"

"I loved the special effects. Re-watched it every few years until the first kid's accusation hit the headlines. Can't stand his music anymore. But that wasn't what I was talking about."

"Which was?"

"The second *Return of the Living Dead* movie."

"Never saw that one."

"I wouldn't bother."

"Did you like *Trainspotting?*" He started his car.

"The movie?" I asked. "Why?"

"Well," he shifted into drive, "the guy who directed that has just released a zombie flick."

"I'm game."

He drove us to Studio on the Square, the city's first boutique cinema, which meant it screened its fair share of foreign films and served beer and wine at the concession stand. We got there in plenty of time for the nine-thirty showing, but the only parking spot he could find was in a corner of the lot far from the door.

Stefano paid for our tickets and I bought our beers and his popcorn. The concession stand worker poured the beers into plastic cups. Before leaving the lobby, I asked him to hold them for a minute. "Okay..." he said, popping a few kernels into his mouth before he held both cups in one palm and cradled the tub of popcorn in the crook of his other arm. I rolled down my sleeves to make sure my skin wouldn't touch the armrests, then I grabbed the beers.

"All set?" he asked.

"Sorry," I said.

"No problem," Stefano grinned. "I just don't know all the rules yet."

As we chose our seats, I searched for Adam, but there were too many people and Stefano was walking too fast for me to be sure he wasn't there.

When the trailers started, Stefano ate a handful of popcorn and offered me some. I shook my head. "If you want any," he said, "feel free."

By the time the movie was over, a thunderstorm was sending rain sideways. A small crowd was waiting it out in the lobby. Lightning branched across the sky. Stefano glanced at his sandals. Thunder pealed. "Up for a race?"

"Do I have a choice?" Another bolt of lightning and boom of thunder drew a few "wows" from the crowd.

"We'll get drenched," I said.

"Don't think there's another option." He got his keys out. "But we'll miss all the traffic once the storm lets up."

"You're a fuckin' Pollyanna."

"It'll be fun, Eeyore." He pushed the door open. "C'mon."

The swelter was gone, gusts strained the treetops, and the rain was chilled. I had a half-foot on Stefano, but he kept a decent pace. I matched him because I didn't want to be standing by his car, waiting for him. The rain slicked my shirt to my chest, my jeans tightened at the knees and shins, and I tried not thinking about how soaked my bootlaces were getting.

Stefano splashed through a deep puddle, and when thunder set off a few car alarms, he hollered. I sped up. He said, "No you don't," and tried catching me.

The taillights of his car flashed and I hopped in. Ten seconds later, he did too with a curtain of rain. I wiped the water from my face, pulled my shirt away from my chest, and rolled up my sleeves. Stefano was catching his breath. He tried drying his hair and face with his shirt, but it was hopeless.

"Ain't that refreshing?" Stefano said.

"If I weren't mostly sober before," I replied, "I would be now."

"Right? And, damn, I need to run more often."

"Like I said, let me know when."

We got to my building's parking lot a little after midnight. With the radio and A/C switched off and the storm holding steady, we sat in Stefano's car. "What did you think about the movie?" He rubbed his forearms.

"I liked it. Great soundtrack. But they're not zombies."

"More realistic, though."

"Not really. Infections don't take over a body *that* quickly."

He said, "You should nominate that for the irony hall of fame."

"And how the fuck do you turn rage into a virus?"

He turned in his seat to face me. "Yeah, that's bullshit, but the bloody projectile puking was cool." I must have made a face because he added, "It nailed how gross that would be if it were real." He paused then asked, "What would you do if it actually happened?"

"Die, I suppose," I said. "If it was hopeless and I had the means, I'd kill myself. Why stick around for your own disembowelment?"

"How much have you thought about this?"

"Ever been bitten by a dog?" I rapped a knuckle against my window. He shook his head. "When I was ten," I said, "a neighbor's German shepherd dragged me a few feet by my right calf."

The rain slacked off a little and thunder clapped. "This was fun," Stefano yawned again, "but I've got a long day tomorrow."

I ignored the weirdest of segues and said, "Same. Working a double. We should do this again."

"Definitely."

I tilted my head to the right and leaned in, but he kissed my cheek.

Rain pummeled the car's roof. "I'll get you closer," he said, driving up to the alley leading to the back stairs. "Good night, Bry. I'll call soon."

"I hope so," I said, hopping out.

Before I made it to the stairs, he was gone. Already soaked, I didn't rush. "No need to slum it with that guy," the note had said. Maybe Stefano really did have a long day waiting for him tomorrow, or maybe the popcorn had been a test, or maybe he was beginning to see me the same way that asshole at Molly's had.

Most likely, he'd expected me to book it up the three flights because of the rain, hoping I wouldn't notice that whatever Chris had told him had definitely sunk in over the course of our date. Now, he was looking out for himself in his own special way.

I should have followed his lead.

# CHAPTER NINE

The storm lasted through the next afternoon. Stefano didn't call me soon. Didn't call me at all. A few days turned into a week. When I called him, while sipping on a highball of bourbon and Coke, he said, "I didn't mean to fall off the face of the earth, but a lot's been going on."

"Sorry to hear that. What's happening?"

"I had to go home to Nashville. My mom was in the hospital, and she's all by herself."

"Is she alright?"

"For now, but it's her heart," Stefano said. "She loves salt as much as she hates exercise."

His excuse reminded me of what Adam had said about Gillian over dinner, but I asked, "How are you doing?"

"Frazzled, man. I ain't gonna lie. I'll be bartending this weekend, if you want to come visit, but I've got a ton of shit I need to get caught up on."

I told him, "I'll think about it."

After I hung up, Chris said, "Give him enough space for the closet he's dragging behind him."

"Thought I had been."

"Soap-Opera hates it when I call him 'girl,'" he said, rifling through CDs, "so he's got some issues."

I took a sip. "More than the few you sent him?"

Chris tossed a CD case on the couch. "I have no idea what that means."

"What did you tell him before our date?"

"Everything you told me." He pulled out the liner notes for one CD, glancing between the lyrics and me like I was interrupting something much more important.

I stared at him, shaking my head.

Chris folded up the liner notes and pointed them at me. "Be mad all you want, Bryan, but if you were in his shoes and I didn't tell you, you'd kill me." As he slipped those liner notes back into the case, his forehead was smooth and his eyes were neither narrowed nor wide open.

I shut my eyes and bit my lower lip.

"Tell me I'm wrong," Chris said.

"You're not wrong." I popped my neck. "But that doesn't make this right. And you know it was a shitty fuckin' thing to do. Tell me it wasn't!"

Chris sighed heavily. "Are you a bisexual?"

"What the fuck are you talking about?"

"I only asked"—he pulled out the liner notes from another CD case—"because you're always trying to have it both ways."

The highball shattered against the baseboard. I looked down at my hand which was still gripping the air where the glass had been. I closed my fist. Shards glittered on the hardwood; bourbon dripped down the plain white walls. Broom, mop, rag. Broom, mop, rag. Broom, mop—

"Bryan!" I looked up. Chris was shaking his head. "*What. The. Actual. Fuck?*"

"I... I—"

"You're goddamn lucky that sailed nowhere near me. Get your shit together and clean up that fuckin' mess."

After I did, I went to my room and switched on my TV, letting the static drown out whatever Chris would soon start listening to. I knew he'd never apologize. If Chris thought he'd done the right thing, your feelings came last in his moral calculation. Take how he policed the fridge. If he wasn't sure when the leftovers had found their way in there, he'd toss the food in the trash without asking. Writing the date on Styrofoam boxes and takeout containers worked for a while, but those also gave Chris a justification if I didn't finish my leftovers quickly enough.

At some point, I'd find out how much trash Chris had talked about me. Until then, I would be patient and stay on my best behavior, giving Stefano however many reasons he needed to begin doubting his choice.

As for Chris and me, we didn't talk that week. The first day I made exactly one cup of coffee, leaving a sip in the pot to burn. The second day, he left my mail on the doormat. The third day, I reset his bedside alarm clock for an hour later. On the fourth, he left me a note: "Since you don't like me being fully transparent, all I'll say is I've touched more than a few things in your room after licking my fingers. Guess which ones." I wrote him a note on the fifth day: "What's the average rent in Taos?" Then, on the sixth day, he said, "Soap-Opera needed to know, but I should have let you tell him," which was the closest he'd get to apologizing.

The following Wednesday night, instead of going out to an '80s-night beer bust at Fantasia, a Midtown club where you could count on at least half the crowd being gay, Chris picked up two pepperoni pizzas and some beer. He yelled my name then said, "Dinner's served."

"What do I owe you?"

"Don't worry about it." He flipped through channels, chewing on a droopy slice. With a full mouth, he asked, "Whatcha-wanna-watch?"

"Your pick," I said.

Movies and shows flickered past until he swallowed, put the slice back on his plate, and backtracked a few channels. On the TV was the late-'70s cheesiness of *Battlestar Galactica*. "My Gramps and I used to watch these reruns. You a fan?"

"All I remember are the skimpy outfits the guys wore when playing whatever that game was called." I took another bite of pizza.

"Pyramid," he said, "and skimpy's the perfect word." After sipping his beer, Chris said, "Gramps called me his little Boomer." On the screen, flattened oval spaceships attacked in undulating waves as more jet-like ships rolled to the left or right, firing lasers this way and that. Out of nowhere, he asked, "What's the weirdest thing somebody in your family ever told you?"

"Going to need a minute for that one," I replied. I'd never told anyone except my mother and the therapist who ditched me what my older half-brother had done to me. But my mother hadn't believed me. This finally came up when she sat me down one day long after Logan had left for college and asked, "Bryan, why don't you ever smile?" I'd looked away. She grabbed my chin and turned my face back to hers. "That was not a rhetorical question, son. I asked it, and I want an answer."

After I told her the truth, she looked elsewhere. I wanted to grab her chin and make her face me, but when she did, her narrowed eyes and tight smile made me ball my fists in my pockets. "You will not tell that lie to your father." She shook her head. "Honestly, I can't believe you told it to me when all I'm trying to do is help you."

Months later, when the day for that year's school photos

arrived, she said, "Don't forget to smile," as if she had forgotten everything else.

"Okay, I'll start," Chris said. "One time when I was six, my Gramps made a campfire behind his house. We all cooked hot dogs and roasted marshmallows. At some point, I got bored and started stirring up the embers with a stick. Next thing I knew, my great-aunt Maribelle snatched my hand and shook her head, saying, "Little boys who play in the fire wet the bed.""

"How's that work?" I started on a new slice.

He shrugged. "You'd have to ask her dementia the answer to that. Your turn."

I finished chewing and licked my lips, deciding to lie. Let this be a test: would I hear this from Stefano, and if so, how soon would that happen? I chuckled.

"This should be good," Chris said.

"One weekend my dad took me with him to the lumber yard. He knew the guy who helped us load all the wood into his pickup. The guy was nothing but smiles and squinty eyes, but as we were driving away, Dad said, 'Some folks you don't want to get stuck in a jail cell with.'"

After a minute, Chris laughed, "What the fuck?"

On the TV, a robot in golden armor monotoned, "By your command."

"Your guess is as good as mine," I said. "Dad never mentioned him again. It didn't happen often, but he had some good lines. A few years later, we had a bunch of neighbors over for a cookout. I was helping him man the grill. After a woman my mother despised walked by, he crouched a little and said, 'She's a sweet lady, but she's got the kind of face that'd send a train down a dirt road.'"

"Jesus," Chris laughed, "your dad's brutal."

"Only when he's whispering behind somebody's back." I

took another bite of pizza and swig of beer, then asked, "Did your great-aunt have any other gems?"

Chris sat back against the couch, a hand on his stomach. "Once, she swore she caught me drinking pickle juice straight from the jar.

"Were you?"

"No, but every time I opened the fridge, she'd accuse me of 'stealing the brine.'"

I opened my mouth but said nothing.

"Wait," Chris said, "it gets better."

"How? She outed you in grade school?"

"Like that was ever a secret." After a moment, he leaned toward me and, in a high raspy voice, he said, 'Keep doing that, Christopher, and you'll thin your blood to water.'" A new episode of *Battlestar Galactica* began. "What are you thinking?"

Without lying too much, and for the first time in forever, I told Chris, "Not a damn thing."

* * *

On Saturday night, Chris picked me up from work and we went to Fugue. This time we didn't get there till half-past midnight. It took longer than usual to shut down Café d'Esyal, so my shower was quick. Chris, on the other hand, took his sweet time.

In Fugue's main hallway, Chris touched my arm above the short sleeve and said, "I'm going to say hey to Puck. I'll catch up." Once he was inside the video bar's bedlam, I went to the jazz lounge, both disappointed and relieved that Adam wasn't there.

I walked to the rear door overlooking the pool and patio. Stefano's bar had a nice crowd. A guy sitting on the last stool on the right was gesturing broadly and people were watching him. Stefano did not look amused.

When I turned to leave, Pamela was in my face. "Bryan!" she yelled, sloshing her drink. "Girl, with all your quirks, I never thought I'd run into you here." She had changed into light baggy jeans and a white blouse but had kept on the Brogues she always wore at work.

"It was my roommate's idea. I was about to take a lap around the dance floor, people-watch a little."

"My friend," she motioned across the lounge, "is apparently catching up with a bunch of her old buddies."

"Want to join me?"

She sipped her cocktail until it wasn't in danger of spilling any more, and said, "Let's."

Using a sandwich bag as a glove, I held a door open for her.

She paused. "Where'd that come from?"

"Outside of work, I pretty much always have one on me," I explained. "Cheaper and more convenient than latex gloves."

"I don't understand how you can wash dishes. You getting help with all that?"

"With what insurance?"

"Ain't that the truth?"

As we walked down the ramp to the dance floor, I offered her my right arm. She scratched her collarbone, her brow furrowed. "I don't believe I've actually ever touched you before."

"It's fine, just keep your hand away from mine." I steered us down the ramp and around the bar to the raised area between the dance floor and the DJ booth. There were many tall two-tops sprouting like mushrooms. Pamela and I stood at the railing and watched the dance floor. Circles cleared here and there for vogue battles. So many queens and preppies, people who shouldn't be shirtless and were, and those who should be but weren't.

"Come here often?" Pamela shouted in my ear.

"What do you think?" Once my eyes had adjusted, I scanned the faces on the dance floor. No sign of Adam. I asked Pamela. "Ready?"

Once we were on the patio, she laughed, "Not a fan of all that."

"Same," I said.

At Stefano's bar, the guy from earlier was still holding court. "Stephen," he announced, "I think I am done."

Stefano served a couple of beers to waiting customers. "You said that twenty minutes ago, Andy. You also said that last week."

"I did not." He slammed a fist against the bar. "But this time I mean it, you fuckin' fucker."

"Say what?" someone in the crowd laughed.

"Andy," Stefano put both hands on the bar, "I won't serve you because you showed up shit-faced, not because we hooked up *once* a year ago."

"I miss you."

"The sex wasn't good, so you must be thinking of some other trick," Stefano said, twisting off a bottle cap and handing over a longneck, then filling up someone's red cup from the keg.

"But I do."

"We were nothing, Andy."

"But—"

"Raise your hand," Stefano asked the crowd, "if you think this sordid little show is done?" Many hands went up, a few clapped.

"*Fine.*" Andy staggered off his stool. He shook his head at the stairs leading up to the lounge, choosing the door to the dance floor.

Pamela sat in the open seat and asked, "Is there a show every night?"

Someone across the bar said, "I've seen that loser make the same scene the last three Saturdays. Hell, it's why I keep coming back."

Stefano sighed, "Glad you came, Bry." He was wearing a black tank-top with white piping around the sleeves and neck and on the chest were two white men's restroom symbols holding hands. His delts were defined and his biceps were pumped, his tan was coming in, and the black chest hair I could see was trimmed close.

"This is Pamela," I told him.

"Nice to meet you," he said before asking what he could get us.

Pamela said, "I'm good."

I slid over a ten-dollar bill. "A Heineken, and keep the change."

"Thanks, Bry," he winked, popping off the cap with a bottle opener and sitting it on the bar in front of me.

I grabbed the beer, taking a drink as I watched him serve other customers.

Pamela asked, "Is that your roommate?"

"He's a friend."

"Okay." She shook her head a couple times. Then she turned around and faced the pool. A few people were swimming. "What are your thoughts on potlucks?"

"You lost me."

She motioned at the twink who was wearing nothing but underwear and cannonballing into the pool.

"I don't trust them," I said.

"Never can tell how clean some folks keep their kitchens." We turned back around as Stefano was making change. After that, there was a lull in business, so he poured himself a beer, sneaking a sip before hiding the cup behind the bar. "How did y'all meet?"

"Work," Pamela and I said at the same time. "She's the head server," I added.

"That I am." She then asked Stefano, "Need another gig? Not that this place isn't... pleasant."

"Actually," Stefano said, "I do."

"What experience do you have, besides slinging beers?"

"Mostly cater-waitering."

"Who with?"

I didn't catch the company's name he mentioned, but Pamela knew it, saying, "That's connected to Paraíso, which is pretty fancy." After Stefano re-filled a couple beer bust cups, she asked him, "How many plates can you carry at once?"

He rubbed the flesh between his right thumb and index finger, "Four to five, depending on the dishes."

Pamela grabbed a bev nap and wrote down her number. "Call me and we can talk about getting you an interview."

Chris exited the dance floor and went straight to Stefano. He waved, and while talking to Stefano, he thumbed back at me.

"Is he another friend?" Pamela asked.

"No, that's my roommate."

"The last time I went to TGI Fridays, I think he was the one that screwed up my order." She examined her nails, then she looked over her shoulder at the lounge. "I should be getting back to my friend." When Chris and Stefano's huddle was done, she told Stefano, "Don't lose my number." Then she tilted her head, and said, "Bry, it was good to see you out in the real world."

As she left, Chris took her seat. "Hey," he said. "Change of plans. Soap-Opera's going to give you a lift home."

"Let me guess," I said. "This is one of those 'break the glass in case of a dick emergency' moments?"

"That's cute," Chris said, "but he is fine. Before you get snippy, he's hosting the sleepover, so I'll see you tomorrow."

"Have fun," I said.

"Always do. You should try it sometime." He walked back inside. "If it's not good for the soul, well..."

# CHAPTER TEN

It was almost two on Sunday morning, the clouds were heavy and low, but that same twink was still swimming in his skivvies. Stefano nodded at the thin crowd and wiped his hands on a bar rag. "Wouldn't be surprised if Jaime cuts me loose soon."

"Who's that?"

"The manager." He looked to my left, his voice getting chipper: "Hello, Jaime."

Behind me stood the man who'd taken the photo of Stefano during my last visit. He was either in his haggard mid-fifties or gritty late-forties. He was slightly shorter than average, but the long hem of his shorts wasn't doing him any favors. "Say cheese," he raised the camera to his eye. I turned my back to him. Stefano stood up straight, held the bar rag in front of his stomach, and smiled.

"How's business been?" Jaime checked his watch.

"Steady, until the last thirty minutes or so." Stefano then said, "Jaime, this is Bry. He's a good friend."

"Nice to meet you," Jaime stuck out his hand.

"No offense, boss," Stefano said, "but he's got an issue with handshakes."

Jaime chuckled, "Dating must be hell for you."

"You have no idea." I took a long drink.

"I'm giving him a lift home, so is it okay if he hangs out while we close up?"

"No problem," Jaime said. He walked around the pool, snapped a photo of the lone swimmer, and dashed up the steps to the lounge. Once the manager was back inside, Stefano refilled his cup from the keg and drank.

"Cheers." He raised his cup toward me, and I tapped my longneck against it.

"If you need me to find a ride, I'm sure I can."

"Don't worry about it," Stefano said, hiding his cup.

A group of four middle-aged men exited the dance floor. "Hello!" said the ringleader. "Aren't you adorable?"

"Be right back," I said, going to the smaller men's restroom in the side hallway. The dance floor restroom was nothing but a long curving wall of urinals without partitions and two measly sinks.

On my return, I zipped through the video bar. Of course, Adam wasn't there. The lounge was empty except for two bartenders and a barback.

"We are closed," a bartender snapped.

"I'm just on my way back to my friend."

"We are *closed*. Your *friend* has probably left."

"He works here." I thumbed toward the pool. "Down there."

"Fine," the bartender sighed, "but I'm locking the door behind you." I hadn't taken two steps before he did.

As I got closer to Stefano's bar, I heard the same ringleader from before saying, "I am completely serious." He and the rest of his group were perched on the stools. I walked around the bar, my back to the wooden fence so I could keep everyone in view.

The ringleader waved a fifty-dollar bill in his left hand. "Show us them tits and this is yours." Stefano smiled but shook his head. "It's a gay bar, for fuck's sake," the ringleader said. "You're not here because you're smart. If you were, you would have already accepted my offer."

"Fine," Stefano said, raising the left side of his shirt. Before he knew it, the ringleader had reached across the bar and wrenched his nipple so hard, he crumpled at the waist, shouting, "Fuck!"

The club's manager stormed out from the dance floor, standing in front of the door with his arms crossed.

"Like I said," the ringleader pocketed his cash, "you're out here because you're not all that bright."

"*Sir*," Jaime said, getting the asshole's attention. "I think you owe my employee an apology, unless you want to get banned."

"I'm friends with the owners," the ringleader scoffed.

"I have their home phone numbers," Jaime replied, taking out his cell phone. "How much you wanna bet they have no clue who you are?"

The ringleader said nothing.

"How's about you wager whatever you were offering my bartender?"

"You have no idea who we are," one guy said, "so how are you going to ban us?"

Jaime smiled. "Didn't all of y'all pay for drinks using credit cards up in the lounge?" He patted the ringleader's shoulder. "Tip Stephen however much you promised him, and none of y'all will get banned."

The ringleader glared at Stefano as he handed over the fifty. He tried leading his faggle up to the lounge, but Jaime whistled with his fingers. "Y'all are walking out the front door with me and my friend," he nodded in my direction, "while Stephen shuts down for the night."

Jaime let them walk ahead of us through the dance floor and up the ramp. He looked around the empty space, giving a thumbs-up to the older bartender. The overhead lights snapped on, and I was as surprised as I shouldn't have been. The maroon carpeting was covered with a patina of overlapping stains, cigarette burns, and patches of what were possibly mold near the walls. My fists and jaws clenched. The dance floor looked treacherous, like your shoes would stick here and slip there. How many people had dropped wallets or keys or cell phones, those items getting stepped on or kicked before they could be retrieved? I bet those people would snatch up their belongings and pocket them, brushing their hands off on their pant legs without a second thought, if they even bothered to do that much, and feeling lucky as they ran their hands through a potential trick's hair or cupped his face while they kissed.

Whenever the place was crowded and the music was thundering, the mirror balls, lasers, and disco lights made the walls seem a much brighter red than they did under the fluorescent bulbs. Like the carpet, there were stains across different spans of the wall. Sweat, water damage, spilled drinks, and who knows what else. The place still reeked of second-hand smoke, but once empty it also smelled stale and sour. If this room were a person, he'd be the tragic mess who was always abandoned, never realizing how stuck he was until long after everybody had left and the lights were flipped on, only to forget his dejection the following night once the music started thumping and his lingering hangover made pre-gaming that much cheaper.

As we walked up the ramp to the main hallway, heading toward the front door, Jaime glanced to his left. The lounge was empty except for the two bartenders sorting their tills. To our right, Puck's bar was a mixture of low lighting and bright TVs. Jaime shook his head and muttered under his breath.

The door-whore said, "We ready?"

"We are," Jaime turned this attention back to the ringleader and motioned to the door. "I hope you all have had a great evening."

The group walked out, but the ringleader held the door open with a foot. "What's your name?"

"Jameson Alastair Hitchens. Be safe, gentlemen," Jaime pulled the door shut and locked it. The ringleader was yelling about the owners, but Jaime nodded at the door-whore who flipped a switch, lowering the metal security gate.

"Follow me," Jaime said as we started back to the dance floor, where we went through the main restroom. It was all clear, if you ignored the splattered piss and the slap of your soles against the tiles. One urinal was dangerously close to overflowing. Judging by his choice of footwear, Jaime didn't care. He was wearing the same brand of Tevas that Stefano had worn on our date. Jaime's toenails were thick and yellow. With each step he took, I wondered how often he washed his feet.

Then we went up the side hallway and through those restrooms. Jaime laughed, "This is my least favorite part of the job."

Surely, barbacks were the poor souls unclogging toilets and mopping up puke, so I asked, "Why's that?"

"Bad nights mean I have to wake up a drunk who'd passed out in a stall, or I have to break up a couple who'd decided to fuck in one."

"How romantic," I said.

"That's never been my scene, but different folks are inspired or desperate in different ways."

Jaime had a point. I mean, I knew the places my desperation had taken me. These days, though, I'd never be able to get hard with the smell of piss and second-hand smoke and the tinge of vomit all around me.

As we exited the women's restroom, Stefano was lugging a keg on a dolly through the video bar. Jaime unlocked the walk-in cooler for him. "Thanks," Stefano winked, slinging open that door. His left triceps was flexed from the weight and between that and the veins on his forearm, it looked like he'd been hitting the gym hard. I knew the wink was little more than friendly flirtation, but I stared at the closed metal door. If I went into the cooler, how warm would his left arm feel wrapped around my neck?

Jaime continued to the end of this hallway, fumbling with a ring of keys. "Bryan?" he said. "You okay?"

"It's been a long day," I laughed, rubbing the back of my neck.

Once he unlocked the door, we entered a storeroom that was as big as a two-car garage. To my right, a shelf was lined with unopened bottles of liquor, a spectrum fading from dark brown to clear, the bottles tall and fat, short and skinny, cylindrical and squared off. Behind me, the interior door clanged shut. Straight ahead, there was another heavier-looking exterior door, beside which there was a monitor switching between the security cameras scattered throughout the parking lot. If I ignored the aboveground location, the storeroom felt like the perfect spot to hole up and wait for the end of the world. As long as the security cameras kept working and the liquor lasted, you could waste all the hours you had left watching anyone unlucky enough to be locked out, all while fueling your buzz until time no longer mattered.

Jaime walked to the monitor and watched for a few moments. I couldn't explain why, but I checked the room for other cameras. There was just the one perched high in the left corner and aimed at the door to the parking lot. "Where are all the inside security cameras?" I asked.

Jaime grabbed a huge bottle of bleach off the lower rung of an industrial shelf, saying, "The owners are real old school."

"How do you mean?"

"They remember having to take their license plates off their cars when they went to gay bars. Cops and private eyes would lurk around the lots, writing down plate numbers." He locked the storeroom behind us. "Lots of guys got extorted or wound up divorced and jobless, if they were lucky."

"How long ago was that?"

"This is Tennessee, so it ain't ancient history." He opened the door to the video bar for me. "It was all I could do to get the owners to agree to the outside cameras. Puck!" he announced. "Let there be light."

The last customer winced at the sudden glare.

"Damn it," Jaime said. "Not again."

"Boss, this isn't my fault," Puck sighed

"Duke, my boy," Jaime said.

Duke shook his head and stared at the bar. "What do I owe you, Puck?"

"I haven't served you a drop of anything 'cept water."

Duke tried putting his wallet back into his pocket, but he dropped it. When he stood and bent over to retrieve it, he knocked over his chair.

Jaime shook his head, flipped open his phone, and hit speed dial. A few moments later, he was saying, "Yeah, I need a pickup at 2866 Poplar Avenue."

Duke stood his chair upright and sat back down.

"Fifteen minutes? Thanks." Jaime shut his phone and told Puck, "Get me a coffee and my new pal whichever beer he wants on me."

Puck served me a Heineken. I took a drink and held the bottle on the seat between my thighs.

Duke perked up. "Could I—"

"This should be your third strike," Jaime interrupted him, "but I'll give you one more chance *if* you can tell me who kept serving you tonight."

"That new guy," Duke said.

"Which one?"

Duke pointed at the side hallway. "Downstairs."

Puck handed Jaime a steaming mug. He took a sip of coffee and cringed. "Guessing that's a vintage pot." Jaime had a murder of crows wrinkling the corners of his eyes even when he wasn't smiling, and he had a deep artificial tan that could camouflage any number of maladies.

Puck took off his top hat and scratched through his long blond hair, avoiding his bald spot. Now, his smirk was gone, replaced by pursed lips.

Unlike the first time I'd seen Duke at Ntropé, his eyes didn't look like he had been crying, but his face sagged more than it should on someone as skinny as he was.

There was a mirror behind Puck's bar, but I didn't look at my reflection.

After several minutes of silence, Jaime's cell phone started ringing. "Yello... no kiddin'? We'll be right out." He stood. "Duke, my boy, fortune's smiling on you for once. A couple canceled rides put you at the top of the list. Give me your driver's license." When Jaime had it in hand, he studied the address. "This cab ain't gonna be cheap." He gripped Duke's shoulder, saying, "Let's go," and led him to the exit via the storeroom.

I slid Puck a five. He blew me a kiss, grabbing the cash with one hand and setting a couple bev naps on the bar with the other. "Rough night?" I asked, sitting my beer on the napkins.

"It wasn't 'til that mess showed up and ran off half the bar. This should've been his last rodeo, if you ask me."

"The first time I saw him was after-hours at Ntropé. My roommate warned me about him, calling him 'Dire Duke.'"

Puck started counting his drawer. "Used to be a decent customer, but every time I see him now, he's a little bit worse."

Jaime returned and sat a few chairs down from me. He sipped his coffee, then he pulled a stack of Polaroids from his shirt pocket.

Puck plinked pennies back into his till, I took a drink, and Jaime played his own little game of Solitaire. Puck flipped down the bill holders, wrapped his credit card receipts with the register's summary, and asked, "Why are you grinning, boss?"

Jaime handed the stack of photos to Puck.

"Oh, this year's cabana-boy." Puck glanced at me and began dealing the photos one by one.

In the first, Stefano was sitting atop his bar after-hours, his blurred feet swinging back and forth, smoking and smiling, a wired expression on his face. In another, one hand was on the door frame to the dance floor, the other on the open door itself, his torso was angled forward, an "M" drawn in a vanishing perspective.

But when Puck got to the last Polaroid, his chin drew close to his neck. "Not what I was expecting, but alright."

"What's that?" I asked, scooping up the snapshots in front of me and handing them back to Jaime.

"And there he goes," Puck thumbed to his right. Stefano was carrying his till down the main hallway to the office right by the front desk. Puck held the final Polaroid to his chest and leaned toward Jaime. "Tell me, boss—*sir*—how'd you get the cabana-boy to do this?"

"He was having a pretty dead night, so I told him to help himself to the keg. When I dared him, he dropped trou."

"Is that all it took?"

"He's proud," Jaime chuckled. "Go ahead."

Puck handed me the snapshot facedown. I flipped it over. The image was washed out from a bright light to the right, and the background was the walk-in cooler in the side hallway. Off-center stood a bleary-eyed Stefano, who was sticking out his tongue, raising his shirt to his chin with his left hand, while with his right he waved his semi-hard cock in front of his jeans.

I stared at it for two breaths before tossing it down the bar to Jaime. "I've seen it in person," I said, trying to act blasé.

"And y'all are still talking?" Puck smiled. "Will wonders never cease?"

"In-person's always good," the manager chuckled, "but photos last longer." Then he slid that Polaroid into the middle of the stack, which he returned to his shirt pocket.

When Stefano entered and sat next to me, Puck smiled, "Hey, cabana-boy," before taking his till to the office.

Stefano raised his arms above his head, stretching his back until it popped.

"Thirsty, Stephen?" Jaime walked around to the bar flap, lifted it, and opened a reach-in cooler.

"I'll have what he's having," Stefano nodded at me. Jaime handed him a beer.

I had half a bottle left. Stefano chugged his, his Adam's apple bobbing twice.

Puck walked back in and saw Stefano's beer, then shook his head. "Jaime, quit fuckin' up my shit."

The manager waved him off. "I'll take care of it."

Stefano held his bottle toward me and we toasted. "We should get going," he said, so we finished our drinks.

Jaime walked us to the storeroom exit, watching the security monitor long enough to go through all three cameras before he unlocked the door. It opened onto a concrete porch wide enough for two people to stand side-by-side, with a thick railing on the right as you walked down the steps to the parking lot. Stefano's car was a few spaces away.

"Have a good morning, y'all," Jaime said.

"Thanks for the beer," I told him. Stefano gave a quick wave. Jaime waited until we were buckled up and Stefano was backing out of his parking space before he returned inside. When we reached Poplar Avenue, Stefano paused, the blinker clicking. "Are you hungry?"

"I could eat," I said. "As long as it's not CK's."

"I'm thinking pizza." So he drove to the Madison Avenue Tavern, which was a late-night spot that catered mainly to bartenders and servers. Most people called the dive the Mad Tav, and its decor looked like the owners had either given up or run out of paint—half of the brick walls were a faded purple, the other a dirty mustard. It was always dimly lit and packed, with a busy pool table and a surprisingly good jukebox. The food was good too, but the place reminded me of what I didn't want to look like in ten to fifteen years, bruised and jaundiced and tired.

We sat in a booth near the back, Stefano facing the front door. We split a pitcher of PBR and each ordered a small pizza. Stefano got his with pepperoni, sausage, jalapeños, and onions, and I got a plain pepperoni. In silence, we ate a slice and sipped our beer. The jukebox was playing ELO's "Don't Bring Me Down." Teams of two were shooting pool, and the bar was packed shoulder to shoulder. In this fine establishment, it didn't matter what you ordered or drank, it came with sides of second-hand smoke and fryer grease.

Stefano finished eating his first slice before I did, and he waved to someone behind me. Enter Ian and Viv and a woman I hadn't met. All three were wearing white button-downs and black slacks. Ian's shirt was unbuttoned all the way, his tie hanging loose, a sweaty white tank-top hugging his torso, his belt was buckled but not drawn tight. Viv and the other woman's shirts were unbuttoned a little, their sleeves rolled up. Viv wore her tie as a headband, and the other woman's tie was knotted but hung loose.

"Stephen!" Ian said. "What's up, dude?"

"Another night of slinging brews to fags." I must have made a face, because he said, "It's not a lie," before telling Ian, "And I about got a nipple ripped off, so that was new."

"Compared to our gig, I'd settle for losing a nip."

"How's Beatrix doing these days?" Stefano asked. Then to me, he explained, "She's the catering company's manager."

"Dry as ever," Viv said. "Get the job done, or get gone."

"After tonight, I miss cater-waitering. Where were y'all?"

"A plated dinner at the Botanical Gardens," Viv shook her head. "Two hundred needy-as-fuck-all diners."

The other woman told Stefano, "There were three protein options and one vegetarian, and they were allowed to sub sides."

"And let's never talk about butter again," Viv laughed.

I was hiding behind my beer mug, but Ian said, "You look familiar?"

Viv said, "He does."

"Oh, right, right," he said. "The special case."

"No, the fluffer."

I sighed, "I'm not a 'special case' and I wasn't a—"

"We took your advice," she interrupted me, "and you should learn how to take a joke."

"I apologize, because if I gave you advice, good lord."

"You told us we should audition for a Tennessee Williams play," she explained. "We got cast as Maggie and Brick in next month's run of *Cat on a Hot Tin Roof* at the Circuit Playhouse. The director's got a unique vision."

As Ian put his arm around her, Stefano took a drink of his beer and stared at the table, mouthing, "unique vision."

"I'll check it out," I said.

Ian waved at someone then asked, "Mind if we join you?" All the other booths were full.

Stefano pushed his pizza and pitcher over to my side and blocked me in. The woman I didn't know slid onto the other side first, with Ian in the middle, and Viv on the outer seat.

I mumbled, "A Viv on the edge."

Viv, Ian, and their friend all went silent. Stefano was chuckling.

"A me on a what?" Viv raised a hand.

I said, "On the edge. Sorry—"

Ian yawned and grabbed a slice of Stefano's pizza.

"No," their friend said, "that's a good title."

Ian kept chewing a mouthful.

Their friend slapped both hands on the table like she was trying to get the entire dive bar's attention. "So, what kind of edge do you see Vivian standing on?"

Ian, Viv, and Stefano all swiveled their heads toward me. Stefano's eyes were bright but commiserating as he bit his lower lip to keep from smiling. When I put my left hand on his knee, he crossed his ankles, shaking his head.

When Ian and Viv's friend grabbed a slice of my pizza, I lost my appetite. I finished my mug, took a moment to refill it because I knew the pitcher wasn't going to last long. "Hi, my name is Bryan. What's yours?"

"It's Audrey."

"How's the pizza?"

"It's good, why?"

"Because it's mine." She stopped chewing. "Anyway, Audrey, what literal edge do see Viv's toes curling over?"

"It's a good question," Ian rubbed his chin like someone who'd never grown a goatee but wished he could.

"Why am I standing there?" Viv grabbed the pitcher.

Stefano was taking a drink, but he started coughing and covered his mouth with his right hand. I slapped his back.

Audrey was squinting. "Think I got it." Viv and Ian looked at her, then at us, then back at her.

Stefano grabbed my forearm, sliding from the booth, "We'll catch y'all later." Then we found our server and tabbed out.

"You're good at that," he said as we walked to his car.

"At what?"

"If I told you, I'd ruin it."

"Go ahead," I laughed, "what's left to ruin?"

"Right," Stefano rolled his eyes and drove me home.

When he pulled into my building's parking lot this time, he found a space near the row of mailboxes. He didn't notice that his blinker was clicking until I told him. He switched it off, then leaned back in his seat and rubbed his thighs.

"Thanks for the ride," I said. When I unclenched my hands, there were pale crescents on my palms.

"No problem," he said, looking at me for a few breaths. His hands kept moving from his thighs to his knees. I unbuckled my seat belt, leaned over, and tried kissing him. He didn't return it. I felt his hand on my chest and tilted my head to my right. He gently pushed me back. I opened my eyes. He sighed. I stared out the passenger-side window.

After he said my name, I faced him.

"I like you," he said. "It's just…"

I held my breath, expecting him to bring up what Chris had told him, but he surprised me.

"Every time we go out, I catch you glancing around, like you're looking for somebody else."

He massaged his temples with his right hand. "Whoever

you're waiting for, I'm pretty sure it's not me." While I was gritting my teeth, Stefano said, "I wish it was me, Bry."

"I wasn't looking for someone better," I said. "I was watching out for somebody."

"That's not how it felt."

"If you're tired, we can talk about this some other time."

"Don't get me wrong, Bryan," Stefano shook his head. I stared at the floorboard. Nothing good ever follows *Don't get me wrong*. "You're a great guy," he said, "but I don't think I'm ready for anything serious. I need to get going, but I'll catch up with you later."

*Catch up.* No matter how bad his pace was, even I couldn't run in whatever direction he was headed. After what Chris had told him, did he assume I'd been infected, which meant he might catch it? If so, I couldn't blame him when that would be exactly what I'd be thinking. But if I told him everything that had happened to me and every last thing I had done, either he'd never look at me the same way again, eventually disappearing from my life, or he would immediately cut me off. That had happened before, and even though I knew this was futile, I didn't want to fast-forward to that moment.

"I'd like to stay friends, but I think that's all I got in me right now," Stefano said.

"Yeah," I muttered. "I'd like that." *Yeah* was much more casual than *yes*, but *yeah* still felt like an intestinal tumor, a vascular lump of red, gray, and black glistening in my bloody palm.

"Glad to hear it." He patted his thighs. "We should go running some time. You don't need it, but having a running buddy makes me more consistent."

"I never need an excuse to run." I made myself sit up straight. Before I realized it, I said, "And if you ever change your mind," which I regretted as soon as he began nodding slowly, with raised eyebrows and a thin smile.

"Will do," he said.

* * *

I couldn't fall asleep for a while because of that tumorous *yeah*, so I opened my journal and turned it into this:

*To pay off the loan shark, Mitchell got his kidney removed at a dive bar. A geezer from one of the local motorcycle gangs laid Mitchell on the pool table. The worn felt was mottled green and brown, pockmarked with cigarette burns, and stained from spilled drinks and prior operations.*

*Using a scalpel that had seen better days and had been held by steadier hands, the geezer sliced down along Mitchell's left rib cage. The old man's cuts were good enough, but the cigarette dangling between his lips sprinkled ash onto the moist red of Mitchell's viscera. After his first gasp and cringe, the sizzling smelled good.*

*"Sorry 'bout that." The geezer let him take a drag.*

*Mitchell exhaled, then said, "Barkeep, two shots of whiskey."*

After I closed my journal and hid it between the mattress and box spring, I shut my eyes and drifted into a dreamless sleep.

# CHAPTER ELEVEN

What a difference the season makes. When I moved here, locals would often recount how destructive the previous year's ice storm was. How every intact branch was sheathed in a perfectly clear and heavy outline. How those limbs crashed wherever gravity demanded. How the police ignored adults who went "asphalt tubing," kneeling on circular sleds as they were towed by trucks across parking lots, flat roads, and in Overton Park. How there was so much beauty despite the loss of power and the city's general shutdown. And how there was so much silence besides the groan of snapping branches.

One of the worst things about Memphis was how, being situated near a fickle northernly curve of the jet stream, you never knew which season's storms were going to wreck a good portion of your year. Two days after Stefano cut things off, Memphis suffered what was later dubbed "Hurricane Elvis." That derecho hit Shelby county and its neighbors with straight-line winds exceeding a hundred miles an hour, toppling and snapping trees that had cast shade for centuries. Parts of

Memphis and the surrounding towns were without power for weeks.

All over Midtown, trees had turned major roads and side streets into obstacle courses. If I were a kid whose home had been spared, I would have been thrilled by this make-shift playground, so many boughs I could now reach with little effort. At night, though, I knew that same child-self would be frightened by this real-life thicket from *Sleeping Beauty*.

That afternoon, I walked around the neighborhood, heading west down Poplar. Car after car and roof after roof had been crushed. On the way back, when I crossed Cooper, Chris was trudging home in last night's outfit. He was frowning and his shoulders were drawn high.

When I was in earshot, he asked, "How are the cars in our parking lot?"

"Fine."

"Naturally," he yawned, continuing to our building. "I'd swear my trick's place was in the eye of the storm. He was cool about letting me stay while things cleared up, though."

"Who is he?"

"Brett-something." When I arched an eyebrow, he waved me off. "The same guy from Saturday night."

"Twice in one week? Sounds like it's getting serious."

"Shut up," he said.

"Where does he live?"

"On Barksdale." When I frowned, he explained, "Behind the Walgreens on Union." That wasn't too far from our place, but there wasn't a direct route even when Mother Nature hadn't left clusterfuck after clusterfuck in her wake.

"Where's your car?"

"Crushed under an oak." He started up the rear stairwell. "Which is a good enough metaphor to describe me. Between our first fuck, us getting woken up by the storm, then him wanting another go-round, I didn't get much sleep."

"Priorities," I said as we started up the second flight of stairs.

"Don't be jealous. Anyway, when I rounded the hedges, I couldn't believe that that was my Miata crushed by a tree. I hit the alarm remote and nothing happened."

I opened the kitchen door for us.

"Thought about asking Brett for a ride home," Chris said, "but his street was a disaster, so I knew I'd have better luck hoofing it."

When he noticed I had all the windows open, I told him, "The power's out. Trying to get a little circulation going." We had gas heat and a gas range, so we weren't totally shit out of luck, but neither of us would be taking hot showers in this heat any time soon.

Because the cordless and my cell phone were nearly dead, I dug an old corded phone out of the closet and plugged it into the kitchen outlet. Chris tried calling his insurance company a few times but never got through to anyone. After he hung up on the last attempt, the phone started ringing.

"You better be FEMA," he said. After a couple minutes, he cupped the receiver, "It's Soap-Opera," then he got back into the conversation. "Ours is too... No shit," Chris laughed. "Damn, that's horrible."

I asked, "What happened?"

Chris told me, "Fugue's patio was wiped out. Stefano says the manager has no idea when the club's going to reopen." Then he forgot me and asked Stefano, "How's your car?" A few moments later, he said, "No, mine's pancaked, and let me tell you what..."

I went to my bedroom, took off my shirt, socks, and shoes. From the open window, I heard chainsaws and sirens and a car alarm spiraling through its melodies. I willed myself to feel cool, but I couldn't ignore Chris's pacing. "No, feel free. You can sweat alongside us," he said as I joined him in the living room. "Not sure what your neck of the woods looks like, but in these parts, all the stoplights are either out or down, and unless you got a sugar-daddy you haven't told me about, most roads will require a Hummer." He sighed. "No, smart ass, not that kind, unless this turns *Mad Max* on the quick. But this is Memphis, so... be careful, girl." He chuckled, "Sorry, *man*. Be the manliest of men getting here in your ever-so manly base model Corolla. Yeah, I love you too. Mean it." Chris hung up. "So... as the world turns," he looked me in the eye, "Soap-Opera's coming over. Hope that's okay."

"If he's cool with it, so am I."

Chris sighed, "I am exhausted. I'm going to take me a cold shower, and for once, I'm going to be fine with it. Carry on glistening, or whatever it is you're doing."

A few moments later, Chris started the shower. I heard the curtain rings slide against the rod, then Chris shouted, "Praise Jesus." Someone was grilling out nearby. I went to my bedroom and lay down atop the covers. I smiled and shut my eyes. Soon, I was lying naked on my back in Antarctica. It was summer and the sun never set. With no human souls for thousands of miles in every direction, it was heaven. I made a snow angel then got up and walked a few feet before making another. I felt melt-water collecting beneath the small of my back, then a door was slammed and the dream ended.

I sat up, scratching the back of my neck and yawning. According to my alarm clock, my coma nap had lasted a couple hours. I had to shake my head a few times before I was fully awake. When I checked my watch and realized there were at least two more hours before dusk, all I wanted was another nap.

I heard laughter and Stefano's voice. I rubbed the sleep

from my eyes with the butts of my palms, toweled off the sweat, and put on a tank-top. After I checked my hair in the bathroom mirror, I went to the kitchen. Stefano had brought a rolling cooler. He and Chris were sipping beers.

"And he comes bearing gifts," I said.

Stefano was sitting on the countertop but hopped off when he saw me. "Don't get too excited. All I've got is some hot dogs, a package of buns, and a twelve-pack. I had to stop at three different gas stations, but I found a bag of ice. Lucky for me, I hadn't deposited the weekend's tips yet, 'cause I couldn't find an ATM that worked."

I walked to the fridge, but Chris said, "I've already moved the beers we had left into the cooler." Stefano played bartender, cracking the lid wide enough to grab a beer, twisting off the cap as he stood and handed it to me. He lived near Park and Highland, which would be quite the trek under these conditions.

"Did the University District get demolished?" I asked before taking a sip.

"Our place is fine, but my older brother is a lot to deal with when things aren't fucked six ways to Sunday."

"What's his name?" Chris asked.

"He goes by Jack, and he has a major inferiority complex that he disguises by never admitting he's wrong. About any-goddamn-thing."

"My half-brother's the same way," I said, taking a sip.

"We're getting off-track," Chris cut in. "What's his real name?"

"Giacomo Matteo Malatesta, Junior."

"Bet all of that means something," Chris said.

Stefano laughed, "Every name means something."

"What's your middle name?" I asked.

"Uberto. Y'alls?"

"Keeping up with the paisanos," Chris said, "mine's Dante."

Several pops and booms sounded. A dash of normalcy amidst the calamity: were those gunshots or fireworks? They were both staring at me. "It's Scott, the most vanilla of vanillas. Like your brother, Stefano, I'm also a junior." Then I asked, "Speaking of, what's going on with him?"

Stefano yawned. "I didn't sleep much last night, but after Jack had polished off a bottle of bourbon by two in the afternoon and started accusing me of stealing his booze, I decided I'd rather stay gone 'til he dried the fuck out."

"Maybe this heat will get that done," Chris said.

"Doubtful, but it couldn't hurt." When Chris went to the bathroom, Stefano asked, "Is everything okay?"

"Yeah."

"I don't want to make this weird."

"You're not the first guy I've heard the 'let's just be friends' line from, Stefano. Don't worry about it, and if you still want a running buddy, I'm game."

Deep into dusk, we carried Stefano's cooler and Chris's portable charcoal grill out to the front courtyard, where an impromptu block party was happening. We cooked our hot dogs while others grilled burgers and bratwursts. Many were swapping food, but I stuck with what we made on Chris's grill.

The neighbor directly across the hall from us had a cooler but no ice. He had moved into the building in January, I think, but I didn't learn his name until he traded two warm PBR tallboys to Chris for two hot dogs.

After he ate the first one, he said, "I am Hugo. Two of you I have seen often. The third, a few times."

"I'm Chris," he said, "this is Bryan, and that"—he pointed to his left—"is Stefano, our little refugee from across town."

"Stefano? Where are you from?"

"Nashville, roundabouts. My dad was from Italy."

"A nice country. Me, I'm from Portugal." He had hazel eyes, straight black hair that hung to the middle of his ears, and tan skin.

Stefano pulled out his cell phone and dialed a number. "Hey, is this Pamela?"

More fireworks sounded in the direction of Overton Park. Hugo yawned.

"What do you do?" I asked.

He took a bite of his second hot dog. After he was done chewing, he said, "I am getting my PhD in audiology at the University of Memphis. And you?" He bit off another chunk.

"I wash dishes."

He paused chewing, brought his right index finger to his lips, and swallowed. "Are you joking?"

"Sadly," I began, but Chris cut me off.

"Sadly, he's a writer."

Hugo finished his hot dog and wiped his lips with the back of his hand. "No writer is sad except the one who never writes." He opened his cooler grabbed two more tall-boys and handed them to me. "Someone left these in my refrigerator," he leaned in, "but they are no good at all."

"You're right," I said, "but we'll take them." Stefano was shutting down the grill. Chris was watching the sky, chewing, his head lolling side to side.

"We have different palates," Hugo winked, patting my upper arm.

"It's an acquired taste, for sure."

"I am certain I will get accustomed the local tastes," Hugo said. "It was nice to meet all of you, but especially you, Bryan."

After Hugo walked away, Chris narrowed his eyes and smirked.

"What?" I asked.

"He was flirting with you."

"Doubtful," I said. "Chalk it up to him being foreign."

"'Local tastes,'" Chris shook his head, "'but especially you.' C'mon, Bry. He's suspect."

"What'd I miss?" Stefano asked.

"Chris is seeing things that aren't there."

"Right," Chris said. "That's *my* problem."

We hauled the cooler back inside, leaving the portable grill on the back porch. Chris and Stefano would stay up late playing cards by candlelight. I didn't close my bedroom door to keep the air flowing. Around three in the morning, I woke up sweaty and parched. I went to the kitchen as quietly as I could and poured a tall glass of water, drinking one at the sink and re-filling another to take with me.

On the way back, I saw Stefano asleep on the couch. He was shirtless and lying on a beach towel, both arms above his head, one leg on the couch, the other foot on the floor. His snoring was soft and I watched his stomach rise and fall until he coughed and stirred. He didn't wake, but I headed to my room and sat on the side of my twin bed closest to the window.

A weak breeze blew through the screen. I packed a bowl and lit up. The usual noise of Poplar Avenue was missing. Sirens sounded from a distance, but they didn't last long. The chainsaws would start screaming at dawn like the newest and most annoying species of songbird, so I should get as much shuteye as I could. But it took forever to fall back to sleep because I kept listening for tentative steps that never creaked on the hardwood floors.

# CHAPTER TWELVE

During the third week of August while I was pushing a dolly stacked with boxes of new plates into the kitchen door at work, Stefano pulled into the lot. His hair was slicked back to the left, and he was wearing a white button-down, a black tie, black slacks, and brightly polished shoes. I stared at his starched and brilliant shirt.

He had ended up staying at our place for a week. After a few days, pretending everything was fine and dandy wasn't that difficult. Funny how sharing a single bathroom can slam the brakes on an infatuation. Once the roads were clear, he drove Chris around to different car lots; Chris ended up buying a used Honda Civic hatchback.

I stood the dolly up, my foot on the axle as he fussed with his outfit. "You clean up well," I said, checking my watch. It was a quarter-to-two.

He buttoned his sleeves. "I try."

"Here for an interview?"

"Yup. Any pointers?"

"Don't say 'yup.'"

"What else?"

"The manager's in a good mood today," I said, "but he's not big on smiles. As in, he rarely does, and he thinks you shouldn't trust people who smile all the time."

"Okay..." Stefano checked the tuck of his shirt. "And this is him in a good mood?"

"He may crack a joke or two, but I wouldn't tell him any. Answer him directly, call him 'sir,' and you'll do fine. Seriously, after the storm we lost two servers and a cook, so he's getting desperate."

"How do I look?" Stefano asked.

I almost said "scrappy." Instead, I told him, "Admittedly, I'm biased, but handsome."

"Can I put you as a reference?"

"Sure. That shouldn't hurt your chances."

He patted my shoulder and began walking around to the restaurant's front door.

"Break a leg," I said, tilting the dolly and pushing it inside. I unpacked the new plates and ran the first rack through the dishwasher. While that cycled through, I walked to the kitchen door and peeked at the interview. They were at table thirteen, a two-top, and the manager was sitting with his back to the wall. I couldn't hear what Stefano was saying, but he was talking with his hands. The manager was reading Stefano's application. When he looked up, he saw me and motioned to move on with one leftward jerk of his head.

I returned to the dishwasher, rolling out the clean rack and rolling in another one. I held up a plate. It was handcrafted, with dark blue lacquer and gray swirls. My reflection was sharp. After three more loads washed and put away, I took a smoke break, hidden from view behind the dumpster. I'd gotten halfway through the joint when I heard a car door slamming. I took a quick drag, stubbed it out, holding my breath as I left my hiding spot. Stefano was leaving, but he stopped and pulled back in when he saw me. He left his car running and got out.

I exhaled. "How did it go?"

"It's weird how such an elfin guy can be so intimidating."

"After a while, you get used to him and ignore it. But you didn't answer my question."

"I start training tomorrow."

I extended my left elbow and he bumped it with his right.

"How much longer are you working today?" Stefano asked.

"I'm off at three. Why?"

"Wanna go for a run?" he opened his car door, one elbow on the frame, the other on the roof.

"Sure." I popped my neck. "Let's meet at my place around four. We can run around the park."

* * *

By a quarter-to-four, I'd made it home and changed into shorts and a tank-top. From today's spam, I added this clipping to my collection before heading to the parking lot:

*Most famous for hydrocarbon haberdashery and Euclidian anaplasmosis, the grand exasperator sits ready with his bourgeois gavel... the fleet messenger, that ingrate what calls himself Erbium, exits from the Eigenvector arboretum*

As I was finishing a long set of toe touches—my ass against the back wall of the building, my forehead on my shins—I heard keys jingling and someone say, "Hello, Bryan."

I glanced up and saw Hugo. After several more steps, he stopped walking and turned around. His eyes were squinting from the sun, but he was grinning.

"Hey, Hugo," I said, standing and stretching my left arm across my chest.

He spun his keys on his left index finger. His squint deepened as it shifted from my tank-top, to shorts, to Mizunos, then back up to my face. "Jogging? In this swelter?"

"I am."

"God be with you," he laughed.

"It's not so bad," I lied.

He quit spinning his keys and attempted to touch his toes. As handsome as he was, it looked like he rarely stretched. When he quit trying, he laughed, "Never have I been that flexible."

"You should practice," I said. "It helps to keep you from getting hurt."

He started spinning his keys again. "I will keep that in mind," he said, "but for now I must get groceries."

A few minutes after Hugo drove off, Stefano pulled into the parking lot. It was in the mid-nineties and hairdos were collapsing all over Bluff City. When he walked up, I told him, "Hope you're ready, because this isn't going to be fun."

"I'll do my best." He stretched his quads in turn, grabbing the toe of each shoe and pulling that ankle toward his ass.

From the parking lot, we ran to Cooper and then to Poplar, heading west down to Tucker. There we crossed Poplar and entered the park. I led Stefano past the Parkview Apartments and down Kenilworth. After a curve, that road turned into Overton Park Avenue.

Stefano said, "The park's the other way."

"Trust me." I kept my pace, taking a right on McLean. "We're taking a long way to the loop." At Prentis, we took another right and followed that road—which, of course, changed its name before long—back into the park. Then we ran south, taking a left behind the Brooks Museum and heading toward the limestone running trail.

I jogged in place and waited for him. "How are you feeling?" I asked.

"How far have we gone?"

"Barely two miles. The trail is a mile-forty, if you're up for it."

"Let's do it." Stefano took off.

I followed him for a minute then matched his pace. "Excited for the new job?"

Between breaths, Stefano asked, "How can you carry on a conversation?"

"If I'm pushing it, I can't, but this pace is doable. No offense."

"None... taken."

We ran in silence for a while, and when we rounded the loop near East Parkway, I said, "We can slow down if you need to."

"How... much... farther?"

"Little less than a mile, give or take."

"Let's keep... going. Finish... the trail."

I slapped his back with my right hand and focused on my breathing. I noticed a swarm of gnats just ahead of us and closed my mouth. So many bugs died stuck to my sweaty skin and apparently in Stefano's mouth.

"Fuckin' gross," he coughed and spat.

After a laugh, I peeked at the teardrops above his knees, then at his crotch. I rolled my neck and noticed something about his stride. "Keep running," I said. "I need a head-on view." Before he could make a joke, I was off. After a long sprint, I slowed down and turned around. He favored his right leg and he was landing on the outside of his soles and rolling inward.

When he reached me, I resumed jogging, and he asked, "What's wrong?"

"If you're serious about this, you need shoes with better arch support."

Near the end of our run, a stocky guy was jogging toward us. He was shirtless and led by two Rottweilers on leashes. He was built but not ripped, a hairy chest and stomach. He carried his weight well and he was running commando. He pulled the leashes short and nodded as he passed us.

Stefano pulled off his T-shirt and wiped his face with it. Then he tucked it into the waistband of his shorts, and laughed, "Poor guy."

With the Brooks in sight, I slowed to a walk and checked my watch. A little over thirty-five minutes. "Looked fine to me."

Stefano had his hands on his head. "Imagine the massive turds he has to scoop up."

"That's a pleasant image."

"How was our pace?"

I did some quick math. "Close to eleven minutes a mile."

"How long's that route usually take you?"

We walked back toward Poplar. "Not counting having to wait on traffic, I can get it done in under thirty."

He chuckled, "I'm a fuckin' turtle," wiping his chest and back with his shirt.

"You'll get faster," I said. "This humidity isn't playing around."

We raced across Poplar, but then we took our time heading back to my place. He never put his shirt back on, and as we neared Cooper, a car sped past blaring its horn.

"The fuck was that about?"

"I'd bet it was Mr. Fifty Bucks from the bar," I said, "getting excited for the full show." I didn't mind either, but I kept that to myself.

"That'd be my luck," he wiped down his chest again, "and thanks for reminding me of that piece of shit."

We walked to the first Poplar Avenue driveway of my

building. At the alley that led to my rear stairs, I asked, "Want a glass of water?"

"I'm good," he replied, adding a "will do" about our next run and continuing to his car.

When I reached the third floor, Hugo was struggling with two armfuls of grocery bags and having trouble unlocking his door. "Need help?" I asked.

"Yes, Bryan," he said, "please," offering me his left arm. I took those bags, and when he unlocked the door, I followed him inside his apartment. The screen door slapped shut behind me, but the wooden door was wide open. The A/C from the window unit blasting in his kitchen was a welcome relief. "Set those there," he pointed at the counter. "Are you thirsty?"

"I'm fine, but thanks."

"No, no. Sit." I did as he told me, my back to the door. He grabbed a large glass from the cupboard, used tongs to fill it halfway with ice, and poured water out of a pitcher from the fridge. I guess I took too large of a first drink, because a freezing rush tumbled down my torso.

He shut and locked his kitchen door and began putting up his groceries. "How can you run in this sauna?"

"You either resign yourself to the humidity or you move."

When he was done with his groceries, he sat across from me, his left knee too close to my right. Because our kitchens were tiny, so were our tables. His was a metal bistro with two folding chairs. I remembered what Chris had said about Hugo, and asked, "Have you gotten used to the local tastes yet?"

"The music is great," Hugo said, "and some barbecue is good. The weather, not so much."

"Sounds about right," I said, thinking, *I told you, Chris,* until Hugo placed his firm hand on my knee. The back of his hand and knuckles were covered in dark hair, and there were calluses on his fingertips like he played guitar. He wasn't smiling, but his face was open. Before I knew it, I was half-hard. "I have to go," I said.

"My apologies," he pulled his hand back. "I must have been mistaken."

After I took another drink of water, I said, "You weren't."

"Would you like to have some fun?" I said nothing. "Always safe," he raised his hands in front of his chest. My face must have done something, because he grinned and glanced down. "I would very much like to suck your dick." There was no hiding my erection at this point. He grabbed me through my shorts. "Follow me, Bryan."

# CHAPTER THIRTEEN

Over the next month, Hugo and I fucked around. I didn't tell Chris because I knew he'd blab it to Stefano. Things were casual and careful, and Hugo wanted nothing to do with anal. I'd never gotten so comfortable with someone as quickly as I did with him. The first few times he kept asking me if he could do this or that, and the man could give a mean blowjob through a condom. I'd tried doing that in the past from both ends, but until Hugo it had never felt good.

Because of his grad school, we hooked up whenever he was burned out from studying or from writing papers. But he was the horniest after finishing major exams. Everything was fine until the first time we ever went anywhere in public together, which was also our last.

We'd walked down to Overton Square and ate dinner at the Cajun restaurant on the backside. His body language in public wasn't reserved exactly, but there was a distance. I thought that was fine. Overton Square and Midtown were cool places, but some bigots flew under the radar until it was too late.

When the server took away the plates and brought another

round of beers, I asked why he was studying audiology. "I have family members who are deaf. I've often thought about what their lives would have been like if cochlear implants had been around when they were children."

"According to my mother," I began, "I couldn't hear for the first year-and-a-half of my life. Now, this is what she told me, so take it with a pinch of salt."

He perked up a little.

"The story goes, I was born temporarily deaf because of complications from my premature birth. Eighteen months later, my father still didn't believe anything was wrong with me until one evening my mother sat me in front of the TV, grabbed a pot and metal ladle from the kitchen and banged the ladle inside the pot. After I hadn't startled, my father said, 'Maybe you're right.'"

"So," Hugo frowned, "your hearing was fixed how, with a myringotomy or tympanostomy?"

"If you mean tubes down the ears, then yes. Four times, I think."

"This sounds like a family myth," he said, people-watching, "and your mother, you'll forgive me, she sounds misinformed. You didn't hear what they were saying clearly, but at some level you could hear. It sounds like you had chronic ear infections causing hearing loss above thirty decibels." He motioned around the slammed restaurant. "I'd say this is approaching eighty. If the pot and ladle tale is true, then I am not surprised it took multiple procedures. By the way, human hearing does not finish developing on average until we have nine years of age. Could she have embellished things to make for a better tale?"

"I wouldn't be surprised."

When the server came back around, Hugo asked for the check.

"Let's split it," I said.

"No, no. I am paying because I asked you out to dinner, and because I need to tell you the truth."

All the other conversations fell away, but the scrapes of forks and knives against plates grew louder. Hugo took a long drink and said, "I like you, Bryan, and I have very much enjoyed hanging out with you."

"But?"

"My fiancée, she is moving here next month."

"Fiancée, as in your *future wife?*"

"It works the same for us as it does in this country."

I sat back in my chair, took another swig of beer. Of course, there was a catch. Always was. I popped my knuckles. "If I had known you were engaged, Hugo, I never would have—"

"No," he interrupted me. "It is fine. Honestly." He leaned in close. "We are both bisexual, and I have told her about you."

"*What?*"

"Yes. She and I do not keep secrets."

*From one another.* I looked anywhere else.

"Are you... freaked out?" he asked.

There were no photos of her in his apartment. "Taken by surprise," I said. "This... this has never happened to me."

"That is why I wanted to tell you now, before she arrives and you two meet."

"How long have you been together?"

"Almost four years."

"How long have you been in an open relationship?"

"Almost four years."

"And you're getting married?"

"Yes," he smiled. "We love each other, so as long as we agree, what's wrong with sharing that with others?"

"So meeting her would be an interview of sorts?"

"I suppose," he shrugged with his hands, "one could put it that way."

While thinking—*How's about that? The catch has its own catch*—I finished my beer. In normal situations, I sucked at job interviews. I couldn't imagine how much worse I'd do while answering the questions of someone who knew the size of my cock and my proclivities.

*What would your previous boyfriend say about you,* Clarissa might ask, *and may we contact him?* Or, *Tell me about a time when you solved a problem in bed that you hadn't caused?* And the interview would surely end with this question: *On the off chance this sticks, where do you see yourself in five years?*

When I stood, Hugo did the same. Outside, the air was cooler, but that was a false lull before summer ended. The stroll back was a good ten minutes, but Hugo wasn't in a rush.

"I'm just curious," I asked, "but why didn't you tell me this on the front end?"

"I was worried you would be upset. While Clarissa and I don't keep secrets, we do value our privacy. Too many people do not understand."

Wasn't that the truth? Since I came out, I'd seen a few gay couples who tried having open relationships. They were usually older and stalked the clubs for their newest third like grizzled trappers collecting pelts. Admittedly, my sample size was small, but I had never seen it work out in the long term.

This made me wonder: if Curt had been okay with me fucking other people, would I have wound up here? Then again, if we had been open, he would have definitely been more popular than me, and I knew my jealousy would only fuel my OCD. In the end, I would have ruined us in some other pathetic manner.

Hugo broke the silence once we reached our building's parking lot. "You do value the privacy of your thoughts, Bryan."

"That's one way to put it," I said.

"Know that I am grateful to have met you," Hugo touched

my shoulder when we reached our floor. "If you want to keep seeing one another, we can, but Clarissa wants to meet you. I will respect your wishes, but I would like to keep hanging out. Please let me know your decision."

I unlocked my door, telling him, "I will," but I knew I had already made up my mind. What possible point could there be in meeting Clarissa?

How long would it be until either Hugo or Clarissa realized their openness was the weakest dam holding back their denial of insatiable desires for something the other would always lack? Without her in the picture, would Hugo have been satisfied with only me? That was what the past month had felt like, and now all that time and vulnerability had amounted to less than nothing. Still, as much as I wished Hugo would realize he'd been lying to himself, I knew he wasn't the only liar.

I would bet my life that Adam and Gillian didn't have an open relationship—that she had no fucking clue he was playing for both teams. In that sense, he was carrying on the long tradition of cowardice masquerading as masculinity.

With that thought, my stomach clenched so hard I had to stop walking. I realized I'd been distracted by Hugo. How long had it been since I'd last searched for Adam? Since I'd gotten mad at Chris for telling Stefano the truth?

Then I realized something else: I'd hidden the truth from Stefano, even if it was a lie of omission, and there was nothing a lying coward hates worse than his true self being reflected back at him.

My stomach lurched. I wanted Adam to experience a revelation as uncomfortable as this one. I would love to find Adam and Gillian having a pleasant date in a restaurant, pull up a chair, and cause a scene that neither would ever forget.

While holding onto the bathroom sink, I stared at my feet, the left one wouldn't stop tapping. Adam, Stefano, Hugo.

Adam could have been nothing more than a fling and, at best, maybe a way to begin getting over myself. Had he been only that, I would have met Stefano much sooner. Then, upon entering any crowded room or dance floor, I would have focused on him at the expense of everyone else.

When I finally looked up and stared at my reflection, my lips were thin, my nostrils were flared, and my jaws were clenched. I'd let Hugo distract me from Adam and I'd let Adam distract me from Stefano. A knot within a knot within a knot, every last one threaded by my mistakes.

To unclench my jaws, I started whispering, "That won't happen again," over and over, like I was thumbing through the decades of a rosary.

# CHAPTER FOURTEEN

A week before Thanksgiving, I was returning from a ten-mile run around Overton Park and the Evergreen District when Hugo and Clarissa were one flight above me on the rear stairwell. She was beautiful, with light brown skin, dark eyes, and wavy black hair that hung between her shoulder blades. She had been civil, but until that day Hugo had avoided eye-contact. When he saw me, he whispered to Clarissa, who continued on without him.

"I owe you an apology," I said before he could get a word in edgewise.

"No, you don't, Bryan." His smile seemed sincere. "I had fun. You did too, in spite of yourself. I told you I would respect your wishes, but all I heard from you was the same silence during our walk home from dinner. I assumed that was what you wanted, so that is what you get. And now we are just neighbors, which is for the best, I think."

After that, I was little more than a spectator to frequent get-togethers Hugo and Clarissa hosted. Study sessions? Dinner parties? Four-ways? All I knew was how tired I was of people mistakenly knocking on my door.

Like God was rubbing it in my face, everybody but me was pairing up. For a couple weeks now, Chris had been dating a male cheerleader from MTSU whose name was Dallas, because of course it was. And while me and Hugo had been hooking up, Stefano had started seeing a guy from Little Rock named Benji, whom I called the Mutt. Stefano told me that that was a shitty joke and I should try harder.

After showering, I opened my bedroom window and smoked a small bowl, letting myself cool down. Before I'd finished, my cell phone started ringing. It was my mother. I let it ring a few more times before answering.

"Don't hang up," she said before I could say hello.

I nearly addressed her by her first name, Cecily, but laughed, "Mom, I wasn't going to."

"Good."

"Why did you say that?"

"I hope you've been doing well," she ignored my question. Obviously, she hadn't heard about the summer storm. I couldn't blame her. National news coverage was zero to none.

"I'm fine," I said, thinking, *It's amazing how much weight you can lose while sweating through your bed sheets*—and—*it's amazing how quickly you grow to love cold showers*—and—*warm beer is like unsweetened iced tea: you acquire an ability to ignore your taste buds and gag reflex, if you hadn't already learned the latter.*

"How are you?" I asked.

"We're doing well," she said, "but your brother just broke off his engagement. I really thought she was going to be the one. How is Memphis treating you?"

"The same," I played along. Maybe she'd heard about the storm, but since I hadn't called home, I must have been spared.

If I told her the truth, she probably would have said, "It couldn't have been that bad if we didn't hear about it right away."

"Bryan?" she asked.

"What?"

"Did you hear what I just said?"

"Sorry." I shut the window. "There was a jet flying right over my place."

"Funny. I didn't hear that." I stayed silent. "Well," she continued, "what I'd said was, I'm just planting seeds, but could you visit this Christmas?"

"What's wrong?"

"Nothing, Bryan, but it's literally been years since you came home. I'd love to see you. So would your father."

"I'll think about it," I said.

"I love you, son."

"Love you, too."

"I mean it," she said.

I told her, "So do I," and hung up. So many questions never asked, so many answers chosen out of convenience. For some reason, I began thinking about all the things I ruined at home between puberty and leaving for college.

When I was twelve, I gained six inches in height and was imprisoned during the worst summer vacation of my life. One morning after exploring the woods behind our house, I woke up with my shins and calves and forearms and elbows and face ridged by rashes and seeping welts, a raised relief map that would never answer the question my mother would ask once her shock wore off: "Damn it, Bryan, where did you get into all this poison ivy?"

My left eye had been sealed shut by a blister that seeped so profusely I "cried" orange tears, the run-off's color matching my hair. Blisters littered my skin, but no part of my body was as caked as the bridge of my nose. My reflection resembled some obscure alien race from *Star Trek* that had been featured only once because the prosthetics were too expensive and their otherness was too unsettling.

As disgusting as my flesh felt, it was nothing compared to seeing how others saw me. Waiting in the pediatrician's lobby, children either pointed at me in fascination or hid their faces in their mother's sleeves and cried. Then things got worse.

"You don't want *that* down *there*," the doctor warned, addressing my mother more than me. "So, make sure you wash your hands extra good *before* going to the bathroom."

Soon, though, soap wasn't strong enough. To compensate, I would:

1. Strip naked, get in the shower, and pour bleach straight from the bottle onto my welts.

   a. Welcome the acrid smell and cold sting.

   b. Lie when required: "*Mom*, I have no idea where all the Clorox has gone! What would I need it for?"

2. Take a shower, alternating the water between scalding and freezing.

   a. End on freezing.

   b. Last as long as I could.

3. Air dry as much as possible, then pat dry as gently as possible using different towels for different body parts.

It took the rest of that summer for the welts to heal. I spent most of it cooped up out of the sun, when I should have been in a pool, letting the chlorine dry out the blisters. My mother never said anything, but I caught her sideways glances during the girl-trips she missed after being unable to find me a babysitter. The scars felt as plentiful as my freckles and, like those glances, didn't fade until the following winter.

During the autumn I was sixteen, after I finally told my mother what her first son, my half-brother, had done to me, her voice was as calm as her enunciation was condescending: "Are you sure that's *exactly* how it happened?" When I told her yes, she shook her head and the two syllables of my name crossing her lips made me long for the swelter of summer.

In late spring the year I turned eighteen, I showed my father's revolver to my best friend, Ryan. When I pulled the pistol case out from under the nightstand, it shushed against the carpet. The gun's barrel and cylinder were polished silver, the handle a glistening black. It went off while I was holding it barrel-up near my left ear. Ryan fell back on my parent's bed with his arms spread wide and I crumpled to the floor. I knew I was cussing, but I only heard the thundering absence that wouldn't quit pealing for an hour.

When he sat up, I rushed over and hugged him. I knew Ryan wasn't gay, but he was crying and I was crying and I was so glad I hadn't killed him that I kissed him on the mouth. He pulled back. I did too. Tears were in his eyes. More fell from mine. He shuddered, pointing at the wall. After I'd glanced back, he patted my shoulder and shook his head. I couldn't hear what he was saying, but I'd watched the shape of his lips and knew he never called me a faggot.

We raced to a nearby hardware store, where we bought spackle and paint, and then we tried covering up the hole in the wall of my parents' bedroom. All we did was make it more obvious. Nobody had asked me what happened, but my father bought a gun safe that weekend.

As August neared and I prepared to move to Memphis for college, I dreaded all of the questions I was certain were coming, but those never arrived. My parents had obviously talked about it. The gun safe was proof of that. But whatever they had said to one another was never spoken to me. There was so much left to fester, it was hard to keep track of it all.

Once I had finished moving into my dorm room, I collapsed on the creaky twin bed and decided to take their cue. If they didn't want to hear the truth, then I wouldn't bother. What could it hurt?

\* \* \*

Talking to my mother reminded me of my time with Hugo. She never asked questions she didn't want the answers to, and he hadn't told me the truth he didn't want questioned. I'd gone along with both to distract myself from realities I didn't want to face, which reminded me of the liar I had seen in the mirror the night Hugo finally told me about his fiancée.

Because I had today and tomorrow off, I decided to search for Adam in a place I hadn't considered before. Once dressed, I set out for The Oil Well, the closest thing Memphis had to a leather bar.

It took a good thirty-minutes to walk down to the place, which was near Poplar and Cleveland, right by the Jack Pirtle's Chicken and the sketchy Kroger's. When I entered, twilight and second-hand smoke replaced the bright afternoon and fried chicken. The guys playing pool squinted at me, cigarettes hanging from their lips.

Near the front door and blacked-out windows, along the bar's shorter curved arm, were three empty chairs. I claimed the last seat, my back to the wall. Once my eyes adjusted, I'd have a good view of everything. The TVs above the bar were playing a porno with the volume muted, the jukebox was blaring Matchbox 20's "Long Day," and the small talk was punctuated by the sharp clang of a cue ball breaking a new rack.

The lone bartender sauntered up. I didn't catch his name, but he was in his early sixties at the least, with sunken cheeks, a mustache several decades out of date, square glasses, and short parted hair. I had my ID out, but he didn't check it. "What can I get you?"

"A Heineken, and I'll start a tab."

As he returned with my beer, I heard a familiar laugh and knew it was Curt before we saw each other and his smile flat-lined. I watched condensation trickle down the side of my bottle until he and two other guys relocated to the patio.

I knew he hadn't been laughing *at* me, but I gripped the cold longneck, wishing I could make Curt laugh *with* me once more. There was nothing I could say that would bring him back to my side, but I couldn't stop myself. I might begin with, *I am sorry,* and follow up with something like, *I didn't deserve you, and you didn't deserve what I did to you.* But the last thing Curt wanted was my apology. *Words are so cheap,* I could hear him scoffing. *No wonder you're such a spendthrift.*

An old man with a cane ambled over, sitting two chairs down from mine. He pushed back from the bar loudly and spilled some of his cocktail. The bartender walked over, lifted the glass, wiped off the bar, and set the highball on a couple of bev naps without a word.

"Haven't seen you here before." He took a sip of his drink. "New in town?"

"Sadly, no. I've come here a few times."

"And how often have you visited?" He smiled. He was bald, but the hair on his sides was silver and thick, meeting an unkempt beard. His eyes were puffy and bloodshot, his nose was lumpy and red. He wore a yellow golf shirt that had a ketchup stain on the chest. His gut strained the shirt's fabric, and I'd bet his acid-washed jean shorts were older than me.

"Whatcha drinking, son?"

I told him and asked the same question.

He chuckled, "A bottom swill martini. I like 'em dirty. How's about you?"

"Sorry?"

"How d'you like your cocktails?"

"Those are about the only thing I'll take dirty."

He harrumphed and slapped my back. "Smart man. Stay that way." He drained his drink and slammed the highball so hard on the bar I was surprised it didn't shatter.

"Harold," the bartender said, putting his hands on his hips, "have you had enough or are you being an asshole?"

I wished I could scoot my chair back, but the damn wall wouldn't budge.

"What?" Harold raised his palms.

"Are you finished for the day," the bartender walked over, speaking slowly, "or was all that noise just you asking for a refill?"

"Yes," he said.

The bartender shook his head, then made Harold a new gin martini, pouring this one into a clear plastic cup. After he walked away, Harold said, "Never tastes the same outta one of these. But cheers," he raised the cup. I obliged and took another healthy drink.

"So what do they call you?"

"My name's—"

"No, son, not your name. What do people call you?"

"They call me my name," I said before noticing several nearby patrons staring. So many raised eyebrows. A wisp of a guy seated at the bar's opposite end looked familiar. I'd almost placed him, but Harold took a larger drink than he'd planned and started coughing.

I slapped his back a couple times, wiping off that hand on my jeans.

Once he composed himself, he said, "So?"

"I never listen to what idiots call me," I lied.

"Smart man," he said. "Smart man."

"Too smart, and nowhere near enough," I mumbled.

Harold stared at the martini left in his cup. The bartender walked over with the tab. He glanced at me as he slid Harold the bad news.

A tall blond guy with broad shoulders exited the restroom and beelined it to the back patio. His gait seemed wrong, but he could have been Adam. I finished my first beer and ordered a second.

Harold fumbled through his leather wallet. Bloated with receipts and coupons and cash, it was worn and cracked, the bottom edges creased, the seams straining. The bartender opened my new beer. I stood, saying, "Nice to meet you, Harold."

The old man paused counting change out for his tab. "Stay smart, son."

With the chilled reassurance of a new beer in hand, I went to the restroom. There were two side-by-side, labeled "Master" and "Slave." I chose the latter. The exteriors of both doors were painted black to match the bar's decor, but their interiors were painted red. That pop of color was needed because both restrooms were claustrophobic spaces with grimy white floors and shiny black tiles on the walls except for a thin line of red squares placed a little higher than waist-level. The restroom names were likely chosen because the bar's original clientele was in the leather community, but the reason I avoided the

"Master" restroom was its urinal trough. How could anybody have looked at a urinal and thought, *Yeah, let's make this so much worse?* The "Slave" restroom had stalls, in contrast, and even though those didn't lock, there was still some degree of privacy.

In any case, this restroom was cleaner than the one at CK's, and it was stocked with liquid soap, paper towels, and a mouthwash dispenser of all things. I had my tragic moments, to be sure, but I'd never gargle whatever generic Listerine was doled out in those plastic thimbles.

After the flush, I used some paper towels to turn on the faucet, and when I was done, another batch to shut it off. I took the first drink of my second beer and examined myself in the mirror. Every mirror outside of my apartment reflected my face harshly, like they didn't feel the need to lie to me. Staring at myself, I said, "If it is him, you're *not* overreacting. Go."

The patio door was propped open. In its place hung a curtain of overlapping transparent strips of plastic. It was difficult to get through those with my hands unscathed, but I managed it, all while feeling like I was walking into a slaughterhouse. The "Cattle Crossing" sign posted directly ahead didn't help. A tall wooden fenced surrounded the patio, and in the back left corner there was a treehouse that consisted of two platforms. One was five steps above the patio, with another set of steps at the back left leading to an octagonal platform that circled a sycamore.

From my right, I heard, "Bry, Bry, Bry." Curt was smiling like a server visiting a ten-top that had been seated twenty minutes before the kitchen closed and wanted separate checks. "Of all the places I worried I'd run into you, I never thought it would be this fine establishment." He was sitting at a table with the two guys who'd followed him out here and the blond guy who wasn't Adam. One of his friends was grinning as he glanced between me and his watch.

I took a sip of beer, then said, "It's never too late to try new things."

"How's about being honest with yourself? Have you tried that yet?"

"Working on it."

"Bet you are," Curt chuckled. He had a new look. The tousled mop of black hair that had hung to his ears and was better suited to the Grunge era was gone, replaced by buzzed sides, enough on the top to part, and the beginnings of a beard. Which made sense: a cosmetological cure is a hell of a lot cheaper than the geographical one.

After my first slip, Curt had promised me if I ever cheated on him again, he would delete me from his life like an unwanted file. I had to give him credit for sticking to his word. "How are you doing?" I asked.

"No," Curt said. "We're not talking about me."

I mumbled, "I'm sorry."

One of the guys smacked a five-dollar bill on the table. "Damn it, Curt," he laughed, "you called his worthless apology happening in under two minutes."

Curt mock-shushed him and stood, his friends following suit. "Nice to see some things will apparently never change. Happy hunting, Bry." With that, he and his friends pushed through the plastic curtain. The blond looked me up and down with a smirk and a shake of his head.

With the patio all to myself, I walked to the treehouse's upper level. Above the platform, the tree's lichen-splotched trunk bulged toward the front, leaving space for only one person to walk around that side at a time. Instead of cross-beams, the railing had two steel chains. As I leaned my elbows on that railing and took a drink, I kept my feet on the green-painted wooden deck. A police siren wailed past on Poplar and the air was thick with the aroma of fried chicken from right around the corner. My stomach growled because all I'd eaten that day was a bowl of cereal.

*Man cannot live by bread alone,* I swirled my beer, *but damn it if I weren't trying.* Behind the fence sat a two-story house. No blinds or curtains covered the window into a second-floor room. What had the person who lived there seen on any given night?

A new group pushed through the plastic curtain, laughing. Curt's friend was right. He had called it. He always could.

\* \* \*

Curt had also grown up in Ladue, but we hadn't known each other. When we met in Memphis and started dating, he didn't rush things, letting me get comfortable. After a couple months of mostly kissing and mutual jerk-offs, we started fucking. We used condoms for anal, and he didn't care that I wouldn't swallow his load as long as I let him swallow mine. He was the first person I truly felt comfortable being naked with. After being so patient with me, he was energetic and we were a good match. While he occasionally liked to flip-flop, he was more of a bottom, which was fine by me.

We were together for two years, and before those last few months when the sex stopped altogether, him wanting to top me was a blue moon. Either I loved Curt pounding my ass because it didn't happen that often or because my load never hit my face unless he was thrusting fast and deep while choking me as hard as he could. Curt had been the only person I ever let treat me that way, and I loved how simultaneously spent and sated it made me feel. As usual, I was probably overthinking things. Sometimes having a cock up your ass is nothing more profound than having a cock up your ass.

When he bottomed, whether I was trying to pin his ankles to the headboard or he was pumping me dry, I could forget everything and focus on the moment. I loved how much he would sweat, how heavy those drops felt when they splashed, how his knees would buckle when he could no longer crouch, how his thighs would shudder against my hips, and how when he got to that point, I'd grab his wrists, pulling his hands off his cock and moving them to my throat.

Four months into our relationship, he'd asked, "What's a kink you've always wanted to try?"

After a few long moments, I said, "I want you to choke me while I'm fucking you."

"One hand or two?"

"I don't know."

"We'll figure it out," he smiled.

That night, as he rode me faster and faster, his eyes narrowed and his smile widened and his grip tightened. I came too quickly. He let go of my neck and I gasped, my eyes fluttering to stars retreating faster than I could blink.

Curt wasn't far behind me, shooting warm ropes up to the hollow below my Adam's apple. Then he collapsed and hugged me, smearing himself between us. I hadn't started limping yet and was halfway inside of him. "Damn, Bry," he moaned.

I double-checked that the condom was still on before I slowly pushed all the way back in.

He raised up and play-smacked my face. "Easy now."

In time, I didn't have to guide his hands. He grew adept at choking me with one and punching my chest with the other. He'd slap my face if I asked, but never as hard as I liked.

Once, he told me he didn't want to leave a mark. When I said, "You already have," he rolled his eyes, held my wrists over my head with his left hand, and choked me with his right forearm. Nose to nose, he stared at me without blinking. He was frowning and grinning. I started squirming a little. He kissed me on the cheek, then he whispered into my ear, "When I do leave a mark, you won't forget it."

Turns out we flip-flopped on that, too. On a Saturday night in January of 2002, I'd gone out to Fugue by myself because Curt was feeling depressed. "I haven't been to the gym in a month," he said from the couch, "so I'm definitely not stepping a foot inside that place."

Following two weeks of hardly talking and sleeping in separate beds, Curt had said, "I don't want to break up with you." His sigh sounded like "yet." If I had told him that, I'm sure he'd say, "Original recipe Bryan. Listening with his feelings instead of his ears."

But how many times had I offered to blow Curt only for him to decline with, "I haven't showered in a few days"? I should have suggested we shower together, not worrying about another rejection. But I never had. Whenever I asked why he was feeling depressed, he wouldn't give me a direct answer, which made me think it was less about him and more about me.

That night, before Fugue's door-whore stamped the back of my left hand, I was already buzzed. In Puck's bar, I ordered the first of too many beers. Over the next few hours, I caught a guy who kept staring at me. If I were sober, I would have blushed. I didn't go out with the intention of cheating on Curt, but I'd been so lonely for so long. The attention made me realize how much I was starving. The trick was in college and his apartment was somewhere near Highland and Southern.

I couldn't remember his name or what he even looked like, but I do remember how, when a train whistle bolted me upright in his twin bed, he spooned me until I calmed down. I knew regret and shame would rise along with the sun, but I closed my eyes to him nuzzling my neck and slept like a smothered baby.

Late that next morning, the trick gently nudged my shoulder until I sat up, then he handed me a steaming cup of coffee with too much creamer. His smile made me uncomfortable.

\* \* \*

A fire truck screaming east on Poplar made me shake my head. And with that, I was back in the treehouse of The Oil Well and still much too sober.

The patio had filled up a little and a guy walking up the treehouse stairs, asked, "Penny for your thoughts, handsome?"

"I don't like ripping people off," I said before finishing my beer and heading back inside.

# CHAPTER FIFTEEN

My former seat and the two others beside it were occupied. Toni Braxton's "Unbreak My Heart" was playing on the jukebox, and a couple were punching in more selections. The second-hand smoke was getting thicker, but there were two currently empty seats near the well station. The first was tilted against the railing, with a half-full beer sitting in front of it. I claimed the second near the long end of the bar.

The bartender walked up. "Need a refill?" I nodded. "On it." He turned around, rummaged through the reach-in cooler, popped off the cap, and set the bottle on a bev nap. "Are you doing alright?"

"Sure. Why?"

"Never hurts to ask." Someone down the bar yelled for a drink. The bartender smiled and threw an olive, saying, "Girl, we all know your liver's on borrowed time, but it's gonna wait."

"That's a good one," I said.

"I can transfer you, Bryan, but I'd appreciate it if you showed me some love."

"I'll tab out."

147

He served the rowdy patron, pouring out a few shots for him, that guy's friends, and one for himself. After they all slammed their shots, he chatted with other patrons on his way back, printed off my tab, and welcomed the swishy and stocky bartenders who were both clocking in. Then he elbowed up in front of me, saying, "Thanks."

I signed the receipt. "Why did you ask if I was okay?"

"Sling drinks long enough and you can tell when someone's not having their best day."

"Good guess."

"Oh, I don't have to guess," he winked, opening a beer for himself and raising it for a toast. "Hope you have a better night, Bryan."

With a smile, I clinked my new bottle against his. As he walked off, the chair next to me was dragged away from the bar. Its occupant was Duke. He waved to someone on the other side of the room, and then he looked at me.

I pretended to watch one of the TVs, but he patted my shoulder.

"Do I know you?" he asked.

"I don't think so," I said.

"Well, now you do. I'm Duke." He stuck out his hand.

I tapped his palm with the bottom of my longneck.

"Alright," he smirked. "What's your name?"

He took a sip, so did I. "Bryan," I said afterward.

"Are you sure we haven't met?"

I decided not to bring up the night I saw him at Fugue because he'd barely glanced at me. "Think I saw you at Ntropé a few months ago. It was after-hours and you were crying at the bar."

"Yeah..." Duke peeled the label from his beer. "Don't think I ever felt as tragic as I did that night. I'm sure I looked like a fuckin' mess."

"We've all been there."

"Doubt it. Ever think a guy loves you," he chuckled, "so while you're messing around, you let him take some nudies of you, *then* he shares those with all his friends? Oh, and a few of 'em are your coworkers?"

The swishy and stocky bartenders pretended they weren't eavesdropping.

Duke continued, "Turns out I was nothing but a joke. The night you saw me crying was right after the shit splattered through the fan. You seen that movie where the prom queen gets drenched in pig's blood? What I wouldn't give for her psychic powers."

The guy to the left of Duke said, "Sometimes we shouldn't tell all our business to everybody in earshot."

"We don't have to talk about that," I told Duke and took a drink.

He laughed, "Alright. How tall are you?"

As pick-up lines go, I thought that was weird, but whatever. "A little over six foot. And you?"

"Five-even," he declared.

"A ring box?"

He frowned.

At that moment, I'd swear I heard Curt's commentary: *Confused so soon? That's not a promising sign.*

I ignored that. "Good things come in small packages."

"Are you online?" he asked, telling me his AOL screen name and spelling it: "It's w-a-y-two-as-in-the-number-c-u-t." I couldn't figure out what "Way2Cut" meant, because from what I remember he was skinny, not ripped. "You should add me to your buddy list."

"That's not really my thing," I said.

He motioned to the swishy bartender and asked, "How's about some shots? Are they your thing?" I shrugged. He ordered two whiskeys. We tossed those back, and once I finished my beer, he ordered us another round. Soon, I was feeling good and buzzed.

"I'm going to get some air," I said.

"See you in a couple minutes," he rubbed my back.

The patio was pretty busy now. When I got to the tree-house's upper level somebody yelled my name. I waved, but I couldn't place his face. He asked, "It's Bryan, right? Chris Oliver's roommate?"

"That's me."

"I'm Jason," he said. "I met you at the theatre party. You told me some stories about working at Fresh Springs."

His shoulder-length hair hung loose and he only had a mustache now. "How's it going?" I asked.

After taking a deep breath, he said, "The good days are bad and the bad days are nightmares. Never thought I'd use so much hand sanitizer," he laughed.

"Which cabin are you in?"

"Number one."

"The teenage sex offenders," I shook my head.

Duke walked up with two beers and handed me one. "What are y'all talking about?"

"His job," I told him. "Where I used to work."

I made introductions and Jason cut his eyes at Duke. "I've heard."

"I'll be down there when you're done," Duke said, walking to an empty patio table.

"Does that cabin still have the highest staff turnover?" I asked Jason.

He nodded. "My first week there, an offender told me, 'You won't last six months.'"

"Those kids will play you if you're not careful."

"Yeah," he shook his head. "Wished I'd never read some of

their files."

"Talk about nightmares. Clive Barker's got nothing on them." Then I said, "Nice seeing you," and joined Duke.

When I sat down across from him, he said, "See? What did I tell you?"

"What are you talking about?"

"I've got no idea who the fuck that guy is, but he sure knows all about me."

"Forget him."

"Well, he's not the first to say something like that."

"Fuck him," I leaned across the table, "and fuck the asshole who stomped all over your privacy." Despite himself, Duke smiled. I continued, "Who cares what they think?" When I finished by saying—"It doesn't matter what people think they know about you, as long as you know the truth"—my gut clenched because I wasn't sure I'd ever been more dishonest.

He took a sip, then said, "Are you a counselor?"

I was about to make a joke about how desperate somebody would have to be in order to take my advice, but I didn't want him feeling any worse than he already did. "Maybe I wanted to be one a long time ago," I said, "but things didn't work out."

* * *

I mostly remember buying each other a few more rounds, but then we were kissing in Duke's car. His mouth tasted minty. After a while, we stopped and he lit a cigarette. He took a drag and ran a hand through my hair. "No pressure, Bryan." He rolled down his window a little, blowing out smoke and ashing his cigarette. He started rubbing the top and inside of my upper thigh with his right hand. I felt no pressure but the good kind straining the crotch of my jeans.

Duke's gated apartment complex was fifteen minutes

outside of Memphis proper. How we made it there in one piece, God only knows. He kicked off his shoes and walked out of his jeans four steps into his place. We started kissing and I slid a hand down the front of his boxer-briefs.

When I paused, Duke pulled back and narrowed his eyes. "What?"

"You uncut?"

"I'm normal. Why?"

"Your screen name... I thought circumcision mishap."

"Supposed to read 'cute,' but somebody'd beat me to it."

*Guess he's never heard of the letter Q*, I imagined Curt saying. *Way2Qute but not Way2Brite?*

After a brief mutual jerk-off, Duke went down on me. I lay back on the couch while he made a lot of noise and even more spit. I shut my eyes and relaxed for a good while, until he started straddling me. Slowly, he moved forward, and we began dry-humping. *Play-fucking*, I thought, enjoying the friction. Duke slapped his cock against the drum of my stomach. I closed my eyes and felt him shuffling his position, thinking nothing of it, until he grabbed my cock at the base and sat on it. When I opened my eyes, he was contentedly grinding his ass.

Back then, if I had ever told anyone this story, here was how it would end: it took several seconds before I realized what Duke had done, at which point I jerked my hips back, turned to the side, and shoved him off me. My cock felt cold from tip to base. My whole body shivered.

Duke slumped on the far couch cushion, and we stared at each other for what drunkenly felt like forever but was probably no more than a minute. His forehead was rutted, his eyes were squinting, and his lips were pressed tightly together. I had no idea what my face looked like. What could I say or do at that point? I was stranded in Bartlett and didn't want to have to call a cab, so we jacked off and fell asleep on the couch.

Here was what actually happened: Duke did sit on my cock and it did take me a few seconds to realize what he'd done, but I didn't pull out. I knew I should have, but I felt like I deserved this. He squirmed his ass. "That's more like it," he played with my nipples. "Take it."

He was so warm, and that comfort felt as amazing as it did wrong. When he began riding me, he put his hands on his head and arched his back. I thought of shirtless guys dancing at the club, turned on by how much they believed they were turning on everybody else.

Duke built up speed. I gripped his hips and started thrusting. Might as well, considering how far we'd gone already. He put his hands on my chest and toggled my cock side to side. My eyes rolled to the back of my head.

He chuckled, "Goddamn, you have a beautiful dick," and I told him, "Your ass feels like summer." Then he shifted from his knees, crouching on his heels, and spread his cheeks with both hands.

My body grunted and happily bounced his ass on my cock. He sat back, looking at the ceiling and laughing "Yeah-ha-ha-fuckin'-yeah" in time with the flat smack of my hips against his thighs, and he started punching my chest, moaning louder and louder. I was so close so fast. Duke knew it and told me to pull out, so I traced his spine with the largest load of my life.

"That's okay," he hugged me, kissing my neck. "Knew alls you needed was some encouragement." My body tensed, but he didn't notice. I hated that he had been right about how simple I was. But more than that, I hated how I could only do the right thing in a story I'd completely made up.

Near dawn, I awoke to him jerking me off. "Morning, handsome," Duke said. "Looked like you could use some attention." Thankfully, it was over soon enough. I was so dehydrated that this ejaculation was less life-affirming than the sneeze that vanishes on the cusp of happening.

Duke grinned, "Wanna hit the showers?"

"I need to piss," I excused myself. My urine was a pungent canary. Several pink Daisy razors littered the tub, light brown curlies winking from so many blades. I imagined the hot water running out as he shaved.

"Whatcha thinkin' about that shower?" he asked as I finished washing my hands.

"Thanks, but I'd just get in the way." While he cleaned up, I got dressed and waited on the couch. My mind kept asking, *If crabs could think, would they consider the transfer from one person's pubes to another's the equivalent of faster-than-light travel?*

Then Duke drove me back to my apartment, chain-smoking and small-talking the entire way. He meant well, but I pined for the louse's version of FTL. In the parking lot of my apartment building, Duke kissed me on the cheek and asked for my number. I almost gave him the landline, but that would have been a disaster. God, if Duke ever left a message on the answering machine and Chris heard it, he would never let me live that down. So I gave Duke my cell phone number, and he drove away, waving. I raised my hand but didn't wave back.

"Chris," I yelled after closing the kitchen door. Nothing. I stripped right there and bagged up the clothes I was wearing. Then I got one of the RID kits from the top shelf in my bedroom closet and lathered up the worst shampoo ever from head to toe. Did it smell and feel so bad because the manufacturer was shaming you, because it was that toxic, or were those one and the same? For ten minutes, I crouched in the shower and hugged my knees. Then I rinsed, repeated, and began to worry in earnest.

What stood out the most about our hookup was how, when

I had smacked Duke's nicely shaped ass, it felt about as firm as a sponge. In that moment, I had thought, *Go... I should go*, but all I did was stare at the front door.

Beside it stood a two-and-a-half-foot tall ceramic rabbit with a flat shelf atop its head. I knew the rabbit's height because it only reached up to Duke's waist. He'd dumped his keys on it after locking the door but before stripping. The misplaced garden ornament looked godawful.

He noticed me staring and bragged, "Got it for next to nothing at the outlet mall off exit twenty."

*When it comes to you, Bry,* I had heard Curt, *what's the difference between being a bargain and just being real cheap?*

Duke snapped his fingers. "Earth to Bryan."

And all I did was shake my head and go through with it.

# CHAPTER SIXTEEN

Thanksgiving arrived with colder winds rustling the red and brown leaves that hadn't fallen yet. Chris went home to Atlanta, Stefano left for Nashville, but I stayed right where I was.

Since Duke, I'd dodged the waking world for as long as I could. Eventually, sleep would spurn me, so I would drag myself out of bed. If I had to work, I'd show up and talk to as few people as possible. If I didn't have to work and didn't want to pick up extra shifts, I'd head out for longer and longer runs. But it didn't matter how fast or how far I ran because I couldn't forget the trajectory of my life those past few months.

Stefano had been nice for a minute, and then out of nowhere, Hugo had seemed like a great consolation prize. I could have stopped there, but, no, I got drunk enough to fuck Duke. Dire Duke. If he was the local joke, what did that make me?

A Thanksgiving dinner of leftover frozen pizza awaited me in the fridge when I returned from a fifteen-miler with a six-pack under my arm. As I walked up the front staircase, I smelled ham, some kind of fish, and onions roasting. An ostensibly straight couple were knocking on Hugo and Clarissa's door. While I unlocked mine, Clarissa welcomed them in and the aromas set my stomach to growling. My dinner was going to taste even cheaper than it already was.

Duke called my cell phone twice between seven and seven-thirty. The second time, he left a voice mail. I hit delete without listening to it. I called my mother and told her I would come home this Christmas. Soon enough, the pizza and beer were gone, the phone stayed silent, and so went my Thanksgiving.

# PART III

*Automaticity*: Just like computer programs, people have subroutines. These schemas allow us to complete habitual actions with little conscious attention. If these cognitive reflexes could talk, they would tell Descartes to go fuck himself. In more practical terms, have you ever driven home from work without thinking or had sex that bored you so much your mind wandered, only returning with a sense of amazement that you'd somehow finished the chore? Time passes and you're not consciously aware of those individual steps, literal or not, or how you wound up wherever your subconscious has led you.

See also: catastrophizing, denial, drinking, and jogging.

*I'm acting absent-mindedly, not instinctually or reflex-*
*ively. If only my thanatos required conscious intent.*
*Honestly, it's probably more effective when it's left*
*running in the background. Think of how many facets*
*it's polishing while I'm distracted by a new trigger.*

— 9 DECEMBER 2003

# CHAPTER SEVENTEEN

It was December 20, the temperature was hovering near freezing, and I had the rare Saturday night off. I should have walked the few blocks to Studio on the Square and caught a movie. But I didn't have plans. Hardly ever did anymore.

On my nightstand was a letter from the Health Department that had arrived a week ago. I hadn't opened it yet, pushing that off for as long as I could. It might be nothing, or it could be everything. Memphis wasn't a big city, yet it seemed filled with Adam's shoddy Xeroxes, while the real thing had vanished.

I lay on my twin bed shirtless and going commando in a pair of checkerboard Umbros. I'd turned off all the lights but left my TV on after switching to a channel of snowy static and dialing the volume to zero. I was watching the rise and fall of my stomach. I liked how the rabbit-eared reception drenched my body hair and freckles in an eerie slate.

Chris's newest compilation of techno blared from down the hall. His prep for a night out was a regularly measured thrum less imaginative than the refrigerator's compressor.

On my turntable spun the Dead Boys' *Young, Loud, and Snotty*, the volume cranked. Stiv Bators was growling the lyrics to "Not Anymore," a lament about being homeless and cold. So, when I heard the creak of a floorboard and someone besides Chris asking—"Can I check out something?"—I was thrown for a few seconds. Stefano's voice sounded unfamiliar because I hadn't been expecting him and because he hadn't been over to the apartment much since he began dating Benji. Still, *scrappy* would never not spring to mind.

He flipped on the overhead light and shut the door. "What is that? Proto-emo shit?"

"Hardly. But I've got Joy Division," I dialed down the volume, "if that's how you want to pre-game."

He ran a hand through my recent haircut, then playfully shoved my head and sat at the foot of the bed. "Lowered your ears?"

I sat up, yawning. "Didn't hear you come in."

"Not surprised," Stefano squeezed my left calf. "How're you?"

I flexed the muscle, "What mood of a read are you looking for?"

Stefano's dark eyes shifted from my lap to my chest, blinks mapping upwards from the scar to the corner of my lips.

"Wanna venture into the wild," he smiled, "with me and Topher?"

He meant Fugue. "The Mutt will be there, right?" I leaned in.

Stefano reclined, draped his arms over the footboard. "*Benji* will be there. He's driving in from Little Rock."

"He sounds nice—"

"He is and you need to come up with a new joke."

"What I meant was," I stared at the hollow where Stefano's

neck and collar bone met, "Fugue is bad enough without being a third wheel."

"You could actually go out once in a while," he raised his hands palms-up, "have a life."

"Hearing about how yours is playing out is *funner*."

"Bry, c'mon."

I squeezed Stefano's right calf through his jeans and felt him flex it. "All that from running?"

"And," he smirked, "from monopolizing Jack's bike lately."

"How brotherly." I slipped my hand up Stefano's pants leg, tickling through the hair above his sock. "Have you changed your mind?"

"About what?"

I leaned in close. "Hanging out as more than friends."

"Bryan, no." Stefano shook his head. "I'm dating Benji."

"Thought you didn't want anything serious."

"Don't know how serious we are, but who said I couldn't change my mind?"

"Sorry," I squeezed his calf once more and reclined. Several moments of silence passed while he stared at a stack of books, searching for a story that better suited him.

Times like that, I felt ghostly, lacking someone or some-place to haunt. But my last real haunt, Curt, had been gone before we were through. Without the outline of another, I felt as insubstantial as the mercury-shimmer of an air pocket over a summer road. I liked to imagine I could pass freely between the layers of stratum through which were threaded my desires and fears, fantasies and shame. And all of those god-fine strands were strung between every conceivable point, like power lines weaving through the low sky, beautiful if not for a humming fear insinuating every cell with a fatal unraveling.

Although this grace saved nothing so much as it was pathetic, I'd only ever wrecked my own home. And although

Stefano and Benji would probably never have a home to wreck, I wanted to demolish whatever foundation Stefano thought he was laying.

What was Benji, after all, but a "For-Rent" ad Stefano had circled in the local weekly? A listing he'd check out but ultimately decide against because the rent was too high for the space. Not to mention Benji lived two hours away, so how long would it be, really, before that distance led Stefano's eye to wander? But I couldn't tell Stefano this, no matter how right I was. I'd have to wait for that *ultimately.*

Instead of opening my mouth and ruining any future chances, I opened the nightstand drawer and rummaged for supplies. Quickly, I lit up a joint and passed it. Stefano hit it twice, closed his eyes, and passed it back without coughing. He smelled nice, not overpowering, comfortable, undeniably him. The taste of his spit I transposed.

After I cashed the roach, I dug my bronchial inhaler out from under the covers, took two pumps. Stefano patted my right shoulder then traced two fingers over my scar before standing.

When I stood, I kept my back to him until I'd shifted myself. Manners and all. When I turned around, Stefano had dug some change out of a pocket, counting it as he exhaled. "Good night, Soap-Opera," I took another pump from my inhaler, "if that's what you want."

"Yeah, yeah." Stefano smiled. "You're welcome to join us," he said as he opened the door. "Topher!" he yelled, walking down the hall.

His exit made me think of the pretense of afterglow. At some point, somebody will shatter it by scratching himself, passing gas, or doing both with a smile and a chuckle (followed by a joke that is funny if intimacy has replaced familiarity), or by getting up to take a piss or a shower, or to let the other drip into the toilet.

Then there are the sounds: the bathroom fan, his weight settling onto the toilet seat, and if not that, then his pissing, the toilet paper being unrolled in banners and ripped off, followed by the toilet's raucous flush, the open tap steaming a mirror.

When the techno died, Chris said, "Bye-bye, Bry-Bry."

Stalled and stuck in the mud, I was the venerable cliched Memphian: someone who likes the city well enough but needs to move because it's a dead-end for them, yet years pass and they stay put.

Once I had the apartment to myself, I turned off my record player and went to the living room, hearing the party that Hugo and Clarissa were throwing. I grabbed a beer from the fridge and decided to make spaghetti.

While salting the bubbling water, there were several loud knocks. I opened the front door to find a drunk straight couple. They were laughing but that stopped when they saw me.

"Is this... Hugo's place?"

I pointed behind them. "Turn around and follow the noise." As Hugo opened his door and the drunk couple forgot all about me, the water started roiling over the pot. After the noodles were cooking, I added four cloves of garlic I'd swiped from work to the simmering sauce.

The music and stomping from Hugo's apartment got louder. I finished that beer and opened another, feeling bad for the people who lived in the unit under his. I flipped on the TV, catching the tail-end of a *Star Trek: The Next Generation* rerun.

Apparently, it was a marathon. That episode finished when my dinner was ready, so I watched a second as I ate way too much pasta. During a third episode, I lay on the couch, sipping on a new beer and feeling bloated as fuck. I was calculating how much I'd need to run tomorrow when there was a commercial for a nearby outlet mall, which made me think of Duke.

The noise from Hugo's apartment ended with a slammed front door. It was a quarter-to-midnight, and I was tired but nowhere near sleepy. When I checked my email, there was a piece of spam stripped of images, anonymous, and fragmented:

*safeguard the remitting pearlstone ... a funeral in Germany and a baton horse on the esplanade ... the hypodermic's servitude ... indulge and salivate about the frugal promiscuity of cerulean polyglots*

I added this to my collection and went to the kitchen. I opened the Midtown alt-zine's newest issue, uselessly checking out the event listings for tonight. If I hadn't procrastinated, there was a movie and a band I would have liked to see. Flipping back to the letters to the editor and political cartoons, an article's title caught my eye.

## PUBLIC HEALTH by Alek Mina

### BLUFF CITY PLAGUES: THEN & NOW

*How Memphis reacted to outbreaks of Yellow Fever during the 1870s, how it's reacting to the ongoing HIV/AIDS epidemic, and what these responses could tell us about how we should proceed.*

Facing the sandbags of festering corpses, local legends from the 1870s tell of how our city government—unable to stem the flood—paved over the bodies instead of removing them for a proper burial. While stories of such practices abound in antiquity, contemporary parallels are sparse.

This macabre tale relates how the corpses were stacked high on once bustling streets, certain to be joined by many more mothers and fathers, sons and daughters, brothers and sisters, neighbors and strangers, blacks and whites—united once and forever by the inescapable equality of decomposition. In truth, the city's historians assure us, most were buried in Martyrs Park.

Wrecked first by the Civil War then haunted by the perennial fear of Yellow Fever, Memphis was the first municipality in the nation to implement a modern, citywide sewer system.

According to Dr. John H. Eskine, president of the Board of Health, this was necessary because "the local conditions surrounding this portion of our riverfront were such as to have originated almost any disease and

certainly to have intensified one naturally as malignant as this one."[1]

Or, to put it more vividly, consider the learned remarks of an unnamed Northerner: "I've been to Cairo, and there's dirt for you.... I've been to Cologne where it's pure smell—but they all back down to Memphis."[2]

In any event, such public health reforms were largely ignored by the industrial chiefs of the day. This is a disregard that, by 1880, had set Atlanta well on its way to surpassing Memphis's regional significance. And this persists even now, with both Atlanta and Nashville drawing attention away from the Bluff City.

## Losing to the House

The Bluff City. A more apt nickname there isn't, for wasn't this city called on its most arrogant of bluffs? While most non-locals will admit Memphis's historical significance as the cradle of the Blues, they ignore how it's a strategic shipping hub for both North America and the rest of the world.

Many Memphians are guilty of this as well, disregarding

much of what the city has to offer and a new flood, one which is not seen as a deluge because it is so slow in spilling over, because to the people on dry land, those who are unlucky enough to drown are little more than sandbags abandoned a few at a time and swiftly swept downriver.

## An Antediluvian Port

By all accounts, Memphis had been a cosmopolitan city until the late 1870s. The impetus for both shifts—from urbane to provincial, and from the rank, wet gutters to the immaculate, dry sidewalks—was then dubbed the "yellow-jack's sting."

In the decade following the Civil War, Memphis suffered three separate outbreaks of Yellow Fever...

I closed the weekly, deciding to save the rest for later when I could give it my full attention. I pulled my journal out from under my mattress and opened it. On a blank page, I wrote:

*"[R]ank, wet gutters" and "immaculate, dry sidewalks"*
*and the dead buried beneath streets we stroll down*
*unaware, "united once and forever by the inescapable*
*equality of decomposition." Every city must be the same.*
*Still, with what Memphis saw during the 19th century,*
*imagine if the dead rose, tearing up sidewalks and*
*cobblestones, terrifying yuppies in their overpriced*
*condos and inspiring a new exodus from downtown as*
*the dead shambled about, surprised by everything that*
*has changed but even more so by all that hasn't. Could*
*make for a cool story.*

After hiding my journal, I went for a walk. There were two

different convenience stores several blocks from my apartment, with a third chain a half-mile farther west. But this third store—which was a broom closet of cigarettes, chips, soda, and beer—neighbored the liquor store that owned Sputnik.

The moon was brilliant. And that was a good thing, because the streetlights along westbound Poplar, on the Overton Park side, weren't working. The darkness rendered the park's mostly skeletal forest immense and solid.

I crossed Cooper and saw that giant man from the summer bundled up in a coat, hat, and scarf, leading his two Rottweilers across Poplar into the park. I slowed my pace, disgusted that I was considering following him, for assuming that he was doing anything other than letting his massive dogs drop their tremendous turds somewhere other than his tiny lawn.

*I'm a weak, weak man.* I shoved my hands into the sweatshirt's pockets and jaywalked across Poplar. I didn't have a plan, but I headed in his direction. Soon, he'd turned around, two full plastic bags in one hand, the leashes in the other. When he saw me, he nodded but gave me a wide berth. I kept walking in the same direction, hoping I wasn't being as obvious as I felt. After a few minutes, I headed west, resuming my trip. I trudged past the first two convenience stores, crossed at the Evergreen intersection, lit by the orange streetlights of eastbound Poplar.

Sputnik came into view, its spikes rising above the rooftops of an independent bookstore, the Circuit Playhouse, and the third convenience store's metal awning. Moments later those were replaced by spikes from the other half. I quickened my pace.

I lingered by a pay phone and watched Sputnik. Yes, it was kitsch, but its dynamic and seemingly contradictory revolutions made me feel not so much myself. I liked how it only appeared that things were being pulled in opposite directions: a dog-and-tail routine, so busy but accomplishing nothing.

A bearded, barrel-chested man exited the convenience store, a cigarette dangling between his lips. He began struggling to unfold a road map without ashing on it. Any hopes I had for continuing to enjoy Sputnik's revolutions shriveled and died as he began hawking phlegm. "Here we go," he grunted, jabbing the road map. "East Parkway runs north-south? That's some shit." Having found his way wherever he was headed, the man began the origami required to return his guide to its rectangular bellows.

It wasn't until I set the case of beer on the counter and readied my ID that I realized I'd forgotten to bring hand sanitizer or a sandwich bag. My chest tightened and my mind raced. When I was given my change, I pocketed it with my left hand and started back home, carrying the beer with my right.

Told myself, "You'll be alright," told myself, "hold out until you're home," told myself, "home, home," and this worked well enough.

When I passed Overton Park, the westbound streetlights were still dark, and the dog walker was nowhere to be seen. Odds were, he was sitting on his couch, the TV droning, one dog at his feet, the other resting its skull in his lap, all three drowsing.

Once I started up the rear staircase, my chest tightened so quickly it burned. I held the case between my knees, got a can, popped it open, chugging it by the time I reached the kitchen door.

Like a child who just couldn't hold it any longer, I stumbled from the kitchen to my bedroom. I used my inhaler to pump myself into a sigh. Next, I drenched my left hand, the change, and the lining of my left front pocket in hand sanitizer. As much comfort as my rituals gave me, they could also crash me until I'd complied with the stepwise directives issued by a reflexive and super-cooled-swift quarter of my mind.

Even worse, I always hated it when I forgot my own fuckin' rules. I could understand it happening when I was drunk, but when I was sober (mostly, anyway) I questioned how much I was holding on to, and whether or not these lapses were nothing more than my subconscious ridiculing my exaggerated fears and hypocritical actions. Curt had once phrased it this way: "You'll rim me, but you won't hold my hand or touch a doorknob? What the fuck is wrong with you?"

A few minutes and another beer later, I checked the answering machine. There was one message from my mother, which she left about six hours ago: "Hello, Bry. I wanted to remind you about your flight Monday morning. It's at twelve-fifteen, so you should get to the airport at least—" I erased the rest.

By this time, my cell phone was done charging. This was the only phone number that mattered, the one that never changed, the one I had used to call Adam all those many times. After I flipped it open and powered it up, there were no voice mails. That was fine. The past few years, I'd been panning this river-town, sifting through people, discarding those who had less value than pyrite. Not that I had anything to show for it, certainly no gold nuggets.

If anyone really wanted to call me, they could. Most never did, but every so often one would, and it was never a call I was glad to answer. Meanwhile, the people I wanted to hear from had written me out of their lives because I wasn't worth it. Later, I would wonder if that was why I had declined Stefano's invitation.

I flipped on the TV in the living room and channel surfed. There were so many options, but any time I found a show or movie I might have wanted to watch, it was either on a channel that wasn't part of our cable package or was almost over. So I kept switching from station to station. On this one, there was a guy who looked like Adam, on another there was Curt, on the next was someone who resembled Stefano, and in the background of every show I saw Duke lurking like a clueless extra. I should have turned the TV off and done something else, but I kept on switching channels.

# CHAPTER EIGHTEEN

After thirty minutes, I settled on a documentary about books bound in human skin. There was a thriving illegal market for "contemporary anthropodermic bibliopegy." I raced to my bedroom, repeating the phrase until I found my journal and wrote it down. The covers of a few recently bound books showed evidence of human bite marks. After DNA testing was performed, the FBI found matches and solved three cold cases. The oldest of these cases only dated to the late 1980s.

The content of these books included: a collection of recipes, none of which called for human flesh, which was good because the Bolognese dish sounded tasty; one of St. Paul's letters and a hodgepodge of Old Testament passages; and the last text mixed two of the final cantos of Dante's *Inferno* with a previously unpublished tale of a cannibalistic coroner from 19th century Providence, Rhode Island.

As I finished a lukewarm beer, I wondered what book someone might use my skin to bind. What text would be hidden between my hide? I couldn't decide what book would be best suited for my flesh, but I was sure Curt would have several options at the ready.

Five beers in since those first two after I got back from the store, I decided to call him. I got his answering machine: "This is Curt. I'll get back to you." After the beep, I said, "Hey, it's Bryan. It's late, I know, and I shouldn't be calling you now or at all. You're right to think so little of me after... everything I did, but I'd like to talk. I want..." I fell silent for a few moments. "I need you to know how I—"

The machine cut me off, which was for the best. I'd apologized to Curt the morning after I'd cheated on him and many more times before he moved out. I knew he didn't want to hear me grovel yet again, but God I wanted to hear the deep inhale and exhale preceding his calm and thorough vivisection of my failures, to hear him sigh as he butterflied my rib cage and took a long, withering look at my heart.

Hopefully, Curt would erase the message and never ask me what the fuck I'd wanted to tell him. Whenever he had choked me, of course I couldn't talk, but I also didn't think a damn thing. That silence was so rare. By the end, maybe Curt had loved the silence just as much.

An hour later, my cell phone rang. It was Duke. I took a chug, then said, "Hello?" There was silence except for a long inhale. "Bryan?" he finally asked.

"That's me." I stood, rolling my eyes. "Who is this?" I played dumb.

"It's Duke. Sorry for calling so late, but I found your number while cleaning out my place, and I took that for a sign."

"A sign?"

"Yeah. How're you doing?"

"Alright," I said. "And you?"

"I've been better, I s'pose." Duke let out a tiny laugh, which meant who knew what.

I flicked the beer can's pop-top back and forth with my thumb, thinking about those pink razors and that ceramic rabbit. I finished my beer and didn't catch what Duke was saying. "What's that?" I asked.

Duke said, "I was talking about the night we hooked up."

"What about it?"

"I wasn't in a good place back then," he said. "Made bad choices more often than I wanna admit."

*Back then* was barely a month prior. "Where are you going with this, Duke?"

"I'm not saying it's you that infected me, could be a few guys, but I thought I should give you a heads-up."

*"What?"*

Rationally and medically, if he were positive when we fucked, my risk for getting infected was on the low end, but that didn't keep the apartment's floor from plummeting, like my mind remained at the peak of a rollercoaster as my body fell away.

"You there?" Duke asked.

"When did you find out? Did you know this the night we fucked?"

"I swear I didn't, Bryan." I heard the chimes of several instant messages in the background.

I thought for a moment before saying, "It's fuckin' late."

"I'm sorry—"

"Forget what I said," I interrupted him. "What I meant was, how far down the list am I?"

Duke's huff sounded like a frown. I walked to the bay window, flicking the pop-top. All too often I had lived in concurrent windows, those overlapping frames fogging up and obscuring everything else. If I never let those panes clear, what did that say about me? Regardless, whatever this phone call was about, I thought it should be difficult. So I chugged the rest of my beer and waited for him to speak. There was nothing from his end of the line.

I thought, *Smile*, and actually tried to. I'd heard how people can somehow hear your smile over the phone, which had always sounded like nothing more than propaganda for those unlucky enough to work in a call center. Early on, I had learned my family expected me to smile, like I later realized that when they asked me how I was doing, all they really wanted to hear was a "Fine, and you?"

Listening to the silence stretching out on this call, I couldn't actually make myself smile. Duke and me were both as maculate as the urinal trough at a football stadium. *A shame I'm not into that*, I thought, making myself smirk and shudder. "Unless there's something you need to say..." I crushed the can for punctuation and switched off the TV.

"Guess not," Duke replied. "Fuck it—"

I pocketed my cell phone, gathered up the empties, and carried the armful to the trash can. It was nearing last call at Fugue. Even if it weren't, I didn't have a ride. The Paris Adult Bookstore was less than a mile-and-a-half from my apartment, but I would never walk down that stretch of road this late at night, and even as drunk as I was, I would never set foot in there again.

Back at the bay windows, I stared at Overton Park for a few minutes, noticing how little traffic was passing by on Poplar Avenue. *Best to stick close to home.* I'd probably see nothing, the cold cutting down on the cruising, but you never knew. There could always be someone more desperate than me.

# CHAPTER NINETEEN

I didn't have a route planned, but I wanted to feel the air turn sharp in my throat and chest, for my nipples to shrink painfully, for my legs to burn. I hadn't left my apartment yet, but my heart raced with the same urgency that had compelled me to the adult bookstore until the night my car was totaled. I ignored that gravitational pull and took my time, dressing for the weather and the hour. Then I slowly drank a small glass of tepid water.

I stashed a small bottle of hand sanitizer, a travel size bottle of mouthwash, and a brand-new sandwich bag in my jeans pockets. If I had to remove my gloves wherever I wound up, I would want to wash away as much as I could without a sink and soap. Last, I pocketed two beers in my zip-up hoodie.

After I exited the front stairwell, I wanted to start running. I patted the chilled roadies and reminded myself I was too drunk to try. At best, I would have twisted my ankle and ruined those beers. But walking while drunk or high had never been a problem.

My fifth summer in town, I went to Memphis in May while

tripping on two tabs. After a thunderstorm drenched the venue and turned the park into a mud pit, I got separated from my ride. I'd tried running in mud-caked shoes for a few blocks. It did not go well. When I rounded a corner, my feet slid out from under me. A tourist took a photo of me laid out on the sidewalk with a disposable camera. After I had picked myself up, I walked all the way back from the riverfront to my apartment in Midtown. Granted, it'd taken me six hours, but the acid allowed me to witness an entirely different Memphis. Everything was foreground and background at the same time, breathing whenever I did. The roaring in my ears was louder than the planes undulating like humpback whales on their way to the airport.

Tonight, the planes overhead were as loud as usual, one momentarily blocking the full moon. Once that plane had passed, the moon's glow compensated for the busted streetlights on the other side of Poplar. The road was empty. At the corner of Cooper, I accidentally stepped in a small pile of dog shit. I rubbed my sole in the brown grass and kept thinking about the dog walker, recognizing that this was no different from another midnight destination which had, for a few years, often kept me from sleeping.

In my teens, based on my father's small collection of porn and those I swapped with friends, I'd learned how to get what I wanted. I would narrow my search by selecting the nostalgic, salivating hue of 8-mm film and tan lines. Note: copyright dates can be unreliable. Often the date listed on the box was when the tape was released, not when the footage was shot. The mid-1970s was the best window. A time before anyone had any inkling of how pervasively the population had been converted.

Weaned on my father's collection of straight porn from its polyester heyday, I could only come watching skin slide against skin, knowing in all likelihood I was jerking off to ghosts. Preserved on video, there remained then-carefree bodies long since whittled to marrow. Men whose ranks I'd surely have been counted among had I been born a decade earlier and whom I might be destined to join despite myself, because of myself.

Before I had lost interest in porn, I liked to imagine myself as one of the guys on-screen, sampling men at a bathhouse. I'd replace propriety with a towel, my street clothes folded neatly and secured in a rented locker. There, all distinctions would be forsaken for friction's varied splendor, or at least that's how I'd romanticized it.

Picture the tangled bough of a tree: some twigs would bend effortlessly, while the girth of other branches would demand the same of me. And when the branch I was straddling grew tiresome, all I had to do was find another.

Before meeting Curt, I had often suffered from insomnia. I would wake up between two and three a.m., painfully erect and my body shivering. Once this feeling had kidnapped my will, I could never fall back to sleep. So, I'd dress quietly and drive from my apartment to an adult bookstore named after the City of Lights, a name whose irony repulsed me. I'd purchase the required number of tokens, pocketing these quarter-sized coins as I pushed through the turnstile at the back and made my way through the darkened maze of broom-closet-sized booths.

After selecting an empty booth, I'd use my gloved left hand to open and lock the door and deposit tokens and channel surf. With my right hand, I'd unzip my pants and masturbate, ignoring the stale, ever-present smells of bleach and piss and incense.

Some booths had glory holes, but I avoided these because most men got irritated if all I wanted to do was watch or be watched. Some men liked to watch me, though, and I liked seeing their dilated eyes through the tiny peepholes drilled into the walls of every booth. Liked how some men would extend their hands through the slender space between the booth partition and the floor, palms jingling with tokens, bidding me to last a little while longer. Liked how some men, when I said I was close, would extend an empty hand through the space and whimper, "C'mon," while opening and closing their palms. What I didn't like was how some men would knock on the door or slip the toe of a shoe beneath the partition. No matter how shiny the shoes were, I never answered the door until the last night I lost myself in the labyrinth.

On my way to find a booth that night, I locked eyes with a man around my age, both of us appraising. He was five-eight or so, with short-clipped dishwater blond hair and a thick beard. His cargo shorts hung to his knees hiding his quads, but his calves were bulging and hairy. My whole body chattered as I catalogued his sneakers. I was completely sober, but that wasn't going to stop me.

As much as this place was disgusting, it made me feel the best kind of frantic, buzzed but sharp, swept along by the inescapable surrender to one of the deepest urges. The first booth I walked into smell liked puke, so I found a different one. I locked this new booth's door, deposited eight tokens into the video console, and started switching between channels. A few minutes later, someone knocked on the door three quick times. I looked down and recognized his shoes.

With my hands shaking, I unlocked the door. The man rushed in and sat on the swivel chair, saying, "Show me, show me," and I did, and he swallowed me whole. I didn't lower the monitor's volume, but the blaring moans weren't louder than the wet sounds the man made, and too quickly, before I could warn him, I came. I stood and stuffed myself back into my jeans.

"Wait," he spat and unzipped his shorts, "let me—"

Out of the booth, the maze, the bookstore, back home, home, home. All I wanted was a scalding shower. I was anxious but didn't speed. At that hour, the MPD suspected everybody. After I turned left on East Parkway, I started to calm down.

Less than a mile from home, however, a drunk driver ran up on the eastbound curb of Poplar, then swerved across four lanes and slammed into the space between my front left tire and driver's-side door. My seatbelt cut into my right armpit, and when the other driver tried reversing, my neck felt worse than it already did.

Unluckily for him, our cars were stuck together. Unluckier for me, a crack was branching diagonally across my windshield and my driver's-side door was bent in its frame. The drunk driver kept trying to free his car. I didn't want to be sitting there when the glass shattered, so I pulled up the parking brake, switched on the hazard lights, unbuckled my seatbelt, and climbed into the passenger seat. Between the initial impact and the drunk fuck's repeated attempts to uncouple our cars, my head was pounding. I sat there for a few more moments to steady myself, then I opened the passenger-side door.

This was before I had a cell phone, but as I got out of my car, a police cruiser rolling through Overton Park flipped on its blue lights and siren. I put my hands on my head and waited. After the cop boxed in the drunk driver, he quit trying to flee the scene.

Over the speaker, the cop announced, "Shut off the car's engine and drop the keys out the window." I heard another set of sirens behind me. "Westbound driver!"

I turned back around to face the first cop. "Yes?"

"Stay where you are."

The cop exited his vehicle, his gun drawn. "Driver in the eastbound vehicle! Shut off the engine! Drop your keys out the window! Now!"

The drunk driver started complying with the instructions when a second cruiser pulled up behind my car. I held the back of my neck with both hands. A second cop walked past me and helped the first one yank the other driver out of his car.

"Damn, boy," the new arrival said, "you smell like a fuckin' distillery." The drunk driver struggled, so they pulled his arms up behind him, slammed his chest against the trunk of his car, and handcuffed him.

The first cop took the drunk driver to his cruiser and had him blow into a breathalyzer. The second cop returned to me. "What's your name?" he asked, standing way too close, his right hand near his holster. I told him. "Have you been drinking tonight, sir?" I shook my head. "Always good to hear that. Now, say the alphabet backwards."

"Are you kidding me?"

"Do I look like a comedian?"

"No, sir." I took a breath and began. Any other time, I would have raced through it, but I went slowly because my neck was killing me and I didn't want to screw up. By that time, two more cruisers had arrived to direct traffic. The cop who'd been questioning me must have noticed me rubbing my neck.

"Are you hurt?"

"Think I got whiplash."

"Give me your license." He pocketed that and patted me down before saying, "Have a seat in my car. I'll be back in a few minutes to get your statement." He peered at my driver's license in his cruiser's headlights while speaking into his shoulder CB.

Fifteen minutes later, he returned holding a breathalyzer.

"Exit the car," he said. "I don't smell any alcohol on you, sir, but we're going to check you on this to make sure." I had to blow for ten seconds. "You're good." He handed my license back. "Now, tell me what happened." After I did, he said, "What were you doing out so late? Just getting off work at the hub?"

"No, I don't work at FedEx," I told him. "I woke up and couldn't fall back to sleep. Thought if I drove around for a while, that'd help."

"Where were you coming from before here?"

"East Parkway."

"And before there?"

"Summer Avenue."

"Around Rhodes College?" My face must have done something, because he chuckled, "So it was the less scenic side at *three in the morning?*" He popped his neck. "I'm going to be a minute finishing up your paperwork, so you can chill on the sidewalk."

I walked across the eastbound lanes and sat on a short ledge that ran in front of an apartment building. After the wrecker towed away my car, the second cop drove me back to my apartment, dropping me off with his card, instructions for how to get a copy of the accident report, and what would turn out to be a correct prediction: "Bet your car gets totaled."

Then I took a scalding shower and reminded myself: the freedom of my bathhouse fantasies and bookstore realities was more akin to the plummeting atmospheric pressure preceding a storm front. From that night forward, I never watched porn anywhere but home.

\* \* \*

My teeth began to chatter, my chest tightened in a good way, and my upper thighs shook. After I jaywalked across Poplar, I dropped into a culvert that led to the forest.

When the shadows were deep enough, I scrambled out and chugged the first of my roadies. The forest was oddly bright as I padded along. I crumpled the can and tossed it aside. Light pollution was hemorrhaging from everywhere, reminding me of a "forest at night" scene from a '70s made-for-TV film. Once, while seeing a band at Hi-Tone on Poplar, I'd overheard a guy who had a clean-shaven face but a neck-beard, like some low-rent Thoreau, joke that Overton Park should be renamed "Sodom's Trails." Couldn't fault him there. Was it homophobic if it was spot-on? But on that night and at that hour, the park was as purified as the pillar of doubt which had once been Lot's wife.

The emptiness was a license to proceed, but what did I want? Honestly, it wasn't physical contact. To watch, to only be as decadent as my mind would allow me: a part of, yet distanced and safe. I frowned. It sucks being a living contradiction. *Smile. Embrace the joke I am. Isn't that sliver of overlap in the Venn diagram me?*

I opened my second roadie and took a gulp. The sky was a putty nothing. Wind knocked branches against one another, making hollow and clumpity thuds. With two more gulps, while wondering how Foley artists would replicate those sounds, I finished that second beer.

I lengthened my stride: arms and footfalls slipping into a readymade pace, breath steady and low. I closed my eyes and began to run. After a few seconds, I could feel myself drifting too far to the right.

I opened my eyes, steadied myself, and sped up. My sweatshirt's hood was flopping. My jeans tightened with each step. The only time I was certain my asthma wouldn't bother me was when I was running. As I glanced between the dark forest on either side, my mind veered dizzy.

My breathing was getting louder, but I kept my ears alert. After a quarter-mile, I slowed to a walk, then stopped completely. With my hands on my head, I caught my breath. I heard nothing but the traffic along Poplar and the planes flying above. I raised my hood back up, pulled the drawstrings tight, then crouched and checked my shoelaces. When I stood, my head swam for several moments. A dog started barking, but I couldn't tell how close it was.

I exited the park as quickly as I could, following the route I took into it. Once I crossed back over Poplar, I could have headed east and been back in my building in a few minutes, but I turned west and walked down to Tucker. There, I took a left, figuring I'd make a long loop around the square and head back home.

Halfway down Tucker, I started jogging again. The cold was really sobering me up, my sight felt sharp, and any wooziness from earlier was gone. Now that my lungs were used to the chill, my breathing was quiet and steady, and I thought I'd keep running until I was completely sober, and—

I was no longer a mid-twenty-something existing in Memphis. I was a twelve-year-old languishing in a middle school cafeteria in St. Louis, a vast room that was always too loud and filled with too many eyes and too many mouths declaring challenges disguised as questions.

Before I knew it, I snapped, "I can't. I've got asthma!"

"How do you know you can't till you fuckin' try?"

"'Cause my Mom, she—" I was interrupted by Drew's laughter.

"Aww, I guess Bry-Bry does everything his mommywommy says." Everybody at the table joined in. I stared at their trendy Lunchables.

"Betcha five dollars you're too big a chicken-shit to show up at the starting line." Drew continued, "I'll throw in another five if you can actually finish the race."

"If we're betting," I tried to save face, "what's in it for you?"

"How about the entire *Inferno* series, including all the crossovers."

"Ten bucks ain't enough for that many comics."

"Then how much?"

"It's split between—what?—twelve different books, so..." I glanced at the ceiling, under-bid, "at least another twenty."

"Another ten," he countered.

"Sure." I smiled despite not remembering how long a five-K was and only owning a pair of hand-me-down sneakers.

The race took place in late April. The sky was overcast, the clouds a low and solid ash, but it was warm so there were many shirtless men. I was exhilarated. Drew was stuck far behind me in the middle of the pack, so I got his attention by yelling and waving my arms. Drew pointed me out to his friends and they started laughing.

I turned around, drumming the sides of my legs with my fists. Since puberty had crashed into me, I'd grown half-a-foot taller. Maybe that was why I had crept as close to the starting line as I could. There was a man in front of me—a tall, shirtless redhead. His freckled body resembled one of the leaner super-heroes in my comics, except his looked lived in, used in a good way. When the pack could sense that the start was near, some-body shoved me, bumping me into him.

He turned, frowning at first, then his face relaxed. He hadn't shaved for a couple days, so the start of his beard mingled with his chest hair, all of it the same dirty orange. At that moment, I wanted to be as handsome as him when I grew up.

"Aren't you eager, little man?" he laughed.

"Yeah," I said, trying not to stare and hating how much I wanted to.

He noticed my sneakers, "Is this your first race?"

"No," I lied, trying to act normal.

He laughed, leaning in close. He smelled warm: a little sweat, and beneath that, a trace of whatever cologne he'd worn the day before. "When the gun's fired, keep your feet moving, and you'll do fine."

"Runners!" shouted someone through a megaphone. "Take your mark!"

"See you at the finish line," the redhead said before facing forward and setting his stance.

When the shot was fired, I pushed and elbowed exactly like those around me were doing, taking short steps until the knot of knees and ankles loosened, then I ran as quickly as I could. I lengthened my stride, ignoring the licks of cold flame weaving between my ribs. While I lost sight of the redhead long before the first mile marker, I kept my pace, finishing first for the twelve-to-fourteen-year-olds.

Although Drew wouldn't pay up, I wasn't mad. Along with my low-numbered Popsicle stick, I'd won a $50 gift certificate to a local running store. As for the chintzy "gold" trophy, I tossed that in a restroom trashcan. From then until the day I left for college, my parents viewed my asthma attacks the same way they viewed me having to go to the bathroom whenever my half-brother Logan and I were told to do our chores.

Every day after school, I'd lace up the shoes I bought with the gift certificate and race down the trails in the woods behind our house, dodging weeds and branches, running until a four-chambered grenade exploded in my chest. Then I'd collapse on the trail—a calm, oblivious god of dust angels—and stare at the rustling canopy. I got good at avoiding poison ivy, but I made mistakes occasionally when I got distracted. In high school, I joined the cross-country team, thinking I could train myself to run forever—

But I wasn't running. I wasn't even standing. The wind froze my sore wet face and the sidewalk chilled my scraped left palm and right knee. I looked around but saw nobody. Since my left hand was already touching the ground, I used it to steady myself as I stood. My hoodie was half-on-half-off, my right arm out of its sleeve. The rest of my body was numb. The collar of my shirt had been stretched out, and two fingers poked through the sandwich bag like a hobo's glove.

My left eye was swelling and my jaw felt sore. I tasted iron right before several heavy drops of blood fell from my nose. I'd been punched in the face before, so that was familiar. I patted my pockets, felt my wallet and cell phone, so I didn't think somebody had tried to mug me.

My stomach churned. I hunched over, clutched my knees, quit breathing, tried not thinking, and waited for it. A warm sensation floated up my throat. I imagined my lower jaw unhinging and a nice fat balloon slowly rolling out, remembering some nature documentary of an egg snake earning its living but running the film in reverse.

My eyes teared up, but no drops fell and the urge to puke sank, leaving behind nothing but a sour burn in my throat.

I looked around. *Where was I?* This was Midtown, but it wasn't my neighborhood and it wasn't that close to the park.

I pulled my sweatshirt back on, zipped up the front, and raised the hood. If my face looked anywhere as bad as it felt, I didn't want anybody seeing it. I pinched my nostrils and hawked out bloody phlegm. The scenery was familiar, but it took me a few minutes to realize that. I was way down Evergreen, not far from Overton Park Avenue. I headed back toward Poplar, past Café d'Esyal and CK's Diner, where the brightness of Sputnik was too much for my one good eye.

Every step was painful. My left palm throbbed even after I clenched it and stuffed it in a pocket. My aching jaw made me shut my eyes for a few moments every time I spat. I checked my phone. No missed calls. No voice mails. I arched my eyebrows, trying to lessen my headache. That did not work.

When I thought, *If Curt could see me now*, I couldn't help but smile, and somehow *that* made the rest of my walk home bearable.

# CHAPTER TWENTY

I attributed my wobbly ascent up the rear stairwell to my injuries, but after my key missed the lock five times, I grabbed the knob with one hand and guided the key in with the other. When I shut the door behind me, my mind reeled. I held onto the counter until that passed.

Every step I took sounded like a stomp no matter how carefully I walked. Chris's bedroom door was shut, but the stereo's volume was dialed low enough that my mind could translate the hushed moans and the tapping of his headboard into a vague jealousy.

When I pulled back my hood, the bathroom lights were glaring. My swollen left eye was already mixing yellow and purple. It would be black soon. When I peeled back the lids, they slid like sandpaper. The sclera from the cornea to the outer edge was more red than white. My bloodied nose was also swollen, possibly broken. Though my jaw ached, it looked normal for now, and I still had all of my teeth.

As I stared into the mirror, a translucent image of Adam's face floated over mine. Every blink sharpened the focus. I ran the faucet full-blast and washed my face for several minutes, enjoying the steam while spitting blood and phlegm. I couldn't help but think about the night Stefano stood on his tiptoes and how his freak-out had been both endearing and irritating, a different kind of mirror, one that was all too familiar.

The suds swirled pink. My left eye stung. My nose continued to drip, so I stuffed it with toilet paper from a new roll under the sink, because I never grabbed from the current roll unless I was wiping my ass. The face I saw in the reflection seemed fitting, expected. If I could see how well it suited me, then everyone else would too.

My heart was racing like I'd just finished a marathon, and I couldn't get it to slow down no matter how I breathed. My eyes darted around the bathroom, like the answer to what had happened to me was hiding between Chris's various skincare and hair products. I gripped the porcelain sink and stared at the drain.

When I had moved in, the stopper was already gone, and we never bothered buying a new one. The sink was a bright white, but I'd never peered down the drain. It shouldn't have been surprising that what helped keep us clean was filthy, but in that moment, I was disgusted. Each breath I took squeezed me tighter.

Back in the hallway, the noise from Chris's room was getting louder. I didn't bother being quiet closing my bedroom door or rummaging through my desk, where I found a bag of moldable earplugs I hadn't used in months. The last few times I did, I'd heard things: either klaxons, or snippets of eaves-dropped conversations at a crowded cocktail party. I had awakened tired, certain I had missed something, an absence that nothing during the following day would answer.

I put in a pair of earplugs, but all I heard were my pulse and breathing. I'd never paid too much attention to either except immediately after finishing a run. Both sounded awkward, and that awkwardness was compounded by the embarrassment I felt whenever I was completely alone.

*Quit thinking already.* I crawled into bed and cocooned myself in the comforter. My left eye throbbed in time with my pulse. The streetlights, the few passing headlights, and the Venetian blinds sketched faces across the ceiling.

Outside, an ambulance raced down Poplar. Fumbling head-long, the lullaby teased me to sleep. I slipped my left hand around my cock and held it there.

*Smile,* I wished myself to sleep. *Smile.*

# CHAPTER TWENTY-ONE

My alarm clock was buzzing. For what seemed like hours, I had dreamed it was the roaring of an animal, then the screaming of sirens, then a naked man yelling at me.

While I couldn't remember exactly who he was or what the argument was about, it felt so slow-motion and tense and real that, in the middle of the dream and to the frustration of this man, I'd searched the room for the light switch, which was almost hidden behind a bookcase. When I finally found it, I flipped it down and up, and the light went off and on accordingly. The man told me to concentrate, to pay attention. I told him, "I am."

Most of the time, the dreams that I could remember felt so deep, like I was walking on the bottom of a pool, the effort and will required to hold myself down there considerable. But as soon as I woke, coherency rippled, erasing itself.

When I sat up and shut off the alarm clock, the sheets fell from my naked body, which surprised me because I didn't remember deciding to sleep nude. My eye and jaw were throbbing, so I put my feet on the floor, hoping the chill would distract me from the pain. My left palm was still scraped, but it was no longer burning and it didn't ache as bad as my skull.

The TV in the living room was blaring, and two people were talking as they padded past my door. One was Chris, the other I didn't recognize. At a quarter-to-nine, Chris's overnighter must have been accomplished, lingering well past first light. I pulled the tissue out of my nostrils; the tips of both plugs were a dark, crusted red.

My shift started in ninety minutes. Well, the first of a double, and Stefano would be working too. I put on some underwear, a sweatshirt, and then found my Umbros near the foot of the bed and pulled them on.

Outside my bedroom, the aromas of bacon, toast, and coffee grew stronger as different sounds clarified. Plates clinked as they were taken from the cabinet and set on the table. The silverware drawer screeched when it was opened and utensils jostled. Beneath it all was a slight laughter, the kind attached to a nascent inside joke.

Nudging the bathroom door open with a foot, I reached in with my right arm, feeling for the medicine cabinet. I turned its mirrored door all the way to the wall so I wouldn't see myself on the way to the toilet.

The quantity, color, and pungency of my piss brought back the morning-after with Duke. All around me, the bathroom was heavy with condensation, droplets tracing bars down the walls. The long shower Chris and his guest had taken meant that I needn't have bothered with the mirror.

I flushed the toilet and washed my hands. With each lathering, my heart began to race and I got angrier. Had they opened doors or dialed up the hot water using hands still smeared with spit and lube and come? Which light switches had Chris or his trick flipped? I wanted this guy to leave not because he'd fucked Chris, but because this was my home, of a sort, and this new presence introduced any untold number of variables. And while they had both cleaned up this morning, none of us were closed systems devoid of contaminants.

A list unrolled in my mind, the minimal steps demanding immediate action. #1: WALK TO THE KITCHEN, MAKING AS LITTLE EYE CONTACT AS POSSIBLE. Chris and his trick watched me; I gave them a little wave. #2: FOLD SEVERAL PAPER TOWELS, MAKING A THICK SQUARE. REPEAT TWICE. With one of those in hand and the other stashed in a pocket, I completed #3: GRAB THE SPRAY BOTTLE OF BLEACH-BASED COUNTER CLEANER AND SATURATE A SQUARE. ENJOY THE SMELL, and #4: WIPE OFF CABINET EDGES, DRAWER-PULLS, AND REFRIGERATOR DOOR HANDLE, which I did as quickly as I could.

Chris's guest watched me, but my roommate kept eating and chitchatting between bites because this was our normal. I tossed the first thick square in the trash, and next up was #5: RETURN TO THE BATHROOM, CLOSE THE DOOR, AND SIGH-SIGH-SIGH IN PRIVATE. Once there, I went through #6: SATURATE THE NEW SQUARE AND WIPE OFF THE BATHROOM DOORKNOBS, LIGHT SWITCH, AND SINK AND SHOWER HANDLES.

After I was finished with all that, I stayed in the bathroom for a few minutes, breathing deeply. In the mirror, my left eye was black now. My nostrils were caked with blood, but my nose wasn't broken. After blowing my nose, I washed my hands while staring at myself in the mirror and prepping for the last three steps:

#7: RETURN TO THE KITCHEN, SAY, "HELLO," OR "GOOD MORNING," OR WHAT-THE-FUCK-EVER.

#8: MAKE YOURSELF BREAKFAST—IT'S IMPORTANT, AFTER ALL, BECAUSE WHO KNOWS HOW MANY RITUALS TODAY WILL DEMAND.

#9: ENGAGE IN SMALL TALK AND TRY NOT TO APPEAR COMPLETELY ODD. GOOD LUCK WITH THAT.

With my mind quieted, I sat the bottle of cleanser on the countertop and poured a cup of coffee. Chris and his trick were sitting at the two-top wearing nothing but boxers, which meant two more things to clean once they were done. Their clear glass bowls and ceramic plates were empty, and they were drinking coffee and chain-smoking.

When Chris's guest pointed at me, I thought I knew what was coming, but he asked, "How did that happen?"

"What did you forget?" I asked Chris while making myself a bowl of cereal.

"He's old-fashioned." Chris grinned at his guest, then said, "Dallas, this is my roommate Bryan. Bry, this is Dallas."

Right, the cheerleader. To him I said, "Which 'that'? I've been quite blessed lately."

"Jesus," Chris said, "Caught sight of yourself in a mirror today?"

"Hours and hours ago, when I got home." I could see my distorted reflection in the chrome toaster. I poured milk over my cereal, lying, "I imagine it's looking better."

"How's it y'all are so synched?" Chris took a long drag.

Dallas asked, "So?"

To him: "I've run into every door that life has opened for me." And then to Chris: "What?"

"Seriously? No tumble down the stairs?" Chris chuckled. "Oh, but Soap-Opera, he had himself a sweeps-week brawl."

"Yeah," the cheerleader said. "But at least he held his own."

"I forgot to quit turning the other cheek." I spooned a heap of corn flakes into my mouth, crunching out. "I'm a masochist like that."

"Bry, please. Manners."

After swallowing the mouthful, I asked, "What happened with Stefano?"

"Benji's ex picked a fight."

I leaned on a stretch of countertop next to the sink, farthest from the small table that was too cluttered with dishes and an artificial, boxer-clad coziness. "Did Stefano get arrested?"

"It was over too quick. The other guy left with a bloody nose. It started when Soap-Opera was walking away and Benji's ex threw a cheap shot. Stefano stumbled into a couple who were sucking face like hagfish. Afterwards, you'd have thought those two queens were the aggrieved party, the connip-tion they threw. All that fuss over a couple of watered-down Cosmos. And judging by their Millington couture, I'm sure the chipped tooth was nothing new."

"Chris, focus. I'm pulling a double today."

"Right, right. So, Benji's ex rushed Soap-Opera."

"That was all kinds of awesome," Dallas said.

"Totally ninja, right?"

"*Chris.*"

"Whatever. Benji's ex rushed Stefano, fist raised. At the last second, Soap-Opera crouched, wrapped him around the waist, spun, and slung him into the cigarette machine. Dude was holding his side with one hand as he threw another punch. Soap-Opera ducked it, landed two southpaws, was rearing back for a third, *and* that's when the bouncer decided to do his job."

"Who's the ex?" I spooned in another mouthful.

Chris quit staring at his trick's spread legs and looked me in the eye. "Adam."

I coughed, half-choking on and half-spitting out the mouthful. The most sizable lump landed in the sink with a wet plop. "Sorry," I mumbled.

"You should have been there," Chris said. "Would have done you a world of good."

"Fuckin' Adam." I turned around and ran the faucet, rinsing the lump of corn flakes down the drain and began washing my dishes. Adam had become a ghost, everywhere out of the corner of my eye, but nowhere when I looked head-on.

"Wasn't sure it was him, because he goes by Dex these days," Chris said. "Stefano had to explain things afterward. Don't worry. Our boy Soap-Opera tooled that piece of shit for the two minutes the fight lasted."

Two minutes. Stefano hadn't lasted that long in my mouth before he'd bloodied my nose. If I had gone out with him and Chris last night, I could have seen him "tool" Adam. I would have probably found it hot until I remembered that Adam was haunting me from both the past and a possible future. If Adam had infected me, I might have exposed Stefano. If I was infected but hadn't exposed Stefano, he might still get infected if Adam had infected Benji. But would it matter who he got it from? Wouldn't he still blame me? If I were in his shoes, I knew I would.

"He's a professional dish washer," Chris said, snapping me out of it, "so he likes to be thorough."

When I shut off the faucet and turned around, my hands were red. Chris nodded and mouthed, "You okay?"

Dallas said, "Y'all got a nice place."

As Chris went through his spiel, I pocketed my hands in my hoodie and mouthed, "Yes."

Chris and Dallas (and Stefano for that matter) were all about the same height. Stocky but muscular, the cheerleader's build reminded me of Stefano's, only a hairier and rougher beige instead of smoother olive. I was glad I'd decided not to go commando. While Chris's light brown skin was shiny with lotion, his guest looked like he was still sweating from the shower. Whether Chris knew it or not, his extended trick was mocking Stefano's decision to call things off.

There were a few more questions, mostly about my bruises. "I'd rather not talk about it," I lied, not wanting to admit that I knew little more than they could assume.

"Would you believe he's a cheerleader at MTSU?" Chris changed the subject. "I didn't buy it," he took a drag of his cigarette, "but when we got here and you were getting a facial, he told me to turn around."

"Subtle."

"Right? But I did. He grabbed my hips and told me to jump on the count of three. Next thing I know, he's holding me up by my calves, and my hands are flat against the ceiling."

"Did he have any pompoms?"

Chris took a sip of coffee, then said, "Oh, he's got a pair."

When I asked about the life of a closeted male college cheerleader in Murfreesboro, Dallas started complaining about his coach making them run loops around a set of tennis courts at a recent practice and having to do a set of four back tucks between each loop.

"It pays off, obviously," I returned the spray bottle to its place beneath the sink, the cupboard door crying as I opened and shut it.

Dallas cleared his throat slightly and pointed at the cupboard. "How's all *that* work?"

Chris yawned. I could guess what most of his trick's questions about my OCD would be, annoying and familiar like so much spit gathering behind his lips.

"Since I've known you, Bry," Chris sipped his coffee, "this is what, your third black eye? And not all that long ago," he looked at his trick, "he got shot."

"Damn," the cheerleader said. "That's horrible, but I was talking about the cleaning stuff."

"Nice meeting you." I drained my mug and sat it in the sink. "But I've got to get ready for work. Trust me, Chris's version of that 'stuff' is bound to be more entertaining than mine."

# CHAPTER TWENTY-TWO

Before my shift started, I went to the employee restroom and squeezed four drops of Visine into each eye. Hopefully, the right one wouldn't be as bloodshot soon. As for the left, *rough* was an understatement, but the bruise was a distraction from my hangover. With my hands washed, I went to my station where my head throbbed from the sounds and overlapping stenches of melted butter, syrup, and batter battling the frying sausage and eggs Benedict. I was queasy for over an hour.

The brunch that followed was busy, if unexceptional. When I helped bus tables as things were wrapping up, I noticed many eyes that were bleary from the previous night and others that were glassing over from the bottomless Mimosas and Bloody Marys. It was probably my hangover and the longing to lessen it with some hair of the dog that made me jealous of the socially acceptable alcoholism happening all around me. Lugging the full tub, I reminded myself it was better to let my hangover run its course than postpone it for a few hours by getting drunk all over again.

Upon my return to the kitchen, the manager stopped me. "Jesus!" he grabbed my chin and tilted my head. "What the fuck did you do?" I pulled back and adjusted my grip on the tub. "Until all that's less obvious," he drew a circle in the air with his index finger, "you're grounded during the dinner shift. Stay back here, so your lovely mug doesn't ruin the appetites of our guests."

After taking out the trash, I washed my hands, but whatever relief I normally felt was repeatedly punctured by the manager's voice.

He was talking at Stefano: "You'll work dinner?" If Stefano had any bruises from his fight with Adam last night, they were hidden beneath his button-down.

Hoping to hasten his rise from expediting and bussing to serving tables full-time, Stefano said, "Sure," but since all the side work was done, could he leave and come back?

"Of course," said the manager. "This isn't grade school."

I was done too and ready for a break. "Soap-Opera," I said, turning the faucet off with an elbow, "where are you headed?"

"Somewhere private for a while." Then he said, "Actually, I need to talk."

"I know the perfect place."

Soon, we were strolling along the Old Bridge's eastbound walkway. Downtown Memphis was upstream and the day was too bright, a false warmth tempered periodically by the strong gusts of wind high above the river.

After some small talk, he asked, "So, what the fuck happened to your face?"

"Somebody's malice."

"Looks like it was personal," Stefano chuckled.

"Feels like it, that's for sure."

"Please explain this to me: you won't go out with us, but you'll go out by yourself and get beat up?"

"I don't remember any of it happening."

"Start with what you do remember."

"After you guys left, I cooked some pasta and watched TV until the asshole across the hall ended his party, then I walked to the store and got some beer. After a few cans, I went for a jog around the neighborhood."

"How shit-faced were you?" he asked, kicking at a Styrofoam cup.

"I didn't think I was," I told him. "It hit all at once. When I came to, I wasn't too far from home. And apparently, Fugue isn't all that safe."

"Alls I can say is, I didn't seek mine out."

"And you said nothing to provoke your fight?"

"Oh, no, I totally told Adam to fuck off and leave Benji alone."

I said, "Alright." *Leave Benji alone.* Benji who was safe in public and lived two hours away in another state. Benji who had apparently dated Adam for who knows how long? Benji, on whom Stefano was doting so much attention. Benji, not me. Never me.

"I've seen Adam occasionally at Fugue," Stefano said. "Even before Chris told me what he did to you, I thought he was sketchy."

"Wish I had your radar," I said. *Even after Chris told you what he'd done, what did you do except keep pocketing whatever little tip he left you?* I looked south, wishing I could teleport myself beyond the horizon. *That was enough to make you bite your tongue? And when tips no longer mattered, you still said nothing about me?* I exhaled and tried to give Stefano the benefit of the doubt. No one ever talks about how much disbelief you have to suspend in daily life to keep yourself functioning. That almost made me chuckle.

"On one of my last nights at Fugue," Stefano continued, "Adam kept flirting with me. Because I was on the clock, I couldn't say what I really thought about him. Each time he ordered a beer, I imagined punching his face. If I didn't need the job, I would've."

I hated to admit it, but that felt good for a few moments. Until I thought about the limits of Stefano's chivalry, a half-full tip jar on a cheap pool bar. Last night, Benji was the pretext for the fight, but—benefit of the doubt, after all—maybe I had been some part of the subtext, and maybe Stefano carried a sliver of guilt from not doing anything for me when he was a bartender and Adam sat within arm's reach. Admitting that, however, could knock over the first of many dominoes, each tracing a path that circled down and around to the center of how much he actually cared for Benji. At best, Benji was serving the same function as Hugo had for me. I didn't know how long Stefano would keep using the Mutt to distract himself, but I knew standing up to Adam would fuel his infatuation for a while. After all, he loved people seeing him as a man and not a faggot.

The more I thought about it, the angrier I got with myself for declining Stefano's invitation. If I hadn't, I could have thrown a few punches. While it would have been amazing to watch Stefano beat the shit out of Adam, I also would have loved the opportunity to take every dirty shot I could. Let me punch one of Adam's kidneys so hard he would piss blood. Better yet, let me put one of the club's heavy glass ashtrays to its best use by slamming it against his temple.

But if I were there, things would have played out differently. Would my presence have made Stefano focus on Benji that much harder? And with Stefano being so preoccupied, would Adam even have had the chance to confront him? Last, if Adam had noticed me and not disappeared, would I have had the balls to actually start a fight without Stefano by my side?

"So last night," Stefano was saying, "when Adam got in my face and told me I didn't have what Benji needs, I smiled. I amped up Adam's accent and said, 'Right, *Dex*. I guess what Benji really needs is some brainless skuz what's got a gangrenous tallboy for a dick.'"

"Did Benji like you putting his business out there?"

"Funny you say that, because the next thing I said was, 'How's business these days?'"

"I don't want to know."

"Oh, I'm sure he's doing well. What I can't figure out is why he goes by 'Dex.' Benji says Adam's middle name is Kevin or something like that. Whatever you want to call him, he's got himself a website now."

I said, "That seems risky," but it gave me a good idea. "What's the name of his site?"

After telling me, Stefano said, "He doesn't show his face, and the graphics and pics suck, but he's got a cam-feed and does out-calls. Reasonable rates, I suppose." Stefano started knocking a fist against each girder.

A barge piled with three sloppy pyramids of sand was inching down the Mississippi. A gust from the south raked us with some of its grit. How many other names had Adam used with suckers like me? In straight Memphis, he was Adam; in gay Memphis, he was Dex. I wondered if he had different names in Bartlett and Germantown and Millington, and if he did, how easy was it for him to keep each identity separate?

A tourist-laden steamboat passed the barge, heading north. The muddy water was smooth one moment and swirling with an undertow the next.

"Can you imagine doing that?" Stefano asked.

"Doing what?"

"Paying for sex."

"You've never bought a porno?"

"Yeah, why not compare apples to fisting?" he said.

I stopped walking to catch my breath from laughing. "That's surely something somebody could say."

"Figured that'd get your attention."

We resumed walking. When I saw two people standing by the far shore of the river, the sounds of the wind and traffic and Stefano's voice and rhythmic knocking against the girders all faded. How easy would it be to disappear on either side of the bridge or to jump off the stanchion and vanish beneath the water that never ran clear, lost beneath the filth until my corpse washed ashore somewhere downriver?

But this trip wasn't about that bullshit. I looked at Stefano and asked, "What did you need to talk about?"

"Last night was weird. Chris and that cheerleader were raring to go. Felt like a third wheel all night. With them and with Benji. After my fight with Adam, Benji swore he was only waiting for his best friend to drive them back to Little Rock and he'd call me today."

"Let me guess: he stuck around."

"*And* he had it out with Adam. Woke me up a couple hours later, drunk and stutter-crying his ass off. It took forever to get the story out of him. I was so glad his best friend was doing the driving. When she got on the phone, I gave her directions. I was mad he'd lied to me, but it felt kind of nice that he came back." He paused, shaking his head.

Having the man he thought he was dating in his bedroom was significant to Stefano because he wasn't completely out yet to his older brother. Not officially, anyway. Giacomo learned about Stefano bartending at Fugue after two of his frat brothers had been "drug there" one night by their girlfriends. "As long as you pay your share of the rent, what do I care?" was his older brother's bored comment.

Stefano had come out to one of his straight best friends, to whom he'd often joked his inevitable disclosure to Giacomo was the reason he'd been hitting the gym religiously: a preparation for the worst possible reaction.

"Your major's drama, right?" his friend had asked.

"Pretty much."

He laughed, "Perfect."

Getting back to the end of Stefano's night, if I listened to more details than I liked, to watch his face relax, to hear his deep voice lighten somewhat, to imagine him talking about me like this, well, that was enough to make it tolerable. Better still, he was noticing red flags in himself and Benji. Which was to say, I knew Stefano was about to ask a question, but I didn't know if he actually wanted it answered.

"Benji's friend crashed on the couch and he slept in my bed. So that's fucked up, right?"

"Which part? Him staying behind after lying to you, or him sleeping in your bed, or you liking the latter?" He scrunched his lips and looked at the walkway. "Do you mind," I said, "if I ask what all you did?"

"Just oral, mostly him sucking me off." He tapped another girder. "I can't figure out if I did anything wrong." He was still staring at his shoes, his forehead furrowed.

Stefano had grown up Catholic like me. Who knew how much of this was recycled guilt from all of that? Then I remembered Stefano hated being called "girl." How much he was struggling against *that* to enjoy himself? His hang-ups probably ran deep. Aside from my bloody nose during our solitary hookup, he didn't seem to have my germ issues. In those days, though, I couldn't get myself past any of that unless I was fucked up. How some people could feel lust while sober and not detest themselves was light years beyond me, so distant no telescope would ever see it. I couldn't imagine how those same people could ask for what they truly wanted without shame or regret. In other words, I had no clue what I could say to help him.

By then, we'd crossed into Arkansas. When I turned around, starting back toward Tennessee, the wind was building. After I was sure Stefano was following me, I asked, "Where's all this coming from?"

"When I came out to my mom, she said some things."

"This should be good," I chuckled.

"First, she knew I was gay long before I did."

"Isn't it funny how they *always* knew but still got upset once we made it official?"

"Ain't that the truth? Next, she said, 'Oh, Stefano, why would you do that? It hurts.' I was speechless, until I told her, 'Thanks for assuming I'm a bottom, and I never needed to know that about you.'"

"Did she say anything else?"

"She told me, 'Son, I will never stop loving you, but please don't get it. That would just break my heart.'"

*As fucked up as that is,* I thought, *it still might have been nice to hear my mother say it.* All I could say was, "Wow."

"Yeah," Stefano sighed, "getting back to my question."

"What exactly do you think you did wrong?" I asked him.

"Maybe I took advantage of Benji. He was upset and drunk and..."

"When did the oral start?"

"When he woke up—I mean, when he woke me up."

"So he wanted whatever happened to happen, right?"

"I guess."

"And he got off too?"

Stefano stared north toward the glare of the reflective panels on the Memphis Pyramid. Finally, he said, "But when we walked to his car the morning after, it was like he felt ashamed, or..." Stefano paused, tapped a girder. "I don't know. He wouldn't look at me."

Without thinking, I said, "You need to buy yourself a map."

Stefano stopped to gaze at downtown Memphis. He was smarter than most people gave him credit for, but he didn't like improvisation. He liked knowing where he needed to stand, what he needed to be doing, what he needed to say, how he should react to what was said to him, and making those tiny lies as honest as possible—all of that was what he was good at. Subtract drink or confrontation or a clear role to play and Stefano could be reserved. "I'm not the one lost, I'm just..." he trailed off.

"Not that well-traveled?"

"Plus, I don't know all the tourist traps like you do," he laughed under his breath.

"I was joking."

He checked his watch, "Or something like that, right?"

"If there's one thing I know," I told him, "most of the time whatever people are saying about you is less about anything you said or did, and more about some loop they're trying to drag you into, to convince you it's yours."

With more than an hour before the dinner shift, traffic hit a lull. At the next service access hatch to a stanchion nearer the eastern shore, I knelt and got the plastic sandwich bag out of my pocket. "And now for the real reason we came here," I tried lightening the mood, "one of Memphis's little-known gems. The hatch was rusted stiff but unlocked. I opened it, let Stefano climb down, and followed.

Unlike all the times I'd been in the Gateway Arch—staring down at the stadium, or standing motionless at the dead center of that narrow gallery, with my eyes closed and feeling the monument's negligible sway in the wind—I never felt unsafe beneath this bridge. Falling from any of the Old Bridge's stanchions meant you had either leaped or you couldn't keep somebody from tossing you over the railing.

"Nice," Stefano said as a tire floated south.

I wasn't worried about us getting caught, so I zoned out watching the Mississippi whose currents rippled into one another and against the bridge's stanchions. Unlike trying to remember my dreams, when I concentrated on how these permutations strengthened or diminished in their collisions, somehow things became clearer, more definite. Randomness could be so beautiful, so maybe "chaos" was the beauty our limited imaginations wouldn't let us reconcile.

We sat and rested our forearms on the low-set handrails, and though neither of us talked we kicked at the air and each other's feet. The night before, I'd told Stefano, more or less, how I felt about him, probably sounding worse than desperate. After playing the bit part of the gay best friend who always had an ear to lend, I didn't have any doubts about where I then stood. Since it didn't seem like he had really been listening last night or today, I chose silence.

As much as I wanted to look at Stefano, the river was beautiful, perfect for a swan dive were it not from this height as hard as eddying sheets of concrete that would transform into undertows swifter than you could regain your consciousness or catch your breath, or for being downriver from too many sewage treatment plants.

A freight train was crossing the Harahan. The screech of wheels against braking clamps and rails sounded as though it were feeding upon itself: from high to low and back again, a series of sluggish ovals. Underscoring that bedlam was a rumbling counterpoint, a thousand cellos slowly bowing the ugliest, deepest note.

Whenever I remember the last decent conversation I had with Stefano, the clamor of the braking train punctuates his every word, until that is all I can hear.

# CHAPTER TWENTY-THREE

During the dinner shift, d'Esyal's manager was testier than usual. He shouldn't have been. The restaurant was busy but not swamped.

One large-party reservation arrived five guests shy. Another would saunter in two hours late with twice as many people in tow, but the reservation was for one of the owner's old friends, and the local news anchor tipped well. With Stefano waiting tables, there was more than enough coverage.

Pamela was delegating freely so we could go on another smoke break. "Soap-Opera," she said on her way out, "Twenty needs refreshing. After that, bus five, three, and nine. Thanks."

I pouted my lips in sympathy to the expression on his face, fishing in my pockets for a lighter and winking before pulling the door shut. Lighting up our respective joints behind the dumpster, Pamela tilted her head and narrowed her eyes. "Don't take this the wrong way, but you've been looking a little tired. Might wanna do a Candida cleanse. Could be you're too yeasty."

With as much as I'd been drinking lately, she'd hit too close to the mark. I exhaled, then said, "Add water, hops, and malt, and there's your bull's-eye. But I prefer my metaphors cosmological."

"Like what?"

"A black hole."

Pamela laughed. "You remember I grew up in San Francisco, right? Let's play free association. You say 'black hole,' I hear 'this little piggy.'"

"Yeah, that's me." I took a hit.

"I wouldn't be surprised," she stared at the lit end of her joint, "if some deep part of you is secretly into scat."

"Sometimes our chats are nice," I exhaled. "Other times, you make me want to never leave my sink."

"Please," she laughed, "explain your metaphor."

"There's this thing called an 'event horizon,' which is the point of no return. Once you cross it, your destination is inescapable. It's not so much a horizon as a sheer cliff."

"Gotcha."

"After you fall off the cliff, your body gets spaghettified."

"Now you're making shit up."

"No, that's what astrophysicists call it: 'spaghettification.' The different parts of your body, down to the atoms you'd been leasing, start stretching farther and farther apart."

"Okay. You're cut off," Pamela said. "You're too high for me." She cashed her roach. "Funny, I used to think of myself as a 'Lifer,' as long as I've been here, but from now on I'm going to tell people I've been 'spaghettified.'"

"And *I'm* too high?"

We laughed and returned inside—she to the front of the house, me to my sink.

As I slogged through the backlog, I kept thinking about the event horizon. For example, let's consider a tall and skinny man, like myself, who was shoved off that cliff. At that point, his fate would be sealed, but how would the event horizon appear to him before spaghettification? How deep would his regret be? How steep was that slip? Irrevocable as the math, I'd guess. Frozen forever, any light that hadn't been ensnared alongside him would illuminate his worst moments. His identity coalesced, an immortality achieved through the stasis of light itself.

Stefano walked back into the kitchen. There were no orders to expedite, but the manager yelled his name. "You have a call," he grumbled.

I sent a full rack through the dishwasher.

"Whoever it is kept rattling about it being an emergency, so I'm going to put it on speaker-phone. Keep it short."

"Hello?" Stefano asked.

Giacomo slurred, "Where'd you lose my bike lock?"

"That's the emergency?"

"It is to me!"

"Oh, dear," the manager shook his head, "this does sound quite grim."

Stefano pinched the bridge of his nose. "I think it's in my backpack—"

"Which's *where?*"

"Drop the tone and try my bedroom! Jesus, if it wasn't on the bike, or anywhere downstairs, or in your room, then where's that leave?"

"Said you could borrow my bike a couple days ago, and that was fine. We're brothers. I don't mind sharing. But it was nice out today, and I thought I'd go for a ride, and guess what?"

"You couldn't find—"

"I couldn't *find* the lock!"

"Jack, settle down."

"Shut up, *Stephen*, this ain't about me."

"Yo, newbie!" a chef shouted. "Six's up!"

214

"This's about you *acting* like you ain't got a goddamn brain."

"Yeah, coming!" Stefano answered the cook, then: "Don't call here unless it's—" The dial tone cut him off.

The manager hung up the phone. "Next time he calls, I won't bother taking a message. Tell him that, please, whenever he's sober-ish."

I was unloading the dishwasher when Stefano picked up table six's entrées—balancing two on his left arm, holding the third in his left hand, the fourth in his right—and started walking out to the floor. D'Esyal's towering and stout owner stopped him, pressing his broad palm against Stefano's chest.

"Young man," he exhaled in his thick accent, "forget all that —You!" He startled a server named Cindy. "Come." She scratched her left eye with her left middle finger before whispering something to Pamela and taking the plates. The owner explained: "I need you to help out Cindy for a moment. There are four men at table twelve who'd like a better look of you." His voice sounded as slow as a spilled bottle of olive oil. "They say they remember you from your bartending days by some pool." He wrapped an arm around Stefano's shoulders and walked him toward the floor. "Young man, it will be all right, no? They have ordered an overpriced bottle of some Pinot swill and have asked about you twice. Go get the wine, prance over to their table, and flirt a little. It's good for tip, no? Good, good!" the owner slapped Stefano's ass, the third-stringer getting called off the bench. "Go, young man!"

"Freud!" Pamela said. "I need your help on the floor." I buttoned up my utility shirt, grabbed a tub, and followed her to a table far enough from twelve that we weren't completely obvious. On the way out, she whispered, "Cindy told me I should hear the shit they're saying about Soap-Opera." Pamela carried a new square of white butcher paper and stood with her back to

Stefano, eavesdropping while I cleared the table from the other side.

Sitting before Stefano was Mr. Fifty-Bucks and his crew. "How has everything been tonight?" Stefano presented the wine, smiling as he uncorked the bottle and poured four glasses, the first going to the ringleader.

Usually when I bus tables, I aim to be quick but quiet. Never was I as careful and silent while clearing as I was that night.

After taking a gulp, Mr. Fifty-Bucks arched both eyebrows, propped his elbows on the table, right hand atop left, chin atop knuckles, and remarked, "Just wonderful." He looked Stefano up and down. "All this—the clothes, I mean," Mr. Fifty-Bucks said, "*this* is different."

"One must dress the part," Stefano said. "And thank you."

"Still not too bright, are you?" He frowned and turned to his friends. "Did you hear me give him a compliment?" One of his friends arched an eyebrow, the other shook his head. The third feigned interest in a table on the other side of the restaurant.

Stefano set the bottle on their table.

"How would you like to earn a huge tip?"

I pulled off the soiled piece of butcher paper and loudly folded it.

Stefano glanced at me. "Fool me once."

"What was that?" Mr. Fifty-Bucks asked.

Pamela made a show of placing the new square of butcher paper on the table and I lifted the tub with little care for the plates and glasses.

"Let me know if I can get you anything else," Stefano bowed out, following us to the kitchen. He popped his neck.

"Isn't he a pleasant piece of work?" Pamela said.

Cindy replied, "Told you," then said to Stefano, "I wouldn't let them get anywhere near your ass."

The manager was taking a smoke break, so I called Stefano over. "I forgot to ask you this on the bridge," I said, "but when are you going home for Christmas?"

"Day of. Returning Friday."

"You've got the weekend off, right?"

"Thankfully."

"Could you cover my shifts tomorrow through Wednesday?"

"Why?"

"My parents have bought me a plane ticket home. With the restaurant closed Christmas day, that would allow me to stay until Friday morning."

"Aw," Stefano chuckled, "you miss Mrs. Meigs?"

"Careful now." I quick-sprayed the front of his pants. He flinched, more from surprise than from the water pressure.

"Man," he stared at his crotch, his hands out to his sides.

I could have joked about getting him wet, but I tossed him a hand towel. "It's not that bad," I said, washing dishes instead of figuring out which side he was dressing on.

# CHAPTER TWENTY-FOUR

Behind the restaurant, the wind was knocking trees against one another. I didn't shut the kitchen door entirely, leaving a tall thin rectangle of light that turned itself into a right triangle on the wall.

Smoke from the stoves wove against the sky. I heard the abrasive squirping of starlings, the rotating-mockingbird melody of a car alarm, and the first roar of tonight's FedEx flights slicing the skies above Midtown, compounding the vrumm of traffic and freight lines snaking through various neighborhoods. You live here and it often escapes you how much cargo passes through this town until a plane drowns out your conversation and you both fall momentarily silent.

I carried a full trash bag in each hand, my little scales, enjoying the slight strain on my shoulders and arms as I kept them from dragging on the pavement. Sitting one bag on the ground, I slung open the half-lid and swung the other over my shoulder. As I was swinging in the second, I heard footsteps and a grunt. I landed hard on my ass and the butts of my palms.

Backlit by a streetlight, I couldn't make out who this man

was until he spoke: "What were you thinking?" Curt. My haunt. *Reverse that, subtract him, and factor in nobody but me.* "I could have had you arrested," he muttered.

"When?" I squinted my eyes. "How have you been?" and "I miss you" were long since pointless—humiliating to me, irritating to Curt.

"Last night," he spat. "I knew you wouldn't remember."

I touched my face.

"If I'd known it was you," Curt shook his head, "I wouldn't have done that. Most of it anyway."

"I went running last night," I said more to myself, trying to remember the time I'd lost.

Curt laughed bitterly, glaring an all-too-familiar expression that combined disgust, pity, and resignation.

I turned my back on him and closed the dumpster's lid, hoping he'd take the shot. But all I felt were the wind on my neck and Curt's heavy presence a few feet removed. *What do you want? What do you want?* scrolled across my mind. But I wasn't sure who was supposed to answer the question.

"This is what I get for falling asleep naked with the door unlocked, but I swear, Bryan, I can't live like this."

Curt stepped closer, the faintest sound of his teeth chattering. I turned toward him. His shoulders were tense, and his fists were clenched. His jaws were working from side to side, and his breaths were loud and quick. He was thinking.

I wanted to touch him, wanted him to want me to touch him, and knew he wanted anything but. Still, I hoped I was mistaken, that Curt had—

"At first," he whispered, interrupting my thoughts, "I didn't realize it was you."

I said, "Whatever it was, it's my fault"—then, "Saying 'I'm sorry' is worth that much less each time it's said"—then, "Sometimes, penance needs to be more tangible than one's guilty conscience—"

"*Shut up!*" I did. He scrunched his lips, nodded, and sighed deeply. "You've already told me all of this. More than once. I have the voice mails." Curt stepped closer. "It's rehearsed," his face lowered, his shoulders drawn up tight, "a script, and I fuckin' hate reruns." He opened and clenched his fists.

The wind had stuck my damp T-shirt to me in places, highlighting a shoulder, an arm, a few ribs, my stomach. I stepped closer.

"Curt, I..."

His shoulders canted forward. His fists punched both sides of my chest at the same time, slamming me against the dumpster and popping several of his knuckles.

My breath escaped in a small cloud.

Curt's dark eyebrows crowded one another, his eyes were slits, and his lower jaw was working back and forth. He was pressing his fists into my chest, grinding the left one deep into the scar.

"What were you thinking?"

That was the same thing he'd asked the one time he visited me in the hospital after I'd been shot. Before The Oil Well, that was the last time I'd seen him (or remembered seeing him). He'd run into my parents in the hallway and asked what had happened. I was tired, but I could hear them clearly.

"The police report said the woman he was with when they got shot had 'a long history of solicitation.'" My mother said, "I made it a point to remember that phrase."

"Is she okay?" Curt asked.

"All the police told us is she took the brunt of the buckshot. If Bryan asks, tell him his father and I are getting some fresh air and lunch somewhere besides this hospital's horrible cafeteria."

Then, slouching in a chair next to the bed, Curt shook his head. "Bry, what's wrong with you?"

"Why are you here?"

"Your mother called me, and don't change the subject. What were you thinking?"

Back behind d'Esyal, Curt's hands never left my chest, lesser shoves these, stutters.

"I didn't mean to," I apologized reflexively.

"Breaking into my place was what? A slip?"

I grabbed Curt's right wrist. Guided his hand to my throat. Curt closed his eyes, sighing as his elbow bent and he pressed his face into my chest.

*We are both of us weak, weak men.* I couldn't remember the last time Curt had choked me.

A plane thundered overhead.

Curt nuzzled a nipple, his grip tightening.

I shut my eyes, concentrating on the increasingly desperate and empty pulse in my own neck. I pushed him. Curt pushed back. He squeezed my right thigh with both of his. The wind made me shiver.

Curt choked me harder.

For so long, I'd wanted him to know how much I regretted all the ways I had failed him. I'd often watched him while he was sleeping or distracted in thought. How many times had I lost sleep because of his teeth-grinding? How much had I loved the boyish grin that softened his face whether awake or unconscious? Or the uncharacteristic thickness of his neck and the hollow above his collarbone? I never stopped laying my cheek on his chest, the hair tickling my nose, even if it took me forever to fall asleep listening to his heart, the pace of which I could never match no matter how I staggered my breaths.

D'Esyal's back door was kicked open. Stefano stepped out and asked, "Feel like hitting up Mad Tav?"

Curt and I shared an expression that was a mixture of annoyance and shame.

Stefano had a stack of collapsed cardboard boxes under one arm, a trash bag in his other hand. "Think I want some pizza..." he trailed off, staring.

Curt let go of my throat and took several long steps away, turning his back on Stefano. "Fuckin' Jesus," he muttered.

I rested my right foot against the dumpster. "I'll be back inside in a few."

"You need help?"

"Leave the trash. I'll get it, and pizza sounds good."

Curt stared southwest. Sputnik crested and dipped below the restaurant's roof.

"Are you sure—"

"I'll get it. Give me a few minutes."

Stefano sat the trash down but didn't leave.

"And close the door."

Blocking the light, his shadow was one of many intersecting patches in the parking lot. Stefano slowly pulled the door shut behind him.

"Thank God for the holidays, right?" Curt mumbled.

"What do you mean?"

"At least there's no chance of running into you back home."

"The Meigs," I couldn't help but laugh, "have sprung for roundtrip fare."

"I wouldn't be lucky enough that that means 'by bus'?"

"My flight leaves tomorrow morning. I return Friday."

"What time's your departure?"

"Quarter-past-twelve."

He shook his head

A heart-punt, this—so familiar, so readymade. To the certain disapproval of Chris, I said, "I miss you."

Curt's posture straightened and his face hardened. "And

we're still not talking about that." For once and without any doubts whatsoever, I knew I was a moron. "And don't you dare tell me you're sorry," Curt said. "How does it feel being the cliched guilt-ridden Catholic *several* times over? I deserved more than that—more than some fuck who couldn't realize *he* deserved more for himself."

I opened my mouth.

"No!" He shoved me. "Whatever you were thinking last night, try anything like that again and a black eye will be the least of your worries. And if it comes down to that, Bryan, I'll never apologize for anything you make me do."

\* \* \*

At the Mad Tav, Stefano and I sat in a small corner booth—our backs to the wall, legs stretched out—watching the familiarly fatigued faces slumming after their shifts. This time, should Ian and his crew show up, they wouldn't have the room to invite themselves to our table.

Pamela waved when she arrived and sat at the bar. Stefano and I were splitting a pitcher of PBR and a pepperoni and jalapeño pizza. I recognized one guy in the booth to my right.

His table was laughing, and I guess he caught me glancing at him while trying to figure out where I'd seen him, because he said, "Yo, fire-pecker!"

Stefano laughed so hard he nearly shot beer out of his nose.

"Maybe you can help us," the guy said. The people in that booth faced me.

I handed Stefano some napkins. "How's that?"

"I'm Caleb, by the way, but my friends and me are trying to figure out where all we should take somebody from back home who's visiting Memphis for the first time."

Then it hit me: he was the hotter server from that day at

Cocina Sabroso. His hair had grown out, his coils a little longer but not as orange. "What's on the list so far?"

"The obvious spots. Graceland, ribs at Rendezvous, the fuckin' ducks at the Peabody. I'm sure we'll go to Beale Street at some point."

"If you're going to be down there," a woman in that booth said, "you should take 'em to Raiford's. That place is a blast."

"Sounds like you got it covered," I said.

"Nah," Caleb shook his head, "the tourist bullshit will last, like, a day or two at most. What's a cool spot nobody's heard of?"

Stefano said, "Tell him about the bridge," so I did.

After I was done, Caleb nodded. "Sounds cool, but that bridge is surrounded by some sketch."

"You said from back home," I asked, "where's that?"

"St. Louis," Caleb said.

"Me too. Been here over eight years. Still haven't gone to Graceland."

"What part did you grow up in?"

"Ladue."

"Shit," he chuckled, dragging out the word for several sylla-bles. "Man, that might as well be a whole other city altogether. Ain't it funny," he continued, "how alike there and here are? So many little siloes of sameness. Anyway, thanks for the tip about the bridge. We might check that out."

As he and his friends moved on with their own conversa-tion, Stefano was finishing a mouthful of crust. "Earlier," he said, "I assume you knew that guy. Seemed like y'all were having a moment. Was it his malice that wrecked your face last night?" He grabbed another slice, covering it with crushed red pepper, folding it, and taking a bite.

"That's Curt, my ex. He says he didn't realize it was me, not at first." I took a long drink.

"And what the fuck's that supposed to mean?"

I tapped my fingers against the sweating mug. "Believe me, this isn't a cycle-of-violence-theory-moment, and I'd explain everything if I could, but I deserved *at least* this."

Stefano shook his head and chomped his slice.

I downed my mug. "I need to get home. Still have some packing to do."

"How many bags are you checking?"

"None. I'm only taking a carry-on."

"But I thought," Stefano grinned while re-filling his mug, "you weren't allowed a carry-on."

"Alright. I'll bite," I could guess where this was going, like listening to a child trying to impress an adult with a knock-knock joke. "And why's that?"

"It's just, with all the baggage you've got, it seems like you'd have to check any actual luggage."

I refilled my mug. "Tell Chris that was a good one."

"Oh, he wishes he thought of it," Stefano chuckled.

*Nice to be the butt of an inside joke between two of your only friends.* If I told Stefano and Chris about Duke, how much harsher would their jokes be, or would they quit joking altogether? God, I wished I knew how filthy and tragic Stefano already thought I was. Then I might be able to gauge how much filthier he would see me if I were ever completely honest with him. You might not like where you stood, but it was always better to know where you were. At the least, you wouldn't be surprised by the scenery.

Knowing how easily Stefano could overlook certain variables in others only to put the same ones under a microscope when they involved me was the worst feeling. How much more suspicion did I deserve?

Stefano pointed his slice of pizza at me. "But let's get back to Curt."

That was a distraction, so I said, "How's about we don't." I wondered what Stefano and Chris had said about me after Stefano decided we should be nothing more than friends.

"No," Stefano said. "Seriously, you're fine with him strangling you?"

He didn't say that loudly, but it felt like the whole tavern was now listening to us. "It's complicated," I told him.

"Makes me think about what all you might have asked me to do."

A statement that was actually a question, one which told me how tainted I was in his eyes. I glanced around. No one was looking at us, so I focused on my mug, wondering how long it would be before this would turn into another inside joke between Chris and Stefano. When he said my name, I looked at him and asked, "What?"

"Will you be honest with me?"

My right eye twitched as I stared at him.

"What really happened with Adam?"

I translated that to mean: *if you were so worried about what he did to you, then why weren't you worried for me, or do you only care about the risks you face?* I didn't know what I could say that would make sense. "I will, if you'll do the same. Did you friend-zone me because of what Adam did *to* me?"

He shook his head and whispered, "Whether or not you might be poz doesn't matter to me, Bry. If we ever got past oral, we'd wear condoms regardless. It'd be as easy as that. What isn't easy is what I need to ask you," he said. "Sorry, but there's no way this isn't going to sound harsh."

"Just say it already."

"What did you ask Adam to do to you?"

I imagined Curt on one side of him, my mother on the other, both of them shaking their heads and smirking. *What were you thinking?* Stefano took a drink. I clenched my fists and stared across the room. At a tiny table directly opposite from us, a straight couple were holding hands and gazing into each other's eyes. With her talking and him smiling, the rest of the world had fallen away. When the second-hand smoke finally made me blink, I looked at Stefano again. He was eating another slice like nothing was wrong. My stomach lurched. And after an inhale, I unclenched my fists. Four deep crescent moons were imprinted into each palm.

"So, nothing, huh?"

"Soap-Opera," I said, "you have a gift for understatement. There's harsh, and then there's the shit you just asked." Now it was my turn to shake my head. "If you don't know by now that there are certain things I'd never ask anyone do to me or somebody else, does it matter what I say?"

"Bry, I'm—"

"Speaking of baggage," I laughed, pushing my plate away and pulling my mug close. Stefano stared into space. "You're not wrong about my luggage. Forget about ever finishing unpacking all those bags, where would I even begin?"

"Bry, I'm sorry for making that joke," Stefano said, reaching across the table with both hands.

"And where'd your harsh question come from? Another inside joke at my expense?"

He said nothing. I sat up straight. "I'm about to ask you to do me a favor, Stefano, so pay attention."

"I'm listening."

"If you never bring up Adam again, I'll forget this entire conversation." I took a long drink, neglecting to tell him I was also going to do my damnedest to forget whatever attraction I still felt toward him. If he only wanted to be friends, then I'd play along, knowing he was simply another person around whom I had to censor certain parts of myself.

"I get it," he took a deep breath, "and you got it."

* * *

A small collection of leaves was circling the rear stairwell, each leaf chasing the stem of another, getting nowhere but around until being stranded in a corner. Sputnik trailed across my mind. I paused, my keys in hand.

*The sooner I find Adam, the better*, I thought. I would ask him first what he'd done, but I was certain he'd lie. While I didn't know what all it would take, I would get Adam to admit the truth. Then and only then, maybe Stefano would realize how wrong he had been about every-fuckin'-thing.

To get started, I logged online and eventually found Adam's website. It was a crappy little thing, just like Stefano had said. While the poorly lit torso and back shots were headless, I had no doubt it was Adam.

I clicked on the "contact me" link and filled out the form, faking everything except my email address:

- Name: Paul B.
- Age: 30
- Position: Vers bottom
- Phone #:
- Email: bouillablase@hotmail.com
- Interests: Looking for a hung jock who can be patient but knows how to work this fag over once he's warmed up. Love sucking cock. If we click, we can take it from there.
- Date(s) Requested: 12/26/2003

After I shut my bedroom door, I edged my dresser away from the wall as quietly as I could. Then I pulled out the second drawer from the bottom and reached to the front left side where I'd duct-taped a Manila envelope. I emptied its rubber-banded contents: four stacks of cash with sticky notes summing up their respective worth, and one much thinner stack of fake IDs, which I'd acquired during my first couple years in town.

How easily I'd been able to come up with entire backstories based on each alias's hometown and state, especially the one based on a kid named Brad who had my same birthdate and died before he was five. Figured it wouldn't be too difficult to remember or recreate one or all of those old identities, Brad most of all.

I counted my tip-out, then set that cash aside to be washed. From those sticky notes and tonight's haul, I had $7,439. I was going to pay my mother back for the airfare, and I had to buy presents. My father never expected much from me beyond a solidarity of some sort I had never been able to decipher, while Logan expected all too much.

Nevertheless, I took my time in the shower, deciding to get them gifts they'd never expect. That would definitely cost me more than I'd like, but I had a strong feeling this would be the last time I ever visited them.

# PART IV

*Object Permanence*: at our scale, reality doesn't depend on being observed. And yet, when various parts of it are hidden, never are those things truer or more certain. We develop object permanence by eight or nine months of age, but our adult brains seem hardwired for that earlier stage in as much as denial and selective attention drive so many of our actions.

See also: familial alliances, disappointments, and expectations.

*If only I could see the humor in my OCD, but it's like whatever I can't see must exist, which makes my condition doubly ironic. Peek-a-boo, I always see you. I still haven't gotten tested yet. My HIV status is a gay guy's version of Schrödinger's cat. There's so much I imagine, so many contaminants that I'll never be able to prove don't exist. Picture a wall plastered with photos and newspaper clippings stretching both ways into infinity, and here I stand with a single bundle of yarn knowing I'll never be able to map it all out. And even if I could, it would never make sense to anyone else.*

— 22 DECEMBER 2003

# CHAPTER TWENTY-FIVE

The morning of my flight back home, Chris and I woke up around the same time, but he got to the bathroom first, which meant I had a good hour to myself—if I ignored the tunes blaring from his CD boombox. When it came to house music, my roommate was like a sommelier, detecting subtle differences in the same programmed electronic drumming, dissecting a terroir I couldn't imagine because it all sounded the same to me. Remixes of remixes to help fags dance by number.

God, I needed coffee. After a first cup, my frown subsided, and I grabbed ten sandwich bags and rolled them up. I slid those into an outside pocket of my carry-on. Hopefully, I wouldn't need that many, but you never knew. In movies, I often noticed how people would throw their luggage onto their beds. Why would you do that? Did it magically become clean when it crossed the threshold of your home? Let's say it was checked luggage. How many hands had tossed it, and how many other suitcases from complete strangers did it rub up against? And what about hotels and bed bugs?

With a second cup warming my hands, I returned to my

bedroom. I packed six shirts, two pairs of jeans beside the ones I would be wearing, and ten pairs of underwear and socks. Last, I wrapped my dress shoes in separate plastic grocery bags and lay them soles up atop my clothes. I would never understand how some people tossed their shoes into their luggage, not caring about them soiling every piece of clothing. All I had left to pack was my toiletries kit, but I couldn't do that until Chris was finished. While waiting, I checked my email and found this gem in a new spam:

*Grandmother is a collusion grade dimethyl cartographer, and downslope from Appalachia, in a mastodon shack, stands the felicitous salesgirl, her handmade alluvial inferno...*

At some point, I might try to stitch all of those snippets together into something coherent. Until then, it was just another text clipping on my computer's desktop.

The end of Chris's beauty regime was a slung-open door and him announcing, "It's all yours." With one towel around his waist, he dried off his upper body with another. I stripped down to my boxers and headed to the shower. Before I got there, he asked, "Wanna split a cab?"

I yawned a yes and shut the bathroom door. I dialed the water to scalding and stood under the stream, head hanging, eyes closed, staying in there for as long as I could, a few more minutes of peace until I was on my way to the Show-Me state.

Before we walked down to the driveway to wait for the cab, Chris separated his car keys from his key ring and left them in the coffee table's drawer.

"Why are you doing that?" I asked.

"Don't need 'em."

"I wouldn't feel right without mine."

"Of course you wouldn't," Chris laughed. "But they'll be fine, and I've got a spare set squirreled away in my bedroom." Chris's backpack was stuffed full, reminding me of an elementary school kid bent double by their textbooks, and he dragged a full-sized suitcase he'd have to check. He wasn't coming back until the thirtieth.

After we were through security, we walked down concourse B. His flight was at 11:50 a.m. at gate B-40 and mine was twenty-five minutes later at gate B-18. Because our gates were on opposite branches off the concourse and there was an hour until Chris's flight boarded, we found a restaurant before the split and sat at the bar.

One thing I liked about airport bars, besides how easily most people will drink much earlier in the day than they would normally, was how difficult it could be to figure out who was arriving and who was departing. A liminal space where no one really noticed you because their attention was focused on their watches and how much beer or liquor was left in their glasses.

In a few minutes, he had a bourbon and Coke and I had a tall beer. "Cheers," he said and held his glass up.

"What are we toasting?"

"To a better year than the shit-show this one's been."

I raised my mug, "And may certain people get everything they deserve, whether they are blood or not."

"May they all rot in Hell," he chuckled and we clinked glasses. After a moment, he said, "You've never talked much about your family."

"There are plenty of reasons for that, but if you think I'm a 'special case'—"

"Fuck Ian, 'cause I never called you that."

"Well, Stefano mentioned a baggage joke last night, so..."

"That's different. We're your friends. First, I'm not going to trash you to random folks, and second, Soap-Opera and I weren't trashing you. Good Lord, he's got some baggage of his own. Who doesn't? But you were saying?"

"About my family?" I asked. He nodded. "It sucks being stuck with people who have the market cornered on denial."

Chris checked his watch and took a drink. "What won't they believe?"

"It doesn't matter."

"Pretend I'm a perfect stranger. Somebody you'll never see again." Chris motioned around the crowded bar, the murmur of so many conversations overlapping like the currents colliding with the Old Bridge's stanchions. "What could you tell me that you'd never tell another soul?"

"I get what you're trying to do, Chris, but we're roommates. Some things you never forget, and sometimes, after those who are supposed to love you have chosen to never believe you, it's all you can do to tell one other person." What I didn't tell him was how much I didn't want Stefano to ever find out what my half-brother had done to me. Sure, Chris had been helpful at times in moving on with my life after Curt and gently pushing me out of my comfort zones, but at that point I knew how little I could trust him to keep a secret. Some stereotypes are bullshit, but one thing Chris had made clear to me was how some gays loved their drama.

Chris pushed his drink away and turned to face me.

"I've already told somebody *that* truth," I continued. "He believed me, and while that wasn't why he wound up leaving, it might have been in the back of his mind every time he looked at me."

A few minutes of silence passed. Chris paid for our drinks, glancing at his watch. "I was going to tell you this in January," he said as he grabbed his cocktail, slowly swirling the glass, "but I'm cutting back on drinking next year."

"Definitely couldn't hurt me," I said with no intention of following suit.

"Do one thing for me, Bry." He stood, placing a hand on my shoulder.

"What's that?"

"Don't let your fucked up family fuck you up any more than they already have."

"I'll do my best."

Chris put on his backpack, awkwardly squeezed my shoulder, and left the bar. I finished my beer and ordered another, settling my tab right away so I wouldn't have to stay any longer than it took to empty this new mug.

\* \* \*

Curt didn't board the plane until a few minutes before the gate closed. He was seated four rows ahead of my perch near the left wing. With the headrests and the holiday flux and my slouching in the fully upright position, he didn't see me.

As the flight attendant began the announcements, I rested my forehead against the portal's frigid glass. The wintry daylight shifted between pewter-dull and magnesium-glare, the iridescence of an oyster shell fumbling between my fingers.

The flight was around four hours long and at full capacity. Once we were at cruising altitude, the man sitting in the middle seat of my row wouldn't shut up: "Real glad I got to the airport two hours early. Still not used to all these new rules. Can't believe we have to take off our damn shoes. How long until you think we're stripping down to our skivvies?" When he took a breath, I plopped in my earphones and cranked up Archers of Loaf's *All the Nation's Airports* on my Discman.

The term *cruising altitude* always made me smile. Guys trawling parks and rest stops probably felt a vertiginous thrill as they literally lowered themselves to grimy floors and shit-splattered toilets, inescapably linking sex with waste. The guy in the aisle seat alternated between glowering at the middle-seat guy and trying to will the beverage cart's arrival. I started staring at the thousands of feet between me and the patchwork fields we raced past, ignoring all of the middle-seater's attempts at small talk

Upon landing, I powered up my phone. I had a voice mail from my mother: "Hello, Bry. I am *sooo* sorry, but I'm going to be a little late picking you up. The day I'm having, I'll be an hour late, I'm—"

I erased the rest. I found a seat at a bar on the concourse, ordered a tall beer, opened the alt-zine and picked up where I'd left off.

*Bluff City Plagues – continued*

### An Illusory Reprieve

As paradoxical as it seems, many of us actually take comfort from, if not like, the disease model. It provides a framework for treatment and communities in which we can find some measure of solace. While every disease cannot be cured, one could argue the disease model gifts us with an illusion of control. And should the best outcome be a dignified death, that can be a goal unto itself.

Plagues are a different story altogether. In the past, those pestilences rippled across continents, over walls, around hearths, and into the eyes and noses and mouths of people huddling in fear. Sometimes, people spread these intentionally during wars or colonization (which are essentially the same thing). Other times, plagues recurred annually because people did not know how to slow their spread, how to treat them, and/or because their sanitation and water purification were woefully insufficient. Plagues destabilize society to varying degrees, unmasking cultural and social distinctions as the arbitrary conventions they have always been.

Which is to say, those who are uninfected or unaffected by plagues will cast aside the pain and guilt and shame and suffering, striving to restore the status quo, for their unease may be a nagging conscience, but it is more likely the discomfort of inconvenience.

In our country, what would eventually be named HIV/AIDS was initially seen as a gay plague. A legion of lazy preachers *reasoned* that this had to be a curse from God because of how easily it could be spread via unprotected anal sex. Ignoring the women who contracted it through vaginal sex or transmitted it to their children during birth or through breastfeeding. Ignoring the adults and children who were infected from compromised blood supplies. Ignoring those who got it from sharing needles. Ignoring anything that might keep them from yet again re-making God in their limited, twisted image. If our queer souls were corrupted, wouldn't it make perfect sense that our blood was too? In other words, they will never not find an excuse to justify their homophobia or any other hatred of those they deem to be the *other*. But I digress.

The first news article discussing what we now call HIV/AIDS appeared in *The New York Times* in July 1981.[1] Physicians and researchers remained at a loss for so long because the virus mutates so swiftly, so continuously, infecting so many different systems within the body, setting up a seemingly endless series of reservoirs from which it can begin its onslaught against the body anew.

According to a 1998 study published in the journal *Nature*, the first confirmed case of HIV infection and death from AIDS is believed to have occurred in 1959 in what is now the city of Kinshasa in the Democratic Republic of

Congo.[2] More recently, a research study published in the *Proceedings of the National Academy of Sciences* has placed the spread of HIV subtypes A and B sometime in the 1940s, with a plus-minus range that could mean HIV found its way from monkeys to chimpanzees to humans as early as 1924 or as late as 1959.[3]

Then in 1981, like the tremors that precede a volcanic eruption, AIDS emerged slowly but gained speed exponentially. The pyroclastic flow that finally billowed down the mountainside overtook too many who had no idea that they'd already been entombed.

Since then, if you're fortunate (that is, if you can afford it and if your doctor isn't a self-righteous bigot like the preachers I mentioned earlier), HIV has largely transitioned from a plague to a chronic condition. It is true that the advent of protease inhibitors and the "cocktail" in the late 1990s produced the so-called "Lazarus effect" in many people who were almost as hopeless as that eponymous man was before Jesus wept. But even in industrialized countries like ours, access to life-saving medications is by no means equal.

For a more striking contrast, consider the inequitable access in countries struggling to industrialize and/or recovering from centuries of colonial rule. That said, as miraculous as the "cocktail" has been, it is by no means a cure. For some it was too little, too late.

And that brings us to Selynn.

I had no doubts about her fate, but I'd deal with her later. It might take me a while, but I'm the kind of person who finishes everything they begin reading no matter how predictable the ending may be because other people's tragedies can be useful distractions. Was that parasitism or commensalism, or was it simply the cost of being human? Somehow, it felt more like an entirely different kind of Lazarus effect, raising our spirits, if only for a few moments when our lives might seem not so bad by comparison.

Speaking of which, what was life like for Lazarus after he had been resurrected? Once all of the tears had been wiped away and the hugs had ended and the feasts had been eaten and the wine had been drunk, I imagine him feeling both thankful and unmoored, doing his best to conceal how uncomfortable it was to be Jesus's final sign (well, except for the most important one of all). Ripped from Sheol, maybe he realized how much he had savored the bliss of the deepest, dreamless sleep. Only now, he awoke early on every new day he had been blessed with, each dawn too bright and surreal, burdened by a fatigue that would never cease darkening his eyes until they closed again for the final time.

It was rush hour so I ordered another tall beer. That was a good choice because my mother ended up being ninety-seven minutes late. I would have taken a cab if I'd been in any rush and wanted to waste some money. As it was, it felt nice to accept her empty excuses—some errand this, some traffic that. She couldn't help but stare at my bruised face, but she never asked what had happened, which both felt nice and reminded me of those months before I'd left for college when neither she nor my father ever demanded I explain how a bullet hole wound up in their bedroom wall.

When we pulled into the circular driveway of my parents' home, I realized I'd forgotten how much front yard there was, all of it perfectly manicured like her nails. The house had a basement and another two full stories aboveground, a long face topped with a pair of vacant eyes in the dormer windows of the converted attic.

She drove around the side and clicked the garage door

remote. Her spot was nearest the inside door. She led me through a "mud room" that had never seen a speck of dirt, then through the laundry room into an open kitchen that wasn't much smaller than my apartment. She opened the fridge. "What would you like to drink? We have wine, beer, soda, and juice. I could make you a spritzer."

"A beer's fine."

She reached far back into the fridge and pulled out a Budweiser. My mother was in her late-fifties and as tall as me. Her light brown hair was a bit grayer, the same shoulder-length style she'd worn since I was a teenager.

In her late-twenties, she had given birth to my half-brother Logan. Seven years later in her mid-thirties, following two miscarriages, she'd had me. Both pregnancies were long hoped for and difficult to bring to term, so after me, she declared that she was done. Did she regret not taking another chance? Third times the charm, they say. I didn't know much about her first husband, except she had met him when she was a sophomore in college, which also happened to be her final year in college. He died unexpectedly before Logan had turned four. Within a year, she'd met and married my father.

Our poisons of choice in hand, she led me downstairs to the bedroom between the den and a storage hallway. After Logan had left for college, this windowless room was mine. It was as close to a sensory deprivation tank as I'd ever been in.

Two cardboard boxes were awaiting me in the room, my name scrawled on the sides of both in thick black marker. I foolishly hoped my parents had decided to forgo wrapping paper and exchange gifts early, saying as much.

"No," my mother explained, "we need the space in the storage hallway. These boxes have to go, so take whatever you don't want thrown away or donated."

I leaned my carry-on against the dresser, unable to imagine how I'd save everything I might want.

Nearing four p.m., I took a break from sorting through things and sat on the floor. I paged through the first comic I'd ever bought: a poorly drawn version of *The Three Little Pigs*. I'd read this so many times that it was held together by tape. One particular page kept sticking, stiffened by time, water-damage, and something else.

I set it aside with the many other comics I'd rediscovered. Then, as I sifted through the strata of my childhood—rusty Matchbox cars; perfectly balanced Weebles; G.I. Joes and Transformers, some whole, most missing an arm or a leg—I found the blanket. My chest felt like I'd been buried under a rockslide, each breath bringing more weight down upon me.

I dug through my carry-on, found my inhaler, and after a few pumps, I could breathe. I picked up the blanket with two fingers, holding it away from me. I had tossed this in the trash before I left for college. It should have disintegrated long ago in a landfill, but here it was, packed away like a threadbare keepsake, with all of those memories still woven through it like a raggedy counter-stitch.

\* \* \*

*Bry, you can read that later, I need you to listen. We're gonna play a game.*

*It got any pigs in it?*

*You can be whichever's your favorite.*

*What about a wolf?*—I ask as Logan crouches to unbutton my Garanimals, his fingers fumbling.

*I'll be the wolf. Now you go over there, stand behind the dresser.*

*But why do I gotta have my bottoms off?*

243

*Do the pigs in your comic book wear pants?*

*No.*

*Now, I'll be hiding under your sleeping bag. You be quiet and try real hard to make it from the window to the door without making any noise. If I hear you, I'll try and catch you. Remember, buddy, you gotta be quiet: pigs don't talk, do they?*

"Oink," they say, "oink."

*But do they talk?*

*It's cold, Loggie.*

And I try to yell when Logan catches me and won't let go. With one hand, he chokes me. With the other, he wraps the blanket around my head. The fabric has the burn of grass blades on my summer-sweaty skin. The grit of a zipper. The rustle of jeans falling to the floor. His stomach and thighs feel feverish, but in the center of everything there is the tiniest cold slick that burns as it expands. I want to puke but there's nothing, nothing at all.

Since Logan is holding me down, I escape the only way I can. I imagine I'm outside, and the day is bright and there's a cool breeze struggling against the heat's oppressive weight. I do my best to ignore how that breeze keeps getting thinned to nothing. I'm in the backyard, looking for night crawlers, or hidden treasure, or the baseball trophy Logan said he'd buried back there because it'd been possessed by the Devil-Himself. And he had warned me if I ever dug it up, the Devil-Himself would leave the trophy and tear into me, and it wasn't real gold anyway, something fake to look fancy on a shelf. And without even trying, I find the trophy and the backyard catches on fire while I'm facedown. And Logan hadn't lied. When I whimper, he chokes me harder.

*You can't talk remember?*

I try to say his name, but it devolves into a snotty string of consonants and he boxes one of my ears. When he quits raping me, the sudden absence burns and shivers at the same time.

Coughing, gasping, I open my eyes: the blanket's blurry fabric darkens in several places as a warm and viscous liquid seeps through the wide-weave, drips onto a cheek, smelling like bleach. Hold my breath. Don't breathe, not until Logan leaves the bedroom.

As soon as the door clicks shut, I rip the blanket off my head. With a wet plop, it lands on the open copy of *The Three Little Pigs*. I bite my lip but sounds and spit sputter through and my chest feels like it's about to explode and I'm drowning. Like the prior summer when my father had thrown me into the deep end of our pool, I'm clawing toward the surface, but there's no hold anywhere, and while I should conserve what little air I have, my heart races, wasting everything doubly.

\* \* \*

My jaws were sore. I stopped grinding my teeth and wiped my eyes roughly with a sleeve. Though I tried not to, I could trace outlines of numerous faint stains within the blanket's faded blue. I held it close to my face. How ironic was it that, now, most of my close friends associate the smell of bleach with my cleaning rituals?

I tried to pin each ghostly stain to a different instance, but I couldn't tell what was foreground, mid-ground, or background. I held it up to the ceiling light. Touched it with my bare hands. But none of that mattered. Each instance was present, no matter how long after the fact. I folded the blanket, laid it on the bed, and sat on the floor, my face hanging below my knees.

Heavy footsteps descended the basement stairs. "How's it coming?" my mother asked, entering the bedroom.

I looked up, rubbing my hands on my knees. "Getting there."

"How long till you think you'll be done?"

"I don't know. Why?"

"Bry, we both know how you are." She paused for a beat. "I would appreciate it if you'd get this finished before you take off anywhere."

"I will."

She sighed, eyeing the forty or so comics I had stacked on the bed. "Still can't get over how much money you wasted on those things. Sure glad you grew out of that phase."

I started digging through the nearest box, wanting to reach the bottom, but there was just so much shit.

"Oh!" She walked to the bed, grabbed the blanket, unfolding it as she brought it to her face. She shook it away, her nose crinkling in an exaggerated washing detergent commercial's "before" scene. "Hmm." She dropped it unfolded onto the bed. "Logan told me you'd want this later. Why did you throw it away in the first place?"

"Because," I gritted my teeth, "I didn't want it."

Her voice lightened, "Then why have you saved it with the rest of this junk?"

"To keep from losing the rag—"

"So you've changed your—"

"—before I take it out back and torch it."

"*Bry!* This was your blinky!"

"Which he used to"—I fiddled with one of my broken Transformers which wouldn't transform as it should—"Never mind. It doesn't matter."

With a weird smile, my mother closed her eyes and shook her head. "I'd be more willing to believe you, Bry, if you'd said it was somebody else. A boyfriend of one of your babysitters, a soccer coach, or even a priest. But I cannot accept that Logan did that to you. Why can't you let go of things that are long gone? If you had ever bothered to ask me," she continued, "I would have said that you were exaggerating things while minimizing your guilt, all so we'll feel sorry for you. Like how you were trying to help your little hooker, or like I'm sure you'd do if I bothered asking about the fight you obviously lost. If *that* happened, it was harmless curiosity. All kids do that. You never played doctor with any of your friends?"

*Played doctor?* In her mind, because doctors take an oath to do no harm, no harm could have possibly been done to me, just forget that my assailant wasn't a physician. I sat there, staring at her, my mouth slightly open but completely silent. When Stefano came out to his mother, she had told him that if he got infected with HIV it would break her heart. After what my mother had just said, I knew that if Adam had infected me, her heart wouldn't break. She would pity me, of course, but any sadness would be more about what her friends would think of her than about concern for my well-being. Still, whatever degree of sorrow pained her would more than be balanced by the satisfaction of having been right all along.

She walked to the door. "Whatever happened whenever is nothing right now." Her voice, the crackle of late autumn underfoot, "And it hasn't been for *how* many years? Please, Bry, this is the first time you've been back since leaving for college, and it's the holidays, and I want things to be nice. I want both of my boys home and happy, and I want you two to get along, and I don't want to have to worry about you. That's all. I don't need any other present from you than that. If you want to burn your blinky, fine, just use the grill out back." She shook her head. "Oprah's about to start."

She climbed the staircase, but all I *heard* was AND—AND —AND—AND. My sight blurred on the blanket. I shut my eyes. *Breathe.* After an exhale, I told myself, "You're about to go running." I fumbled for my inhaler and took two pumps. In the nightstand's top drawer, I found an old cigarette lighter.

It took several grinding flicks. My thumb began to singe as I stared at the wavering flame. When I touched the flame to the blanket, I imagined specks of ash spiraling, flames creeping along the lines of thread that segmented the bed's comforter into squares, flames licking the headboard, the bedposts, and the walls. But the fire would not catch.

I threw a pullover on the blanket, smothering the pathetic smoldering, and changed into my running gear. The pullover wasn't even singed.

Upstairs, my mother was sitting at the kitchen table. A rich, warm aroma filled the room. Her face looked placid. Whether that was from the theme of Oprah going to a commercial break or the half-empty highball, who knew? She took a drink before noticing me.

Reflecting light from the TV, the condensation pattern that her glass left on the table evoked Jupiter's storm bands and its Great Red Spot. In '94, the Shoemaker–Levy 9 comet fractured and crashed into the gas giant. I'd read somewhere the combined force of these collisions was equivalent to a hundred million megatons of TNT. The resulting cloud of debris was roughly the same radius as the earth, a ghostly satellite in Jupiter's upper atmosphere.

She swallowed her drink. "You can't be through."

"It's through." I unlocked and cracked the kitchen door, bent at the waist, grabbing my ankles. "You can trash it all. What's cooking?"

"A pan of chocolate fudge brownies with walnuts and macadamia nuts."

"Smells good," I said, stretching.

"Those were always your favorite," she said. "Would you like to watch Oprah with me? She's doing a good topic today."

I raised my head off my shins. "What's she tackling?"

In unison with the ice cubes, her voice clinked, "Forgiveness." She took a sip and set the glass on the table. "And not starting the New Year with old grudges."

I stood, doing ankle rotation stretches. *Nothing about the necessity of accountability?* No, my ability to suspend disbelief only stretched so far. "Thanks, but I need to get a run in."

"After you're done, do you think you could run to the store? We need a few things for dinner." She took another sip. "And, Bry, I'm sorry, it's just..." She waved her right hand in front of her chest. I was about to respond, God help me, when she asked, "What's burning?"

"I dropped a cigarette on my pullover."

"Smoke outside from now on."

"Will do."

"How's your asthma?"

"Better."

"So, the store?"

"Make a list. I'll be back in an hour or so."

My stride was long and smooth. Away from the house. Away from the trails. Away, away, away, focusing on a horizon I could never reach. I quickened my sprint with an image: a man seen running toward a waning sun, his silhouette losing its outline, blurring into the watercolor shades of orange and red rippling into and through one another as indigo from above waited to drown him.

# CHAPTER TWENTY-SIX

When I returned, I poured myself a glass of water and grabbed a corner brownie. The edges were a perfect level of crispiness and the fudge was gooey and warm. I closed my eyes and chewed. Maybe the sugar rush was heightened because I'd pushed myself during the run, but in that moment, I was a child warming up after playing in the snow, fudge smearing my face, mom laughing at the mess I was making.

"Guess my recipe's still good," she chuckled.

I opened my eyes and finished chewing the last bite. After I took a gulp of water, I said, "I didn't realize how much I missed these."

She smiled and pointed at the edge of her lips. I grabbed a paper towel off the roll and wiped my mouth. "There are clean towels in the downstairs bathroom."

"Thanks," I told her, meaning it.

During the run, I'd decided I was tired of merely existing chained to various age-appropriate security blankets, those damn rituals most people think are either me acting out a part or trying to get attention. They are scripts of a sort, but nothing in the way people imagine.

While remembering the theatre department's party at Fugue and how easy it was to tell the truth and lie at the same time, I peeled off my sweatshirt, track pants, and socks. My family knew a version of my past self, so for the duration of this visit I'd hide how much I hated handshakes. After all, the Meigs were not a hugging family except in times of great distress. When I was nine, my maternal grandmother died. While I faintly heard my mother crying behind her closed bedroom door at night, I never saw her tears. At the viewing, she shook so many hands, always placing her left atop hers and the mourner's. I tried my best not to cry too much in public, but near the end of the viewing she sat next to me and gave me a side-hug, flattening her skirt with her other hand and laying her head atop mine.

As for my father, I couldn't remember the last time he hugged me, but I do remember the Saturday morning he taught me how to tie my shoelaces and shake hands like a man. With the former, he said, "Always double-knot them, unless the shoes are old, and then you triple-knot them. You always want to keep your shoelaces from touching the ground." Regarding the latter, he instructed me that, "Real men should test the other guy's grip. If you can't beat him, at least match him."

Getting back to handshakes, mine would be vigorous and firm, and of course, I would smile when I gripped their hand, getting much closer to them than I would normally. I wouldn't be the one to stop shaking first. Also, I would not use my sandwich bag gloves for doorknobs. People opened door after door after door with nothing tragic happening to them, so why not give it a shot? What was the worst thing that could happen?

To be clear, I wasn't going to be the kind of guy who whipped out his cock, began pissing, then used the same hand to flush the urinal mid-stream and shake off. Nor would I let myself get drunk enough to bareback anybody. But for the duration of this trip, I was going to ignore my OCD. Occasionally, I might even drop things on the floor, pick them up, and dust them off. I wouldn't even count to five-Mississippi. I would only wash my hands before every meal and after pissing or shitting. Whenever a major trigger happened, I would remind myself it was patently ridiculous, willing myself to be calm while catching my mother's reaction to my lack of one. Let her believe I'd grown out of one of my "phases." Let her believe she'd been right, even though I knew how wrong she was.

As for the literal security blanket, I'd burn it later. For now, I decided that using the towels in the downstairs bathroom, which were neatly folded and smelled cleaned, would do nothing but dry me.

The bathroom was small, with a low ceiling, but the spacious shower stall had two projecting shelves that connected with the floor and doubled as seats. I lathered up and rinsed off, adjusted the shower nozzle so the stream hit the nearest seat. To test my new resolve, I did something I'd done before leaving home without giving it a second thought: I sat with my ass on the very edge of one ledge and faced away from the shower, letting myself hang heavily under the hot water and curtains of steam.

In turn, the shower's sudsy swirls revealed and obscured a filthy drain. When it came to my triggers, out of sight was a curse and out of mind was a saving grace. But that salvation ceased as soon as I remembered or was reminded of whatever I'd forgotten, at which point a maw that eclipsed the horizon would open beneath me. Like every one of my fears was an individual fish in a school being corralled by the net of bubbles that a humpback whale had exhaled. Trapped by the shimmering mesh, each fish would frantically swim upward and around but never through the bubbles, until all were swallowed by the lunging gulp.

I stood and lathered up for a second time. This final trip to my childhood home wasn't about my triggers. Besides the anonymous tricks, how long have I held those who were, or should have been, closest to me at arm's length, letting them slip to my toes, then down the drain, losing them to all the muck beneath the grate?

I shut my eyes and leaned back into the stream, letting the water pummel my scalp. *Selbsthaß*, one of the few words I remembered from two years of college German, popped into my mind. It was a masculine noun that meant "self-hatred," because of course it did.

For so many years, my *Selbsthaß* felt like a thicket spreading and branching from my chest, wooden knots and thorns choking out the light, but after my mother's last lecture it seemed like that had been done *to* me instead of being one of my defining traits. Still, I wondered how much I played into the way she acted toward me.

Until this visit, the last time I'd seen my folks was in the hospital a few days after getting shot. That happened shortly after Curt dumped me. He'd moved out of our apartment in a hurry, so many cabinet doors and drawers left open and empty.

Newly single sounds optimistic if you're the one who broke it off or you're banking a fat alimony check. I should have been getting sober and staying celibate. On the night I was shot, I'd arrived early and alone at a mostly lesbian bar on Madison Avenue near the Midtown Piggly Wiggly. I went there for their "Karaoke Xperienz." Yes, the flyers stapled to telephone poles were in Comic Sans, but the host had songs you would never expect a karaoke DJ to have.

Before the sidewalk sale began, I left with a guy who'd sung both the Dead Boys' "High Tension Wire" and The Lemonheads' acoustic cover of "Skulls" by the Misfits. During the latter, he'd leered at me while doing his best impersonation of Evan Dando's Xanaxed-out Glenn Danzig. Despite the lyrics, despite his scraggly beard, I found the serenade sexy.

Our small talk was little more than crude logistics: Scraggly was a bottom, great, but we couldn't go to his place because he lived in his grandmother's basement. My place was out too, because Curt still had his keys. We walked to Scraggly's '89 Ford Escort, which he'd parked in the rear corner of an adjoining two-story parking garage.

He had hoarded clothes and small appliances in the back-seat. I hadn't been in any forests or off any unpaved paths in I couldn't remember how long, but I began to itch. I was about to tell myself to stop already, but Scraggly shoved me against the wall, unzipped my pants, and pulled down my underwear. For three literal head-bobs, I was hard inside his mouth. Until the moment he paused and, without a hint of irony, moaned: "I want you deep inside me."

With a silent laugh, I asked, "Anything I should know about you?" I expected the usual, "No, man, of course not."

"Do you mean," he stepped back, "am I clean?"

"If you want to put it like that," I said, "sure."

"I have herpes in my ass," Scraggly looked to the side, "but it ain't flared up in years. Honest. And that's it."

Zipping up, I wondered how I hadn't noticed the parking garage's great lighting. "Let me check something out." I walked forward far enough to see across the street: one block down, a police cruiser was idling in front of a strip mall. "I need to get home," I pointed out the cruiser. "And you should be careful driving back to yours."

"You're right. It's late." Scraggly dug an envelope and crayon out of his car's midden. "Can I get your number?"

I wrote it wrong by the last digit, memorized the forgery in case he asked, then walked away. After the cop began trailing Scraggly's car, I felt relieved. He'd been up front with me, and good for him, but most guys weren't. By stopping the proceedings, I'd likely saved both of us from getting arrested for public indecency.

When I cut through an apartment building's parking lot on the way to my duplex, a white woman was leaning against the mailboxes. Her crossed arms puffed up a pink feather boa jacket. Her stringy shoulder-length dishwater-blond hair was wet.

*The answer: This wears a micro-mini, fishnets, stilettos, and has a chronic U.T.I.*

*Alex, what is Big Bird in drag?*

"Hey!" she whispered in clouds of smoky frost. "Can I get a favor?"

"Depends." I clutched my keys

She pushed off the mailboxes. "Could you walk me home?" She twitched a smile, her lips shattered pottery sloppily glued back together. "I live real near here. I'd walk by myself, but my date... he kinda went off on me."

"And?"

"*And* I had to jump out the goddamn car!" She made a sweeping arc with her left hand, resting it against her forehead in a stock woe-is-me. *Sunset Boulevard* flitted across my mind. *Pick a story whose narrator isn't dead from the start.* "He was circling the block," she continued. "That's why I'm hanging out back here. My place is three blocks down and a couple over."

I stared at my keys while she kept saying, "Please." I pocketed my keys and walked her home. We hadn't gotten far before a car screeched to a stop and blocked our way, the driver throwing his door open and aiming something squat and gleaming—

—then I was squinting as fluorescent lights raced overhead.

Someone to my right drawled: "A John with a GSW in his upper right chest." The paramedic's forearms were thick and tanned. The massive hands in purple latex looked surreal. Then everything went black. Until I started hearing people arguing about me.

"We're taking him back to Missouri," said my father. "*Our son needs help getting his life in order.*"

"He's an adult, Bryan," my mother told my namesake. "He's lucky we're paying the bill."

I got angrier the longer my father kept silent. For a few groggy seconds, I considered sitting up and ripping out the IV like people do on TV, but it was all I could manage to open my eyes and keep them open, so much sleep crowding the corners.

Two commercials played before my father said, "Cecily, he's our son, and we are his home."

"*Home?* Bryan, please quit deluding yourself. How many times has he visited since he left for college?" Silence. "Exactly. He'd never move back now. We're not home to him anymore, if we ever were."

They didn't notice I was conscious until I rasped, "Neither of you are wrong."

Still wasting hot water in Ladue, I was disgusted by how much of myself I had exposed to complete strangers, yet I wouldn't shake hands with those I actually cared about.

*There's a world of filth, and the world's filthiest people think you're nothing but,* I thought. *Why not fuckin' embrace it? Quit expecting the worst to happen and sometimes it won't.*

I shut off the lukewarm shower, deciding I would give my mother another chance. Might as well add her to my systematic desensitization list. After all, doing so couldn't hurt me any worse than everything she had said a little while ago.

# CHAPTER TWENTY-SEVEN

I left the bathroom with a long towel wrapped around my waist while drying my hair with a second. I felt the trace and trickle of water beads along my chest and back. The TV in the den was blaring a basketball game, but I didn't think much of it as I went to the bedroom. The door was cracked and the light was on, neither of which I'd left that way. I draped the second towel over my shoulders and tightened the first.

As I pushed the door open, a shadow was cast on the wall by the closet light. From behind the closet's folding slat doors a kneeling Logan poked his head out and got a good look at me. "Damn," he shook his head. "Is that from a fist or a baseball bat?"

I grabbed both ends of the towel around my neck, yoking it, as if the harder I pulled, the straighter, the taller, I'd stand. "I need some privacy."

"Never could duck, could you?"

Until I saw his grin for the first time in nearly a decade, I hadn't realized that I wanted to punch out his teeth more than I wanted to bash in Adam's face.

Since I'd left for college, the bedroom's closet had become a catchall. Apparently, Logan was also looking for things to save from the dump.

"Hurry up," he stood, pointlessly brushing off his knees. "Mom's list is getting longer by the minute. And she told me to tell you the water isn't free."

Having different fathers, we resemble cousins more than brothers. What hair Logan had left was more salt than russet, but that seasoning had started before he graduated high school, an advantageous camouflage for his dry scalp. While both of us had our mother's emerald eyes, his were weighed down by thick brows and flanked by murders of crows, all of which was only accentuated by his perpetually pale skin. He was at least a head shorter than me, not that that had ever kept him from adding a few inches to his height just like he had always inflated his SAT scores.

*Smile*, I thought, *smile*, but I couldn't fake it. I pulled the towel from around my neck and put on a T-shirt.

"Mom told me it looked rough," Logan stared at my face, "but damn."

"Some guys have tattoos or piercings. Some have scars."

"It's all the same," he said, walking past and squeezing my left trap, "except you didn't choose any of yours." When he pulled the door shut, the push-lock knob made a hollow click.

A blink. The dresser mirror reflected the drum-tight flexing of my stomach and the barely noticeable but unmistakable stirring in the middle of the towel around my waist.

* * *

At this point, since I'd hadn't driven in a couple years, I was used to riding shotgun. For a long time, I couldn't stand not driving because I would get motion sickness. Logan's driving, much like his presence, was taking me back to some place I didn't want to go.

He sped the rental Audi TT down the driveway, swinging the car onto our street in a wide arc. Of course, he drove like an asshole.

"I have this year's model," Logan spoke. "It looks pretty much the same, but there's so many little differences most people would never notice." He drummed the steering wheel. "This loaner baby will suffice for a few days."

"How you manage to cope is beyond me."

"Probably the same way you do," Logan chuckled. While the store wasn't that far from the house, Logan took each turn and curve like he had an unfulfilled dream of being a Formula One racer. Along the way, he was trying to explain the intricacies of hedge funds, but all I heard was jargon like "directional" and "tail-risk" and "two and twenty."

I was trying my best not to puke all over the car's silver and black interior. There were so many circular gauges and buttons and vents, and a bright red hazard button in the center of the dashboard. I pushed my seat back, but the dashboard still crowded my knees. Being so close to Logan wasn't helping things, either. With my eyes shut, I imagined the store's aisles crammed with dutiful sons getting their mothers' last-minute groceries. The parking lot, however, was mostly empty and he had his choice of spaces. He parked in the middle of two. "I'm not trying to be a jerk," he said when I frowned, "but there's no one here, and this will keep some ass from bumping the baby."

I thought about asking—*If there's no one here, what are the chances of that happening?*—but there was no need to waste a breath.

Logan held the two-sided grocery list our mother had scrawled in his right hand. With his left, he tugged on the front of the shopping cart. "We need vinegar, chicken broth, marsh-mallows and... Can you read this?" He stuck the list in my face.

Our mother's left-slanting penmanship was cramped, erratic. I stared at the hatch marks for several moments. "It's either Crisco, or"—I grabbed the list from him, tilted it to the right—"Jell-O. But what flavor?"

"Crisco," Logan sighed. "What's she trying to do? Help you get ready for a date?" Before I could respond, he said, "Let me borrow your cell phone."

"It's dead."

"Figures." Logan patted his front and rear pockets before finding his phone. "Mine's getting there too. Hate wasting minutes." He walked off, dialing.

I pushed the cart toward the rear of the store, near the meats and cheeses. Including checkers and baggers, there were fifteen people scattered between produce and alcohol. With my left foot on the undercarriage, I kicked with my right foot, building speed. The front left wheel wobbled, so I corrected the drifting with periodic jerks to keep from sideswiping endcaps.

The few other shoppers and employees paid me little mind. I couldn't wait until I was outside, where I could get a running start and ride the cart down the drainage dip in the middle of the parking lot. Between aisles five and twelve, I scooted along. When my phone began vibrating, I hopped off the cart and came to a stop. "Liar," Logan said when I answered. "Grab a few bags of chips, some soda, and get to the checkout."

"Sure, Dad," I replied, pushing the cart to aisle fourteen. As kids, that was how we called each other "mother-fucker."

"That gets better every time you say it."

"Likewise."

In the snacks and soda aisle, I selected bags of chips at random, then snagged a couple of two-liters. I was about to begin scooting again when Curt walked into the opposite end of the aisle.

He stood lopsided, carrying a full basket with his left hand, as he consulted a list written on a torn rectangle of newspaper. He was wearing an oversized wool sweater he'd had for years—its sleeves hung to his knuckles—and olive-green fatigues that fit him well. He turned to the side. The sweater draped him so that while the middle was obscured, the pull of gravity on the heavy fabric highlighted his chest and shoulders.

He wadded the newsprint into a ball, tossed it onto a shelf, and reached for a twelve-pack of soda. When Curt noticed me, he laughed, "Yours got you out too?" His smile appeared genuine, but his eyes cut me up and down. "Thought I saw Logan. Man, what the fuck happened to him?"

"Karma, I guess."

"From the look of things, I'd say she's been putting in overtime. Why hasn't he shaved his head yet?"

"Beyond vanity? You got me." My phone vibrated. When I answered, Logan said, "Let's go already.

"Still got the same number?" Curt asked.

"I'm coming," I said to Logan, flipping my phone shut. Then I told Curt, "It's never changed."

He walked off, nodding. "Good to know."

Logan waited by an open checkout lane with several boxes of Lime Jell-O and two six-packs of beer. "Bryan asked for these," he grinned, meaning my father. "Who were you talking to?"

"Nobody." I emptied the cart onto the conveyor belt, the cashier scanning barcodes as quickly as I could unload our purchases. "Just somebody I knew for a while."

Logan sat the beer down on the conveyor belt, the bottles clinking, and stared at me like I could ever owe him an answer. "You lie so needlessly."

# CHAPTER TWENTY-EIGHT

Even though my mother had said my presence was the only gift she wanted from me, after she learned that the Meigs boys didn't have a present between us, she began cleaning house. As she vacuumed, her movements were quick and efficient. Her face was stone, her lips sealed.

The house didn't need to be cleaned any more than I needed to wash my hands as often as I did. The carpet had been shampooed recently, and the air was thick with the competing scents of lemon, pine, and bleach. As winsomely sentimental as baby pictures are to some, that miasma was my childhood. Diffused and insinuating, pressing and burning, invisible but for a slight wavering.

"Nice for once that it's not about me," my father said as he, Logan, and I threaded our way through the other desperate shoppers at the mall.

"Hey," Logan said dismissively, "she's the one who wanted everyone home. That adage about wishes, don't you think, Bryan?" Logan referred to my father by our shared first name, but I was Bry, dip-shit, bastard, or whatever epithet suited the moment. He said, "The airlines swear my luggage is intact but on its way to Juneau, along with the gifts I'd bought for you two."

"At least you had an excuse for showing up empty-handed," I said. Neither acknowledged that they'd heard me. I was lagging several feet behind them, looking from side to side at this new mall, its faux marble everything and potted plants and fountains. I was carrying two shopping bags in each hand, swinging both arms, using the weight of the gifts as momentum.

My father and Logan began debating which stores to hit up next, not that there were many left. Me, I was done shopping, one nice gift for everyone, but they were intent on outdoing each other. No prize to be had other than that. If you asked me, my father had always looked at Logan like his step-son was a sales rep, one he'd been forced to feign friendliness toward but had never fully trusted.

And if I were projecting, why were their conversations always more superficial than the worst snippets of workplace blandness? Or was Logan that way with everybody? If he asked you how you were doing and you actually told him, he would interrupt, saying, "Quit whining already. You think you have it so bad?" While you might think you were having an actual conversation, he was only waiting for the chance to explain how you were uninformed, mistaken, or naive. Listening to Logan's "punctuated monologues" with other people was interesting because I liked to guess the moment he would pounce.

This was our second pass on the lower level. We were marching down the middle of the hall. Above, the fuzzy silhouettes of shoppers on the upper level were passing in both directions, looking like the two-dimensional stage props of an elementary school play.

Logan was gesturing with his free right hand. I had no idea what they were talking about now, their voices a slightly more distinct buzz than the background noise. I was swinging the shopping bags, like an overgrown five-year-old. My front left pocket began thrumming.

"Hey," I swung the shopping bags in my left hand against the back of Logan's legs, "take these for a minute." That annoyed him, but he kept talking to my father and grabbed the two bags. The call was listed as "private." When I answered, there was a pause. "Hello?" I repeated.

"And it works," Curt replied. "Can you believe it? Us talking two days in a row?"

"My bills are current."

"And the rest?" There was nothing to say, so I said nothing. "Look up," Curt chuckled. Several stores ahead, he was leaning on the railing. We exchanged nods.

"So," I said, "you're waiting for your sister to quit trying on clothes she's ostensibly buying for your mom, you're hungry but she's asked you not to go anywhere, and you're bored and wondering how much longer this will last, and you see me?"

"Sounds good, Run-On. But it's weird, seeing you from this vantage point. It's like a third-person shoot-'em-up and I'm the sniper. What can I make you do? How's about you swing the two heavy-looking bags you're still holding into the back of Loggie's fat skull? Don't lie. You know you wanna."

"It wouldn't matter. Like my mother says, 'Whatever happened whenever is nothing right now, and it hasn't been for how many years?'"

"She can tell herself whatever she wants, but it doesn't mean she's right."

My father tapped me on the shoulder, motioning that he and Logan were going into a store that sold overpriced items like back massagers, golf ball cleaners, and automatic shoe polishers. I leaned against the wall next to the store's entrance. Logan dumped the other two bags at my feet.

"I can't see you anymore," Curt whined.

"That's what you wanted."

"You can't blame me." He sounded bored. "How many was it in the end?"

"What?"

"How many times did you cheat on me?"

"That I told you about?"

He laughed softly. "What's left to lose, Bry?"

"How much of this is about loose threads?"

"They're none but yours," he said, "and you did the unraveling."

"I may be a terrible Catholic, but I'm still better than you when it comes to owning my bullshit, and that's where we differ."

"I'm not sure why you think I'm competing with you," he chuckled, "especially when it comes to that, but when was the last time you went to mass?" I stayed silent because I couldn't remember. Curt said, "That's what I thought. Contrition's your true drug of choice, Bry. Sure, you feel great in the moment, but nothing will ever feel as good as the first time you felt lower than the muck that even hogs won't roll in. Let's be honest, what problems have your little confessions ever solved?"

"At least I admitted my trespasses."

"And where has that gotten you?"

I couldn't explain why, but I almost told Curt how he'd only begun choking me as hard as I wanted *after* telling him what Logan had done to me. I bit my tongue because if I did, he'd never talk to me again. "We are nothing alike, no matter how much you're trying to make us," he might say before hanging up on me forever. And then there was me—stupid, stupid me who kept clinging to any chance of keeping Curt in my life some way or another.

"You still there?" he asked.

"Yeah."

"I was saying your confessions aren't about penance or reconciliation or whatever the Vatican's marketing it as these days. No, Bry, all ironical, you like feeling dirty, and what's the best way to feel *absolutely* filthy except to tell somebody your lowliest trespasses so they'll condemn you?"

He had me there, but I changed the subject. "Thought you were going to grad school for philosophy, not theology."

"I had to take a seminar on Aquinas. Then I saw you and figured I'd put that bullshit to use."

"Whatever you're driving at, Curt, get there already."

"Tomorrow night," he said, "I'm going out with an old friend. Clubs should be packed, and we'll all be needing a break. When are you flying back?"

"Friday, mid-morning. I have to work that night."

"Perfect. We'll have you back home by six, at the latest."

"Why are you doing this?"

"We're out of our zip code and it won't be just you and me, so quit jumping to conclusions. I haven't forgiven you, but that doesn't mean we can't have some fun."

"But why?"

"Maybe I feel bad for what I did to your face despite you breaking into my place. Maybe this is as much of an olive branch as I can manage. And maybe, just maybe, for once in your life, you shouldn't be asking me so many goddamn questions."

When my father and half-brother exited the store, I said, "I have to go."

"Tomorrow night, we'll pick you up around ten. Be ready."

# CHAPTER TWENTY-NINE

To the joy of no one but my mother, our family's Christmas began promptly at eight a.m. My father seemed resigned to it. But for once, Logan and I were on the same page, both of us wishing we could have slept in a little while longer.

Still, the danishes and coffee were plentiful, and our mother looked genuinely happy. When it came to her selective denial, I realized it wasn't about me. It was about who she thought she was, about the mother she had believed herself to be. That morning, I wouldn't bring up anything to challenge her self-image, letting that be an unspoken gift she might never recognize.

"Open this, Bry," she said, handing me a present. Her wrapping was immaculate. "I hope you like it."

"Thanks, Mom." I handed her my present. "And here's yours." My wrapping would never not be sloppy. The corners of her lips momentarily sagged downward. "You didn't have to, Bry!"

In the background, Logan and my father swapped presents

they'd probably picked for themselves in that gadget store. Then Logan topped off his wine glass. He was on his second super-sized Mimosa. My father frowned at that, but he shook his head and opened his present.

My mother slowly peeled apart my "tapemanship." I ripped through hers. In the department store box, whose top and bottom were taped together, were an envelope and a Bible —King James, of course. Inside the envelope, also taped shut, was a card. It was unsigned and the readymade cursive script proclaimed, "In this time of joy & praise, in this season of peace & grace, there's no better chance than now, to say all you must, but do so in love." The sentiment was too millennial for my tastes, but I was sure that was neither what its author nor my mother had intended. Inside the card was a $300 gift certificate to Oak Court. I guess my eyes widened, because my mother said, "That's the fancy mall close to the university, isn't it?"

"It is."

"I don't know your taste in clothes these days, so I hope you can find yourself a few nice outfits." My gift for her was a Coach purse. Her mouth fell open when she opened the box. "Bry, you can't afford this. Can you?"

"I've been saving up for years. But if you already have that one, I have the receipt."

"No," she shook her head. "This is from the latest season, isn't it?"

"Of course it is, Mom. Bry knows these kinds of things," Logan said. "He's always been special like that."

"Not always," she said. "That gets me thinking, whatever happened—"

"He used to be a *real* shit." Logan interrupted her, then laughed.

"Language," my father said. "And slow yourself down."

"Sorry," Logan said. "Figured since we're all adults, no

harm, no foul. But let's be honest, he was. There's no denying that."

"Dad, it's funny," I said, "because he's talking about me like I'm not here, and because," I thought about Curt, "he's being *ironical*. Or, that's what I'm going to assume. Benefit of the doubt."

"What I was trying to say is," my mother glared at Logan, then winked at me and asked, "whatever happened to whatshername? That girl you dated your first year in college."

"Her name was Janet—"

"*Damn it!*"

"Logan!"

"Come on, Mom, it's a reference to—"

"That didn't even last a full semester," I cut in. "Think she's married now and has a couple of kids by the guy she cheated on me with, so I guess he was worth it."

"From what you told me back then," my mother switched gears, "I never did like her. Who wants some brownies?" She left for the kitchen.

My father patted my shoulder as he followed her. Before he started up the stairs, he stared at Logan. "Hit the brakes."

Logan pressed his lips together. When our parents were out of earshot, he chuckled, "Please tell me you two actually fucked."

"Yes, and why are you interested in my sex life?"

"How was she?"

"Not great, but not the worst."

"Let me get this straight."

"Please endeavor."

"So, you've had pussy, but you'd rather resort to ass?"

"Apparently, nowadays, most straight guys do too. In any case, it worked for you for long enough, didn't it?"

"What the fuck are you talking about?"

"You know," I said, "I think I'm in the mood for a brownie."

"That always was your favorite color."

"I bet if we argued about taking a dick up the ass," I laughed, "you'd try to tell me—as a straight man who *isn't* into getting pegged—what's what."

"Why does everything come back to sex with you?"

It was weird, being sober around someone so buzzed. So much to say and no chance of tangling the thread before I said everything. "Yessiree, that's me. The filthier the sex, the better it is. If you—now, I'm using the 'generic you,' so don't get any ideas—but if *you*, as a random trick, show up to my place without a can of Crisco, I'll slam the door in your face. If you do, though, it's all good because I have rubber sheets. And after you leave, I'll finger-paint with whatever you work out of me. Let's hope I'd eaten corn, you know, for the texture."

"You're disgusting," Logan sipped his mimosa and stared at the ceiling.

"Since we're on the topic of cognitive dissonance," I continued, "is there any chance you and your fiancée will get back together? If so, I should start saving up for that gift. Ever heard the saying, 'the more expensive the wedding, the quicker the divorce'? I have a corollary to it: the grander the spectacle, the worse the relationship."

Logan chuckled into his wine glass. After he resurfaced, he sat his drink on the coffee table, and said, "There's not a chance in hell of that happening. When my ex cheated on me, I dumped her worthless ass."

"Sounds like she made the choice for both of you."

"Fuck you." He shook his head, looking at the Christmas tree across the room. It sparkled and flashed.

"No, Logan, never again."

He clenched his fist and I hopped off the couch as he threw

a punch that missed. He returned to an upright position with his head lowered, but his eyes were trained on me.

"Throw another punch and see what happens." He said nothing. I continued: "I have no patience for your bullshit, Logan, because you won't admit what you did."

"For fuck's sake, there's goddamn nothing I need to—"

"Keep lying to Mom all you want. She'll believe you. And my father? No worries there. He'll change the subject and forget whatever you said before his segue. While you can tell yourself that your fiancée 'made her choice' and you made yours, she probably sensed there's something off about you. Everybody always has. That's why so many keep you at arm's length."

A teakettle started crying in the kitchen.

"It'd be better if we don't talk to each other unless the folks are around," I said. "It'd be best if we didn't talk at all."

"Same, faggot."

"That's good, Logan. Honesty is good."

Then I went to the kitchen, got a couple brownies, a glass of soda, and headed back to my bedroom, where I locked the door. If he wanted to continue this "conversation," he'd have to break the door down. Sure, my parents could keep ignoring the truth, but the door would be busted, and how would they explain that away?

As I scarfed down the brownies, my mother's question made me think about Janet, my first and last real girlfriend and the person with whom I squandered my virginity. She was a year older, in a sorority, five-foot-three, and a decided non-tanner. The only color to her face was a bright band of freckles across the bridge of her nose and cheeks. I was always self-conscious around Janet, unsure if I was fooling anyone, worrying the worn-down blue of her eyes saw more about me, and more clearly, than most did.

Take the night we'd dry-humped in my dorm room, how her eyes had narrowed when I'd asked her to lick my nipples, a narrowing that never lessened until our last night together, when those shut altogether. Our relationship, for lack of a better word, was summed up in that moment.

Until that night in mid-December, I had apparently been too insistent about having sex, while she'd been seeking a more meaningful relationship. The first time she'd allowed my cock to be in the vicinity of her pussy was a month earlier, when I spent a night at her off-campus townhouse. After giving me a weak hand job, she'd dragged my cock over her clit, down between her lips, parking me in line for a straight shot. I clumsily thumped at her clit while slowly pushing myself inside. Janet moaned twice, made a face, said, "No. Stop."

I'd pulled out, thinking, *Won't be long now.* Surprisingly, when I grabbed my cock, there was some gelatinous substance stuck to the head. I flicked off whatever that was and kept stroking.

Back then, my OCD was more like a mosquito buzzing, coming and going, and had little to do with sex. I'd never been a fan of handshakes or doorknobs, but a glob of hand sanitizer would calm my mind in most cases. The worst it got was right after I'd jerked off to gay porn, which usually involved me shoplifting a *Playgirl* from the Bookstar on Poplar or, when I was the most desperate, renting a video from an adult bookstore on Getwell Road.

A week after Thanksgiving, Janet picked me up at my dorm and drove around campus, finally pulling into the parking lot across from the law school. There, with the engine idling and without being prompted, she said, "We need to talk."

"I already figured that out."

"It's bad, Bryan."

"Go ahead and say it."

"God, it's awful."

"It's better to dive into the cold pool," I stared out of my window.

"When I went home last week, my friends took me to a party. And of all the people I didn't want to run into, my high school boyfriend showed up. I ignored him and asked my best friend, 'Did you know he was going to be here?' She pleaded the fifth. Later on, she said, 'Janet, he's changed.' I told her to fuck off and found the punch bowl. Besides going to the party, that was my worst mistake. I've been to enough frat parties, so I knew I should've never drunk the punch. But I did. I was mad."

"At your friends, right?"

"I guess... I wanted to scream. I felt out of place and since I hadn't driven there, I kept getting refills. If I got too sloppy, my friends would take me home, right?"

"And?"

"*And* eventually everything felt like a tilt-a-whirl at the county fair. Then I felt hands on my shoulders and heard someone saying, 'I think this party's over,' not so much to me, as I was walked away from the lights and noise, into a dark room. When I heard the door shut and lock, I think I asked where my friends were, but he laughed, 'You don't have any friends.' I started to cry, 'That's not true,' and he said, 'You hate those bitches,' which made me laugh, and when he asked if I wanted to leave, I laughed again and shook my head."

Janet looked at me, but I said nothing.

"The rest is a blur. He fucked me. I didn't want to, but he was the love of my life for four years, and he'd cheated on me so many times. I think he raped me, but I don't think it was *rape-rape*."

"What the fuck?" I said. The car's heater hummed. I shifted in the passenger seat, trying to hide my semi.

"I told him to stop, I did, but he kept saying I wouldn't have gone to the party if I didn't want him. I was so drunk and nervous I couldn't stop laughing. That's the worst part. The piece of shit probably thinks he was right." She shook her head. After a minute, she asked, "Can you forgive me?"

When I said, "I need to think," she started crying. I remember feeling glad she wasn't as frigid as she'd acted with me, and I figured her guilt might be my chance. Fuck it, right? She had cheated on me after all, so why not treat sex like a mercenary transaction?

Janet was wearing a sweater and a long, billowy skirt that was slit up to the knee, the fabric too thin for this weather. Her attire was like our relationship: nothing but mixed signals. I kissed and hugged her, and then lay my head on her lap, facing the steering column, nuzzling against her warm thighs. She ran her nails through my hair, tickling my scalp. She began scratching from my widow's peak down to the base of my neck and around the knob of bone behind my right ear.

"God," I grunted, "let me eat you out."

Her hand left my head. I heard her tap a fingernail against her teeth. She said, "Bad timing." I continued rooting until Janet pushed my face out of her lap, and said, "*Stop*. Trust me. Right now's not any good."

And even after all that, we wouldn't fuck until mid-December, on the night of her sorority's formal. To be precise, as she had corrected me once, she was in a "female fraternity." I knew little about the university's Greek system other than a joke some drunk frat guy told me while we were ordering drinks at the formal's cash bar: "What goes down quicker than an anchor?"

"You got me," I said. "It's obviously not the ship."

He laughed, "Yeah, relationships can sink pretty damn fast, but only a Dee Gee goes down quicker," and I laughed along with him, even though Janet had never given and would never give me a blowjob. He punched my shoulder, "I like that: 'the ship,'" and walked off.

Speaking of "ships," a few hours later, Janet and I were both high and tanked on Champagne, and she was ready. I was ecstatic. *This is it,* I kept thinking as we stumbled out of our formal wear and crashed onto the hotel bed. I wanted to feel myself slide inside someone, to cause reactions which were entirely alien to me. Was I truly attracted to her? No. Was she attractive? Yes, but she was more like a goal I hadn't scored yet because the posts kept shifting.

By fifteen minutes in, I knew I'd never put any points on the board. Janet—a tired, disappointed spectator tapping a zealous fan on the shoulder, hoping the asshole would finally quit screaming since the game had been called—politely asked me to stop, rolled onto her side, and passed out. Most likely it was the alcohol, but I chalked it up to her suspecting who I truly was.

With my mouth open but silent, I had sat back on my knees, squeezed my eyes shut, and ran a hand through my hair. When she began softly snoring, I pulled the covers over her and locked myself in the bathroom. Everything except for the faucet fixtures and mirror was white. I stared at my reflection: my eyes were floored wide, the corners of my lips were drawn low, and my jaws were gritting. Lowering my gaze, my chest was rising and falling from quick, shallow breaths. My cock was glistened slick and deflating. It felt as useful as my appendix.

Rushing down the hallway on our floor, I could hear a drunken clamor. I felt angry and jealous of being denied yet again. I closed my eyes, grabbed myself, and concentrated on the deep, bourboned-drawls of frat guys, not any particular voice, just the timbre. Soon, in relief and shame, I came into the sink. Then I hopped in the shower and cleaned up for ten minutes, like I somehow knew a week later I'd be pissing fire.

After we had checked out of the hotel the following morning, I began the drive from the downtown hotel to Janet's place near St. Francis Hospital, which was not a quick trip. I had hoped Janet was simply hung over, but it was only then that I felt the distance I should have noticed all along had I not been so focused on the prospect of fucking a woman. Like that could have ever erased my past.

While I was merging from Union to Poplar, Janet asked, "Can we get some fast food?"

"No problem." I made a right into the Wendy's across the street from Fugue, though I didn't know about the club back then.

"I'm starving," she said, staring out her window. She wanted a combo meal, and, "You mind?"

"No problem," I muttered, ordering a soda for myself. My wallet would be empty after paying for lunch, my sole credit card almost maxed, and it was over a week until payday. I felt queasy. I pulled up to the window and paid for the food.

Then, as though she hadn't liked an entree I'd suggested at dinner the night before, she said: "I don't think we should see each other anymore."

The cashier plinked the change into my hand as I stared at Janet, who adjusted her seat belt.

"Here's you go," said the cashier, handing over the food and two mammoth yellow cups. "Y'all want some ketchup with all that?"

Janet leaned forward in her seat and told the woman, "Do you mind?"

I caught a whiff of her perfume from the formal, noticing for the first time how rank it smelled. For whatever reason, the scent reminded me of unsweetened iced tea: the taste just wrong, a lacking that draws that much more attention to its absence. I smiled, letting my car roll up to the exit, and patted Janet's knee.

"Wait, I need ketchup!" She sat back against her window, the skin beneath her chin wrinkled, a defensive expression wrenching her face.

"I'm sure you have some at home."

"But they'll be cold by then, and there's nothing worse than soggy fries."

I idled at the exit for longer than I needed to and looked at her, the turn signal clicking, the eastbound lanes clear. Finally, I snagged a few fries, saying, "Oh, I could think of a few things that are much, much worse."

At a quarter-past-eight, as I was walking upstairs to get another glass of water, my cell phone rang. "Hello," Curt said, "This is a friendly reminder to make yourself presentable. Be there in an hour or so."

"I'll be ready."

After I hung up, my mother asked, "Who was that?"

"Curt."

"*Curt*-Curt?"

"Yes."

"And what are you getting ready for?"

"I'm going to hang out with some friends."

"The first time you've visited *at all* in eight years, and you're going out with friends to get drunk?"

"At the least."

"Well then," she said, "you have yourself a nice time."

I headed downstairs and prepped. Then adjusting for gay-time, I waited until 9:40 before I went back upstairs.

Five steps from the top, I heard Logan: "Mom, this is what

he does. He always makes everything about himself. He has to be the depressed little center of attention or he's not happy, however the hell he defines *happiness*." She must have made a face, because he quickly added, "Let me put it this way, has he paid you back for the hospital bill? What about the airfare you popped for? Has he ever even said thanks? No, because in his warped little mind, he deserves all of that and more."

"I'm not sure what I was expecting," my mother sighed, "but you're right. Always have been. He's as moody as he ever was and won't talk that much, but when he does..." She sighed.

"What is it?"

"He blames you for—"

A glass was sat on the table roughly.

"The little faggot—"

"*Logan!*"

After a moment, he said calmly, "I've earned the right to call him what he is. You ask me, that little *faggot* was attracted to me, so he made up that convoluted story to keep himself from feeling guilty. I do not care, because it did *not* happen. And if he won't stop dredging up that lie, I'm done with him, Mom, and you should be too."

I padded back down to the bedroom, and as I took a last glance in the mirror, Curt texted: "We r trning on2 ur str3t."

I replied, "I'll be waiting with those missing letters," and by the time I had stomped back up the stairs, the kitchen was empty.

# CHAPTER THIRTY

Like almost all of my nights out, this one began the day before. It was now the morning after Christmas, the miracle spent, pushing four a.m., and I was naked except for the towel wrapped around my waist and the cheap flip-flops I'd purchased at the bathhouse's front desk. That you could rent a towel but not flip-flops felt like one of my OCD's Byzantine rules.

It was funny how I could be comfortable in a place I would never have imagined stepping foot in, much less with my toes millimeters from the floor. Each flap of my flip-flops was wet and brought the smell of bleach, which made me both thankful and disgusted.

While Curt had reserved himself a private room, I'd opted for a locker, not that he'd offered me an invitation to share his temporary digs. After the last several hours, I expected nothing from him except getting abandoned like his street clothes.

The towel was neither stained nor comfortable. I focused on that to keep myself from itching. The first time I went to the arcade of an adult bookstore, my heart galloped and my body shook from fear and excitement. In the bathhouse, I heard my heartbeat in my ears and didn't have to check my pulse to feel it in my neck. My cock was half-hard, straining against the towel.

All around me were surfaces I would never touch. The inanimate ones were easy to ignore, but the men cruising by me were another matter. A part of me wanted to take Curt's cue. If there was a more perfect place to live out the cliche *When in Rome* than while visiting a bathhouse in a city you haven't lived in for years, I didn't know what that was. Like Stefano had said, all of those months ago, "actors gotta commit." Really, what did I have to lose at this point? I'd guess Curt's goal was to make me admit that my OCD was sometimes selective, to let go and fuck a random stranger with a mostly sober intent. No relationship was at stake, and no names were needed. There would be nothing to regret except the chances I didn't take for however long we stayed here.

* * *

At the first of two downtown clubs, Curt and his friend had bought each other a few drinks, alternating between people-watching and dancing. The guy's name was Kyle, I think. He was taller than me and on the chubby side, but he seemed a little frantic, his hands twitching, feet tapping. I stayed near them, but when I tried to join in with their gossip, they ignored me. The clubs were noisy as fuck, sure, but they weren't so loud you couldn't have a conversation.

Once, at the second club, we were leaning on the railing of an area a few feet above the dance floor. While Curt was slowly scanning the crowd, Kyle had pointed to a spot vaguely ahead of me, and said, "She is shameful."

"One must respect oneself more than that," Curt said before taking a sip.

Yes, they were talking about me and whoever else was in their line of sight. I'd never been a huge fan of gay clubs, but after my months-long systematic desensitization searching for Adam, I was about done. The same conversations, the same manipulations, the same resignations. None of those went anywhere, but I found myself there time after time, because I like nothing more than disappointing myself.

Kyle excused himself to go piss or snort a line, or both.

A few moments later, Curt held his cocktail out. I clicked my beer against his glass. "Are you having fun?" he asked.

"You're speaking to me now?"

"Until Kyle gets back. I'm not a complete asshole."

"Well..."

"Want to be even-Steven?" I nodded. "Good. When we're done here, you're tagging along to our last stop of the evening. It's so far out of your comfort zone, you're going to hate it."

"Where are we going?"

"It's a surprise."

"Fine," I took a swig, calculating how many more beers I'd need to drink to get through whatever he had planned. "I'm in."

"If you're lucky, yeah. But if you back out, you'll need to get your own ass home and I'll never talk to you again. And the next time you try to start up a convo, because we both know you can't help yourself, I won't pull any of my punches."

After Kyle returned empty-handed, I asked, "You guys need anything?" He said they were fine. So I walked to where the crowd was densest on the dance floor, hiding within the swirl of skin grazing skin and generic drumbeats. Souls desperate for attention had a number of raised platforms to choose from, every perch filled with writhing, half-naked men lost in the throes of how sexy their go-go-routines must have appeared to us insecure groundlings. I danced and stared at the mirror ball's twirling reflections.

For an hour, I ignored the elbows and arms brushing against mine until Curt found me. He gripped my throat from behind, grinding against my ass and cupping my ear. "We're leaving. If you're ready to be even-Steven, now's the time to pay up."

\* \* \*

From the parking lot, the lesser of St. Louis's bathhouses appeared to be a split-level, ranch-style home. Where I was walking now, though, more closely resembled a mixture of a warehouse, tanning salon, and quarter-booth labyrinth. The bathhouse had showers, a steam room and sauna, Jacuzzis, a small gym, a TV room, and (closed for the season) a pool and deck.

The ceiling was high, naked, and the walls of each private room didn't reach the ceiling. The space was well lit, the floors cleaner than I'd assumed they would be. When I smelled the barest trace of bleach, I felt both vaguely reassured and repulsed.

Once properly undressed, I kept my distance from Curt, who was cruising. Ostensibly so was I. Like the clubs, the bathhouse was crowded with a mix of attractive, average, and ugly men. Whether real or another kind of drag, wedding bands were more plentiful than I'd expected. I fell into the slow lane of traffic, keeping Curt in sight, tailing him like an amateur detective. I was sure I was as obvious as it is on TV.

As soon as I'd checked in, I reminded myself: *There's a world of filth.* Men brushed against me. A few attempted to grope me, but the rest were, well, polite. No, that was me being too gracious. Not everyone liked the scar or the shiner. There was rough trade and then there was trade that had been too roughed up.

So, damaged goods I was. Most men gave me a wide berth, disappearing into private rooms, sometimes closing their doors, sometimes not. A married man gripped the hips of the guy bent in front of him, his golden band shining as he fucked the bottom like he hated the guy more than he hated himself. So many fingers tumbling down tight stomachs, under towels. Three men huddled around a fourth who knelt, his appetite whetted, mouth opened wide. Over there, an even luckier man was getting railed from behind while sucking another man's cock.

Picture life as fast-forwarding through the preview trailers of a VHS porno. I watched whoever wanted or allowed me to. A few guys gave me weird looks when I draped my towel over my shoulders instead of letting it drop to the floor. *When in Rome* only took me so far, because no matter where I went, there I was.

I edged through a few different scenes, and when I finally shot a few ropes, my head swam like I had just been choked or taken a huge hit of poppers. Blinking, the lights were too bright. I wrapped the towel back around my waist and resumed cruising. Based on pornos I'd seen, I always imagined there would be more steam: the distance obscured in a fog, men appearing and disappearing, torsos and arms floating disconnected from lower legs until you were so near that the towels no longer blended into the steam. But here, you could see what you were doing or what was being done to you, so you couldn't lie to yourself. Or if you could, I knew the psychiatric diagnosis for you.

Then I saw Curt leading someone back to his private room. He looked at me, arching his right eyebrow and nodding. I'd seen that look so many times during our relationship whenever he wanted me to take charge. His trick was olive-skinned and furry-chested, the bulge in his towel substantial. He was hot

and sweating, grinning like he'd won the best prize at the
county fair, his eyes zeroed-in on Curt's ass. Mine were too. I
followed them, not surprised when Curt left the door cracked
wide enough for someone to watch and winked at me one final
time.

I crept up, keeping the slap of my flip-flops to a minimum.
Beneath the sloppy, moist sounds, I heard Curt's deep moans.
The door halved my face, which Curt would have seen if he'd
ever bothered glancing back. But he was lying face down on the
bed—his left leg drawn up, his ass raised—while the man who
knelt behind him was gripping, spreading, and licking. Here an
open door was an invitation, right? Did Curt want me to join
them? I reached out my hand to push open the door, until I
remembered what I'd forgotten.


My open hand hesitates an inch before the doorknob to Curt's
apartment, the Venetian blinds half-dialed at a decline. He's
been renting a small studio apartment on one side of a detached
garage. He's lying on a mattress, bathed in the light from his
TV. He has fallen asleep naked on his stomach, his head facing
to the left. His right leg is straight and his left knee is bent,
those toes making a figure-four with the opposite knee. The
crevice of his ass and spine, an unbroken line.

Shadows flicker across his muscular frame, and the doorknob's right there, and from the sliver of TV that's visible you
can tell he's been watching a porno, like he passed out shortly
after coming, the unmistakable flash and hammering of tanned
skin. Men and women? That wouldn't surprise you. Men and
men? You can't tell and you don't care.

Your left hand reaches, grasps the doorknob silently, and
turns it slowly. It's unlocked. A part of your mind asks: *What
exactly are you going to do?* And though you cannot begin to

answer this question, you keep turning the knob, inching the door open, a creaking of wood, the hesitancy of hinges, the thought of how you'd feel if someone did this to you never crossing your mind, until...

I shook my head and withdrew my hand. This place was an Iron Maiden in the good old Inquisition style. So many unavoidable triggers piercing me from every angle and inescapable. Still, this wasn't about revenge, I didn't think. It felt more like Curt was trying to get me to strip away my OCD, however briefly, with only this scratchy towel to remind me of my limits, as arbitrary as they were.

Sure, I could step into that room and Curt might not kick me out, but beyond admitting he'd always been right, what else would I have to surrender? I didn't know the particulars, but I knew they would coalesce into the lens through which Curt would forever see me. Only then did I realize I hadn't been breathing, my pulse growing as desperate as I didn't want to make myself. *Not ever again.* So I used the bottom of my towel as a make-shift glove to softly pull the door shut.

Done pretending, I washed my hands, got dressed, and went to the TV room, where I'd wait for almost two hours, the upholstered furniture making me think about Fugue's lounge. I began itching everywhere. But when I checked and rechecked, fingering through my pubic hair, there was nothing. Though I wasn't exactly sure why, I almost felt disappointed.

On the drive home, to be on the safe side, I made Curt stop at an all-night drug store under the pretense of thirst. I bought three sodas, a RID kit, and a pack of disposable razors. I handed Curt and his friend a soda, then opened mine and chugged it.

Curt's friend laughed, "Some aftertaste, huh?"

"Like you wouldn't believe." I stared out the window. The

farther we got from the bathhouse, the more I could feel my anxiety building, and the less I wanted to be anywhere around Curt or in these clothes.

* * *

I got a trash bag from under the kitchen sink, stripped right there, laying my wallet, phone, and keys on the countertop and bagging up the rest.

Downstairs, the TV in the den was off. I'd worried Logan would be sleeping on the couch. Still, I locked the bathroom door. I lathered up with the lice-killing shampoo and waited, then showered and repeated, washing myself several times with regular soap and shaving front and back from belly button to knee.

Like Curt and I had actually kissed and my tongue weren't dulled by so much beer and soda, I could taste him on my lips, my tongue, the back of my throat. Like we'd actually touched this morning, last night, whenever, and I hadn't washed myself as many times as I had, I could smell him all over me. I had never felt simultaneously so wearied and wired.

As Curt was leading that trick to his room, he'd winked at me. Translation: *Just how desperate are we nowadays, Bry?* I hoped he had heard the click of the door and the slap of my flip-flops walking away as the equivalent of me shrugging: *You only wish you knew the answer to that question, and what will you think when you realize it will never again include you?*

Once I was dressed, I packed. As much as I had loved them, the toys and comics could go wherever my mother felt fit. Each was a costly reminder of how much I had tried to escape from Logan and how often I had failed. Wasted capital? Apparently, my mother had never paid attention to the wet beds. And then there was my "blinky." With it in hand, I grabbed my other bag of trash, tossed the latter into the roll-out, and took the blanket to the gas grill on the back deck.

The stars and moon were gone.

From what I could tell, the grill hadn't been cleaned since the Carter administration. I stretched the rag across the warming rack and sprayed it with lighter fluid. The Bic was flimsy at first, but it lit eventually. I held the flame to the blanket's center, then to each of its corners. Watched those curl and shrivel and crackle. A hole formed in the center, where new red edges raced outward, meeting those sprinting inward.

Back inside, I got three hundred bucks out of my wallet, found a palm-sized note pad near the telephone in the kitchen, and sat at the table.

Mom,

By the time you read this, I'll be at the airport. This will seem rude, I'm sure, but hopefully it will make things less awkward.

Last night, I eavesdropped on you and Logan. It's funny, hearing people who are supposed to love me tearing me apart because the true story I've told for a decade now has *never* changed. The simplest truth must be that I am the liar, right? It's late, so the simple truths that follow may be a little jumbled. All I ask is that you bear with me, this one last time.

Once, I loved getting lost in forests. Knowing the risks, I'd still love to hike deer paths no hunter has ever found, letting weeds and leaves and branches brush against me. Remember the morning after I caught poison ivy the first time? I wish I'd never learned how unwelcome urushiol will make itself after it secures the tiniest foothold.

Since that is impossible, I'd love to shake somebody's hand and lose myself in a conversation instead of worrying about the last thing they touched and questioning how on this good green earth they could ever think the soles of their shoes weren't absolutely filthy.

Sometimes, I fantasize about licking barbecue sauce off my fingers and not caring about door knobs or salt and pepper shakers or the pens the server leaves with the check, bothered as little about picking up things off the floor as you are about tipping well.

Do you remember when I was sixteen, right before I told you what Logan had done to me, and you asked why I was always depressed? I had said something like this: "I hate myself, Mom, all the time. I have these thoughts that will not stop. By washing my hands, I can quiet them to a whisper, for a little while." You said it couldn't be that bad. And, yes, I did try following your golden boy's advice: "Quit worrying about shit you can't control." But I could never be as oblivious as him.

Likewise, I will never understand why you took Logan at his word and not me at mine. How did he earn your unfailing trust? And if I ever had it, how did I lose it?

Here's some random trivia: Do you know that pyrite—a.k.a. fool's gold—can only form in oxygen-free environments?

Like the rest of whatever life I have left, I'm not sure where all of this is headed, but I'll wind things up. As tired as I am of seeing doubt slice your eyes, here's the precious little I'd settle for, which I'm sure you'd never guess in a million years. I'd love to make friends with random dogs, letting them smell and lick my outstretched hand, scratching them behind their ears, then picking up a knobby stick and throwing it, never giving their slobber a second thought as I endlessly toss that stick and never stop smiling.

I don't have a clever segue from that, so despite everything, Mom, I love you. I can't not. But I also can't forget whose side you took and how you weren't there for me when I needed you the most. And yet, I love you. And I always will. If you don't believe that after all of this, I hope you will one day. Because I wasn't lying then, and I'm not lying now.

When you read this, remember why I haven't visited since leaving for college. Until you can admit that *why*, it's better for me to stay gone.

~ Bryan

P.S.: The cash beneath this letter is paying you back for my flight. Whether you ever believe this or not, just like you couldn't believe the gift I bought you, I was already going to do that even before I overheard every goddamn thing Logan said about me.

I ripped off the sheet of paper, wrapping it around the cash, and wrote my mother's name on it. Seeing the keys to Logan's rental, I decided to get to the airport terribly early. I drove the speed limit, occasionally taking my hands off the wheel to test the car's alignment. Each time, it would drift gently to the left. I kept thinking about the shopping cart's wobbly wheel.

After I'd parked, I got the tire iron from the trunk and slightly loosened the lug nuts on the front driver's side tire. With that finished, I almost slung the tire iron back into the trunk, but I hadn't worn gloves, so I kept it out, grabbed my carry-on, and slung the keys under the passenger seat.

I pocketed the parking receipt and dialed Logan's number. It went straight to voice mail. "Hey, I needed to get back to Memphis early, so I borrowed your rental. I would have woken you up, but I don't think about anybody but myself. Need to work on that, so I'll add it to my list of New Year's resolutions, which is already as long as the OED. So much needs a-changing. Look at me go. Me, me, me. Don't worry, your 'baby' is fine. I parked it in the Terminal One garage. The keys are riding shotgun—well, beneath it." After I hung up, I dropped the tire iron behind a trash can, wiping that hand on my jeans as the automatic doors whooshed open.

The one good thing about heightened airport security was Logan couldn't confront me at the gate without buying a ticket. Maybe he would find his rental and use this as yet more proof of how selfish a piece of shit I was.

When he drove his "baby" back to my father's home, how long would it be until that rental's wheel sought its own path? How far would it stray? The car might not even make it back onto the interstate, with Logan becoming the asshole slowing down all the recent arrivals ready to get as far away from the airport as possible. Or maybe he'd wind up in a ditch or stranded on a median. Or maybe nothing would happen until a few days after he returned the rental, when he'd receive a telephone call from the location's furious manager, demanding an explanation and threatening to sue him.

Because I was never going to see Logan again, I decided to quit wasting any more time thinking about him.

# PART V

*Apophenia:* some say human beings are natural storytellers because that's how we collapse reality into comprehensible threads. But all that does is deny the world's chaos, compounding what we seek to control by imposing patterns onto the wind.

See also: agency, narrative arcs, and fate.

*Rationally, yes, most of the threads I notice and the connections I make bear the same relation to reality as my obsessions do to actual threats. But there I am, and there I'll be, hoping for the opposite while seeing what I dread everywhere I look.*

— 26 DECEMBER 2003

# CHAPTER THIRTY-ONE

As the plane neared Memphis, my thoughts would not stop ricocheting off one another. Even if I ever wanted to go back home again, after stealing Logan's rental and leaving without saying goodbye to the folks, they wouldn't have me. Maybe they hadn't woken up by the time of my flight, or maybe they'd already written me off and that was why nobody had called my cell phone.

I'd said everything I needed to tell my mother in the letter. And I was so tired of worrying about whether or not she believed me and whether or not Logan would ever come clean. She wouldn't. He wouldn't. The way of the world was as it should be. They both had their own North Star, guiding them to a truth they had decided was *the* truth because it led them where they had always wanted to arrive. I was no different, walking with my head on backward, so focused on the past I was always stumbling over shit I could have easily dodged.

The plane would be making its final approach soon and so would I, to a life I no longer wanted to live, to remain the person Curt and Chris and Stefano thought I was. They'd probably never be able to see me as anyone but the joke I'd made of myself and the one they had made out of me, but I was done with all of that now. I was going to move on. At the very least, I would move out from Chris's place, cutting him and Stefano off for a while. I had heard people say, "fake it till you make it," but couldn't you also fake it till you forgot it? Had I never learned my family's most important lesson?

To distract myself, I opened up the alt-zine and decided to finish "Bluff City Plagues."

## Coda: How Many More Hopeless Cases?

Selynn (not her real name) sat propped up by several pillows, her elbows too large in comparison with the rest of her arms, over which her ashen skin was stretched too tight.

Her case manager, Gillian, said Selynn had been a hard-working single mother of two children, holding down three jobs.

"I often wonder," Gillian said, "how much the stress she was under worsened her health. She hated asking for help. I had to reach out to her more often than other clients because by the time Selynn would ask for assistance, things had usually gotten pretty bad."

I paused reading because I thought I knew who Selynn was. If I was right, she had been on my case load at MFLAG. She'd been in good health back then, with a consistently high T-cell count. She smiled all the time, but I wonder if she did that so people wouldn't worry about her. If I was correct in recognizing a former client from this description, whoever this particular

Gillian was, she was right about Selynn's hesitation to admit she needed help.

Many might call that pride, but I saw a fear of being powerless in certain situations like getting laid off from one of her jobs and not making rent the next month. Which must have reminded her of how little power she had over her health and how quickly opportunistic infections could take root.

Selynn coughed up a glob of tarry and yellow phlegm into a wad of tissue. Then, in a staccato voice, she said, "Always loved me some oranges."

Her case manager started Selynn's snack because her client's hands shook too much, a sticky atmosphere coalescing as Gillian peeled back the rind. Gillian recalled seeing individual bubbles of citrus spray, floating until bursting, shorn by a draft of breath, their remnants reminiscent of an unrolled condom or a halo. ("I know how that sounds, but...")

Selynn crossed her forearms in her lap and let Gillian feed her slices. Gillian knew that Selynn knew she was going to die, perhaps not in this hospital but painfully and soon. That was why Selynn had asked to borrow Gillian's Bible when she called the day before, pleading with her not to forget it.

Gillian hadn't. Upon arrival, she'd handed it to Selynn, telling her to keep it. And Selynn would, dying with it in her hands, her sister would later tell Gillian, being buried with it per one of her last requests.

When Gillian hugged her client goodbye, Selynn began to cry, tightening her embrace. "A death-grip," Gillian said, "isn't only a turn of phrase. It's a terrifying strength." She also reported that Selynn asked many, some might say inevitable, questions like, "Why's this happening to me?"

Or this: "I don't wanna do my baby girls wrong, but no matter what I do, now that I'm up in here, I'm afraid I'll only do 'em wrong."

And last: "How's this my fault, when he lied to me—when he knew damn well what he was doing, who he'd been doing, and lying to my face, my back, my everything, so he could get all he wanted, served up hot on a plate, waiting, so... you spell it out: how's this mine? How is any of this mine?"

After her questions dried up like a puddle in the Sahara, the statements came: "I'm a godawful person, and I'll tell you why, Gilly. If I could go back in time and not have to worry about God, I'd kill the man who did this to me, sure as there's a dawn every morning till Judgment Day. Here I am in this bed, all these tubes running outta me like extension cords, every last one waiting for MLG-and-W to cut the juice. I keep waiting to find out this's been a mistake, but I keep on waking up in this damn bed."

When Gillian opened her wet eyes, she saw down the back of Selynn's gown, vertebra and rib after vertebra and rib, like her skeleton was doing its best to abandon the rest of her body.

After a mere seven months in the field, Gillian had witnessed the passing of too many clients, her first within a week on the job. Selynn had been a tall, thin woman in good health, but after her T-cells plummeted and she was diagnosed with several opportunistic infections, she dropped below a hundred pounds and lost most of her hair.

"Every client is different, but Selynn," Gillian said, "she faded so fast it was a shocking reminder how this isn't a manageable disease for everybody."

§

As it's going, it's likely to continue going. Women are the fastest rising group of new HIV infections, with African Americans representing the majority of this group. Women are more susceptible to this infection than heterosexual men are, for who is sullied more by use, the mortar or the pestle? It's the latter, for it remains a solidity upon which is ground either one's poison or one's medicine, but never both.

So it will fundamentally remain an either/or proposition: either you trust people or you don't, and if you do, then be prepared to submit to the benefits and the consequences. Because people will never stop, because some people lie, and others will have (read: cause) accidents, the sum of which is a lottery with ever-increasing odds.

Everybody's a winner with nothing to collect and a lifetime to pay out. Born with a ticket, entered with a lie, an "I've never done this before. Now, shh, babe, shh."

So what's my point? If you feel that this piece has shifted focus or changed directions too frequently, if you feel that these are distractions, then ponder hands trying to cup water.

Hands cannot keep the ground from getting wet. Hands, no matter how tightly you press your fingers together, cannot form a watertight seal. And should some water remain in them, it slakes no thirst, definitely not a thirst which is so much worse than being stranded in a desert, one which makes you long for the day when you can swim in the ocean, where, though immersed in the undrinkable, you are drenched, you are as saturated as a sunken cork, and should you recognize that things are indeed through, you are also able to recognize that you are beyond thirst.

Approximately 60 percent of our bodies is water and we will perish within three days if deprived of it, so it's not in the least bit surprising that those like Selynn, until their deaths, seek to sup that much more life for as long as they are able.

I closed the weekly, thinking, *Amen*. How many people never thought about confronting their regrets and the people who'd wronged them until they were on their deathbeds? Regret was a black hole. If you orbited it too closely, time slowed, letting all of that sorrow and guilt and shame and remorse and impotent anger loom larger and larger, heavier and heavier, reducing any progress you thought you were making until you made none at all, and while you were worrying about that, you wouldn't notice oblivion had already ensnared you.

Once we landed, the pilot's voice crackled over the PA: "There's been a runway incident. It's nothing serious, folks, but we are facing a bit of a traffic jam. Your patience is appreciated."

Thirty minutes later, I stopped at a crowded Applebee's on the concourse and ordered a Heineken draft. After checking my ID, the server asked, "Sixteen or twenty ounces?"

"Twenty."

She grabbed a frosty mug from the reach-in cooler and filled it up. I was gladdened by how many other people were also seeking a distraction. I took my time with it, ignoring the conversations happening around me. I tried powering up my cell phone, but it was dead.

Sitting in that uncomfortable chair, I felt exactly how I had while waiting for Curt in the bathhouse. I focused on my mug, watching the suds disappear, letting the background noise fade to nothing. In so many ways, I didn't want to end up like Selynn, withering away in a hospital bed, knowing who had killed her so many years before but unable to do anything about it. Chris had said "nothing's set in stone" when I'd told him about Adam. Admitting that his point still stood made me feel guilty. I was nothing like Selynn and her story wasn't about me, no matter how much I projected myself onto it.

I took my first drink from this new beer, and my own projection made me think of some of Stefano's. With my first deep breath afterward, I realized I would never forget what he had asked me about Adam. I needed to find out what the fuck had prompted that. If I could, I was sure I'd learn a few things about my roommate too, which would require us to have a serious conversation. But focusing on Chris felt like going backwards, and nothing good was waiting for me there.

While confronting Adam might not fix anything, at the very least I would be doing *something*. I had waited so long to stand up to Logan that no one would believe me, and I had never said a damn word to help that kid in Cocina Sabroso. I wasn't going to repeat either of those mistakes. Whether or not he ever acknowledged what he had done to me, Adam would hear me out.

First things first, I had to figure out exactly what I would say when I finally found him. I knew I wouldn't have the chance to ask too many questions, so I needed to avoid the obvious one. After all, asking a rapist why he raped people was like asking why the owl swooped down on the field mouse. It might be better to ask in what moment he had decided to rape me—what weakness had he seen that I'd been unaware of?

I was in the middle of a long drink, wanting nothing more than to be finished with all of this before 2004 dawned, when a middle-aged woman to my right said, "Coming or going?" After swallowing the gulp, I faced her. She inclined her head, looking at my black eye. "Or sent packing?"

"Coming home," I tilted my mug of lukewarm beer, "which is where I should be headed." I paid my tab but didn't finish the mug.

The woman said, "Hope your New Year's doesn't involve any fisticuffs."

I paused. "Fisticuffs?"

"Sounds better than getting your ass kicked, don't it?"

Finding a cab didn't take too long, and thankfully the driver wasn't talkative. His driving, on the other hand, reminded me of Logan's during our trip to the grocery store. As we headed down East Parkway back to Midtown, I watched homes and apartment buildings race past my window. The brick buildings looked much older than they had before I left, the roads felt rougher, the potholes more plentiful, and the lanes were too narrow for how many cars were squeezed in on each side of the parkway.

After tipping the driver the last seven bucks I had on me and walking up the rear staircase, I entered the apartment and sat at the kitchen table, trying to relax. I couldn't stop looking around, though. I knew how small the apartment was, but like many other things in my life, until I'd visited my parents, this place hadn't felt so cramped. Whatever charm it had before my trip was now nothing more than the shoddy upkeep of a complacent landlord.

A single beer was in the fridge. I opened it, took a drink, and grabbed the cordless phone, blocking my number before calling d'Esyal. There was no way I was wasting tonight in that kitchen, with the manager's shrill voice slicing through the clamor.

When he answered, I said, "Hey, this is Bryan."

"Would this be bad news?"

"Sorry, my flight's been delayed twice already. They're telling us we'll make it home tonight, but it's going to be late. I promise I'll be in tomorrow."

He sighed. "What can you do?"

No messages were blinking on the answering machine, and

when I'd charged my cell phone back up, there were no voice mails. I switched on my computer and drank the beer. Once the modem connected, I checked my email. There were two new messages: the first a spam so pointless it didn't warrant a text clipping, and the second was from Stefano.

> To: bouillablase@hotmail.com
> From: s.malatesta@memphis.edu
> Date: 12/26/03
> Re: Happy X-mas
>
> Hope your trip's gone well, a nice stash of cash and gifts to return and all that. But seriously, I want to apologize for what I said to you on Sunday night. I was out of line. End of story. With mom and everything else going on at home, the extra shifts helped me out.
> As short as it was, the trip was nice, but I'm already about to get the hell out of Dodge. I'd been thinking about what all you said on the bridge, so I called Benji, and we had a great conversation. He's invited me over to Little Rock for the weekend. I tried calling your cell phone a couple times, but all I got was that "out of service" message, which is why I'm emailing you. We'll catch up when I get back to town, but my cell phone service sucks too, so if I don't get your calls or messages, that's why.

What had I been expecting? For Stefano to be waiting for me? When he had questioned me about Adam, it shut me down and put me on the defensive. If I had explained that part of me and Curt's sex life, would he understand or think I was profoundly more fucked up? I laughed at myself because I already knew the answer to that question.

I finished that beer and made a run to the liquor store. Thankfully, I had Chris's car keys. I drove down Poplar, surprised by how responsive his car's brakes were. I parked near Sputnik and watched it for a few minutes. Then, I bought a cheap cabernet.

On the way back in to our apartment, I checked the mail, carrying the stack of bills and flyers in my left hand. I opened the wine in the kitchen and let it breathe while I sorted through the mail. Most of what wasn't junk was addressed to Chris. The sole piece of mail for me was a second letter from the Health Department, a glaring red "URGENT" beneath the stamp.

That cinched it. I was going back to Fugue. The holiday influx was sure to draw Adam out of hiding.

I poured a full glass, my thoughts feeling less hyper with each sip. After two glasses, I called Stefano's cell, but all I got was an automated message: "The wireless customer you are attempting to contact is currently unavailable. Please try again later." I took my letter, the bottle, and my glass to my bedroom and sat on the bed.

While drinking the last glass of wine, I stared at the purplish-red film dripping down the bottle's interior. Poorly rendered stage-blood. I took another drink, not caring if my smile was redder than a vampire's after quenching his thirst. I licked my lips and set the bottle on the floor. A new year was fast approaching, but how could I start fresh if Adam had infected me, the pain long gone but reminders and remainders of him mutating as they colonized me down to the marrow? There were so many shades of red, but every time I closed my eyes, I saw the red of that "URGENT," and when I opened them, all I could think about was that anonymized Selynn. About how everything wasn't all right, but it had been good enough. And how, with no warning, that *good enough* had been wrenched away and how swiftly she had been unmade in the end. At the funeral, did her pallbearers whisper how light her casket was?

I rolled a joint, started smoking, then turned the television to a channel without reception, cut the volume, and stared at the snow. At first, I thought I saw columns of black, gray, and white fluttering forward and backward. Squinting turned those into pinwheels spinning into one another. A blink ruined it all, but the thought that some of this static was caused by the background radiation of the Big Bang, attenuated by an incomprehensible time and distance, made me feel not so entirely separated, not so insignificant. I let my sight glaze over and grew drowsy.

I started watching motes in the weak sunlight slanting through the window. So many faces were hidden within the wood grain, too many for me to gauge how big of a crowd was gathered in my room. Face after face after face. I touched my black eye, wishing I had needed stitches, wishing I could feel the creepy texture of that stitching. Might as well let the outside match the inside, like my carpet does the drapes. Smiling, I closed my eyes...


I'm at the Studio on the Square, except the screen is four stories tall. On it is the Protagonist. He is a lanky high school basketball star with stringy brown hair that hangs to his chin and looks like it hasn't been washed in a couple weeks. His arms and legs are stretched out and too bony, knobby protrusions where no joints should be. He sits on the orange-tiled floor of a restroom that resembles a Hardee's shitter two decades behind the need for remodeling, his back slouched against the wall. He pulls a straight razor out of the gym bag sitting next to him, flicks it open. The reflection on the blade is bright in this dark room, and I am helpless, stuck in this cone of light, forced to witness it all.

Using his left hand, the Protagonist drags the razor from his right shoulder blade to the middle of his chest, then he slices downward and back out, tracing the pectoral past the pinch of his armpit until he meets the cut's mouth. So many rivulets fleeing their headwaters.

He's glad he hasn't cut his fingernails in a while. His eyes open wider and wider as he peels away his flesh. When he does the same to the other half of his chest, his eyes shut, and his bottom lip disappears entirely.

The camera zooms in on the opposite wall where he slings the strips of his skin. As those slap against the wall, they split into sentences, but the letters fall at different rates, making it impossible to read any of them before they tumble into a pile. The camera pans back to the Protagonist, focusing on his torso. His exposed muscles are red, weeping, and shiny in the flickering fluorescent lighting.

There is one other man in the theater a few rows ahead of me. A metronome counting out the steady, perfect beats of hand to popcorn tub, clump of popcorn to his mouth, and chew-chew-chew.

Back to the screen, our protagonist places the razor at the bottom of his right ear and traces the lower edge of his jaw, skating around the left ear, following his hair line from sideburns to widow's peak to sideburns and around the right ear until the blade reaches the initial cut. He feels his nose for the spot where bone ends and cartilage begins, then he traces a deep, swiftly reddening line around his nostrils and across the bridge of his nose. "How much worse is this going to get?" I say out loud before I can stop myself.

Mr. Metronome, still chewing, cranes his head around to leer at me for as long as it takes to fill his mouth with a new handful of popcorn. When he returns his attention to the screen, I do too.

The Protagonist hits the tip of his nose with the razor's handle until it breaks away from the rest like the end of an apple slice. He's now breathing through an open cavity, but there's no sound. The Protagonist outlines his eyes. He grips the edges of skin at the back of his jaw, then he pulls forward and up. It sounds like greasy burlap being ripped in half. But off his face comes, save for the flesh around his eyes. He slings this mask against the tiled wall. The camera does a slow pan from this back to the Protagonist. When he slices off a piece of flesh from his stomach and eats it, I gasp. Mr. Metronome turns all the way around in his seat, scowling.

I am about to open my mouth—while on-screen the Protagonist slices strip after chewy strip from his belly and crams them into a mouth that cannot keep up, bloody cheeks swelled into the most nightmarish chipmunk ever—but an emergency alarm on the side wall starts flashing and blaring. Mr. Metronome looks at me. "Well, ain't that a fuckin' sight?" he screams. "Ain't that—"

By the time I remembered who I was and found the phone and answered it, the ringing had stopped. Caller ID read: "Unknown." I rubbed my eyes and tried making sense of my dream. I'd heard it said that every person in a dream is some part of yourself. If that were true, which version of myself should I focus on: the guy who was mutilating and cannibalizing himself on screen, the man who was watching the spectacle with glee, or was it the one who was forever out of place and ruining things? The last version of me seemed like both the most obvious and least correct choice.

When I checked my email again, there was nothing new from Stefano. Honestly, what did I want to find? A regretful, post-coital postmortem? For him to confess that I'd been right all along—that Benji had been a distraction, and a puerile one at that?

Right before I closed the browser, a new email arrived. It was from Adam's rent-boy account, and it read: "Hey man. Sorry for how long it's taken to get back to you but it's the holidays. If you'd like to meet up in public and feel each other out, I'll be at Fugue probably around ten-thirty. I'll be wearing a sweater that's maroon on top and black on bottom. After you say hi, ask me why I hate olives."

I logged offline and sorted through the clippings tiling my desktop. There was no poetry to be found in any of these small bowls of word salad. Dress it up however you want, each was the equivalent of wilted iceberg. I highlighted the clippings, dragged them to the trash, then typed shift–command–delete.

In the shower after my jog back home, I remembered thinking, *Quit expecting the worst to happen and maybe it won't.* I picked up the letter from the Health Department, weighing its heft. I imagined it was a stone, sitting squarely and heavily in my palm. Before Chris and Stefano made it back to town, I wanted to be done with Adam. I should have opened the letter, read what it said, but I couldn't. Not yet. Regardless of what Adam had done to me, nothing the letter said would change that, and I didn't need to be curled up in the fetal position.

It was almost nine-thirty. In an hour or so, Fugue should be packed with a crowd desperate for a few hours away from their families when they could be themselves. Puck would definitely be working. I chose an outfit I hoped would make me forgettable to everyone else, then I cranked up Chris's techno and danced my way to the shower.

# CHAPTER THIRTY-TWO

I smoked a joint in one of Fugue's spill-over lots, but it didn't help much. And with all the regular smoking happening around me, I felt like I'd need another hit of eye drops before long. As I walked to the club's entrance, I patted the front left pocket of my jeans for that bottle, worried I'd forgotten it, but it was there.

Inside the video bar, I nursed a beer and backed into a corner behind the pool table while guys who were cruising eddied past me. On one hand, I was glad I didn't have to move. On the other, should the place catch on fire, watching the crowd stampede through either door until I blacked out from smoke inhalation would be fun.

So many guys looked vaguely familiar. *How many of them are dying?* I shuddered. *Quit projecting,* I smiled between sips. *Catastrophizing is never a good sign.*

I downed the rest of my beer and slowly made my way to the bar. Duke was flirting with the man seated to his right. He kept leaning too far, his hand gestures and facial expressions too large for his small frame and the tight space. He looked shit-faced, so whatever answers I got from him might make little sense, but if I ran into Adam tonight, I should get a little practice in first. Duke reached toward the man, knocking over an empty longneck. By this point, I was standing behind Duke's intended mark.

"Fuckin'-A!" The man shoved his chair back and stood. "It's *never* gonna happen, you shit-faced Oompa-Loompa!" He stormed out the door to the side hallway.

Duke stared in the opposite direction, his right elbow and upper arm stretched across the bar, the fabric getting dampened by the well mat. His chin teetered on his left hand.

When I sat in the empty seat to Duke's left, I remembered *fremdschämen*, that lovely German notion of being vicariously embarrassed for those who are too clueless to realize how much they should feel humiliated. I'd never had that luxury, not even when I was fucked up. There was always a part of me keeping track of every-goddamn-thing I'd hate myself for the following morning, afternoon, or whenever.

Puck was headed over to Duke when I asked, "How's your night going?"

He halted, sighed, and glared to my right. "When it comes to certain individuals, much slower than I'd like." Puck sat my order on the bar, not releasing his grip on the bottle's base until I grabbed its neck.

Duke's face slipped from its perch, dropping momentarily before jerking back up. Bored with people-watching, he signaled Puck who moved nothing except his left eyebrow, which arched to the brim of his top hat.

"You've more than enjoyed your evening, sir," Puck told him.

Duke stared at his empty drink, saying, "Dunno *what* you gotta do..."

"What's that?" I took a swig, waiting for Duke to recognize me.

"...get decent service here," he raised his face. "Are we friends?"

"Not really, Duke."

He blinked and shook his head twice, then focused on me. "Whatever I did, I'm sorry." He inclined his head. "Oh, it's you... the guy from The Ink Well. The counselor... Brad, right?"

"Yeah," I laughed, "that's me." I didn't want to hang out with Duke, but I needed an answer, and he was drunk enough to let the truth slip out. "How's about we relocate to the lounge? The crowd's not as bad, we won't have to scream to hear each other, and"—I waved Duke in, brushing my cheek against his—"I'm pretty sure Puck's about to have your ass thrown out. This time, I don't think the manager is going to give you another swing at bat."

"Never played baseball," Duke said, "but sure, let's talk." He bumped into several people during the short distance from his barstool to the main hallway.

As I stood up, Puck grabbed my forearm, ignoring several customers waving cash. He leaned in close, "There's rock bottoms, Bry, and then there's holes like him."

"Remember what you said when I told you about Adam?" I pulled my arm free. "No use fretting now."

"And you remember this," he adjusted his hat, "it ain't an accident if you seek it out."

A customer, fanning a twenty, screamed, "I have been *waiting.*"

Puck lolled his head in that direction and screamed, "Ain't you a Christian?" The customer raised both hands palms-up. "Then you should be used to waiting, with the sweet-ass time Christ is taking."

"Thanks," I patted Puck's arm, glad he was misconstruing this.

"Never mention it," he replied as he walked toward his heckler.

"Will do," I said, but I couldn't tell if he'd heard me.

With a smile as fake as his hair dye, Puck bussed a couple of empties, then he walked to the opposite side and served someone who'd just walked in from the hallway, all while keeping eye-contact with his impatient customer.

When I caught up with Duke, he was failing to order from the lounge bartender. I wrapped my right arm across his shoulders and steadied him to a corner far from the oblong bar, where I sat him in an upholstered armchair. "What were you trying to get?"

"A Tom Collins."

I stifled a laugh.

"What?" Duke's expression was the same one he'd put on when I asked if he was uncut. "I like 'em."

"Sorry, I had a professor named that and he was quite the lush. I'll be right back."

The first thing the bartender said to me, thumbing toward the pool, was, "Don't think your little friend is working tonight, so what'll it be?" When I told him Duke's order, the second thing he said to me was, "Seriously?"

I sighed, "And I'll take another," then chugged my beer. "I have a feeling it's going to be a long night."

As the bartender finished making the Tom Collins, he pointed behind me. "Your stray's a-wandering." Duke was heading out to the patio. I paid for the drinks, watching as he slowly descended out of sight. At least he didn't fall. I carried the two drinks to the narrow porch that overlooked the patio. In the five months since the storm, the back fence, volleyball court, and picnic tables had been repaired, but the pool had been emptied and remained covered. The place didn't look like a disaster zone, but it looked sterile and seldom used. I wondered how long it would be until they filled in the pool with concrete.

On the porch there were three thick wooden posts flanked by evergreen shrubs and a couple of cocktail tables. Two guys were finishing their cigarettes. I sat Duke's drink and my beer on a table, patted my back pockets, pretending I'd lost my pack.

As the two smokers headed back to the lounge, one offered me a cigarette. "I'm always losing mine too," he said. "Think the next time I can't find my pack, I'll take that as a sign to finally quit."

I placed the cigarette between my lips, which he lit without being asked. "Thanks," I exhaled. After a few drags, I wished I'd dressed a little warmer. As far as I could tell, the patio was abandoned except for Duke and me.

I glanced back and the bartender was no longer paying us any attention. I didn't want him calling a bouncer or the manager to check up on us. Hopefully, Duke wasn't the only sloppy mess who should have been cut off hours ago, the lot blending together like the multi-textured vomit from several people in the same unflushed toilet. No one remembers the person holding back the drunk's hair, focusing instead on what's left to mop up. As I smoked the cigarette, I patted my front left pocket and pulled out the bottle of eye drops. For a few drags, I thought about spiking Duke's drink, but settled on stubbing out the cigarette and stirring that to the bottom of the cocktail. Let the tar add a little more yellow.

When I descended the steps and rounded the decorative shrubbery, Duke was pissing into the bushes on the far side by the volleyball court. "Sorry it took so long," I announced, setting his cocktail on a picnic table and taking a seat on the opposite end.

Duke shook off for over thirty seconds. He stuffed himself

back into his pants, then he ran his hands through his hair and turned around a little too fast for his mind. He smiled confidently, the open zipper and piss stain on the left leg of his jeans notwithstanding. "So... you wanna talk?" Duke said.

"How are you doing?"

"How's it fuckin' look?"

"Rough."

"Says you."

"Got me there," I laughed.

"Bet I'm disappointing my sponsor." Duke chugged half of his cocktail. "But he told me, he says, 'I was expecting as much.' Told me I shouldn't call you. Wouldn't do no good. Anyway, I told the folks down at the clinic about you. They said they'd be sending you a letter. But fuck all that." Duke almost spilled his glass as he knelt on the bench next to me, eyes half-closed. "Are you in the mood for some no-good?" Duke blinked out of sync. Was he trying to wink? Did it matter? He started coughing.

I leaned back as far as I could.

A moment later, Duke shook his head and took a gulp of his drink. "That night," he said after swallowing, "I told you not to breed me and you didn't. Most guys didn't listen. But it don't matter no more. You can shoot wherever you want. It coulda been you—" Duke began coughing. After a moment, he took another large drink. With watery eyes, he shrugged, "You could've done it. Still could. Why not?"

My first reaction was to get angry, because he was the one who'd decided he needed my raw cock up his ass, but the way he was taking himself out of the equation was so convenient it gave me pause. Yes, we were drunk and I'd gone along with it, but he'd made the choice in the first place, and now it was as if the choice had been made for him.

Part of me wanted to laugh. That night with Adam, I'd never been given the chance to make any choices. But Duke had been awake and aware enough to know what he was doing. Whatever bad choices he'd made were his own. The same went for Adam. Goddamn Adam. His name meant dirt, but his haunting seemed less real the longer it had been since I saw him last, nothing to rub between my palms or dig out from under my nails, but here was Duke. Dire Duke calling me up in the middle of the night with another tragedy of his own making. And here was Duke newly positive and drunker than I'd ever seen him, which was saying something, not that I should say a fuckin' thing. I ran into him without trying, while Adam was probably haunting some brand-new fool, convincing him that he was a decent guy while doing horrible things. Duke was an easy target, no doubt, but easy targets make for good practice. Was that all I'd been for Logan and Adam?

"How many is 'most'?" I asked Duke. He squinted at me and shook his head. I explained, "You said most guys didn't listen."

"But I liked it when they went right ahead..."

"How many were there?"

"...when they kept going."

"What number was I?"

"I dunno. Three? Five?" Duke shrugged. "Like I said, it coulda been you."

"Sounds like I was nothing special."

"What?" Duke coughed and rubbed the base of his throat.

"Never mind," I stood. "Take another drink."

Duke tried but he coughed and pulled the cigarette out of his mouth. He lay his head on the picnic table and hugged his stomach. "Something ain't right."

Adam exited the door from the dance floor, quickly scanned the patio area, then raced up the steps to the lounge.

"That's it," I started slapping Duke's back. "Let it all out."

He covered his mouth with one hand and hugged his stomach. His cheeks swelled, his eyes went wide as he spurted chunky pink vomit first through his nose, then out of his full mouth, splattering a soggy mess all over the picnic table and himself. It stank of liquor and greasy food and so many abominable choices. I stepped back, my stomach clenching and throat tightening. He laid his forehead on the table and continued to puke into his lap.

"Don't worry," I lied, "I'll find you some help." I followed Adam's path.

Before I had made it inside the lounge, I heard the door from the dance floor open and the club's manager start yelling, "Duke! Wake your ass up!" I paused, hiding behind one of the posts and shrubs. "Well, shit!" Jaime spat, getting out his cell phone. A few moments of silence passed, and then he said, "I need an ambulance at 2866 Poplar."

# CHAPTER THIRTY-THREE

Adam wasn't in the lounge or the main hallway. When I opened the door to the video bar, a small crowd rushed out. If he'd found a customer for the night, I might lose him all over again once they left for the John's place. I couldn't catch my breath and my stomach felt hollow. If I didn't confront Adam tonight, part of me was certain I never would.

I made a circuit in the jam-packed video bar to be sure. Right before I exited the door into the side hallway, Puck saw me. He shook his head twice and wiped off the bar top.

I was about to take the stairs to the dance floor when a redheaded woman fled from the restroom. Adam followed a step behind, grabbing her right wrist and swinging her around. "Gillian! *Wait!*" I recognized her from that day in the cafeteria when I'd seen Adam.

Three guys came out of the video bar, their chatter quieting as they walked toward the cigarette machine and watched the show.

I figured it was better for this fiasco to play out, letting Adam get distracted by the conflict and possibly learning something I could use against him. So I leaned against the wall beside the door to the video bar and waited for my turn. My stomach still felt hollow, but it was the good kind, the kind containing the space for so much potential.

"No!" Gillian backhanded him and ripped her other arm out of his grip. "As if I needed another reason. We're done!"

"Stop it, Gilly. Just stop. I told you I was bi, so what the fuck's the matter?"

"*Stop?* How's about where do I *start?* Oh, right! How's about your promise that you'd be monogamous! You know where I've been interning! How could you potentially expose me?"

A barback exited the storeroom carrying two larger bottles of bourbon in one hand and two tall, frosted bottles in the other. He'd begun trying to lock the door when Gillian slapped Adam and shouted, "How could you do this to me!"

"Is there a problem?" the barback asked, forgetting the key in the lock. The blue wrist coil attached to it was swaying gently.

Adam spun on the guy, shaking his head. "She's a little upset."

"Miss?" The barback walked around him, getting closer to Gillian.

"Oh, I'm not upset. I am fine. No offense, but right now all I need is to finish this conversation and get the fuck out of here. Will you let me do that?" The barback began returning to the storeroom but stopped when Gillian yelled, "I've got this. Go already!" He headed downstairs.

After he was gone, Gillian punched Adam's chest. "Here's something I remember about you: rubbers—you've always hated them. Now, here's a couple things you obviously don't remember about me. First, my dad's a DA. Tomorrow morning, I will have a restraining order out against your ass. Second, knowingly spreading HIV is a felony in this state—"

"But I'm *not*—"

"If you touch me again, I'll get my dad to have his friends in Vice haul your ass in." Adam took a couple steps back. Gillian stepped forward, running her hands through her hair. "If you've ruined my life, you have no idea what kind of nightmare I'll make the rest of yours." Then she slung open the door to the video bar and was a red streak parting the crowd.

The three men loitering by the cigarette machine laughed: "Damn" and "I'd flip for her" and "Girl, I think she'd flip you." Adam glared at them, but the faggle started cackling, purchased a pack from the vending machine, and disappeared down the few steps to the pulsing dark of the dance floor. Adam was staring at the ceiling, fists clenched, thumbs tapping his index fingers.

I pulled out my phone, mimed checking it, while I dug out enough change to buy myself a pack. Adam slung open the storeroom door, then shook his hands and flung the keys behind him before slamming the door shut. Once I'd unwrapped my cigarettes, I lit one and pulled the sandwich bag from my left pocket. I hadn't been using it all night long, but the club's floor was disgusting.

I scanned the hallway. There was nothing that would trip me up this time. Had I gone back into the cafeteria on that day way back in May, I could have saved Gillian what she was going through right now. Then I felt guilty for not confronting the man who had molested the boy in Cocina Sabroso's restroom. What did it matter if no one would have believed me? Yes, I hadn't seen anything, but I knew exactly what I would have seen if the lights had been on. Nothing sharpens hindsight like regret. Which is to say, if I had spoken up, that boy might have begun to understand he was being abused and how wrong that was. My heart was racing like I'd just ended a sprint. I took a swig and pulled up my hoodie.

Using the sandwich bag, I grabbed the keys off the floor, slid them into the lock, slowly turning it, and cracking open the door.

"What?" Adam snapped as I entered. "Didn't get enough of a show out there?" He glanced at me as he kept texting.

I locked the door behind me and wrapped the keys in the sandwich bag, stashing those in my right hoodie pocket. The last time I was in this storeroom, it had seemed wide enough for two cars, but now the tall shelves loomed over me from all sides. I double-checked that there was still a lone camera aimed at the exterior door.

"Hey!" Adam shouted. "What the *fuck* do you *want?*"

"Nothing, man. Figured you could use a cig or swig."

Adam rubbed his temples with his right hand. "A drink would be nice." I handed him my beer. He took a chug, wiping his lips with the back of his hand and returning it to me. "Thanks." He looked away, rolled his neck. After several seconds, his eyes narrowed. "Have we met?"

"Why do you hate olives so much?"

After a moment or two, it registered. "I'm sorry, man, but tonight's not going to work for me."

I took a drink because what did his germs matter now?

"Wait," he tilted his head. "I know you from somewhere. Give me a little help. It's been a fucked-up night."

"The night we went on a date was even worse. We met when you were riding a mountain bike and needed directions to Cooper-Young."

He squinted and scrunched up his lips. Then he chuckled. "Almost forgot about you, which is saying something 'cause, Jesus, you're a piece of work."

"Can I ask you about that night?"

"As long as it doesn't involve me strangling you." I opened my mouth but said nothing. He shook his head, laughing, "You were... a little freaky for my tastes."

I took a sip, trying to collect my thoughts, but I blurted: "Why did you rape me?"

"What the fuck are you talking about?"

"You roofied me."

"Dude." He pointed at me, jabbing the air. "I've never raped anybody! We're in the South, so I shouldn't have to say this, but you can't rape somebody who's *literally* begging for it!"

"Define 'literally'?"

"At dinner you polished off how many glasses of wine?"

"And you weren't drinking?"

"No, but you seemed, well, intent. Yeah, that's the word."

"On what?"

"Fuckin' got me." He shrugged. "Drunks either never need any excuses, or they never run out of 'em."

"Fine. What next?"

"I drove us back to your place."

"Then what?"

"And then you fell up half those stairs, excited because your roommate was out of town. You were tenting your jeans before you unlocked the door. Started blowing me right there in the kitchen, bragging how you could take all of me when you bobbed up for air."

"Right."

"Believe whatever you want, you fuckin' freak, but I did *not* rape you. You kept on saying—"

"This should be good!" I pinged the bottle against the leg of some industrial shelving, surprised it didn't shatter. "Tell me what I begged for."

He motioned for another swig. I handed him the beer. He

took a drink, returned it, then continued, "You told me to choke you and say some shit about the Three Little Pigs."

"I did not, I did—"

"Not gonna lie, man, it weirded me out so much I almost left right then and there. Figured it could turn out to be hot or at least make for a good story, so I stayed. I was wrong."

I brought the bottle to my lips and slowly finished the dregs.

"But the worst part," Adam laughed, "was when you moaned, 'Rape me, Louggie. Do it.' So, yeah, I fucked you hard, but you took it like a champ. When you started crying out of nowhere, I punched your chest, and when you hit back like you meant it, I punched your face and really went to town."

I closed my eyes and felt like I was floating several stories in the air. Looking down, I saw myself spinning, almost puking as the multiple outlines of myself collapsed into one.

"Sure, you didn't ask for that, but you never went limp, so a sign's a sign, right? I remember thinking to myself I should start charging for that sick shit."

After opening my eyes, I walked toward the door, but he rammed me into it. "No you don't, you piece of shit." I dropped my beer and raised my hands just before my right cheek slammed against my forearms. The bottle hit the toe of my boot and thunked onto the floor, rolling away behind us.

Adam pinned one of my shoulders and dug an elbow into the back of my neck. "We're not done yet." His breath was stale against my ear. "Think you can call me a rapist and walk away?" He shoved my shoulder and pressed his forearm into the back of my neck. "How's about I show you what—"

I stomped my right foot on his shin and ankle. He stumbled, cursing and clutching at his leg. The beer bottle was in front of the shelving unit with all the liquor. I raced to it. Adam lurched toward me. I grabbed the bottle, stood, and swung, landing a glancing blow against Adam's left temple. The bottle didn't break against his skull, but I lost my grip and it shattered when it hit the floor this time.

Adam's eyes were blinking and vacant. There was a jagged vertical laceration between his eyebrow and hairline. The trickle of blood quickly became a torrent. More and more red staining all that blond hair. He shook his head several times, flinging blood. I glanced to my left then back at Adam. His eyes were clearing and he was breathing heavily. He clenched his fists and stormed toward me. I grabbed a fifth of bourbon from the shelf and swung. His face jerked to the side and he fell forward, first to his knees, then to a three-point stance. He attempted to balance himself with one hand on the floor while gingerly touching his jaw. It looked dislocated, and when his hand pressed down on the teeth the last swing had knocked out, he started dry-heaving and fell to his stomach. With effort, he rolled onto his back, bloody bubbles sputtering through his lips. I set the fifth on the floor and walked over to the broken beer bottle. Using my sandwich bag glove, I picked up its neck-and shoulders and returned to Adam. He had one hand over his mouth and both eyes trained on me. He struggled to sit up, but he quit trying after I kicked his ear.

His eyes stayed shut for a while. I knelt next to him on my left knee and imagined ramming the broken bottle into his mouth. If I spun it from midnight to noon several times, how much resistance would the glass meet as it crunched through his gums and the jagged stumps of teeth that remained, how much strain would I feel on the outside of my right forearm as I did so, and how close would it sound to the stripped dial on the washing machines in my apartment complex's laundry room?

Nearby, shards of Adam's teeth and the longneck were scattered across the floor, so much bloody white and bloody green, and on every last piece of glass there might be traces of my fingerprints.

I shook my head, checked my hands, and told myself to focus. So far, somehow there wasn't any blood on them. Not literally, anyway. That smile of his was already ruined enough. Why mutilate it any further? Knowing my luck, if I tried to do any worse, the bottle would break again, this time slicing open one or more of my fingers. The last time I'd heard Logan speak before leaving Ladue, he'd been blaming me for what he had done to me, and a few moments ago Adam had tried doing the same bullshit. How many times would I be a victim who had brought it upon himself?

But nobody would see me that way after this. I couldn't remember how many times I had called Adam's cell phone, but the police could easily find out the exact number of calls. It would look obsessive, and that would be all the motive the authorities needed.

My left knee started aching from the freezing concrete floor. I couldn't imagine being surrounded by concrete on five sides, or the stainless and lidless steel of prison toilets, or iron bars being the only things separating me from even more concrete. When Adam opened his eyes—his shredded lips moving without saying anything—I bolted to my feet. Adam's smirk was a grotesque mask. I didn't shut my eyes, but everything went black for a few breaths, each inhale and exhale thundering. My eyes opened to the fluorescent lights buzzing above me. I blinked away my hesitation.

When I knelt on Adam's windpipe with my right knee, his throat was so much softer and warmer than the floor. His hands fumbled for my leg, while capillaries burst across his eyes. Though his grip weakened, his eyes widened as far as they could. Between his blinks, I saw Adam shift between anger, fear, pleading, then a groggy rage clawing onto consciousness.

Prolonging this was cruel, so I shifted more weight to my knee. Adam blinked once, twice, then a flutter, after which his eyes remained open, both irises fully dilated. So much black surrounded by thin bands of green.

After his chest quit rising, I dumped the storeroom keys into Adam's left hand and rolled him onto his side. Using the sandwich bag glove, I pulled out his wallet and removed the thick stack of cash, all of which I stashed in my right rear pocket. I dropped his wallet next to him and stood, deciding what to do with the neck-and-shoulders of my beer bottle. How long would it take someone to patiently reconstruct the bottle and dust for my prints? Only then did I look down and realize I had walked through the blood. These boots would have to go, and I'd need to drive home in socked feet to keep from tracking blood into Chris's car.

On a nearby shelf, there was an open box of bev naps and several two-gallon jugs of industrial bleach-based cleaner. I stuffed a few of those napkins up the bottleneck. Using another handful, I picked up a few larger pieces of teeth and dropped them into the bottle.

The broken pieces of green glass and the puddled blood on the floor were screaming GO! And STOP! I ignored the second voice and cleaned up what I could. First, I needed something to carry the bottle in. I found a plastic grocery bag near the trashcan, wrapped the bottle and napkins inside it. Then, with my sandwich bag, I carefully picked up each and every shard of glass I saw, adding them to the bag before stuffing it all into my hoodie's left pocket.

With another two handfuls of napkins, I opened a jug of cleaner, pouring the mixture on the floor and each of my hands in turn. Just in case. I wiped those off on my jeans, which I knew I'd have to toss along with my boots. Once my hands were dry, I rinsed Adam's blood off the fifth and poured a five-Mississippi shot down his throat. Then I wiped down the jug and returned it to the shelf, placing it behind two that were still sealed.

After I picked up the fifth, I pulled the hoodie fully over my head, hiding my face as best I could, and tightened its drawstrings. My eyes darted from spot to spot, making sure I wasn't leaving anything behind. It was only then that I realized Adam and I had never gotten near the security camera's field of view.

With my back to the camera, I went to the security monitor as it cycled through the outside feeds. The rear entrance on Walnut Grove. The front entrance on Poplar. The front steps and an ambulance, its lights flashing and back doors open. Deciding to risk it, I zipped up my hoodie and held the fifth inside, lodged between my left arm and stomach, that hand cupping the bottom to make sure it didn't slip out. With my right hand safely inside the sandwich bag, I opened the door and jogged down the few steps to the parking lot, keeping my eyes straight ahead as I walked to Chris's car.

In the hatchback, under a blanket, there was a small plastic crate filled with bags from various stores. I nestled the bourbon in the crate and found a Dillard's bag large enough to stuff my Docs into. The gravel was cold and sharp against my socked feet.

After sitting behind the wheel and sighing more deeply than I could ever remember doing, the rearview mirror reflected someone I didn't hate.

# CHAPTER THIRTY-FOUR

Back home, I almost switched on some of Chris's music, but it was too late for a solo dance party. The fridge was empty of anything I might have wanted to eat thanks to Chris's zero-tolerance policy on suspicious leftovers. There wasn't any alcohol left in the house either, as if I needed any more, so I smoked a bowl and started planning my final trip to the Old Bridge. I bagged up the clothes I'd worn to the club and kept smoking, Adam's words echoing in my mind.

On the night of our date, I hadn't eaten, but I'd blacked out after a couple beers and a few glasses of wine. One of the few things I could count on was my tolerance. There was no way that blackout had been natural. The morning after, my head felt worse than the few times I'd tried poppers, those burning fumes that were somehow both clinical and funereal.

When I started fucking men, I liked getting choked, but I had never connected that to Logan. I was mostly a top, but what I loved the most was letting Curt choke me, taking him while submitting to his grip. The stars that flashed across my eyes and the rush of dizziness after getting choked were the best alternative to poppers. But now I wasn't so sure if I would ever do that again. How fucked up was I to fetishize an aspect of what Logan had done to me? How long until I could untangle that knot of contradictions? There was so much I was leaving behind, so much that could have mattered, and so much I'd only deluded myself ever had. The most depressing thing was how rarely I'd been able to figure out which was which.

Since I was never sleeping in this bed again, I laid my back-pack on it, cramming it with everything I'd need along with the second letter from the Shelby County Health Department. No matter how much I'd like to forget it, I placed it on top of every-thing, knowing I'd open it soon.

There was almost a grand in Adam's wallet. How many tricks and in how short a time had he earned it? Like Duke, it didn't matter. If Adam had been the engine, I was the freight car he was pulling across the border between yes and no. Jumping the tracks at this point would do nothing but harm me further. We were unhitched now and it was only a matter of time before I slowed to a halt.

I pulled my dresser away from the wall, snaked my arm under the back, and reached for the envelopes full of money. I set aside Adam's cash, which I was leaving behind for Chris, and put $200 in my wallet. I dug out a few pairs of balled-up socks, unrolling those and splitting the rest of my savings between them and the hidden inside pocket of my coat. I rolled those socks back up and stuffed them as deep in my backpack as I could.

For my whole life, I'd felt shame for so many things, some I'd had no control over, but nothing compared to this. Maybe I *had* asked Adam to fuck me like he was raping me and maybe he *hadn't* drugged me. If so, why did I have no memories of either whatsoever? True, I had been fairly drunk by that point, but each *maybe* was a damnable reckoning. Part of me refused to believe those possibilities, yet there they gleamed in all their hideous particularity. Throughout my life, I had sabotaged so many relationships and opportunities, but this self-sabotage was beyond pathological. Trying to understand it led either to a lie that felt like the truth, or a truth that must be a lie. Denying one meant accepting the other, and I could accept neither.

What I couldn't deny was how I had mentioned Logan's name. Adam never would have known it unless I had brought it up. The only question that mattered, one I would never be able to answer, was whether I'd mentioned Logan to egg Adam on, or if I'd done that because my half-brother was the only person my drugged mind could dredge up in the moment. And if Adam were telling the truth, my "sick shit" had been his inspiration to start hustling.

But did any of that even matter after I had killed him? If Adam hadn't forced my hand, I would have walked away— slinging shut the storeroom's door behind me instead of swinging two different bottles against his face and finally taking a knee. When I knelt, I had felt so certain, but two questions were crowding my small bedroom. Was it truly murder if I was only trying to kill the memory of what had been done to me? And, were the scales balanced now? While absolution was always a gift, a liberation, even if the scales were level, I had no idea where forgiveness might find me. I decided those questions would die in this bedroom, where Adam had raped me, just like he had died in Fugue's storeroom.

Once I'd bundled up in several layers of clothes, I stood before the bedroom mirror, hoping the black eye Curt had gifted me would fade soon. This time, Adam hadn't bruised anything but my forearms. As much as I wanted to take that as a win, I couldn't see it as anything other than a draw.

I laid Adam's cash, my key to the apartment, and the Oak

Court gift card on the coffee table. Then I put on my gloves, shouldered the backpack, and left.

As I drove out of the parking lot, I took Cooper down to Madison and headed west. When the Piggly Wiggly came into view, I slowed and took a right onto Avalon then a left on Court, where I parked.

I retrieved the Dillard's bag from the back of Chris's car, threw in my bagged-up jeans, and jogged across the street. A dumpster sat on the side of the grocery store. I slung the shopping bag into it, brushing off my hands on the sides of my pants, like people who didn't really think about germs do, and walked back to the car.

There was a small concrete wall on the right side of Court. I hadn't noticed this when I got out of Chris's car, but someone had spray-painted:

• • — This is not a Rave Party
I am going to Die — • •

"Serves you right." I started the car. "Who is still going to raves?" I drove a little under the speed limit, using turn signals and worrying that a cop might pull me over anyway because being so careful at this hour was in and of itself suspicious.

Like the letter's contents, what was done, was done. No, that wasn't right. I did what I had done. But I did it because no matter what Adam had said, no matter how much truth he'd mixed into his lies, he had attacked me a second time. Should I feel guilty for going further than I ever thought I was capable of?

*Terrible things happen to people every minute of every day*, I told myself, *what's so bad about me doing a terrible thing to a horrible human being?* I checked the rearview mirror. There was a slight smile on my lips. I switched on the radio and focused on the road ahead of me. *After what Adam had done, why should I feel guilty? There was no reason for that. None at all.*

# END OF THE LINE

Above me, traffic rumbled across the Old Bridge while to my right trains on the other two bridges blared their horns. Far below me, the Mississippi kept flowing, and it would keep running long after all of us were gone, ripples intersecting and overriding each other, none of us ever again ourselves.

How many people had been lost, intentionally or not, in those currents? How many had sought the freedom of death in those waters? If I leaped into that freezing churn and if this life was all there was, I'd likely remember nothing after the splash. But I wasn't willing to chance either possibility.

Still, it would be so easy to jump, yelling the whole way down, to taste as much gritty water as I could before the river replaced me with itself. Doing that, however, would convince certain people that everything they had predicted for me was my destiny and not their hopes. The problem was, I wanted to keep remembering, to keep going, to no longer deny who I was whether or not anyone believed me.

Instead, I opened the second letter from the Health Department.

Dear Bryan Meigs,
We have attempted to contact you once by mail
already, but we have not heard back from you. Please
respond to us about an urgent matter regarding your
personal health at 901-222-9XXX.
You may have been exposed to one or more potentially
life-threatening sexually transmitted infections.
Rest assured that we will ensure your confidentiality.
However, if you do not respond to this letter or our
phone calls, we will be forced to conduct home and/or
workplace visits.

The letter concluded with a mission statement that said, among other things, they were working to make this state "one of the nation's ten healthiest." I crumpled the letter, laughing. There was a better chance of an historically accurate Christ returning and being acknowledged by racists as their savior than Tennessee achieving that vague metric.

But the letter. It said something that could change everything or change nothing. I'd always hated hypochondriacs because who the fuck would ever want to be sick? Yet here I was, either somehow still negative or an asymptomatic fuck with OCD absolutely certain that his fate had been sealed, staring at an answer that wasn't worth the paper it was printed on. I almost pitched the letter off the stanchion, but I flattened it out and re-folded it, because not even the Mississippi River deserved that piece of refuse.

For two separate series of train whistles, I stared at the river unable to steady my pulse or get my mind to shut the fuck up for once in my goddamn life. I'd shackled myself with so many different chains, the heaviest lately tethering me to Adam. Because I'd been so focused on him and so distracted by Stefano and my trip home, I hadn't really thought about Duke. Maybe I'd kept running into him because a chain had been pulling me toward him. No, making it Fate's fault was too easy. That would be no better than Duke blaming the consequences of his choices on everybody else.

Over the last few hours, I had barely sampled the fifth I'd stolen from Fugue. I unscrewed the cap and stood, flinging it away as I took a last long drink. After that, I emptied the rest of the bourbon into the river and stuffed the bottle into the bag containing the neck-and-shoulders of the beer bottle and Adam's teeth. I double-knotted the handles and was about to sling it all into the river, when I paused and smashed the bag atop the stanchion, shattering the fifth. For maybe two minutes, I held the heavy bag over the edge of the stanchion, then I let go.

Several seconds later, the bag splashed into the river, the current dragging it south and then under. Any signs of it were quickly erased, and my sight had never been clearer. While I couldn't change what I'd done, I could stop trying to make the worst possible outcomes happen, and the best way to bring that about was to tell a new story about who I was. Certain things would always trigger me, but maybe I could start ignoring the lesser ones. As for the rest, I would focus on the warmth of the water and patiently lather up no more than three times.

If I made it out of town, I didn't know who I'd become, but I knew I couldn't keep living like I had been. Lying about my name and backstory was going to be vital, but that didn't mean I had to lie about who I truly was. That hadn't kept me safe so far, so I had nothing left to lose by being as honest as I could be.

My new truth was this and nothing but this: I had survived by treating Adam the same way he would have treated me if I hadn't fought back. Better that than letting myself be run through the crucible yet again. After all, how many times can someone be melted down and reforged before he's no longer himself?

I wiped my hands on my jeans and stood. After shouldering my backpack, I walked to the stanchion's eastbound side and checked. Sure enough, that hatch wasn't locked, but it was rusted stiff and took several shoves to open it.

Back on the walkway, the morning was still dark. Past the rich homes on the bluff, beyond what passed for Memphis's skyline, a green-black bank of clouds roiled. Following it were a biting cold and the first missives of snow. That message would be short-lived—the letters overlapping, white-on-white, melting on the ground before they could be read. When I closed my eyes, I was floating above Sputnik, viewing it as if through a time-lapsed video: the acid trails of its neon both blurred and sharp, a multiplicity of contrasts.

I heard a voice urging me to run, to sprint so swiftly that I lost myself to friction. But that was a trap because nobody can outrun night, especially when they carry it within themselves. And once we are finally forced to stop, our hearts racing, dusk's friendly cool will claim us, its comfort a lie we will not recognize as such before it was far too late.

I opened my eyes to clouds streaming in from the west and screamed as loud and as long as I could. My scream was drowned out by a train screeching across Harahan, its braking into downtown a cacophony of violent restraint. *A fitting reminder*, flashed across my mind, so I shut my mouth and took several deep breaths. Once I started walking, I never looked back.

Parking too close to Central Station was too obvious, so I drove down to Tom Lee Park on Riverside Drive. The place was deserted, no joggers or dog walkers in sight. I changed out of my running shoes into an older pair of Mizunos. Then I transferred all of the cash and three fake IDs from the wallet

Chris and Stefano would recognize into a billfold I hadn't used in years. In my wallet, I left my useless bank and credit cards, an expired voter registration card, and my driver's license.

On a faded ATM receipt, I scribbled: "Cold as the Muddy is, can I make it to the other side? Least I could do is try. ~ Bry" I placed that pathetic note in the middle of my wallet. Then, I opened the alt-zine to the last page of "Bluff City Plagues" and underlined "as saturated as a sunken cork" and "seek to sup that much more life for as long as they are able."

Grabbing my backpack off the passenger seat, I opened the hatchback, then I locked the doors with the fob, crawled in through the back, and slung the keys under the passenger seat. When I got out, I took another look around. If anyone was watching me, they were using binoculars.

I shut the hatchback and carried my shoes and wallet to the riverbank. I set my backpack down and got the cash out of my pea coat. Then I folded my coat and lay it on the stones. Atop it, I placed the alt-zine open to the "Bluff City Plagues" article and the letter from the Health Department, using my shoes to weigh everything down. I went through my wallet one more time, making sure there was nothing I wanted to save, then I placed it upright in the left shoe.

After shouldering my backpack, I flipped open my cell phone and called my landline. At the beep, I said: "Hey, Chris. You're probably freaking out right about now, but I had to borrow your car. It's locked up in Tom Lee Park, not far from," I spun around, "the Butler Avenue stairs. I hope you weren't lying about having a spare set in your bedroom, because your main set are lying under the passenger seat. When you get back home, you'll see a wad of cash, a gift card, and my key on the coffee table. The cash is more than my share of next month's rent and utilities, and I won't be needing the gift card, so treat yourself. I'm not going to Taos like your last roomy, because I've already found myself. Moving right along, Stefano's looking for a new place, so give him my room. You guys can do whatever you want with everything I've left behind. I won't need any of it, not where I'm headed. I'd suggest you take what Stefano calls my 'library' to the used bookstore down the street near Sputnik and see how much they'll give you for the lot. Have a good life, Chris. I'm glad I knew you for as long as I did. And if you replay this message for Stefano, well, Soap-Opera, I wish you'd given me a second chance. Anyway, I'm done with regret. Right now, all I want to do is feel the river lap my toes."

Before I walked away from this cache, I slid my cell phone behind my wallet in the shoe. While it felt like I was the only person in Memphis, that doesn't mean I didn't book it out of the park. I crossed Riverside and ran up the Butler Avenue stairs. There were eighty-four of them, and they were steep.

Atop the bluff, I faced away from the river, hands on knees, and caught my breath. To my left were expensive homes jammed next to one another regardless of architectural style. I walked down Butler and was so amused by how much uglier the backs of those same homes were that I nearly tripped on the trolly tracks. Luckily, nobody saw me stumble, and my hands never hit the cobblestones.

Soon, I was crossing beneath a railroad trestle, the walls on either side covered in graffiti murals. On that stretch of Butler, cobblestones were showing where the asphalt had worn away. At the corner of Butler and South Main, Fire Station #2 was straight ahead, so I took a right and walked toward the train station. Behind the fire hall was the Lorraine Motel. Ahead of me were Earnestine & Hazel's on the right and the Arcade Restaurant on the left. The former had shut down for the night several hours before while the latter was getting ready to open. A woman was jogging past Central Station. Across the street, a delivery guy rolled up the back gate of a box truck and pulled out the ramp with a rattling clank.

I went to Central Station's second entrance, up the few steps to the lower concourse. Ahead of me were the ticketing booths. It was just past six o'clock. Before I approached the ticket counter, I went down the narrow and low-ceilinged hallway to the men's room, taking a piss that lasted nearly two minutes. With my hands washed, I sat my backpack on a different, drier stretch of countertop and dug out my toothbrush from the toiletries kit.

After brushing my teeth and gargling, I took off the sock cap and tried to fix my hair. I leaned in close to the mirror. My eyes were so bloodshot they reminded me of Adam's. I found the bottle of eye drops and tried blinking away the red. There were stacks of thick folded paper towels. I grabbed two of those stacks, stuffing them in my backpack along with the rest of my items, and then I got out a brand-new sandwich bag.

Right before I exited the restroom, I realized I needed to figure out who I was going to be. All the fake IDs in my wallet were intermixed with the cash. I fumbled through the lot till I found one that hadn't expired and whose name I wouldn't mind ditching, studying it until I had everything memorized.

By the time I was scanning the departures, it was pushing half-past six. Luckily, the decision was easier than I'd thought it would be.

"Good morning, sir," the groggy matron said when I stepped up to the ticketing counter. "You got a reservation?"

"Nope. I hope that won't be a problem."

"There shouldn't be."

"I'd like a ticket for the seven-thirty train to New Orleans, if there are any left."

"There's plenty. You paying with cash or credit?"

"Cash."

She sighed and patted her right palm against her heart. "I was praying you'd say that. Our machine's acting like me." She lay two fingers on the credit card terminal. "She ain't wanting to wake up. Can I see your driver's license?"

"No problem." I handed her the one I'd chosen, yawning.

"Rough night?"

"You have no idea," I chuckled. "Sorry."

"Oh, please." She eyed my license. "If you're the worst part of my day, Mr. Poston, then I need to up and quit. Save me my last nerve. Now, let's find you a seat."

\* \* \*

While I was leaving behind my old life all those years ago, feeling more and more relaxed as the train neared New Orleans, I had wondered who found Adam's body. I hoped it hadn't been Puck. Let it be some random bartender or a barback who hadn't forgotten his keys in a crowded hallway.

Using computers in different public libraries, I searched for airfares to Memphis and its tourist spots, eventually reading the town's main newspaper. In *The Commercial Appeal*, there was a single police report near the end of section A. The column was short and the leads had dried up. Beyond robbery, there wasn't much of a motive. A few months later, the local gay newspaper did a more in-depth article, speculating on the killer's motivation, seeking any tips. After that, the case grew colder than Adam's corpse. Had any of Fugue's employees let it slip that Adam was an occasional hustler? If so, was that why the police hadn't pursued the case? While I'd probably never know what Puck had chosen not to tell the police, I thanked him nonetheless.

What I found myself imagining more often was what, if anything, Adam had been aware of as he lay dead on the floor.

Everything? Nothing? Had he been stuck inside the storeroom, inside his body, growing increasingly claustrophobic as his thoughts lost coherency the same way his shell was steadily losing its heat? The inescapable equality of entropy. Condemned to stare, for as long as he could, at the ceiling and its buzzing rows of fluorescent tubes, the exposed girders and insulation, wires both coiled and loose, spiderwebs of red, blue, green, and yellow. Or maybe he'd been freed, his soul a mist that the overhead lights degraded to nothing more than the smell of ozone.

If Adam could have seen himself, would his wrecked face remind him of those whose lives he ruined? At the least, I had taken from him the handsome ease he relied on. Would his parents find it difficult to think of him in any other way? What would be worse: their son's physical disfigurement or the grotesque image the investigation had painted of him? But that casket, like all my concerns about Adam, was sealed shut.

Next was Duke. Dire Duke. Dear Duke. Duke in a hospital bed, not dying but feeling like he was about to. I hoped he'd recovered from a garden variety alcohol poisoning, that he had started believing whatever his sponsor was telling him, no longer letting himself be defined by gossip. There was so much he could never forget, so much that others would never let him live down, but let him ignore all of that and all of them. Let him move on. And let me not have left him to die on the patio of a gay club.

Lastly, there was Stefano. Some time or another—long after my stories have warped, if not supplanted, any actual memories of him—at some bar or another, in some city or another, while Stefano is lushed, he'll run into me. Let's say this happens during Decadence. I'll have never seen him this blitzed, but New Orleans does that to too many people. We'll both be genuinely surprised but for entirely different reasons.

Before I'll be able to stop him, Stefano will hug me, saying, "I knew you didn't kill yourself," trying to drag me back into that battle with myself. Then he'll ask, "How are you walking around Decadence without a hazmat suit?"

I'll curse myself for not noticing him and disappearing before he could recognize me, but I will also be annoyed by his joke. During my trip to the bathhouse with Curt, I had realized that the filthiest places are ironically the easiest to navigate. Everything was suspect in one way or another, so I never had to wonder.

Until I abandoned my old life in Memphis, my default was to downplay how fucked up a person I was, how many bad things I'd done, and how often I'd graded myself on the laziest of curves. But sometimes Rome finds you where you are, and if it's been long enough and you're comfortable enough, you shrug and stop fighting because you're tired of punching yourself in the face.

Every time Stefano will call me "Bry," I will reply, "That's not my name," exchanging looks with any friends I'll have by then, and telling them later, "Gotta love shit-faced tourists who convince themselves you're some long lost relation." But Stefano will buy me a round and keep drinking and talking, and eventually I'll say, "Be back in a minute." Stefano will watch me go to the restroom, realizing he has to piss, too.

I'll pick any urinal but the middle. When I was seven, my father gave me the rare piece of useful advice: "Never use the one in the middle. And don't shake off more than three times. Four times, your luck might change. Trust me, Bry, you don't want that type of luck."

Stefano will choose the middle urinal, thinking I want him spraying his piss anywhere near me. He'll say something like, "Whodathunk?" And we'll both laugh: me with discomfort, him with a pitiable eagerness.

After we zip up, we'll wash our hands, Stefano lathering for as long as I do, then he'll grab my shoulders with those wet fingers, balance on his tiptoes, and pucker up. I won't move—eyes open, hands at my sides—because what can you do once the tongue of a man you haven't wanted to kiss in years starts ferreting inside your mouth?

When he realizes I'm not kissing back, Stefano will lose those couple extra inches of height. I will glance between him and the door, lying, "I got to catch up with my friends," and leave the bar. Before I walk away, disappointment will sink his face.

And I *will* walk away. If I don't, I'll be dragged back to, if not Memphis, then into the orbits of too many people who would remember me, too many chances for them to remember all the things I assume they'd neglected to tell the police. The following morning Stefano will wake up with the worst hangover of his life. Should he remember seeing me or the name of the bar he found me in, no one he asks will have ever heard of a Bryan Meigs from Memphis. Better to let him think he had gotten so fucked up that he'd confused another ginger for me. Once the embarrassment has faded, he'll feel like he got off easy.

But back in that restroom, after watching me leave, he'll gaze into the mirror—his doubling twinned by drunkenness, but painfully coalescing—and see me staring back.

* * *

Nine hours after leaving Memphis, with my face reflected in the train's window, I smelled a combination of rotten eggs, brackish water, and oil. Cypress trees, Spanish moss, ill-planned flood control, and kudzu fled behind us, replaced by more and more of the same. My regret had been as invasive as that kudzu. Now I wanted it all gone. And I'd have to keep pruning, unless I admitted defeat and allowed it to cover me, preserving a roughly man-shaped mound until it broke me down completely, my unshackled bones crumbling lower and lower year by year.

For two decades, I'd wanted others to believe me, but I wasn't going to keep trying. Before that day, I would never have believed myself capable of killing anybody. Over my life, there were times I had imagined killing myself, but when those thoughts appeared, unbidden and inexplicable flashes sometimes including a plan that involved a bridge, I'd push them aside because I was worried about eternity. By rights, I should have been more fearful than ever before, but I wasn't. Even though I had killed Adam, I wasn't a murderer. Yes, I could have let his ruined mouth be punishment enough, but if I had walked away, wouldn't I be culpable for any suffering he'd certainly inflict upon others down the line?

*Murderer.* I forsook that label as thoroughly as certain people had abandoned me. Turns out, doing that was as easy as sighing, once I quit denying I had been left behind. If I was lost, then let me be forgotten—in passing let mine be a face that looked familiar enough but could never quite be placed. And a truer prayer had never passed these lips.

I strolled through the train station's courtyard toward Loyola, palm trees clumped on both sides. The sight of those made me feel so much farther from Memphis than the few hundred miles of tracks I had traveled. To orient myself, I reviewed a transit map. With a vague destination and no real clue who I was going to be from here on, the blandly named streetcar I caught—49 Loyola/UPT—seemed apropos.

The Crescent City. That silvered sickle was made all the brighter, all the more distracting, by the penumbra shaping it. How much had been forgotten in that shadow? While the man who loses himself on Bourbon Street after burning down his previous life might be a cliche, I'd stick around for as long as it kept me hidden.

But if New Orleans ever started feeling less like a refuge and more like a trap, railroad tracks rumbling beneath my feet no matter where I was walking, I would vanish before any shadow disembarked from the train.

# ACKNOWLEDGMENTS

First, I must thank my family. Without the influence that each of you has had on my life, I would not be who I am. Mom, I cannot thank you enough for encouraging all of my artistic impulses, for being there to help me when I needed it the most, and for making sure all of your children, but especially your sons, knew that being emotionally honest was always a strength and never a weakness.

Next, a huge thank you goes to Lisa Diane Kastner, Peter A. Wright, and the whole team at Running Wild Press for taking a chance on a novel I thought would never get published. A deep gratitude goes out to my editor Cody Sisco whose insightful comments and unfailing enthusiasm were invaluable in helping me develop this novel much further than I had ever thought possible.

And now, I'll backtrack a bit. Very different versions of Chapter 1 and Chapter 17 were published in *The Citron Review* and *Blithe House Quarterly*, respectively. I thank those editors for the confidence these early publications gave me.

Much more recently, John Purdom, Anne-Geri' Fann, and Eddie Charlton gave me incredible feedback. Purdom, Anj, and Eddie, I owe you all so much. And then there's Jeff Hale who gave me two great lines that I used with his permission. Jeff, you are a doll.

From my earliest days in Memphis until I left, the following people were a part of my life during pivotal moments:

Lucas Trautman, Jayde Smith, Hugh von der Tann, Keith Percefull, and Peter Lacey. I must also thank Dave H. who helped my early efforts in submitting this novel to agents and publishers. He believed in me enough to support me when everything else in my life felt like it was falling apart.

Next, there's Billy Squires. Without him, I never would have pursued my MFA or moved to Nashville. All it took was Billy asking whether or not I wanted to stay in the social work field for me to begin following a different path. Over the years, he has remained a dear friend and has done so much in helping me get to where I am.

While pursuing my MFA at the University of Memphis, many people helped shape me as a writer, from Professors Tom Lyon Russell, Leigh Anne Duckworth, Tom Carlson, and John Bensko, to my peers Scott McWaters, Sarah Maggi, the late Patrick Ryan, Bill Yazbec, and Mary Golias. Last but not least, those two years I raced through the three-year program would not have been as fun and memorable without Amy R. Earhart and Becky Bodenheimer Jenkins. Thanks, gals, for all the laughter and commiseration.

Of all the people I met there, though, none had as much of an impact on me as the inimitable Randall Kenan. Randall chaired my thesis committee and was one of the most brilliant people I have ever known. His close-readings were second-to-none, and he was also one of the most supportive and caring souls I have met. He was the first person to read one of the earliest drafts of what would *eventually* become this novel. Suffice it to say, Randall had so many notes flagged with stickies, all of which I needed to hear. I owe him a debt I can never repay, and the world is diminished without having Randall in it.

Last and most importantly, I must express my most profound gratitude to my husband, Daniel Vincent. Recently, after doing something I thought was quirky, as I am wont to do, he joked, "Mike Kiggins: Keeping it weird since 2010." Throughout our time together, this beautiful, thoughtful man has saved my life in multiple ways, and he's never stopped believing in me or helping me to believe in myself when doubt inevitably creeps in. Together, we have made a home, and I can't imagine my life without him by my side. Simply put, I never would have finished this novel without his patience, honesty, and encouragement.

Daniel, I love you.

RIZE publishes great stories and great writing across genres written by People of Color and other underrepresented groups. Our team consists of:

Lisa Diane Kastner, Founder and Executive Editor
Mona Bethke, Acquisitions Editor
Rebecca Dimyan, Editor
Abigail Efird, Editor
Laura Huie, Editor
Cody Sisco, Editor
Chih Wang, Editor
Pulp Art Studios, Cover Design
Standout Books, Interior Design
Polgarus Studios, Interior Design

Learn more about us and our stories at www.runningwildpress. com/rize

Loved this story and want more? Follow us at www.runningwildpress.com/rize, www.facebook/rize, on Twitter @rizerwp and Instagram @rizepress

# NOTES

## CHAPTER 17

1. See "A Report on Yellow Fever as it Appeared in Memphis, Tenn., in 1873," which was published in *Public Health Papers and Reports* in the same year, p. 385.
2. Quoted in the *Memphis Public Ledger* (Sept. 18, 1867).

## CHAPTER 25

1. See Lawrence K. Altman's "Rare Cancer Seen in 41 Homosexuals," *The New York Times*, July 3, 1981, section A, page 20.
2. See Tuofu Zhu et al.'s "An African HIV-1 sequence from 1959 and implications for the origin of the epidemic," *Nature* 391 (1998), 594-97.
3. See Philippe Lemey et al.'s "Tracing the origin and history of the HIV-2 epidemic." *Proceedings of the National Academy of Sciences*, May 2003, 100 (11), 6588-6592.